Praise for the novels of
New York Times bestselling author Megan Hart

"Hart's beautiful use of language and discerning eye
toward human experience elevate the book to a poignant reflection
on the deepest yearnings of the human heart and the
seductive temptation of passion in its many forms."
—*Kirkus Reviews* on *Tear You Apart*

"[Hart] writes erotica for grown-ups....
[*The Space Between Us*] is a quiet book, but it packed a major punch
for me.... She's a stunning writer, and this is a stunning book."
—*Super Librarian*

"*Naked* is a great story, steeped in emotion.
Hart has a wonderful way with her characters....
She conveys their thoughts and actions in a manner
that brings them to life. And the erotic scenes provide a sizzling read."
—*RT Book Reviews*

"*Deeper* is absolutely, positively, the best book that I have read in ages...
the writing is fabulous, the characters' chemistry is combustible, and
the story line brought tears to my eyes more than once.... Beautiful,
poignant and bittersweet...Megan Hart never disappoints."
—*Romance Reader at Heart*, Top Pick

"*Stranger*, like Megan Hart's previous novels,
is an action-packed, sexy, emotional romance that tears up the pages
with heat while also telling a touching love story.... *Stranger* has a
unique, hot premise that Hart delivers on fully."
—Bestselling author Rachel Kramer Bussel

"[*Broken*] is not a traditional romance but the story of a real and
complex woman caught in a difficult situation with no easy answers.
Well-developed secondary characters and a compelling plot add depth
to this absorbing and enticing novel."
—*Library Journal*

"An exceptional story and honest characters make *Dirty* a must-read."
—*Romance Reviews Today*

Apr 2014

Also by *New York Times* bestselling author Megan Hart

TEAR YOU APART
THE FAVOR
THE SPACE BETWEEN US
ALL FALL DOWN
PRECIOUS AND FRAGILE THINGS
COLLIDE
NAKED
SWITCH
DEEPER
STRANGER
TEMPTED
BROKEN
DIRTY

And watch for
LOVELY WILD
Coming soon from Harlequin MIRA

MEGAN HART

Flying

OFFICIALLY NOTED

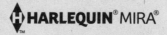

HARLEQUIN® MIRA®

If you purchased this book without a cover you should be aware that this book is stolen property. It was reported as "unsold and destroyed" to the publisher, and neither the author nor the publisher has received any payment for this "stripped book."

Recycling programs
for this product may
not exist in your area.

ISBN-13: 978-0-7783-1622-0

FLYING

Copyright © 2014 by Megan Hart

All rights reserved. Except for use in any review, the reproduction or utilization of this work in whole or in part in any form by any electronic, mechanical or other means, now known or hereafter invented, including xerography, photocopying and recording, or in any information storage or retrieval system, is forbidden without the written permission of the publisher, Harlequin MIRA, 225 Duncan Mill Road, Don Mills, Ontario M3B 3K9, Canada.

This is a work of fiction. Names, characters, places and incidents are either the product of the author's imagination or are used fictitiously, and any resemblance to actual persons, living or dead, business establishments, events or locales is entirely coincidental.

® and TM are trademarks of Harlequin Enterprises Limited or its corporate affiliates. Trademarks indicated with ® are registered in the United States Patent and Trademark Office, the Canadian Trade Marks Office and in other countries.

For questions and comments about the quality of this book, please contact us at CustomerService@Harlequin.com.

Printed in U.S.A.

First printing: May 2014
10 9 8 7 6 5 4 3 2 1

To Johnny, my favorite PITA

And to the Nicest Thing

And special thanks to Laura Hawkins and Lisa and Colm McIvor
for sharing with me their stories about the things that could happen
to make someone unable to fly.

I could write without music, but I'm so glad I don't have to.
Below is a partial playlist of what I listened to while writing *Flying*.
Please support the musicians by buying their music.

"Mistake," Christopher Dallman

"Gonna Hurt More," Aiden James

"Ghost," Ingrid Michaelson

"Cross That Line," Joshua Radin

"Snuff," Slipknot

"Lil Darlin (feat. The O'My's)," ZZ Ward

"Sadist," Stone Sour

"Where We Land," Ed Sheeran

"Give It To Me Right," Melanie Fiona

"Left For You," Nonpoint

"If You Want Me," One Less Reason

"The Fall," Bo Bruce

"Rev 22-20," Puscifer

"Bet U Wish U Had Me Back," Halestorm

"I Don't Apologize (1000 Pictures)," Otherwise

"New York," Snow Patrol

Flying

CHAPTER ONE

Red lips.

Smooth skin.

Perfume.

These are tricks a lot of women know. Men like silky hair and clinging dresses, high heels and gartered stockings like the ones she wears now. In her twenties Stella had taught herself how to be sexy for a man; it wasn't until she was older that she discovered it was so much better to be sexy for herself.

Her feet whisper on the cool industrial tiles as she tips her scarlet-soled pumps into the bin and pushes it along the rollers toward the X-ray machine. Next, her bag, which she affectionately calls the TARDIS. Like the traveling police-box time machine from her son's favorite TV show, Stella's bag is bigger on the inside. It can hold a weekend's worth of everything a woman needs to make herself beautiful, plus a book in case she doesn't find anyone worth being beautiful for.

Her coat goes next. She'd prefer to keep it on, but even if they let her through the scanner with it, the buckle will set off the alarm. Then again, so will the clips on her garters, probably. At this point, Stella knows most of the TSA agents who work at the Harrisburg International Airport by name. They still have to pat her down, of course, but by now it's become sort of a game for them and for her.

"Hi, Pete." She doesn't miss the way his gaze dips to her seam-stockinged toes and lingers on her calves when she turns to add her cell phone to a second bin before pushing that one through behind the first. She can't see him do it, but she's sure he takes a good, long look at her ass too.

This is good.

It doesn't matter that Pete is at least her father's age and wears a walrus mustache. Or that he's married with kids and grandkids whose pictures he proudly displays on his phone. Or even that the gum he chews constantly can't cover up the pervasive odor of bad breath. It doesn't matter that she will never take Pete home and fuck him.

It only matters that she could, if she wanted to. If she tried hard enough. If she let him stand a little too close, breathe a little too hard, if she shifted just the right way so the slit in her dress parted just enough to give him a glimpse of her bare thighs.

Stella is pretty sure Pete thinks she's a relatively expensive call girl, or at the very least some rich man's mistress. It's the clothes, hair, the manicured nails. It's the shoes. There's no way for anyone to mistake anything about her for a woman on a business trip, unless her business is pleasure. Pete doesn't know she doesn't get paid for any of this, at least not with money.

"Where you off to tonight?" Pete lets the wand move

up and down her body as she holds up her arms. The wand beeps around her thighs. He moves it again, slowly. Up and down. "Sorry about this, Stella."

"No problem." Her warm smile isn't forced. He doesn't know it's as much artifice as the fake lashes and fingernails. The only difference is she doesn't need glue to hold it in place. "I'm used to it by now."

He waves her to the side, where a pair of TSA agents will pat her down, explaining the process every step of the way and asking repeatedly for her permission to touch her in places that no longer even feel intimate. Stella makes it easy for them. They're just doing their job.

The agent bending to slide her fingers up Stella's calf is new, or at least has never worked the Friday night shift before when Stella's passing through. Her name tag says Maria. She has dark hair slicked into a tight bun that can't disguise the natural curl. Big dark eyes fringed with lashes that don't need to be glued on. Her mouth isn't painted red, but it's lush and glistening just the same. She does her job efficiently, barely cracking a smile. Not unfriendly, but definitely distant. When she looks up, Stella, who's looking down, thinks she understands why.

Stella's never been with a woman, but that doesn't mean she hasn't thought about it. These tricks—sometimes they work on women too. That gleam of interest, however faint and trying to be ignored, calls to her just as much as it does in a man's eyes, because all of this effort Stella makes isn't so much about the wanting as of being wanted.

When Maria's fingertips skate along the inside of her thighs, Stella's reaction is immediate but not unconscious. Her feet shift on the blue-painted marks on the floor, the rough paint that could snag her stockings if she's not care-

ful. The tiniest movement, not enough to draw attention
to herself, but the agent notices. Their eyes meet. Under
the layers of silk and lace, Stella throbs.

Maria looks away.

What would it be like to hide yourself that way, so the
world can't guess something that is such a basic part of you?
Such a defining thing? Stella understands. Everyone has secrets, and most of them are about sex.

Maria doesn't look at her again, not throughout the entire rest of the inspection, and her voice doesn't falter as
she gives, in monotone, the speech and instructions Stella
could recite from memory. Stella's voice, however, has gone
husky when she gives her permission for every single pat of
Maria's hands against her. By the time it's over, Stella feels
flushed and shivery; she fumbles with her belongings and
Maria has to help with her coat and bag.

"Take your time, ma'am," Maria says in a neutral voice.
"Have a nice day."

Stella slips into her shoes and pulls the bag along behind
her, her coat over her arm. She doesn't look back, keeps
her head high, draws in breath after breath to keep herself steady. In the bathroom, she locks herself inside a stall
and leans against the chilly metal, eyes closed, and pushes
her hands into the slit of her wrap dress. Up the insides of
her thighs, over the stockings and bare flesh, to press her
clit through her panties. Her back arches. Her nipples are
hard. She lets herself imagine for a few moments what it
would be like to have that woman's face against her flesh.
Those lush lips on her cunt. Would it be different than the
beard-rough touch of a man? Probably. She laughs at herself, but silently, and at the sink splashes water on a paper
towel before pressing it to the back of her neck.

She studies her reflection. Dark-lined eyes against pale skin, those red lips. Her hair is naturally auburn and hangs to her shoulders, usually worn with the ends curling up, but not tonight. She wears it in a deep side part now, pinned behind one ear and hanging loose on the other. Because she's alone in the bathroom, she allows herself to give the woman in the mirror a sly smile and an assessing gaze. Stella doesn't stare at herself because she's vain. She does it so she knows how she looks to other people. She does it so she can be sure the expressions she feels on her face look real, her smile bright or sexy or sympathetic as needed and not some Joker-faced grin. She used to never have to think about how she looked, but that was a long time ago. She was a different woman then, one who never worried about her makeup or hair or if she was going to scare someone with her smile.

She's gotten better at it.

She touches up her lipstick and powders her nose. She adjusts her stockings and her push-up bra, opens the neckline of her dress just a little bit more. She slips into her coat and belts it. By the time she gets to the gate, her plane is boarding and she waits patiently in line to take the seat that's left. Sometimes when she gets to the gate she finds out she won't be going where she thought she was, that she'll have to try another flight, but that's the price she pays for flying free. It doesn't happen often. Harrisburg's airport might be international, but it's also very small and hardly ever busy. Tonight, there's no problem.

Tonight, she's going to Atlanta.

It will be warmer there than it is in central Pennsylvania in late September, and that's fine. Stella doesn't plan on sightseeing. She'll barely even leave the airport. One night in, the next out. She has that book if she's not lucky…but she almost always is.

She likes the Hartsfield-Jackson Airport in Atlanta. It has a couple of nice bars and coffee shops where she can sip iced tea or coffee or the occasional hot cocoa, depending on her mood. Like every airport she's ever used, it has a wide selection of hotels no more than a quick shuttle ride from the terminal. She belongs to all the rewards programs. It only ever takes a quick call to confirm a cheap vacancy.

Stella is still thinking of Maria when she sits at the bar in Atlanta and settles her bag at her feet. Having to keep it with her is one inconvenience about these trips, but also the easiest escape route. She can always say she's on her way to catch a plane if she needs an excuse to get away. She's used it a few times, though there's the possibility she'll be caught in the lie when the man whose attentions she's fleeing sees her in a different bar with a different man—but really, what does she care? She doesn't owe them anything, even if they do buy her a drink or three. Even if she does lean a little close, fluttering her lashes, or crosses her legs artfully so that her dress gives them a glimpse of her unspoken promises.

Today isn't the first time she's ever been checked out by a woman. Women look each other over all the time. Women assess each other with bright and knowing eyes that broadcast their approval, envy, disdain. The tricks of gloss and glitter are meant to lure men but impress other women. Stella might have to study her reflection to know if her expression is portraying what she means it to, but all she has to do is look at other women to know if her body's doing the same thing.

Still, there is something different about being looked over

and checked out. That fleeting glimpse of desire in Maria's eyes, coupled with the too-polite way she went about her inspection, have lit a familiar fire inside Stella. Sometimes she likes to flirt and be coy, to dance around her desires and draw them out. Make the outcome uncertain. Sometimes she likes to be pursued. And sometimes, like tonight, she wants to be the one making someone else cross the line they might not even know they had.

A man sits down beside her. One always does. He doesn't try to hide his assessment of her, and it's nicely appreciative. He's conventionally attractive—square jaw, good haircut, a few feathery lines of crow's feet and a glint of silver at his temples. Businessman, suit and tie, white shirt, nice watch. Class ring on his wedding finger. He smells good.

He's not what she wants. Other nights, definitely, but not this one. Stella makes a quarter turn with her body away from him and focuses her attention on her cell phone. He gets the hint, orders a drink and lets his focus fall on a woman on the other side of him. Stella eavesdrops on his opening line. It would've worked on her on another night. Almost all do.

She sees what she wants. He's sitting at the other end of the bar with a pint glass of beer in front of him. He's watching the sports channel on the flat-screen above the bartender. He's youngish, at least a few years younger than her. Clean cut, dark hair cropped close, no hint of a beard. He wears a long-sleeved black shirt and black trousers, and yes, she looks for it—the peek of a white collar from his pocket.

Stella has made an art of observation. She studies him surreptitiously, noting the black bag nestled at his feet like a faithful dog. The bag's the sort you get at a conference, emblazoned with a dove and the words *Episcopal Diocese Fall Clergy Conference* circling it.

Episcopalian, not Roman Catholic. No vow of chastity, but still a priest. Still the sort of man who shouldn't do what she wants him to do.

Guh.

He doesn't look around the bar even when a couple of women pass right behind him on the way to the bathroom. Not even when one of them brushes his shoulder with her bag as she passes. He looks up long enough to move his chair when there's a little bit of a roadblock between the kitchen and bathroom, so he's not totally oblivious or entranced by the week's sports highlights. But he's definitely a guy who's there to enjoy a beer and some food, not company. Especially not random female company. If the tucked-away collar didn't give that away, the onion rings do.

Stella finishes her drink and gathers her things. She gets little more attention from him than the other women did, but when she sits next to him, he does give her a quick glance and a small, polite smile. Stella returns it with the same lack of heat and interest. When the bartender tells her that yes, they do have iced tea, she orders a glass, and when it arrives she makes a show of looking for the sugar.

"Oh...excuse me." A smile with the right amount of friendly, gaze indirect enough not to be threatening. She points to the small dish of packets to his right. "Could you pass me the sugar?"

She's already seen that the dish contains a rainbow of artificial sweeteners. He pushes it to her with a murmured "Oh, sure." Stella frowns. This time when she looks at him, she makes sure to catch his eye completely. Another smile, this one a little slower.

She holds his gaze a little longer than is comfortable before she says, "Is there any real sugar?"

He looks again to his right, but this is a bar, not a diner. She's judged him right, though. Before she can say anything, he's waving at the bartender and asking for real sugar, which the bartender has to hunt for beneath the bar for a moment before he passes over a handful of white packets. They spill from the man's hands, across the polished top of the bar, and Stella laughs as she helps scoop them up and tuck them into place alongside their chemical cousins.

"Thanks," she says. It's enough. She thought it might be. He smiles at her. "You're welcome."

She tears two packets at the same time and stirs the sugar into the tea, then takes out the long spoon and tucks it in her mouth to suck the sweetness before setting it on the napkin in front of her. He looks away, but not quickly enough. She leans a little close, but not too much.

"I hate the taste of artificial sweeteners." This is a dance. Maybe he knows it. Maybe he doesn't. But Stella does, and she's very careful with the steps. "They're terrible."

"Yeah, I know what you mean." He lets his gaze tilt toward her again, but not his body. His hands close around his glass, but he doesn't drink.

Gloss and glitter. It's like dangling a sequined worm in sun-dappled waters, letting it drift and catch the light until the fish decides it wants to bite. The question is, will he bite? Will he?

"Some crazy weather, huh?" The second he opens his mouth to speak, it doesn't matter what he says. It means he's hooked. He points at the TV, across which a banner is running. Freak tornados have swept the Midwest and also odd places on the East Coast that don't usually see them.

He doesn't quite look at her and she's most definitely not looking at him, but she can feel him sneaking a peek.

For one long second, she feigns inattention enough that his words don't turn her toward him. But then… "Hmm? Oh. Yes! Crazy." A soft frown, a crease of concern. "Those poor people. I hope nobody's hurt."

"A few have died, I think." Other men might've said it with a hint of suppressed glee, the joy of the unscathed, but this guy… His sincerity is probably genuine. "And who knows how much the damage will cost?"

Stella angles her body, the smallest twitch, toward him. "Yeah. Scary. Have you ever been in a tornado?"

The question, as she's meant it to, seems to take him a bit off guard. He shakes his head. His body angles toward hers too, almost like an afterthought. "No. Have you?"

She shakes her head. "No. I hope I never am. With my luck, I'd end up in Oz, dropping my house on a witch."

He laughs. He has nice white teeth. Straight. The lines at the corners of his eyes settle him as older than she'd thought. He looks at her now, really looks. There's that gleam, deliciously reluctant, and it sparks a fresh heat inside her.

"I'm Glenn." He holds out his hand.

She takes it. The shake is firm and brief, still utterly polite. "Maria. Should I call you Father?"

He looks almost startled for a second, and when he lets go of her hand, his fingers touch his throat briefly. Then his pocket. "Oh. No. I mean, you don't have to."

Her head tilts, gaze taking him in, like the smile a few seconds longer than is necessary. "Would you *like* me to?"

For half a breath, she thinks she's misjudged him. Either

he has no secrets or he's just that good at keeping them. But then… "You can just call me Glenn. Maria."

There's conversation after that. More about the weather. About the game on TV—he's impressed she knows enough about the sport to keep up. Men always are; it annoys or amuses her, depending on the situation. Tonight, she's amused. They talk of other things, too. Music, for one. Concerts. He's been to see a few of the bands she likes. He shares some of her favorite songs. By the time an hour passes, she has him leaning in to her, getting closer. He offers her an onion ring and laughs when she declines. They order a plate of mozzarella sticks to share.

They don't talk again about his collar…or lack of it. She expects that at any minute he'll tell her he has to leave. They are in an airport, after all. Then he explains his plane's been delayed by those very same storms that had started their conversation. She tells him she's also been delayed because of weather, and as lies go, it's so small it could almost be the truth.

There's a moment when she can tip this the other way. She can thank him for the food and the iced teas he's paid for. She can walk away and let him keep the secrets he already has, instead of becoming one more he has to keep. Stella, momentarily moral, stands to wish him a good night and good luck.

Glenn stands too. He asks her where she's staying. The moment for doing the right thing has passed, and who's to say what's right and wrong, anyway? He's an adult. She isn't forcing him.

All she's done is offer the temptation. He doesn't have to take it. But as she gathers her bag and he helps her with her coat, Stella knows he already has.

"I have a reservation at the Marriott," he tells her.

"Me too," she says, and excuses herself to the restroom, where she makes one.

In the lobby, she gets her key while Glenn studies the nondescript paintings of horses and flowers with the intensity deserving art hung in the Met. She's asked for a room on the lobby level—no elevators, no stairs, just the shortest of walks down a hallway smelling of antiseptic.

At the door, she turns to him with a smile. "Good night, Glenn. Thanks for walking me."

"You're welcome."

Stella's the one who offers her hand. Palm to palm, fingers link. There's a long, slow and lingering squeeze. She tugs him, gently. One step closer. Then another. There's only space enough for a breath between them, and she takes it. In these shoes, all she has to do is tilt her head and offer her mouth, let her tugging hand make him believe she's pulling him when he's the one taking the steps.

She doesn't kiss him. That's important. Stella lets Glenn start the kiss, and she lets him break it too. She keeps her eyes closed and can't stop herself from smiling. Without opening them or looking to make sure they're alone in the hallway, she leans back against the door to her room and puts his hand, fingers still linked with hers, inside her dress. Against her skin. She curls her fingers around his so that his knuckles brush lace and heat. He kisses her again, harder this time.

Glenn's tongue strokes hers. He's an excellent kisser. The hand not between her legs slides up her body, over her breasts, to cup the back of her neck. He breathes a little moan into her mouth, and Stella arches against him.

This is what she likes, what she craves. This is what she

wants. Being wanted so much he'll do anything, finger her in a hotel doorway, maybe fuck her right there, not caring about anything but getting his cock inside her.

"Inside," Glenn whispers against her lips.

She fits the key into the slot without turning around. The door swings open, and they push through it without moving apart. They're already at the bed by the time the door clicks shut. Glenn's hand is still against her cunt, his mouth on hers. His hand on the back of her neck keeps her from falling.

He breaks the kiss and presses his forehead to hers, eyes closed. He licks his mouth. It's Stella's turn to cup the back of his neck, and she feels him shudder at her touch. She's no longer holding his hand between her legs, but he hasn't moved it. His fingers uncurl enough to slide beneath the lace.

She's been wet for hours. His fingertips slide against her. They brush her clit, and Stella groans against him. The sound is low and raw. She doesn't care. She wants him to hear the desire in her voice the same way he feels it between her legs.

She wants to hold nothing back.

Because this is what Stella really wants and craves and needs and seeks. This naked, somehow desperate connection of two people who don't even know each other's last names, but who each knows exactly how the other tastes. Glenn tastes like guilt and fervor. Does she taste the same, or is her flavor more bitter, like secrets and grief? She wants to eat him up, so she opens her mouth and invites his tongue inside.

Should she be surprised when he goes to his knees in front of her with a mutter like a prayer? Still, it startles her enough that if the bed weren't behind her, she'd have backed away. She can't move, and even if she could, his hands move to the backs of her thighs and hold her still. He doesn't look up at her face when he pulls the tie at her side open, nor when her dress falls open to show off her pale blue, lacy bra and matching panties. The garter belt and stockings she loves so much.

The hair, the mouth, the shoes, the tits and ass and pussy no longer matter. When she stands in front of a lover for the first time—and there are only first times, first and last at the same time—she wants to hide herself behind her hands. She wants to fuck in darkness so everything becomes nothing but heat, scent and touch. So she can disappear into those things. So they don't have to see her scars.

Men don't care. She understands this. By the time she's naked in front of them, their cocks are hard and their mouths hungry. They see curves and flesh. Nothing else. That's why no matter how much she wants to hide, she never does. She stands naked in the light even though she'd prefer the darkness, because she deserves this scrutiny and though it's more than a little twisted, she loves and craves the agony it brings her.

Glenn kisses her through the lace. He shivers, his hands moving up to cup her ass and pull her closer. One slips around the front to pull her panties aside, giving his tongue room to find her clit. He knows what he's doing. It's good, oh, fuck, it's so astoundingly good that her fingers have wound into his hair before she realizes it. Her hips bump forward. He sucks gently on her swollen flesh.

Then he looks up at her.

His mouth is wet, eyes bright. There is that desire she

wants to see, along with the guilt she has tasted in his kisses. He swallows, hard. "Maria. I—"

"Shhh." Her fingers twist in his hair for a second before she softens her grip to pass her hand over his head and down to cup his cheek. "It's okay. Nobody will ever know."

God will know, but Stella doesn't say so. She doesn't believe in God, and if Glenn does that's between him and his Maker. Glenn shudders and presses his cheek to her thigh as his fingers dimple her ass. His breath is hot through the lace of her panties. His tongue wet. His teeth press her skin, and she braces herself for the sting. He doesn't bite her. She's a little disappointed.

It took her a few trials to figure out the best way to wear lingerie is to put the panties on over the garter belt, so they can be easily removed without having to take off the stockings first. It makes it so much easier to fuck in places where it might be important to keep most of her clothes on.

Glenn's fingers hook into the lace and pull her panties over her hips, her thighs. She steps out of them, and he uses his hands to settle her on the edge of the bed. Still kneeling, he parts her with his thumbs and finds her clit with his lips and tongue. Oh, God. His teeth. Again, not biting, though the pressure's enough to make her muscles leap.

Stella opens herself to him. Legs spread. One goes over his shoulder, pulling him closer. Her hips rock under his mouth. Sometimes she bites her tongue to keep herself silent, but when he slides a finger inside her, she lets herself cry out again. She blindfolds herself with her hand.

Her pleasure is a spring, coiling tighter. Her world narrows, focused on the finesse of Glenn's mouth and fingers. Even though she twitches and wriggles beneath him, he keeps the pace steady, almost teasing. She hovers close to orgasm, and he eases her off again and again, until in a sobbing breath, she begs.

"Please. Oh, please…please, please, please…"

He's made her blind with desire, but not quite deaf. She hears the sharp intake of his breath and feels it against her. Then finally the relentless swipe of his tongue moving in time to his thrusting fingers. Stella goes over the edge, full force. Her orgasm is brutal. It breaks her open so she's left panting and limp, blinking away stars.

Still fully dressed, Glenn gets up and sits on the bed without touching her. He says nothing. Stella finds her breath and pushes up on her elbow to look at him. His head is bowed, shoulders slumped a little.

"I used to be married," he says. "We divorced. And with my work, it's hard…to find someone… Dating is almost impossible. I'm…sorry."

She wanted him to be reluctant. Not regretful. "Please don't be. I'm not."

His smile's faint, but it's real when he finally looks at her. "Would you be offended if I thanked you?"

Stella laughs, just a little. Shakes her head. "No. Of course not. I should thank you."

When she puts her hand on his thigh, the muscles tense under her fingers. When she slides her hand a little higher, he covers it with his. She lets him stop her.

"I can return the favor," she says, already anticipating the feeling of him inside her.

But Glenn shakes his head. "It was enough."

"But I—" She stops, understanding suddenly and not wanting to make him feel bad.

Glenn looks a little embarrassed, but not too much. "It had been a long time. And you… You're very sexy."

He looks over her whole body so thoroughly that by the time his gaze meets hers, her cheeks have flushed. Again, she wants to cover herself, but settles for another thank-you. When he leans close to kiss her, Stella puts both her hands on his face and holds him to her mouth. Then she hugs him close. His hands stroke her back before he lets her go.

He doesn't ask to stay, and that's fine because then she doesn't have to find a way to ask him to leave. When he's gone, Stella showers, opening her mouth to the spray to wash away the taste of him. Just once, she thinks, maybe some stranger she seduces will ask her about the scars. And maybe, someday, she'll tell him.

CHAPTER TWO

"Mom!"

Stella had been dreaming about the ocean. Soft waves lapping at her toes, scuttling crabs, warm golden sand. In the dream, she'd been wearing a beautiful teal bikini. That was how she knew it was a dream—even in the days before childbirth and everything else that had happened, she'd never worn a bikini. Too much skin exposed to the sun.

"Mom!"

She opened her eyes and groaned. Her sheets had tangled around her feet. The pillow she used between her knees had gone missing, lost somewhere in the abyss of her blankets. Her neck hurt. The lavender oil she'd put on her pillowcase had been the source of the vivid dreams, but it made her sneeze now.

"What?" she muttered, knowing Tristan couldn't possibly hear her. From the sound of his shouts, he was yelling from downstairs. "What, for the love of all that's holy, do you want?"

The elephant tread of her sixteen-year-old on the stairs was enough to force her to burrow farther into the blankets. Tristan had hit another growth spurt, topping six feet now, and his shoe size had gone up along with it. She'd given birth to a giant. A giant with huge feet that tripped him up and left enormous muddy tracks on the floor and couldn't seem to move with anything resembling silence.

"Mom, I need lunch money."

Stella lifted her head from the pillow just enough to glare at her son standing in the doorway. "You have to tell me this *now?*"

"Yeah, well, I need to eat lunch, don't I?"

"What about last night, when I asked you if everything was ready for school and you told me it was?"

"I'm gonna be late," he warned. "I'll miss the bus, and you'll have to drive me."

That would be infinitely worse than having to direct him to her checkbook, since it meant she'd have to get out of bed and didn't even have time for a shower. With another groan, Stella waved her hand toward the jumble of junk on her dresser. "See if I have a twenty in my purse."

At the rate Tristan ate, twenty bucks would last him for only a few days, but she could deposit money in his account later. And in fifteen minutes, according to the clock, he'd be on the bus and she'd be able to sneak back to sleep for another hour.

He rummaged through her bag, couldn't find her wallet and suffered through her grumbling as she took the purse from him to find it. "Dad's picking me up after practice today. I'm staying there tonight."

"Wait, what? I thought I was supposed to take you shopping—"

"Dad will take me."

"Does he know that?"

Tristan shrugged, not caring.

It wasn't that Stella didn't trust Jeff, but she knew from past experience how happy he was to pawn off any sort of parental responsibility on his new wife who, God love her, meant well but was as helpless and fluffy as a bunny rabbit. Cynthia had married Jeff when she was twenty-two. She'd never had children, had never even babysat and had inherited a tween son who seemed to be as foreign to her as if he'd been born on Mars. Even after four years, it seemed cruel of Stella to expect Cynthia to pick up Jeff's slack when dealing with Tristan was so clearly a constant adventure for her.

"Have a good day! Love you!" she called after him as he thundered down the stairs again. Tristan didn't answer. The front door slammed.

Silence, blessed silence.

This was Stella's shared-custody life. In the beginning, Tristan had been only eight, still in elementary school. Too young to go out with friends, still content to hang out watching movies with his mom. Still hopeful, maybe, that his parents were only separating, not getting divorced. They'd decided it was too disruptive for Tristan to move back and forth between households on a weekly basis, so he spent most weeknights with her. Stella had come to enjoy having every other weekend free once Tristan left for school on Friday morning.

Now, if he didn't have a sports practice or a school activity or plans with friends, Tristan spent his time in front of the TV with his video games or an endless stream of movies. Their house had become the place to hang out,

and that was fine with her even if the noise level sometimes became hard to handle. She'd rather he was at home
than have to drive him around or pick him up from places.
Now that Tristan was older, of course, he could get rides
and so had been spending more random weeknights with
Jeff, especially since he now required less "care" and could
simply hang out.

There was no point in going back to sleep now. Stella
stretched and wriggled free of her blankets. Every part of
her creaked and crackled as she stretched. Time for another
visit to the chiropractor. She needed to get there more
regularly rather than waiting until she was in agony, but
somehow time always managed to get away from her. She
winced at the sharp ache in her neck as she twisted her hair
on top of her head—time for a visit to the salon too. And
maybe a trip to the optometrist, she thought as her reflection blurred briefly. She blinked away the sleep, bringing
her face into focus. She leaned on the sink for a moment,
staring in the mirror.

Stella gripped the porcelain until her fingers turned
white. She breathed in. She breathed out. She breathed
until the face of the woman in the mirror stopped looking
as though she wanted to cry.

She smiled.

She frowned.

She looked concerned.

That last one wasn't such a good look for her. It wrinkled
her forehead and creased lines at the corners of her eyes
and mouth. It was almost as bad as feigning interest, which
required a little more sparkle in the eyes. But all of it was
better than the woman with haunted eyes and downturned
mouth that had greeted her a few minutes ago.

Steam had wreathed around the showerhead, so she pulled her nightgown over her head and hung it carefully on the hook. It swung, loose, and she made a mental note to fix it even as she knew she'd forget again until the next time she hung something on it and it threatened to fall. In the shower, she bent her head so the hot water could pound away at her neck and shoulders and back—it was a quick fix that would ease the aches and pains for a while, at least. So would a double dose of ibuprofen and some stretches, if she could force herself to manage them. She should've worked out before she got in the shower, but the morning had already started off upside down—why bother to fix it now?

She slicked her palms full of soap and slid them beneath her arms. Over her belly and thighs. Something stung her there, and she turned to let the water wash away the suds.

A small bruise, the size of a quarter and already fading greenish at the edges. It hurt when she pressed it, but the pain was brief. She pushed it again, making it ache. Then harder. Her fingernail dug into her skin, and that hurt worse. She could've made herself bleed, but stopped before that happened. She had enough scars without giving herself more.

The tears fell before she could stop them, and even though the shower made them invisible, they still burned. The rippled floor that kept her from slipping and killing herself was also impossible to keep clean. The ridges collected all the minerals and iron from the water, forever tinted orange no matter how hard she scrubbed or how much bleach she used. They also hurt her knees and palms as she folded herself onto the floor. She stayed that way until the water began to turn cold. By that time she'd pushed the memory of Glenn's mouth on her so far away she could pretend it had happened to someone else.

CHAPTER THREE

What Stella did would never hang in a museum, but there *was* an art to touching up photos. Smoothing the lines of concern in a forehead. Erasing blemishes bad enough to leave scars. The scars themselves she never took away, unless the client had specifically requested she do so. Consequently, photos that came in with a lot of scars ended up in her queue, and that was fine with her. She knew too well how scars could define a person, no matter how ugly.

Today, her job was to touch up a family portrait taken for a church directory. A set of graying parents, a sullen teenage girl. A young marine son in uniform. The parents and the girl made a triangle, the son slightly separate despite the mother's clenching hand on his shoulder. Her grip had a somewhat desperate look to it that Stella wouldn't be able to do anything about, but she totally understood.

The marine had clearly seen some action. The right side of his face had been burned. The ridges of his scars were still purple and red, the curve of his eyebrow bare of any hair, the lashes missing from that eye. His mouth pulled down on that side. But he stood straight, gaze fixed firmly on the camera. Not smiling, not frowning. It was impossible to tell if he was resigned, ashamed or simply bored.

The clients had requested some shadow removal, along with the standard pimple erasure and taking away the reflection on the father's glasses. The last one was the hardest thing to do, so she left it for last. Stella focused on getting rid of a few flyaway hairs and bulges, things not even checked on the client's list and that they wouldn't even notice had been improved. But they'd notice if they weren't, she knew that much.

Her gaze kept coming back to the marine's face and the digging curve of his mother's fingers. Stoic, she decided. That's how he looked. Not bored or anything else. Simply stoic.

His mother, however, looked faded and tired, her mouth pursed, her hair limp. Maybe she'd sat by his bed while he recovered from his injuries, holding his hand. Or maybe he'd suffered alone, healing enough to be sent home. How terrible it must've been, no matter how it happened, the first time his mother had to look at that ravaged face.

Stella closed her eyes suddenly, fingers stilling on the mouse she'd been manipulating. She took her hand away and folded both in her lap while she gathered herself together. Slow breath. Deep breath. Counting to five, then seven, then ten.

It would never stop haunting her, she thought with a mental shake she echoed with a physical one. Opening her eyes, Stella let out an embarrassed laugh when she saw her coworker Jen peeking around the edge of her cubicle. Wordlessly, Jen held up a coffee mug and an e-cigarette.

"Sure," Stella said. "Give me a minute."

Stella had taken up smoking in college, but quit when she got pregnant. She'd never stopped missing it. She sometimes took a cigarette when she was flying, depending on the situation and who was offering her the smoke. So far as she knew, Jen didn't really smoke either, other than the e-cigarette she'd bought a few months ago and used with nicotine-less cartridges. They'd simply both figured out last year that smokers got breaks and nonsmokers didn't.

Grabbing a fresh cup of coffee from the break room, Stella pushed through the back doors of the building and found Jen waiting. Phone in one hand, coffee in the other, she lifted her chin in greeting as Stella came out.

"Chilly as fuck out here," she said around the e-cigarette tucked between her lips. "My nipples could cut glass."

Stella rubbed at her arms, grateful she'd grabbed a cardigan today. She sipped hot coffee, making a face. "This is swill."

Jen laughed and pulled the e-cig from her lips. "No kidding. I guess they think if they make better coffee we'll drink more of it? And then spend more time in the bathroom, therefore getting less work done?"

"Diabolical." Stella laughed, though it made sense. "Remember when they had the coffee and sandwich service?"

Jen sighed wistfully. "Yes. That guy was so cute. I spent more money on shitty, stale bagels than I made in this place."

Stella didn't want to sit at the splintery picnic table, so she settled for leaning against the brick wall while she warmed her hands on the already cooling mug. "I don't know why they stopped him from coming."

"Because they can take a percentage from the vending machines," Jen said matter-of-factly.

Stella hadn't thought of that.

Touching up photos for the Memory Factory was far from a terrible job, especially if you could get past the deathlike near silence in which they worked. The hours were good, and the pay based on completion of training levels meant that Stella was earning the top rate. More than she'd make in an office anywhere else. But it was no secret that the company itself, which had started off as a small mom-and-pop photography service and was bought by a national corporation, was money hungry. Famished, actually.

Jen drew again on the e-cig, blowing out a plume of mist into the October chill. "I heard Randall's going to be pulling people in for performance reviews soon. Guess we got too many complaints this past quarter."

"I'm not worried about that. Are you?"

"Girrrl," Jen said with a grin, "no way. But some of the temps are shaking in their boots. Which is good, because maybe they'll get fired, and we can get some hours back."

The previous holiday season, the company had hired on a bunch of temps to handle the extra workload that always happened around Christmas and lasted until just after New Year's. For whatever reason, four of the temps had been asked to stay on. None of them were any good, none had passed more than the basic level of training and none of them got along with anyone else in the office. Stella was sure two of them spent most of the day getting high in the supply closet, when they weren't fucking in there. She wouldn't have minded, if their presence hadn't meant, as Jen said, a cutback in some of the overtime that they and the other eight people who worked in their department had come to count on over the summer during vacations.

"They'll just hire more next month anyway," Stella said.

Jen snorted softly. "True. But different ones. Maybe ones that aren't assholes."

Stella laughed at how unlikely that would be. Her coffee had started off bitter, but now it was cold too. She dumped it to the side of the concrete slab and watched it make a stain in the gravel, already thinking ahead to the evening. She was going to dig out her flannel sheets tonight.

"...with me?"

"Sorry, what?" Stella looked up.

"I said, what are you doing tomorrow night? Jared and I are going to hear one of our friends sing at open mic night. Want to come along?"

Stella lifted a suspicious brow. "Are you trying to set me up again?"

"Oh, c'mon. One time. One!" Jen held up a finger. Then another, and after a hesitation, a third. "Okay. Three times. But you have to admit, all three times it was totally legit."

"Jen. I can't date guys who are just a few years older than my kid. Anyway, I told you, I'm not interested. Too much effort." Stella shook her head, looking at the sky, which had gone gray with the promise of rain. Too early for snow, right?

Jen sighed. "How can you not be interested?"

"I'm just not. Boyfriends take up too much time. Too much work." Stella shrugged. "I don't want to deal with a guy on a regular basis. I'm happy being alone."

"Nobody," Jen said darkly, "really wants to be alone."

Stella shrugged again. "Not forever. No. But right now I have enough to deal with at home. Tristan goes to college in two years. I'll have plenty of time to put up with bullshit then."

"It's not all bullshit," Jen said.

"That's because you're in loooooove." Stella grinned and made kissing noises that had Jen ducking her head with laughter. "Things are different when you're in love. You put up with all kinds of shit you'd never tolerate from someone else. Love makes people lose their minds."

"So does great peen," Jen said solemnly.

Stella carefully kept a straight face. "All the more reason to avoid it."

"If you're not careful, your vajayjay's gonna dry up like a tumbleweed and blow away."

"I'll take my chances," Stella said.

CHAPTER FOUR

At birth, Tristan had weighed six pounds, four ounces. He was sixteen inches long. He had no hair, bald as an egg, and had cried nonstop, round the clock, insatiable and inconsolable for the first month and a half of his life.

Sixteen years later he was taller than both his parents, outweighed Stella by about sixty pounds and had the same insatiable appetite, though fortunately he'd replaced the constant screaming with incessant commentary on the world. At least, he used to talk all the time. Now, instead of the hugs and the "love you, Mamas," Tristan's conversations had become stilted and intermittent. He'd replaced his formerly goofy sense of humor with a more sarcastic edge that sometimes bordered on cruel but was nevertheless bitingly funny. Stella hated to laugh at him but usually did, especially when he was making fun of his stepmother.

"That's not nice," she murmured at his demonstration of how Cynthia's mouth was always slightly parted. "Eat your grilled cheese."

She'd made his favorite with thick slices of rye bread and

cheddar, along with a few strips of crispy bacon and thinly sliced tomato. Not the healthiest dinner, but Tristan had grown up and stretched out so much she figured he could stand the extra calories, especially with all the running he'd been doing. For herself, she had a grilled chicken and spinach salad.

Tristan looked at the plate, then at her. "Can't I have what you're having?"

She paused with her fork ready to stab the spinach. "You love grilled cheese."

Tristan said nothing. He cut his gaze from hers, looking so much like Jeff it hurt her heart. Tristan pushed the plate with the tips of his fingers. "No, I don't."

"Since when?" Stella tried to keep the edge from her voice, too aware how easy it would be for them to slip into an argument. He not only looked like his dad; he had a lot of Jeff's personality too. All the things that had driven her nuts about her ex-husband were blooming in her son. No matter how much she'd determined Tristan would never be the sort of man who expected the world to hand him a living on a platter, it seemed nature sometimes did win over nurture. She loved her son, always, with every breath inside her. But there'd been a lot of days lately where she found it very difficult to like him.

"Since always." He muttered something else and moved the plate another half an inch away from him.

Stella stabbed her salad. "What was that?"

"Nothing. I didn't say anything."

"You did," she said. "I heard it."

"Nothing. Forget it," Tristan repeated stubbornly. He got up from the table, leaving the plate. "I'm not hungry, anyway. I'm going out for a run."

He was already through the kitchen doorway before she called out to him, "Hold up. Put the sandwich away for later and put your plate in the dishwasher."

He did, dragging his feet and heaving a sigh as if she'd asked him to amputate all his limbs with a rusty carrot peeler.

"I shouldn't even have to ask you that. C'mon, Tristan." She managed to keep her voice steady and focus on her salad. "You should know better."

"Yeah?" he challenged. "Well, so should you!"

Before she could ask him what the hell he meant by that, he'd stomped away. Footsteps pounded up the stairs and down the hall to his room. The door slammed.

Stella'd lost her appetite too but forced herself to eat anyway. When Tristan thundered down the stairs and toward the front door, she called out again, "Where are you going and how long do you think you'll be gone?"

"For a run, I told you, and I don't know."

There was no way for her to force a different answer from him without a fight, and she was tired of arguing with him. "You have your phone?"

"Yes."

"Don't go too far," she said. "Remember—"

"Yeah, I know, it feels twice as long on the way home as it does on the way there. I know, Mom." Again, the muttered exclamation that probably included the sort of profanity she heard all his friends using when they thought no adults were listening.

She thought of something else as the front door slammed. He was already halfway down the driveway by the time she got to the door. "Tristan!"

For a moment she thought he was going to pretend he didn't hear her, but then he turned. "What?"

"Be back before it gets dark." That didn't give him much time, but the thought of him running alongside the rural roads or even the highway in the dark twisted her stomach. "I mean it!"

He gave her a wave that might as well have been a flip of the bird, and took off down the driveway. She watched him until he disappeared past the trees, then went back inside. She stabbed again at her salad before dumping it in the trash and clearing away the table. She took her time with the cleaning spray and dish cloth, making sure to get all the smudges. She moved to the stainless-steel fridge, then the fronts of the microwave and oven, the stovetop. The cabinets.

Nothing was really dirty, but she cleaned it anyway.

In the days when Jeff had lived in this house, there'd always been too much clutter, too much mess, for Stella to keep up with. It had been like living with a hurricane. Kids, dog, cat, spouse—every other creature in the house had seemed to create a swath of destruction while she ran behind with the vacuum and mop, her laundry basket overflowing. Now, with Tristan spending half the time with his dad, sometimes the only mess in this house was one she made herself.

Sometimes she left her laundry on the empty side of the bed for the whole week without putting it away. She left the cap off the toothpaste tube, didn't put the lid down on the toilet before flushing. She bought the brand of coffee she preferred and played the music she liked best as loud as she wanted. Basically, she did everything she wanted, how she wanted it.

And she did it alone.

In the middle of the worst time, when the concept of

divorce had changed from feeling like a failure to salvation, Stella had turned the idea of being alone over and over until her mind had spun with it. Would she really like it, if that's all she had? In the end it had been Jeff who'd left her, not that she could've blamed him. She'd grown sick of herself by then. But in the end, she'd also decided that being alone was better than wishing she was.

The day Jeff had moved out, Tristan had been away at summer camp, and Stella had opened every window in the house even though a storm was on the way. She'd danced in the backyard, in the rain, risking being struck by lightning. She'd thrown her face up to the sky and let the rain wash everything away and make her clean.

The feeling hadn't lasted long, but it had been long enough. Eight years later, she was still alone and Jeff had remarried. She assumed he was happy in his much bigger house and much younger wife. She didn't really care.

The kitchen was clean. She'd run a few loads of laundry and folded most of it. She took Tristan's, piled high in his basket, down the hall. Passed the closed door between her room and his without pausing. She set the basket just inside his bedroom door with a wince at the sour smell of teenage boy. He wasn't allowed to eat in there anymore, not since she'd had to call the exterminator to deal with an infestation of both mice and ants. And he had strict orders to put his dirty clothes out in the hall every Monday to be washed, or suffer wearing dirty clothes all week. Or do his own laundry. Beyond that, Stella kept out of her son's room. She relished her privacy and figured he did too.

She lingered for a minute or two now, though. It was dangerous to dwell on things the way she had done in the shower this morning. Melancholy wasn't productive. Yet something pulled her in a step or two. He'd long outgrown his twin bed, so one of the first things Stella had done after the divorce was give Tristan her old headboard and mattress and buy herself a new bedroom set. He'd adorned the spindles with stickers and ribbons from science fairs and competitions. A few baseball caps. At the foot of the mattress, he still kept a pile of stuffed animals, shoved mostly between the mattress and the wall.

Mr. Bear. Tigger. Tristan had always preferred the soft plushies to harder toys like action figures or miniature cars. He'd spent hours with them as his backyard companions, wearing them into filth even the hottest setting in the washer couldn't clean. Other mothers had spoken with sighs about kids attached to blankies and teddy bears, some even buying more than one identical lovey toy so their kid wouldn't be traumatized by even a momentary loss. Tristan hadn't ever been like that. He'd loved all his toys equally and also as noncommittally. When limbs were lost or a stuffy simply too ruined to play with, he willingly gave it up in favor of another.

That's why it amused and touched her to see them all now. She'd have thought he'd dumped them ages ago, along with his outgrown footie pj's and the cowboy sheets. Stella nudged the laundry basket inside the room a little farther and reached for Mr. Bear. Her mom had bought him for Tristan when he was a toddler. Mr. Bear had been stuck against the wall next to some unnamed carnival prize snake, green with blue polka dots, incongruously wearing a top hat. When Stella pulled Mr. Bear's arm, the snake came free. So did a few of the other toys.

So did the baby.

It was one of the smallest toys, a soft sculpture baby about the size of her hand. A round, fat body, two stumpy arms and matching legs and a round head without a neck. Dimples and colored thread made the face, two wee eyes and a red kiss-print mouth. Three or four strands of orange hair. It had no gender, really, but the outfit was blue so it was meant to be a boy.

She'd grabbed it up without knowing what it was, but at the sight of that yarn hair, the stubby, floppy arms, she dropped it back onto the bed. It fell facedown, limbs akimbo.

"Where's your baby? Where's your baby?"

He toddles to her, two teeth proudly showing in his bottom gums, the baby clutched in his chubby fists. Blue blanket sleeper. Fluff of reddish hair. Drool in a silver thread she doesn't even mind wiping away as she scoops him up, burying her face in the sweet scent of little boy. Her boy.

"Show Mama your baby."

He holds up the toy, and she enfolds him into her arms, kissing him until he squirms to be put down. And she does, she puts him down, and he stumbles away from her on unsteady feet. Her boy.

Oh, her boy.

Stella left it there and went out, closing the door and locking the memories behind her.

Hours had passed since dinner. No sign of Tristan. No message, no text. Night had fully fallen, not even a hint of setting sun left for her to forgive him by. Her jaw set as she pulled out her phone to tap the screen.

WHERE ARE YOU?

Since she'd personally witnessed her son texting multiple people in different conversations while he played Xbox and watched TV and ate snacks, all at the same time, she knew the only reason he didn't reply to her within a minute or two was because he was ignoring her. Or something had happened to him.

Stella's mother had made a habit of saying, "Be careful" every time Stella left the house. Stella, smart-ass that she'd been, had usually answered, "Nope, I'm gonna take a lot of risks and do dangerous things." Her mom hadn't found that funny.

"You'll understand," she'd say, "when you're a mother."

Stella's mother still told her to be careful every time they parted, and now a mother herself, Stella did understand. She knew all too well how easily horrible things could happen.

She paced in the dining room, looking out the front windows at the darkness. She went to the front door and opened it, looked out the screen door, then went outside. October nights were cool and alive with the sound of crickets or katydids or whatever the hell it was in the woods that made so much noise. Cicadas? Didn't they come out only every seventeen years…?

She was freaking out. She wished for a cigarette, even one of Jen's e-cigs. Instead, she tapped out another message.

ANSWER ME.

Another five minutes passed. An eternity. She was just about to send another message, thinking of calling the police, or at the very least Jeff, when her phone shook in her hand and played its distinctive triple ding.

ran too far

She hadn't realized how slick her hands had become with sweat until her phone slipped from her grasp. She caught it before it could hit the sidewalk. She typed a reply. Where? I'll come get you.

No. I'll come home.

She wasn't going to play this game with him. Instead of another text, Stella called. Tristan sounded out of breath when he answered, and she didn't bother to identify herself. "What did I tell you about getting home before dark?"

She'd jumped on him too hard; she heard it in his reply. "Sorry."

"I'll come get you."

He hesitated, panting. "Pick me up at Sheetz."

She frowned, estimating the distance from their house to the convenience store. "You ran to Sheetz?"

"Just pick me up there. I want to get something to eat anyway."

There was another argument there, a reminder about the sandwich she'd made for him and that he'd rejected, but what sort of shitty mother let her kid go hungry? She sighed and disconnected.

He was waiting for her at one of the outside tables, already drinking from one of those insanely huge fountain drinks and eating a burrito when she pulled into the parking lot. Bugs swooped and swarmed, dive-bombing him and the overhead lights that made him look extra pale. His hair stuck up in the back and clung to his forehead with sweat. He probably reeked.

She kept herself from hugging him by pretending she was angry. The truth was, she was just glad to see him all in one piece. Not that she forgave him—there'd be recriminations for this. There had to be. She'd specifically told him not to run too far and to be home before dark, and he hadn't been.

But maybe she didn't have to really punish him. Maybe her annoyance would be enough. Maybe only a few snakes had to come out of her hair. Half a momdusa, not the full-fledged explosion.

She went inside and got herself a frozen latte, even though the temperature had dropped enough to make a hot coffee drink sound better. They gave her stomachaches, but she couldn't resist. When she came back outside, Tristan had finished his food and crumpled the garbage. He was busy tapping away at his phone, playing a game or texting or Connexing or whatever it was the kids did these days.

The car ride home was silent and stinky. She had to open the windows just to keep from choking on the overripe smell of teenage boy sweat, and Tristan turned the radio up so loud there was no chance of talking. He used to sing along with the songs, but he didn't now. Stella did, fumbling the words, a little bit on purpose to lighten the mood between them even though she felt as though she had every right to be pissed.

She wasn't good at letting go. Not in her regular life. It had been one of the things Jeff had complained about, a flaw she wanted to deny but deep inside knew she couldn't. Stella liked the last word. So when they got home and into the kitchen, she couldn't resist one final poke.

"You can take that sandwich for lunch tomorrow."

Her son, who'd once been a tiny baby, then a toddler dragging his toy bear in the dirt, her boy who was now on his way to being a man, frowned. He shrugged and ran his fingers through his dirty hair in a way disconcertingly like his father had done when they'd first met. It was a panty twister, that move, and he didn't know it yet, thank God.

He looked at the fridge. Then at her, for the first time in a long while meeting her gaze without letting it slide away. "I never liked those sandwiches, Mom."

Stubbornly, Stella shook her head. "You loved—"

"No, Mom," Tristan told her firmly. When had his voice dropped? No more cracking, no more sudden shifts in pitch. "That wasn't me. That was never me. I just never said anything about it until now."

He left her in the kitchen and thudded his big feet up the stairs, and in a few minutes the shower started to run. The pipes squealed. Stella stood without moving, her eyes closed, for a long time, remembering.

Then she threw the sandwich in the trash.

CHAPTER FIVE

Some trips are focused, pinpointed. Specific. Stella arrives, finds what she's looking for and leaves a day or two later. Sometimes she comes home disappointed—Stella might have broad standards and eclectic taste in men, but when it comes to flying she does have standards, nevertheless.

On some trips, like this one to Minnesota, flying is simply a bonus. The Mall of America is a short shuttle ride from both the airport and the luxurious casino hotel where she's booked a king-size room. She's planned a weekend of shopping. Good food in fancy restaurants. Even a little gambling.

Normally, Stella travels carry-on only, but this time she has checked an empty suitcase that she will fill with all of her holiday shopping. The twenty-five-dollar checked-bag fee is worth it, when you consider what she'd have to pay to ship all of her purchases. She spends hours and hundreds of dollars, visiting every store at her leisure and losing herself in the comparison of gifts. Finding the perfect thing for her parents, sister, brother-in-law, nieces and nephews. Coworkers. She even picks up a gift for Jeff and Cynthia, not because she wants to, particularly, but because Cynthia always sends her something and it's begun to feel as though the expectation of receiving one in turn is easier to fulfill than dealing with the unspoken resentment.

For Tristan, she falters. He has so much already. Though Stella vowed to herself she would never play the game of tug-of-war with Jeff about which parent is the "cooler" one, they have both gone overboard with the gifts since the divorce. Tristan owns every device, every video game system with all the accessories, sometimes in duplicate so he has one in each house and doesn't have to suffer the loss of his toys. There've been musical instruments and lessons. Sports equipment. Trips.

But what, she wonders as she goes from store to store to store, would her son really *like?* The problem is, Stella really doesn't know. The sandwich she threw in the trash haunts her, and she second-guesses herself, picking things up and putting them down. She comes away with very little, telling herself there's still time, but she knows too well how that's not always true.

The trip isn't totally without self-indulgence. In the fancy lingerie shop, she springs for a pretty merry widow corset set in a deep wine color. It gives her magnificent cleavage. Paired with matching panties and sheer stockings, her sexiest heels, she's going to shine like a diamond.

In her hotel room Stella packs away all her purchases in the empty suitcase and lays out her clothes for the night. The new lingerie looks even better in the hotel room's far more flattering light than it did in the dressing room. She straightens her back, squares her shoulders. Juts a hip. She

knows how to showcase what she has now in a way she
never did until a few years ago. Then again, until a few
years ago, Stella favored high-waisted cotton granny panties and full-coverage bras, and the last time she'd worn
sexy lingerie had been the first night of her honeymoon.
And that had been no more than a silky nightgown with
spaghetti straps.

Jeff had always said he didn't see the point in spending so much money on something you were only going to
take off right away, and Stella had believed he meant it. Of
course, later, when she'd stumbled on his browser history
and saw the kinds of porn he'd been watching, she could
only chuckle a little at how all the women in his favorite
videos had worn garter belts and stockings, crotchless panties, bras with the nipples cut out. By then there was no way
Stella would've kissed him on the mouth, much less sucked
his cock, and lingerie was out of the question.

No, she hadn't begun wearing sexy scanties for men, even
if most of the ones she found did seem to like her choices.
Stella began wearing these scraps of silk and satin for herself. When she wears something pretty, even under her
rattiest jeans or T-shirt, it reminds her that her body still
works. She breathes, she laughs and sighs; she has orgasms.

She's alive.

In front of the full-length mirror, she smooths the satin
over her belly and cups her breasts for a moment, lifting
them. Her nipples tighten as she watches herself. She tries
on a smile, slow and seductive. She turns to look over her
shoulder at her ass, which will never be her favorite fea-
ture but looks pretty good in the wispy panties. The best
part of this outfit is that there's no hint of it beneath her

regular clothes, but it's almost guaranteed to be an eyeball popper when she gets undressed.

Stella draws in a breath, hands flat on her belly. Her ribs twinge a little as they expand against the corset's metal bones, but it's not laced so tight that she feels faint. She runs her hands up her sides, pressing lightly, waiting for the pain that never seems to go away, though there's no reason for her to ache. Then she slides a hand between her legs, stroking lightly. Her clit pulses. Pushing her fingers inside her panties, Stella finds slick heat. Anticipation is the best aphrodisiac.

She's packed a couple choices, but decides on a simple black dress of clinging fabric. Long sleeves and a demure neckline are offset by the thigh-high slit that will give a tantalizing peek at the tops of her stockings if she crosses her legs just right. Her jewelry is simple to match—a pair of silver hoops in her ears, a matching bracelet of hammered metal and a silver herringbone chain at her throat. She pulls her hair into a careful French knot, sprays on a hint of perfume and she's ready to go.

There was a time when, if she'd seen a woman like herself sitting alone in a high-end restaurant, reading while she ate her expensive dinner, Stella would've felt sorry for her. Now she's been on enough shitty dates to appreciate and understand the luxury of being able to enjoy a good steak and a good book at the same time without having to force a conversation. She declines the waiter's offer of a cocktail, but a few minutes later, he returns.

"The gentleman—" he points to a man several tables over "—would like to send you a glass of wine."

Stella looks up. "Ah. Tell him thanks, but no."

"Something else?" the waiter asks. "We have a great pomegranate martini—"

"No. Thanks. I don't care for anything, but please let him know I appreciate the offer."

By the end of her meal, a truly stellar steak and asparagus steamed to perfection, Stella has almost finished her book and the waiter is back with another offer.

"Coffee and dessert? The gentleman—"

Persistent, she thinks. And horny. She likes that.

Stella sets aside her book and smiles. "Please ask the gentleman if he'd like to join me."

If the waiter hates playing Cupid, he doesn't show it. In minutes, the man who seriously wants to get Stella liquored up and on a sugar high arrives at her table. He's tall, dark and handsome. Just her type, but who's she kidding? Almost all men are her type when she flies.

"Hi. I'm Daryl." He holds out a hand. Warm fingers squeeze hers with the perfect amount of pressure. He has wide brown eyes and a great smile. Straight white teeth. Curly black hair cropped close to his head. His suit is expensive, and so is his watch.

"Lavinia." It's the name of one of the characters in her book.

"Pretty name. Unusual." Daryl looks up at the waiter. "I'll have a coffee and a piece of cherry pie. Vanilla ice cream. And the lady will have...?"

"The same," she decides without looking to see what other delights she might be missing on the dessert menu. "Cherry pie's my favorite."

Daryl is in town for a week to meet with clients, for a business he doesn't describe and Stella doesn't ask about. He comes to Minneapolis a few times a year, always stays at this hotel because of how easy it is to get to the airport and also, of course, the gambling. "Do you gamble, Lavinia?"

"Sometimes. I'm not much for poker or blackjack, but I do like to play the slots. This pie is amazing, great choice. And thank you, by the way." Stella drags her fork through the thick, sweet cherry goo and licks it, watching Daryl's gaze follow the flicker of her tongue.

"How about craps?"

She smiles. "Don't you have to be lucky to win?"

"You have to be lucky to win at anything." Daryl's smile leaves crinkles in the corners of his eyes that Stella likes very much.

She leans toward him. "Tell me, then. Do you feel lucky?"

"Oh," Daryl says, leaning too, "I surely hope so."

She lets him take her to the casino, and she lets him press a hundred dollars' worth of chips into her hand. She also lets him put his arm around her as they take their place at the craps table, and when he asks her to blow on the dice for him, she does that too. Stella has never considered herself lucky, but Daryl wins. And wins again.

Soon the whole crowd is chanting her name—well, not her real name, but the one she gave him. And when finally his streak ends, he pulls her into his arms and kisses her in front of the crowd as though they're lovers and not strangers. He's a very good kisser, and Stella doesn't mind. Not at all.

"Lucky Lavinia," Daryl says into her ear, his hands settling on her hips to pull her close. "You wanna get out of here?"

They go to his room, and he offers her a drink, but she declines.

"Not a drinker." Daryl nods. "I remember now. I could

order us something from room service, if you've got a craving for something sweet."

That's not what she's craving, and she answers him by stepping again into his embrace and offering her mouth. Daryl kisses her slowly, palming her ass and grinding her a little against the growing bulge of his crotch. When he moves his mouth to her throat, Stella lets her head fall back with a small sigh.

"You like that?" Daryl nips a little, sending shivers of delight all through her. "Yeah. I thought so."

Her nipples are tight and hard, her cunt aching. She wants to run her hands all over him, but steps back instead. "Do you have protection?"

She does, if he doesn't. She always does. But a man who expects to fuck without bothering to buy the condoms isn't worth even the small amount of time she's prepared to give him.

"Yeah." Daryl tugs at his tie and the buttons of his shirt, exposing his smooth dark skin. "I'll take care of you, don't you worry."

Stella tilts her head to look him over. "You do this a lot, Daryl?"

"I *travel* a lot." He gives her a nice once-over. "You do this a lot, Lavinia?"

It's a fair question. Her fingers inch up her hem, little by little. For another man, she might play coy or even lie, but she and Daryl seem to have an understanding. "I do it enough."

His warm, full-throated laugh settles between her thighs. "Good. Just so I know where I stand."

It's good for them both to know. She curls her fingers in the fabric of her dress, easing the hem higher. Daryl watches her. At the slide of his tongue over his full lower lip, her clit pulses.

"Why don't you get out of that shirt?" she says in a low voice. "And those pants too."

Daryl unbuttons and tosses his shirt to the chair, but his hands hesitate at his belt buckle. "What about you?"

"You want me to take off my dress?" Stella smiles.

He works open the buckle of his belt, then gets out of his pants and tosses them onto the chair next to his shirt. His body is gorgeous. Fit and lean, with muscles in all the right places. Standing in a pair of tight black briefs, Daryl lifts his chin toward her as he bends to take off his socks. "C'mon. Be fair."

Stella pulls her dress up and over her head, then carefully hangs it over the back of the room's other chair. She strikes a pose, showing off everything she has to its best advantage, and it must be working for him, because Daryl's eyes go wide. He wipes a hand over his mouth.

"Damn," he says. "Look at you."

This is the rush. This is the gasping breath after being underwater for too long. This is coming out of the dark and into the light, if only for a little while.

Stella needs this.

"Kiss me," she says, and Daryl is happy to oblige.

He turns them both so he can sit on the edge of the bed with Stella standing between his legs. He breaks the kiss and leans into her, pressing his forehead to the stiff satin covering her belly. His hands roam over her ass, squeezing. He looks up at her, brow a little furrowed, lips parted and a little wet from their kisses.

"What?" Stella traces a fingertip over one of his thick,

dark eyebrows. His eyelashes are amazing, enviably long and thick, the sort a woman would kill for.

"Didn't think it would be this easy, that's all."

She wonders if she ought to be a little insulted by this. Stella presses her thumb to Daryl's lower lip; when he opens for her, she tucks it inside his mouth. He sucks it gently, biting the tip. She bends to kiss him, replacing her thumb with her tongue. She looks into his eyes.

"We both want something," she says. "Looks like it's the same thing. Is there something wrong with that?"

"No...."

Some men, she knows, want to fuck women who act like whores. Some men think all women are whores. There *is* a difference. Stella's not a slut or a whore no matter how many times she flies with strangers. No man can make her feel that way about herself, no matter what he says or how he acts. She cups Daryl's chin in her palm, holding his face still while she studies him.

"Do you want me to leave?" she asks.

"No!" Daryl laughs and grips her hips, pulling her closer. "Hell no."

"You want to fuck me," Stella murmurs, watching his pupils dilate as she speaks.

"Yeah. Yeah, I do."

She smiles, breathing assent against his mouth. "So fuck me, Daryl."

With a low growl, he pulls her onto the bed, rolling them both so he ends up on top. His weight's a surprise, though the press of his erection isn't. He pushes his hips against her, grinding. His mouth finds hers, a little too hard. Stella puts her hands flat on his chest to hold him back from her for a second. Daryl breaks the kiss to look at her, holding her gaze while he rocks his cock against her clit.

They kiss for a long time, longer than she expects. But she doesn't mind. They move together on the bed, grinding, rocking, rolling.

Daryl moves a hand between her legs at last, slipping his fingers inside her panties. Stroking her clit. Then, pushing inside her. "Shit," he breathes. "You're so wet."

Kissing him, Stella shivers at the press of his thumb on her clit, the push of his fingers inside. One, then another. He fucks into her, and her body responds at once. Muscles going tight, breath short. She writhes under his practiced touch, giving herself up to this pleasure for a minute or so before she opens her eyes and finds him staring at her.

"What?" She goes still.

"I want to watch you come." Daryl licks his lips. "I get off on making a woman come for me."

Stella pushes up on one elbow to reach his mouth with hers. "Sounds like a great idea to me."

Daryl laughs then, relaxing. "Some women... They don't like that."

"They don't like to have an orgasm?" It's hard for her to talk with his fingers working their magic. Her voice is low, throaty, trailing into a moan.

"They like to come, sure, but they want to get right to the fucking. They want to rush things. They want my dick inside them too soon."

Stella arches into his caress, putting her arms over her head to find the solid support of the headboard. She spreads her legs wider, rocking into Daryl's thrusting touch. His thumb slides on her clit in perfectly rough and staggered circles, teasing her.

"I want to watch you come," Daryl says again.

"Keep doing what you're doing," Stella whispers. "And you will."

Daryl pauses long enough to slide her panties down and off, then gets back between her legs to kiss the insides of her thighs. Stella tenses, thinking he'll use his mouth on her and waiting for that new sensation, but Daryl takes her clit between his thumb and forefinger instead. He squeezes gently. Pleasure builds, and Stella rides it. Her orgasm is a column of rising flame, consuming her. Ecstasy floods her, taking away the world and everything else beyond this sensation.

Gasping, breathless, Stella cries out. When she quiets, the soft huff of Daryl's breath caresses her inner thighs. She can't move, doesn't want to even shift to look at him. She is satisfied, replete. Until he begins to gently pinch her clit again. The pressure is soft and steady. It's always harder for her to come a second time, but she's willing to let him try. Stella breathes, relaxing into her desire. There've been times when she's gotten anxious about her ability to have an orgasm, when it's taken too long, when it has slipped away from her no matter how skilled or attentive her lover was being. There've been times when she's had to push a partner aside and take over for herself, or sometimes even simply give up grasping at the elusiveness of her climax. But she's never, ever faked it.

"Wanna see you come again," Daryl murmurs.

Stella sighs. "I'm not sure…"

"Relax."

She tries. When he moves his mouth onto her, Stella lifts herself to his tongue. Lips and teeth press her. His fingers move inside her. It's taking too long, and the first was too strong. She's not going to make it again....

"Shhh," Daryl says against her cunt. "Just feel good."

Stella's flown with selfish men. Egotistical, arrogant men who haven't cared if she's come at all, much less more than once. Not often—it's been her experience that most men, even the ones who pick up women in airport bars, like to be sure they can get the women off. But she's never been with a man so insistent. So determined. And all she can do, really, is lie back and let Daryl try to get her to come.

After another few minutes, he moves up her body to kiss her mouth. "No?"

"Sorry," Stella says, though she's really not.

Daryl laughs a little. "Damn. I tried."

"You did." She rolls to straddle him. He's not completely hard, but that changes after a minute of stroking. "Your turn."

"Let me just grab something." In another minute he's back, shucking out of his briefs and tearing the wrapper on the condom to sheathe himself.

Stella watches him, her breath catching at his look of careful concentration as he smooths the condom onto his cock. How he grips himself at the base. How beautiful men are with their hard pricks in their fists, when their bodies have become tuned toward nothing but pleasure. She loves these moments maybe even more than the actual fucking, these moments when she watches her partner getting ready for her.

Daryl fits himself inside her, keeping his weight balanced on one hand as he uses the other to guide himself. His cock is thicker than she's expecting. Longer too. It makes her gasp when he seats himself all the way. He pauses for a few seconds, looking down at her.

"You feel so good," he says. "I want to fuck you so hard."

He starts moving. Slow at first. Then faster. Harder. He tucks a hand beneath the back of her neck, pulling her closer to his mouth for a bruising kiss. Daryl fucks her hard, his pelvis grinding her clit, and it's this pounding pressure that starts to tip her over the edge again.

He sees it on her face. "Yeah?"

"Yeah," Stella manages to say as she gives herself up again to desire. She comes with a short, sharp jolt of pleasure that cuts off as abruptly as it has arrived, but it's enough to buck her hips. It's all good. So good.

Daryl shudders, grimacing. He bends to bury his face in the side of her neck as he thrusts, then shouts out with his own climax.

A minute or so after that, he rolls off her to stare up at the ceiling. He's put some distance between them, but not enough to make this awkward. She'll be able to get up in a few minutes and get dressed. Head back to her own room.

Before she can move, Daryl looks at her. "Was that okay for you?"

Stella sits, scanning the bed for her discarded panties. Spotting them on the floor, she moves to get off the bed. "It was great."

Daryl's hand on her wrist stops her. "Lavinia."

She twists to look at him, seeing his concern. Thanking him for his performance would feel a little over-the-top, not to mention contrived. "It was great, Daryl. Really."

He doesn't let her go for so long she starts to think he won't. Gently, Stella extricates herself from his grip and gets off the bed to step into her panties. Behind her Daryl takes care of the condom, then heads into the bathroom. He closes the door behind him.

Stella gets dressed quickly. Not lingering. The night has worn on almost to morning, and her plane leaves in only a few hours. She'll have just enough time to get back to her room, shower and change and head for the airport in time to get through security. In the days when she was a flight attendant, a million years ago, traveling by air used to be fun. Now, even with the free trips she still gets as part of the divorce settlement from Jeff, the CEO of an airline, the process of the airplane travel itself is something rather less than enjoyable.

She doesn't want to leave without saying goodbye— Daryl has been a fun flight. But it's late and she's tired and not in the mood for cuddling or, worse, conversation. The bathroom door opens just as she's slipping into her shoes and straightening her stockings.

Daryl looks surprised. "You're leaving?"

"Yes. I have an early plane." She goes to him, offering a kiss because it seems like the thing to do.

Daryl kisses her but looks confused. "You don't want to stay? Have another go-round in the morning?"

"It's already morning." Stella stifles a yawn. "And I'm really tired. This was great, though. I had a good time."

"Not good enough, I guess." Stepping back, Daryl frowns. "Should I even ask for your number?"

"I can give you my number, but that's not what this is. Is it?" She gives him a small smile, trying hard not to sound annoyed, though by this point she's ready to head out the door. "You're not really going to call me, are you?"

This gives him pause. "I guess not. It's just…everyone else always wants to exchange numbers."

Stella laughs. "And how many times do you ever get in touch?"

"You never know. I might call you up, see if you want to be my Lady Luck again sometime when you're out this way." Daryl smiles, but Stella shakes her head.

"I don't think I'll be out this way again for a long time."

"Oh. So it's like that."

"Yes," she says. "It's like that."

She's hurt his feelings. She didn't mean to, but of course that won't make him feel any better. Now this is becoming awkward.

"You won't even give me your number? C'mon." He flashes her a smile meant to be charming, but the desperation in it leaves her cold.

"I don't give my phone number to strangers," Stella says without apologizing.

Daryl scowls. "But you'll fuck one."

Stella doesn't give that the dignity of an answer.

"Was it good for you?" he cries after her as the door shuts, and Stella understands that none of this was really about her, at all.

For a moment she considers grabbing the door before it can close all the way and telling him yes, the sex was good. Fine. She came, twice as a matter of fact. She considers, briefly, soothing his ego.

But then she remembers that none of this was really about him in the first place.

CHAPTER SIX

Mondays. Universally despised, always hectic. This morning Stella had already slept through her alarm, waking up instead to the thunder of Tristan's feet up and down the stairs as he hollered back and forth with his buddy Steven, who'd come to give him a ride. Since Stella had already told Tristan she wasn't sure she wanted him riding with Steven, even if the older boy had been driving for almost two years, this was not the best way to wake up.

"Dad lets me."

Yeah, and then there was that. Too tired to argue with him, especially since he'd missed the bus, Stella waved Tristan into Steven's car and watched them pull out of the driveway with her heart lodged firmly in her throat. She was sure Jeff did let Tristan ride with Steven or whoever else he wanted to, so long as it meant Jeff didn't have to take him to school. Whatever made Jeff's life easier. But Stella wasn't going to dwell on that right now.

Halfway through her shower, the water ran cold. "Son of a bitch."

She twisted the faucet handle, jiggling it, which sometimes worked. Not today. She finished rinsing her hair, shivering, entire body covered in goose pimples, and didn't even bother to shave her legs.

There'd been a time when it was like asking Tristan to cut off his arms and legs in order to get him in the shower, and now he took forever. That was part of the reason why Stella had started setting her alarm for later, to give the aging hot water heater time to replenish the supply.

Downstairs, when she pulled open the dishwasher to get a clean coffee cup, she found another surprise. Nothing was clean. Muttering curses under her breath, Stella stabbed open the soap dispenser...only to discover it encrusted with half-dissolved soap. She checked the dishes. Wet. Just not clean.

"Dammit." She went to the sink to run the hot water. Barely lukewarm, even twenty minutes after her shower. "Shit. Double shit."

Already running late for work, she took the time to run downstairs to the basement to make sure that the water heater hadn't exploded or something equally dire. Staring at it, wishing she knew what to look for, Stella knew better than to fiddle with any of the settings. She did notice the small light by the temperature gauge wasn't lit, but maybe it never was. She couldn't remember ever really looking at the hot water heater before.

No time to deal with it now. She had to get to work. And, adding to the joy that had begun her Monday, the trip that normally took forty minutes took an hour and a half because of an accident.

A car had hit and flipped over the guardrails along the deep, V-shaped gully that separated the east- and westbound sections of the rural highway. It had caught halfway down the steep embankment, the front end a crumpled horror. It had caught on fire. There'd been no way to see if anyone was stuck inside, though the ambulance and fire trucks had given her hope that even if there had been, there wasn't anymore. Traffic had backed up for a couple miles, moving slow, rubbernecking. Stella had been stuck inching along the accident site for a good ten minutes before reaching the opposite side and being able to speed up.

Ten minutes wasn't so long, but by the end of it, she'd been sweating. Her hands shaking. Her breath catching hard in her throat, like needles in her lungs. In the rearview mirror, her eyes were wide and dark, the pupils dilated to cover her irises.

At work, she sat in the parking lot for another five minutes longer than necessary in order to get herself under control. In the office, she went directly to the restroom so she could splash her face with cold water, which had her remembering the frigid shower from the morning.

Frustration, at least, was better than fear.

Despite the morning's rough start, the day itself went smoothly. It almost always did. Sitting for hours in front of a computer, editing out zits and wrinkles, listening to music or audiobooks on her iPod... It certainly wasn't the sort of job Stella had ever imagined herself doing, but it suited her. Her manager was nice and accommodating, and you couldn't beat the hours. Four ten-hour days a week. Jeff had liked to snark at her for that... But again, Stella put that memory aside. It no longer mattered what Jeff thought and hadn't for a long time.

Today's queue of photos was the easiest she'd had for weeks. The customers were all dressed appropriately, nobody had any weird requests and the packages they wanted to order were all standard. Stella worked her way steadily through the jobs, one after another. She worked so efficiently that, despite arriving late, she finished her queue early, and rather than stay and fuck around waiting for more jobs to show up, she decided to leave early.

She called Tristan on her way home, but typically he didn't answer. Nor to her text, which did annoy her, though it was possible he was out running, not just ignoring her. *Benefit of the doubt*, Stella told herself. *Give him the benefit of the doubt.* She called Jeff next, already wincing at the sound of his voice.

"What?" Jeff said.

She shouldn't be offended—it was how he always answered the phone, for anyone but his boss. Even his mother had been subject to his lack of phone etiquette. Stella had never heard him answer a call from Cynthia, though. Maybe she got the princess treatment. God knew she did with everything else.

"Is Tristan with you? I can swing by and pick him up on my way home. I'm getting out now."

"Why are you getting out now?"

She owed him no explanations, Stella reminded herself, but that didn't mean she had to be a total douche canoe to him about everything as a matter of course either. "I finished early. Is he there?"

"Cynthia took him shopping."

"Oh." Stella paused. "Well, I have some errands to run. I can swing by and get him when I'm finished, if she doesn't want to bring him all the way to my place on her way home."

"I'll have her text you."

Stella sighed. They disconnected without saying much of anything else and for a moment, melancholy, Stella tried to remember when they'd loved each other. She couldn't, really. Everything that had happened since colored all the good memories in shades of black.

Her errands didn't take as long as she'd expected, which was why she was surprised to pull into the drive to the blaze of lights in the house and the front door half-open. Irritated, Stella yanked it shut behind her. "Tristan!"

"He's upstairs," Jeff said from the kitchen, where he sat at her table with one of her diet sodas and a pile of her mail, along with her latest issue of *Entertainment Weekly*.

She hadn't seen his car, dammit, forgetting he preferred to park along the opposite side of the street so he didn't have to back out of the driveway. She hated the sight of Jeff in her kitchen—which had once been his kitchen, that was true enough. But by the end she'd hated the sight of him in it then too.

"Did he eat?"

"Yeah. Cynthia made pot roast." Jeff drained the last of the soda and put the empty can back on the table, then tossed the magazine onto the pile of mail.

Of course she did. Stella gave him a tight smile. "Great. Thanks for bringing him home."

Jeff pulled something from his back pocket—a piece of paper he'd folded into thirds. He flattened it on the table and pushed it in her direction. "Here."

"What's that?" Stella asked warily, not taking it.

"I brought over a spreadsheet."

"Of what?" She crossed her arms, keeping her expression carefully neutral. Jeff had always been fond of spreadsheets.

"Of expenses."

Stella's eyebrows rose. "Expenses? For what?"

"Tristan," Jeff said, and Stella's jaw dropped. "I've been keeping track."

Now she took the paper and looked over it. True to form, Jeff had made columns for medical expenses, sports equipment, orthodontia, clothes, school supplies...and gifts. Stella looked at him. "You have to be fucking kidding me."

Jeff looked pained. "Stella."

"You kept track of how much you spent on gifts. For your son." Her lip curled.

They'd hammered out a lot of details in the divorce settlement. Argued over who got to keep the china and how long Stella would remain on his account with Pegasus Airlines so she could get free travel. She'd fought hard for that one. But they hadn't set up anything specific regarding child support for Tristan, mostly because the original plan had been that each of them would be responsible for whatever expenses arose while he was with each of them, and they'd share major expenses. Stella simply tried to take care of whatever Tristan needed, only going to Jeff for stuff like the braces that had come off last year. Like the ski club trip Tristan had wanted to take last Christmas break that had turned out to be twice as expensive as she'd planned for.

Jeff gave her a look. "Of course. I just wanted to show you..."

Stella crumpled the paper in her hands, then thought better of it. She smoothed it. Folded it. Handed it back to him. "What's your point, Jeff?"

"I just dropped a couple hundred bucks on him for gear.

New shoes. He needed clothes too." Jeff paused. "Cynthia made sure he had everything he needed."

Cynthia, who matched her shoes to her belts to her purses. Who got her nails done every week. Hair too.

"Please tell Cynthia I said thanks."

Jeff blinked. "I estimated your expenses too."

Stella set her jaw at that, willing herself not to totally lose her shit all over him, but already knowing she was about to blow. "And?"

"Just wanted to share with you, that's all."

"Because you want to show me up."

Jeff frowned. "That's not what I want."

"No?" Stella waved a dismissive hand. "Really? Then what's this spreadsheet about, Jeff?"

But she knew what it was about, without him even having to respond. Jeff was trying to prove to her in his underhanded way that he was as much a parent to Tristan as she was. That just because she did the majority of the day-to-day stuff didn't mean he didn't do his share too—the money he'd spent evidence of his parenting. Typical Jeff.

Before he could answer, and she could see his desire to reply in every line of his face, Tristan, wrapped in a towel, hair wet, expression stormy, came into the kitchen. Stella's eyebrows rose.

"There's no hot water."

"Shit," she said with a sigh. "I'd hoped it was just temporary."

"Something wrong with your hot water heater?" Jeff asked.

"Maybe." To Tristan, she said, "Just do a pits and privates until I can take a look at it, okay?"

Jeff was already getting up. Never mind that he hadn't

lived here in eight years, and that when he had, he'd been gone so often on business that Stella had been the one to take care of everything around the house anyway. "I'll take a look at it."

"You don't have to—"

But he was already heading into the basement while Tristan stomped back upstairs. Stella gritted her teeth and followed her ex-husband down the stairs to the small utility room that enclosed the furnace and hot water heater. As soon as he opened the door, Jeff recoiled, lifting his feet as though he'd stepped in dog shit. But it was water. Stella heard the squish of it from where she stood, and she almost laughed at the look on Jeff's face when he turned to look at her.

"You have a leak," he said as though it were a personal affront.

"That would explain why we didn't have any hot water."

Jeff squished his way to the hot water heater and bent to study it. "Grab me a flashlight, would you?"

"I said I could take care of it."

He looked over his shoulder at her. "Obviously you can't."

There was a time when he'd been able to read her. When he'd *known* her. Stella couldn't recall exactly when that had changed, but it was never more obvious than in this moment when she was almost ready to punch him in the junk, and all he could do was give her a condescending sneer.

"Get out," she said. "I'll call a plumber. I have a wet vac. I will handle this."

"I'm trying to help you."

"I don't need your help." Stella crossed her arms and

stepped back to let him pass. "I can handle it, whether you think so or not."

"Don't get all bent out of shape. I'm just trying to help you—"

"We're not married anymore, Jeff." Stella could no longer keep her voice steady and even, and she knew it was only going to give him more ammunition to accuse her of being overemotional—something he'd done a whole hell of a lot of during their last days. "This isn't your responsibility, and I wouldn't want you to throw it in my face later. Really, I can handle it."

"Fine." Jeff dusted off his hands and pushed past her, muttering something that sounded suspiciously like "stubborn bitch" under his breath.

She'd been called worse.

Stella followed him up the stairs and into the kitchen, leaving him in there and not bothering to look back when he called after her. Halfway up the stairs she heard the front door open and close. She knocked lightly on Tristan's door, waiting until he answered before she opened it. She had to shove the door against a pile of dirty laundry, but ignored it for now.

"Hey."

Tristan's desk overflowed with miscellaneous junk, but he sat at it anyway. Bent over a sketch pad he closed when she came in, he shoved it under a pile of other things and twisted to look at her. He resembled Jeff more than ever when he scowled.

"I can take all the stuff back," he said. "Cynthia's the one who wanted to buy it all."

"I figured." Stella looked around the room, then leaned

against the bedpost. "You don't have to. Your dad can afford it."

Tristan nodded, his mouth still turned down. "Okay."

She wasn't making it much better. "I'm sorry you heard us fighting about it. It's not about you, Tristan. You know that, right?"

"Yeah. Whatever." He turned back to his desk, but didn't pull out the sketchbook or anything else. He just sat. Dismissing her.

"Tristan."

He didn't turn. Stella sighed. She moved closer to put her hand on his unyielding shoulder. She squeezed gently but said nothing else. Tristan sighed heavily.

A few years ago, their dog, Mr. Chips, had died of old age, at home with his head on Tristan's lap. That had been the last time she could remember her son crying or allowing her to hug him close—he'd grown taller than her in the interim years. And distant. He was becoming more of a stranger to her every day, and she didn't quite know how to stop it.

"No matter what happens between me and your dad, you know both of us still love you."

"Yeah."

Stella let go of him. "I could use your help in the basement, buddy. Can you come down, please?"

He nodded, still not looking at her. Stella didn't push it. Instead, she put in a call to her neighbors to get the name of the plumber they'd used when renovating their bathroom. She called Home Depot to get the prices of hot water heaters, as well as information on their delivery and installation services. And then she went downstairs, hooked up the shop vac and started cleaning up all the mess.

CHAPTER SEVEN

The only real, true time travel occurs in the mind. Scents and music and flavors make memories so vivid it's like being there all over again. This time, it was the sound of her name in a voice that had once been familiar but which she hadn't heard in a really long time.

"Stella?"

It's almost impossible not to turn around when someone says your name, kind of like the way most people will automatically take something if it's thrust toward their hands. Stella wasn't used to hearing her name shouted in a crowd, so she'd have turned even if it had been meant for someone else. Her heart was already pounding.

"Craig. Hi." Her mouth stretched into a smile she knew was too wide. "Wow."

He was smiling too. "Yeah. Wow. It's been a really long time."

Stella could've counted the length of it in months, weeks, days. Hours and minutes, actually, though admitting it would probably freak him out. It had been too long. Or maybe not long enough. The way her pulse leaped and her stomach twisted, she couldn't be sure if she was happy to see him or ready to run away.

"Too long," Craig said after a few seconds passed, Stella unable to speak.

"Yes," she managed, relieved her voice didn't shake. "Way too long. How've you been?"

"Good. I've been good. How are you? You look…great."

Her breath tried to catch in her throat, and she forced a swallow instead. Once upon a time, he'd said other things to her that had made it hard for her to breathe. Time had passed. They would pretend it hadn't happened; they'd been good at that. But she remembered.

"You too."

They stared for too long. Stood a little too close for long-lost strangers bumping into each other in front of the coffee shop. He wore the same cologne, and it still twisted her up tight and complicated inside.

"Let's go in," Craig said. "Let me buy you a coffee."

Coffee. Lunch. That's all it had ever been with them. And once, just once, a conversation in the rain.

The day was bright and clear today with a perfect fall sky, blue and cloudless. Stella wore a short skirt with patterned tights and knee-high boots, a light jacket. She'd dressed this morning in anticipation of cooler weather, but all of a sudden she was far too warm. She had errands to run, places to be, things to do.

"Let's go," she said.

It starts in the coffee shop in the next town, the one she started going to specifically so she could avoid her friends

and get out of the house at the same time, away from anything that reminded her of her failing marriage. It's where
she goes with her laptop and notebook to sit for hours and
make lists and submit her résumé to dozens of places she
hopes won't hire her. She sits and drinks cup after cup of
coffee and makes herself look busy so she can convince
herself she is.

There's a regular crowd in the coffee shop. There's the
woman who sits by the window, typing away and listening to her iPod—she writes books and is, if it's possible,
even more antisocial than Stella. There's a man who stares
at that woman when she's not looking; Stella wonders how
long it will take for him to work up the courage to talk to
her. There's a young mother who comes in every morning with her toddler son to drink a cup of coffee while he
has some hot chocolate. Stella will never talk to her. The
Bible club, its members in matching home-sewn dresses and
prayer caps, would probably love to have her join them, but
Stella's so completely not religious she's also certain she'd
offend them all without even trying. There's the salesguy
who fills the orders for potato salad. He smiles and nods,
but doesn't linger. He, like the staff behind the counter, is
friendly but too busy to make much conversation.

Finally there's Craig, who at first comes in for lunch once
a week. Then twice. Then three times, until finally he is
there every day and somehow, they are sharing a table and
laughing about… Well, whatever he says to make her laugh.
And it becomes this thing Stella refuses to name. This…
friendship. Because that's all it is, she tells herself every day
when she wakes up thinking about him, and every night
when his face is what she thinks of when she closes her eyes

and pretends to sleep. It's a friendship. If Craig didn't have a penis, this wouldn't even be an issue.

It's been so long since Stella laughed, really laughed. Before she knows it, she's looking up every time the bell over the door jingles. When the hands on her watch creep toward noon, her palms start to sweat and her heart to pound. Every day she assumes it's the last time he'll come in. Sometimes he's late and everything inside her goes dark. A weight lifts off her every time Craig comes through the door.

He only has an hour for lunch, and soon that's not enough. Stella believes Connex is the devil, but Craig loves it and "friends" her anyway. She doesn't have much on her profile and hasn't updated in close to a year, though she tries to check in once a week or so to make sure Tristan's not getting into trouble there. Craig has a lot of pictures, an active wall. Stella stalks his profile, checking out the photos of him at the beach, skiing, dressed for a holiday party. She looks at the pictures of him and his family. Two daughters. A wife, now ex, and a dog. Craig was part of a family, and this somehow comforts her. He can understand the challenges of a spouse and kids.

She tells Jeff nothing, and why should she? She doesn't tell him anything about her girlfriends, or the other people at the coffee shop. Actually, she doesn't tell Jeff much of anything anymore. He doesn't ask.

Stella finds work, finally, which means no more coffee shop. She'd taken a basic college course on photo-editing programs on a whim, and the job at the Memory Factory is perfect. Retouching pictures taken for church bulletins isn't what she'd ever imagined herself doing, but with a school-age child and a husband who works sixty hours a week and travels too, she can't go back to being a flight attendant. The hours and money make up for the slightly condescending way Jeff talks about it as a throwaway job.

She also has unlimited access to the internet, all day long, and an instant-message program. So does Craig. This is even better than their single, daily hour. They talk all day long, and even when they're not actively chatting, looking at her contact window and seeing his screen name there is like a touchstone. He's there if she needs him.

And, oh, Stella needs him.

She needs the jolt he gives her with every flirty comment and the small, secret jokes they've created that would mean nothing to anyone else. She needs his perspective on the world because it's different than hers, and even though they disagree on politics and religion, they never argue. He makes her think. He makes her *feel,* and it's been so long since she's had anything but agony or numbness that at first she doesn't recognize what it is that Craig gives her.

Joy.

He doesn't know her, so there are no reminders of the past she needs to forget. No stilted conversations steeped in pity. All Craig gives her is joy, and that's what she needs the most.

Stella knows this…thing…is wrong. But Craig makes her feel as if everything will be all right. As if she hasn't been through what she has. He makes her feel smart and funny. And sexy, yes. There's that. The giddy, floaty, heated rush of knowing someone finds her attractive. She needs that too.

Everything about them together is dishonest, but it's the only thing in her life that feels like the truth.

"Can I call you?" he asks. "I miss talking to you in person. Hearing your voice."

Craig lives alone. Shared custody means he has daddy duty only a few days of the week. The rest of his time is his own. Stella doesn't have that luxury. She has to think about when she can sneak in a late-night phone call. When she can fit him in around the rest of her life.

There's something special about the phone that makes it different than typing instant messages or even texts. Somehow talking on the phone is both more anonymous and intimate than even meeting in person in the coffee shop, in public, where they watch their words and are always so very, very careful not to touch.

"Why do you keep talking to me?" Stella asks him late one night when, feigning an upset stomach, she's sought the dark and quiet of the couch in the basement rec room. She stretches on the chilly leather, reaching for a blanket to warm her.

"I don't know. Sometimes I tell myself I shouldn't."

But he does. Over and over again, he comes back to her, and there is never any reason why they shouldn't continue this friendship other than that both of them know it's becoming more than that. It was already more than that before they ever spoke on the phone. They very specifically do not meet in person. They very carefully do not talk about why.

He complains about his ex-wife, but Stella is carefully, neutrally quiet about her husband. There are things she could complain about, if she wanted, but if she did that, other truths would come out. Things she doesn't want to talk about, not even to Craig. Perhaps especially not to him, because once he knows the truth, there will be no unknowing it. Sometimes things slip out, though. You

can't talk to someone almost every day for hours at a time
without them learning the most important bits and pieces
of you, especially in the darkest parts of the night when it's
so easy to feel alone.

"I miss you," Craig says abruptly when the silence has
stretched on too long. "I miss seeing you."

"I miss seeing you too." She closes her eyes against the
sudden relief of a fear she hadn't wanted to admit she had.

"Maybe we could have lunch sometime."

She should say no, but what comes out is "Yes. I'd like
that."

"It was great seeing you. Catching up." Craig's gaze lingered on hers, and Stella let it.

They'd spent the hour she would've spent shopping lingering over their coffees and a couple very good blueberry
scones he'd bought without asking her if she wanted one.
He'd just remembered how much she liked them. His knee
had nudged hers occasionally under the table, and once
when handing her a napkin his fingers had brushed hers.

There was a time she'd wanted him so much it had been
like fire inside her, consuming every thought. And now...
Now, Stella thought as they stood sort of awkwardly by
her car, each of them hesitating about a final hug...now,
she didn't want him anymore. That made her sadder than
anything else. Once she'd been put to her knees because of
the man in front of her, and it had been a place she'd willingly gone, but in the end it had broken her, just the same.
She had wanted him, and now she did not.

When he pulled her close, she let him, startled but not
resisting. When his mouth found her cheek, Stella closed
her eyes and breathed in his scent. The warmth of his skin

on hers was familiar. The weight of his hands on her. When
he let her go, she swayed, unsteady for a few seconds before
she could open her eyes.

"It was so good seeing you," Craig said in a low voice.
"I've really missed you."

Stella had not missed him. Not for a long time. But she
smiled and reached to squeeze his arm. "Me too."

"Maybe I could call you?"

"Sure. Absolutely." She nodded, smiling, a little taken
aback by how this all had gone. He could call her. She
would answer. It might get awkward, depending on what
he said or asked of her, but she didn't have the heart to tell
him no.

On impulse, she leaned in to hug him again, this time
holding tighter. Craig had been there when she'd needed
someone.

Maybe he needed someone.

"Call me," she said and scribbled her cell number on a
scrap of paper from her pocket. "That would be great."

The awkward brush of his mouth on hers would once
have made her shake; now it only made her smile. She
touched his face and took a few steps back. Craig nodded,
lips parted as though he meant to say more but didn't. He
looked back at her as he walked away, though. Waved.
Stella waved back.

In her car she sat for a few minutes, thinking of how
easily things could change even if it didn't feel easy at all
while you were in them.

CHAPTER EIGHT

"Knock, knock."

Stella looked up to see Jen rapping on the soft edge of the cubicle. "Hey."

"What're you doing tonight?"

"Nothing." Stella swiveled in her chair. "Tristan's with his dad tonight through the weekend."

"Want to go check out the new Justin Ross movie? Jared told me he'd rather poke out both eyes with a chopstick than go." Jen grinned.

Stella hesitated, thinking about the empty house, the laundry she'd planned to do. Cleaning out the fridge. Paying bills. She was flying over the weekend, but tonight she had no plans. "Yes. That sounds great."

"Dinner first?"

"Sure." Stella returned Jen's grin.

They went to dinner at a new Italian place that Stella had heard about but never tried. As she settled into her seat and put the napkin on her lap, Stella realized how long it had been since she'd even gone out with a girlfriend. How long it had been since she'd even really talked with one of her girlfriends.

"Wow," she said aloud without meaning to.

"What?" Jen looked up from the menu. "You don't like what they serve here? We can go someplace else—"

"No. Not that. Just that it's been a while since I went out." Stella held up a hand at the look on her friend's face. "I told you, I'm fine without a boyfriend. I meant with a friend. It's like I haven't even heard from any of them in forever."

She fell silent for a moment, remembering. "I guess I haven't really missed any of them."

The women she'd bonded with in the neighborhood playgroup, the wives of Jeff's friends. Those were the women she'd spent most of her time with. They'd had coffee and dinner at each other's houses. Watched each other's kids. Bitched about their husbands and kids.

But had she ever really been friends with any of those women? Real, strong friendships last through good times and bad, and there'd been some very, very bad times.

Stella looked at Jen. "I guess I lost more than I thought in the divorce."

Jen frowned. "That sucks."

"It's okay." Stella shrugged. "Honestly, I really did just notice now how long it's been since I had, like, a ladies' night out, which says a lot more about me than anything else. So, thanks for inviting me."

"Thanks for coming along. I'm such an enormous Justin Ross fangirl, and Jared will occasionally suffer through watching *Runner* with me, but he's like, 'no way am I going to see that movie.'" Jen laughed, shaking her head. "He'll be waiting up for me when I get home, though. Hoping he'll get secondhand lucky."

Stella snorted laughter. "And all I have at home is a pile of dirty laundry." Before Jen could say anything, she held up a hand. "Hush."

"He has a few cute friends," Jen said, then held up her hands at Stella's expression. "Okay, okay. I'll stop."

Dinner was good. The movie, even better. Stella had never watched *Runner,* the show that had made Justin Ross famous, but she knew who he was. It was impossible not to—he'd suddenly become America's sweetheart. She couldn't say she'd ever be the sort of fangirl Jen was, but she could definitely appreciate his appeal.

"Have fun tonight," she teased as they both got in their cars in the parking lot.

Jen gave her a starry-eyed grin. "Oh…I will. Girl, I definitely will."

Stella's phone pinged just as she pulled into traffic, but she didn't reach to pull it from her purse and check the message. She never checked her phone while driving. Ever. Tristan knew it, and was unlikely to ping again if she didn't answer right away, so when the phone chimed again, Stella glanced at her bag on the front seat, then at the clock. It was just past ten-thirty on a Thursday night. Jeff would've gone to bed. Cynthia would only text if there was a problem, and even then would be more likely to call than send a message.

At the third chime, Stella's hands started to sweat. She gripped the wheel harder, staring down the dark highway. No traffic lights to give her time to pause so she could fumble in her bag and find her phone. She had another twenty minutes' drive to go, and when the phone chimed a fourth, then fifth time, she pulled over to the side of the road to answer it.

The messages, a string of casual conversation ending with "give me a ring when you have a chance," had come from Craig.

First she was relieved that it wasn't an emergency. Then a little annoyed that she'd had to pull over. And finally, as she pulled back out into traffic and finished the drive, Stella realized she was…anxious.

Confused. Anxious. A little excited. But mostly wary, she thought as she dropped her keys in the bowl on the kitchen counter and hung her coat and purse in the closet.

She put her phone on the table while she poured herself a glass of cold water. She eyed it as she leaned against the counter to drink. As if it might bite her, she thought, and laughed out loud.

It was Craig, for goodness' sake.

She had told him to call her, she remembered that much. But, unlike those long-ago days when she'd counted the minutes in between conversations, she hadn't been thinking much of him at all. She hadn't really expected him to call her, as a matter of fact, and now that he had, it would be up to her to return it. Or not.

Still thinking about it, Stella took her phone upstairs and settled it into the charging dock. She showered and got ready for bed, taking her time, but even so it wasn't quite midnight when she slipped into her bed and turned out the light. She turned on her side to stare at the dark, square shape of the phone.

It was reprimanding her.

Not replying to a message was one of the shittiest things to do to someone. She'd always thought that. Not simply

not replying right away, but not replying at all, ever. Toward the end of their marriage, Jeff had started ignoring
her messages, and it had driven her insane with rage.

Craig had always answered her messages…until he'd
stopped.

They've ordered food, but Stella can't eat. She pushes the
food around with her fork and drinks too much iced tea,
but her stomach's too jumpy to put any food in it. Craig
asked to meet her at a chain restaurant where you can create your own pasta dish, and she ordered chicken Alfredo,
a stupid choice because it's far too heavy and rich for her
even on days when she's not a bundle of nerves.

It doesn't matter how many days they've already spent
eating lunch together, or how many hours they've spent
talking on the computer and the phone. This feels different. It *is* different, she reminds herself as Craig tells her a
funny story she finds herself incapable of laughing at. Her
face is frozen. Her fingers clumsy enough to knock her
silverware on the floor so that, blushing, stammering, she
has to reach for her fork.

Craig bends at the same time, his hand taking hers. He
squeezes her fingers, and Stella drops the fork. They both
sit up, facing each other across the small, intimate table for
two. It's a table for lovers, though that isn't what they are.

"Hey," Craig says quietly. "Are you all right?"

She's not. Her hands still shake so much that she tucks
them into her lap, linking her fingers to keep them still.
She manages a smile she hopes doesn't make him recoil.
"Yes, sure. Of course."

Craig carries the conversation all through lunch, and at
the end of it, asks her if she wants to go for a walk with

him along the river. The weather's nice, not too hot. A little breezy. It whips her hair around her face as they follow the black curving path down toward the water. The river's high right now, covering most of the concrete steps leading into it. She's seen it low enough to expose them all.

That's what Stella's thinking about so she doesn't have to think about the way Craig takes her hand as they walk. The height of the water in the river. How fast it flows. What would happen if she went down those stairs and into it… Would she be swept away?

He holds her hand only long enough to tug her to a stop, turning her to face him. "Stella."

She can't look at him. Past him. Beyond him. Anywhere but into his eyes.

"Hey," Craig says in a low voice. "Please look at me."

She does, and it's not as bad as she'd thought it would be. It's worse.

So much worse to look into his deep blue eyes and see the lines in the corners. To lose herself in the way he tilts his head so slightly to the side as he studies her. To note the curve of his mouth and the flash of his tongue inside it when he talks.

"What is this?" Stella asks suddenly, interrupting whatever it was that Craig had started to say. Before he can say anything, she keeps going. "What are we doing? What do you want, Craig?"

He's silent for a moment while the river breeze ruffles the light jacket he's wearing. When it looks as though he's going to reach for her, Stella takes a step back. Craig's brow furrows, but he lets his hands fall back to his sides.

"I don't know." He sounds sincere. "I just like to be with you, Stella."

It's the nicest and worst thing anyone has ever said to her, both at the same time. The look of sudden longing on his face slumps her shoulders. Tightens her throat. It makes her want to leap into his arms and cover his face with kisses…. It makes her want to run away from him and never look back.

"I like to be with you too," she says in a thick, choked voice that embarrasses her.

"Can we sit?" Craig points to a metal bench overlooking the water.

They sit. Their knees touch every so often as they turn toward each other. Stella keeps her hands in her lap so she won't touch him.

She wants to touch him so much.

"Look," he says finally, after long minutes in which neither of them speaks. "I know this is one of those things that is supposed to be wrong. But it doesn't feel wrong. Does it."

He makes it a statement, not a question, but she'd have answered the same way even if he had. "No. It should. I want it to."

For a moment, Craig looks unsure and sad. Then he nods, as though her reply has made something clear that had previously been cloudy. "Do you want me not to call you anymore, Stella?"

This is not at all what she was expecting. It's not what she wanted him to say, not what she wants to hear. The thought of it, of never talking to Craig again…of never seeing him… This is when Stella can't pretend anymore that this friendship hasn't gone too far, and she gets up on numb legs to take a stumbling step away from him.

Her voice is far away and cold. She's made herself an automaton. "Yes," she says. "Yes, I think that would be best."

Craig looks stunned. Then he gets up from the bench. Neutrality slides across his expression, shutting her out, but she can't let herself be upset. Stella lifts her chin. Tightens her jaw. Craig mirrors her stance.

He nods once, sharply. "Right. Okay, then. Well, Stella, thanks for lunch and…good…luck, I guess."

"Goodbye," Stella says, and does not offer her hand.

She watches him walk away from her, his back straight, shoulders square, but somehow, though not a single step he takes is in any way faltering, Craig is limping. There's a moment when she sees herself run after him so clearly it takes her a minute to realize she hasn't moved. Her hand's raised, and Stella forces it back to her side.

She watches him climb the stairs to the sidewalk, and she waits for him to turn around, but he never does.

Hey, Stella typed quickly in the dark without letting herself think too hard about anything. Got your message, but it's too late to call. I'll talk to you tomorrow, if you're free.

She settled the phone back into the dock and wriggled deeper into her pillows and blankets, her eyes at last closing. She was just drifting off to sleep when her phone lit up—it didn't make a noise because of her Do Not Disturb settings, but the glare tickled her eyelids enough to wake her. She already knew who it was before she rolled to check. But even so, she smiled at the sight of Craig's name.

Looking forward to it.

CHAPTER NINE

Not all pilots fool around when they're away from home, but this one is clearly DTF. That's what the cool kids call it—Stella learned it from the Connex account she's basically abandoned. *Down To Fuck*. Actually, the cool kids have probably moved on from that phrase now, on to something else she'll have to look up on urbandictionary.com to understand. It doesn't matter how it's said, the man in front of her is clearly down for something.

This isn't the first time she's flown with Captain Truax, and it's not the first time he's checked her out when she's boarded and unboarded. He has a wide, nice smile for everyone, but his eyes linger on hers when she gets on the plane. There's recognition there, even though today Stella wears a blond wig in a chin-length bob. He's seen her in all shades of blond before. Also brunette. She wonders which he likes better. Maybe he prefers redheads.

"Welcome aboard," the captain says, and Stella smiles.

In the few minutes before they ask everyone to turn off

their phones, Stella shares a few texts with Craig. She'd tried earlier to catch him in a call, as she'd promised, but missed him. Then he'd called back while she was in the shower, and then it had been time for her to get to the airport. She's not sure how she feels about this new development in an old situation.

But she doesn't have to think about it now.

Today's flight is short enough that Stella barely has time to get through a few chapters of her book. She's among the last off the plane. She pauses to pull up the handle on her wheeled bag, and while she does, Captain Truax passes her with his own carry-on. He stops when he sees her struggling.

"Need a hand?"

"The handle's stuck, that's all." Stella steps aside to let him help her. "Don't you have another flight to catch or something?"

Captain Truax, who stands at least six foot three, straightens. His teeth are very white. Very straight. "Nope. I'm off duty. This last little jump was my final flight for a few days."

"Oh. Nice. So you're going home?" They fall companionably into step along the corridor. "You live in Philly?"

"Oh. No. Just taking a little layover, do some sightseeing. Spending some time with my daughter. She goes to Temple. I live in Atlanta." He gives her another grin. "How about you? You make this flight pretty frequently, don't you? Travel a lot for…business?"

And there's the problem with doing what she does. Being noticed. Recognized. She doesn't want to talk to Captain Truax about why she's in the standby seat every other Friday and Sunday. She doesn't like anybody asking her questions.

"Yes." Stella smiles but says no more, and Captain Truax doesn't ask what it is, exactly, that she does.

"Have a great weekend," he says. "Maybe I'll see you on Sunday."

But it doesn't take that long for her to see him again. Stella has also decided to do some sightseeing, mostly because there are sights to see in Philadelphia, and she always means to take Tristan for the day but they never end up doing it. It's only a couple hours from home, but it took a plane to get her here. She's picked Philly because it's convenient and because one of her favorite bands is doing a show Saturday night at a bar downtown.

She sees Captain Truax at the Liberty Bell. He's with his daughter, both of them standing far enough apart from each other to highlight the tension between them, but there's no mistaking the resemblance. Stella, dressed casually, her hair in a ponytail, stands right next to him without him noticing her at all. She watches him try to woo his daughter into a smile, but it's obvious that she's not ready to let go of whatever traumas his parenting has given her.

The night before, Stella had found a much younger man who'd been totally amenable to taking her back to his apartment, if only she didn't mind the fact that he had roommates. That wasn't what bothered her as much as the dilation of his pupils and the too-firm grip of his fingers on her upper arm when he tried to convince her it would be the time of her life.

"I have a nine-inch cock," he'd promised. "And a six-inch tongue."

Stella as a blonde could sometimes be more easily convinced than as a brunette or with her natural hair, but something in the dent of his fingers on her flesh didn't feel right. She put him off with a smile, then watched him move immediately down the bar to another girl, already wasted, who seemed far more inclined to take him up on his offer.

Watching Captain Truax flounder with his kid, Stella feels a pang of sympathy that echoes somewhere in the vicinity of her ovaries. It's so obvious how much he wants her to smile. Or at least take the fucking look of doom off her face. Stella shakes her head as she follows them discreetly past the row of giant plaques giving the history of the Liberty Bell. The bell itself hangs inside a special building. Stella looks at it and waits to feel patriotic, but all she feels is hungry, thirsty and tired from getting up too early. She wanted to take advantage of the whole day.

"Let me take you to dinner," Captain Truax says as he and his frowning daughter leave the Liberty Bell pavilion. "I'm only in town until tomorrow...."

"Sorry, Dad." She doesn't sound sorry at all. "I have plans."

"Maggie..."

The girl shrugs, not looking at him. Stella's heart goes out to him, even though she feels the tiniest bit creepy listening in on the conversation. She keeps herself busy looking at the historical information while she eavesdrops.

"It was good to see you," Maggie says. "I have a lot of studying to do now. Thanks for breakfast and stuff. Call me when you're going to be back in Philly."

It's clear this is an old argument, because Captain Truax shakes his head and steps away from her. "At least let me give you some money."

Maggie shrugs, apparently not at all ashamed of taking her dad's money without giving him anything resembling affection or respect in return. Captain Truax watches her go, his shoulders drooping. Not the man who'd piloted the plane Stella took on Friday, not the man who'd stood so straight and tall and confident, flashing her that sexy smile.

"Hi," Stella says abruptly. "Captain Truax."

He looks confused. "Hi?"

She moves a little closer. Gives him a smile. She has no idea if he knows her name or not, and all the better if he doesn't. She presses a matchbook into his hand—it's from the club she went to last night. "There's a great band playing here tonight. You should come see it. You'll have a good time, I promise."

She takes a few steps back, turning as he focuses on the matchbook and calls after her, "Do I know you?"

"Yes," she says without looking over her shoulder. "And tonight, if you can find me, you can have me."

He'll find her. Stella has no doubts. He might've preferred to be spending time with his daughter on a Saturday night in Philadelphia, but scoping out a stranger in a crowded bar will have to do.

She's blonde again. This wig is one of her favorites, soft and flattering in the cut, hitting her at chin level. She's outlined her eyes in thick dark shadow. Red mouth—of course, it's always red when she flies. She's powdered her skin to paleness that accentuates her dark eyes. She wears a bright blue dress, sheer stockings, matching blue heels that were the reason she bought the dress in the first place.

Devil in a Blue Dress, that's how Stella feels in this outfit. It's served her well in the past, though she hasn't worn it for about a year. It must've been fate that she packed it, since she'd been planning on jeans and a T-shirt for tonight. Denim jacket. Still blonde, though. She'd always meant to be blonde.

The club's the same, but tonight's crowd is different, which makes sense considering the band. It's a better fit for her, this crowd, than the one last night where she moved among them like the Ghost of Christmas Future. Stella likes younger men as much as she likes older ones—she doesn't think of herself as a cougar, which has always sounded so predatory and faintly derogatory. If her captain doesn't come for her, she won't have any trouble finding someone else if she wants to.

She really is just there to hear the band play, after all.

Of course her captain finds her. It's the blonde hair, like a beacon. Maybe it's her ass, the curve of her hips. Maybe it's fate, because when she turns around with an iced tea in her hand, there he stands. In a pair of worn jeans and a long-sleeved, waffle-fabric Henley shirt pushed up on his forearms, his silvering hair catching the multicolored lights from the dance floor, Captain Truax looks even more fuckable than he did in his pilot's uniform. Maybe it's the frown, she thinks as she lights the way for him with her smile. He looks so broken, and there's not a lot sexier than a man who needs fixing...so long as when the morning comes you can say goodbye.

"Hi," he says uncertainly. "It's you."

"It usually is," Stella says.

He smiles then. "What a coincidence."

"The band," she says. "They're going to start soon."

It's a local group she's seen play live at least a few dozen times. She started listening to them during those endless nights when her infant son wouldn't sleep anywhere but tucked against her in the rocker, the singer crooning in her ear through her headphones in those long, long hours until dawn. Certain songs will forever be linked to that time in her mind, sending her back in time as easily and steadily as the Doctor's TARDIS—maybe that's why Jeff always refused to come with her to see this band play.

Stella always makes the time to come and see the group whenever they're booked within traveling distance for her. Dive bars, midsized clubs, renovated art deco theaters, county fairs. She's seen them play in all these places, but never in this one. It's not a venue she'd have thought well suited for the group, which has a folksy rock feel rather than a dance club sound.

It doesn't matter. She's here, listening, and the band's rocking the house, and she has a handsome, damaged man by her side who puts his hand between her shoulder blades when he leans in close to ask her what she'd like to drink.

"Iced tea," Stella says. "Regular. Not Long Island."

Captain Truax doesn't seem put out or surprised by this request, and he doesn't ask her why she's not drinking alcohol. That earns him an instant bonus point. She's met plenty of men who seem personally affronted by her refusal to drink booze. The captain brings her a tall, sweating glass. His is shorter, full of amber liquid, no ice. He sips, grimacing a little, and lifts his glass toward the stage.

"I've heard these guys before."

Stella turns. "You have?"

His gaze skates over her hair and lower, over her breasts and hips, before meeting hers. "Yep."

The lead singer, a burly guy with a full beard and a head of wild red hair, takes the mic. Dressed in plaid and denim, he holds a wooden block in one hand, a hammer in the other. The wood is chipped and bruised. He taps the hammer against it.

"You ready?"

The crowd roars. The band joins him. They play traditional instruments, yes, but also wood blocks. They stomp on boards. They pound on plastic gallon jugs full of sand. Halfway through the first song, the singer breaks the wood block in half and tosses it into a container at the side of the stage, where he pulls out a replacement block.

Stella moves to the music, aware of the captain beside her. She wonders what he thinks of the band. She doesn't care, really, is simply curious. She also wonders what his first name is and, when she turns to ask him, finds him staring at her.

"What?" she asks in a lull between songs as the singer tells a long story about the next song's origin. She's heard the same story a dozen times, could probably repeat it nearly word for word. She has a live recording of the band's set in which the singer told the story, and he keeps the cadence and words almost the same every time.

Again, the captain's gaze takes in her hair. The dress. The liner around her eyes and the red, red of her mouth. She's not surprised when he leans in to kiss her. The slip of his tongue is sweet, not intrusive. She opens for it, greedily.

They slide into an easy embrace. His hands on her hips, hers resting on his shoulders. Her fingers play with the hair on the back of his head, tracing the bumps of his spine at the base of his skull.

His eyes are wide and gray. His mouth grows more insistent. When he presses that long, lean body against hers, Stella feels an answering heat. He surprises her by slipping a hand between them, his fingers without hesitation find-ing her sweet spot.

Surprised, Stella breaks the kiss but doesn't move fully away. "Someone might see."

"I'm discreet." His body blocks hers from any but the nosiest eyes, and Stella knows nobody's paying any atten-tion to them in this shadowy corner by the side of the bar. "And I like to watch you get turned on."

She is, suddenly. Slick and aching, her cunt throbbing, her nipples tight. The captain's an excellent kisser, but that confident stroke between her legs is what sends her over the edge.

"You want to get out of here?" she asks the captain, and is gratified and flattered, as always, when he immediately says yes.

They go to his hotel, which faces the Delaware River and is much older than hers. The rooms are probably three times the price too, she thinks as she follows him into a huge bedroom dominated by a king bed. Fireplace, an-tiques, a river view. She turns to him with a smile as she sits on the bed and smooths the comforter under her fingertips.

"Nice place," she says.

"Thanks." He moves toward her, confident and fully male when he pushes between her legs to bend and kiss her.

God, she loves that.

The way he grips the back of her neck to hold her close. When he pushes her back and covers her with his body. When his mouth moves along the slope of her throat to nip at her exposed collarbones, Stella sighs.

"So hot," he whispers against her skin.

She wants nothing more than to lose herself in all of this, but Stella puts a pause to it with her hands on his chest to push him upward. Truax stands to unbutton his shirt, revealing nicely sculpted abs and pecs covered with salt-and-pepper hair. Stella props herself on an elbow to watch him. She loves these moments. The reveal. She's had to force herself into not feeling embarrassed about her body, so she appreciates self-confidence. He tosses his shirt onto the chair next to the bed and then puts a hand on the button of his jeans.

"Wait," Stella says, and sits. "Let me."

She brushes her lips over his belly, that soft patch of hair. Closing her eyes, she breathes in the warm, male scent of him. For a second or so, Stella lets herself nuzzle his skin while her hands run up the insides of his denim-clad thighs. She cups the weight of his testicles and runs her thumb over the hardening lump of his cock, but doesn't undo the button. Not right away.

She looks up at him with a smile. Truax isn't smiling. His brow is furrowed. Mouth pursed. He cups a hand to her face, then strokes his fingers through her wig.

"Why do you do this?" he asks.

He could mean take men home from bars. He could mean wear a disguise. He could mean a lot of things, but Stella's answer is the same for all the questions she can think he might be asking.

"Because I want to."

His thumb rubs the line of her chin, then tucks into her mouth. She sucks gently, nipping at the tip of it, and is pleased at his reaction. His eyes go heavy-lidded. His lips part, moist from the swipe of his tongue. His hips bump a little forward. Beneath her hand, she imagines the throb of his cock, imprisoned by his jeans. He sighs when she undoes his zipper. When she takes him in her fist, stroking, her breath gusting over the sweetness of his thick erection, Truax gives a small, soft moan.

"I haven't had…this…in a really long time."

Stella pauses, the tip of her tongue so close to his cock he should be able to feel the heat of it. Her fingers twist around his shaft, her knuckles nudging the rim of his head. "No?"

His hand caresses her wig again. She can feel the weight of his touch, of course, but it's different than if he'd touched her own hair. For a moment, she considers slipping off the wig and letting her own hair down so he can tangle his fingers in it. Pull as hard as he wants.

Instead, she takes him slowly into her mouth, sucking gently and using her tongue around the rim. Down, down, she engulfs his cock with her mouth until she can't take any more. His cock is thick but not too long, and Stella's able to brush her lips against his belly before sliding her mouth up and off him. Her hand follows behind and she strokes him while she looks up to see his reaction.

He shudders. "Oh. God. So good."

"Good." Stella smiles and takes him in her mouth again. Slow, slow, she sucks gently at first and then harder. She pushes his jeans and briefs down to his thighs and settles herself between his legs. He bends his knees a little, fucking into her mouth, and she lets him.

The thickness of him, the length, both are just right. Stella lets herself get lost in the back and forth and up and down, sucking and stroking. She cups his balls with her other hand, stroking her thumb along the seam. His moans turn her on.

She shifts her thighs, pressing them together to squeeze her clit with a delightful pressure that makes it unnecessary for her to use her hand on herself. She can probably get off this way, if it goes on long enough. For now, it's enough to let her body fill with slow-growing pleasure.

"I'm gonna come," he mutters, and tries to pull away. "It's too good."

"No such thing as too good." Stella stops sucking him but keeps her grip with her fist. His cock is hard and gleaming from her mouth, gone that yummy shade of on-the-edge red. She lets her fingers drift up and down his shaft, avoiding the sensitive divot beneath the head. She blows a breath across it.

Truax shudders and jerks; he lets out a low, guttural groan. But he doesn't come, and Stella grins. She flicks her tongue once, twice, on the underside of his cock, which pulses.

"Shhh," she tells him. "Not yet."

He laughs breathlessly. "You're killing me."

Stella, his cock still firmly in her fist, leans back. "How long has it been since you've had your cock sucked?"

"Five years," he says at once, no hesitation.

Her fingers squeeze him gently. "That's a long time. How come?"

"My wife..." Truax chokes on the words or on the pleasure in his dick; it doesn't matter. "She doesn't like it."

"That's a shame." Stella rubs his slit with her thumb, covering the head of his cock with clear, sticky fluid. "And nobody else?"

"I haven't...with anyone else."

This stops her. "What?"

For a moment, she thinks he's going to pull away, but the allure of what her fingers are doing, what her mouth has done, keeps him standing there. Never underestimate the power of a blow job, she thinks, and doesn't let herself dwell. She takes him briefly in her mouth again, sucking until he starts to shake.

She stops. Truax lets out a muttered curse. Stella smiles and strokes him, judging how close he is by the look on his face.

"You want me to keep going." It's not a question. "You want me to suck this lovely cock until you come."

"Please," he says. "Oh, fuck. Yes. Please."

He could be lying about it being five years since a woman sucked his dick. He could be lying about not fucking around too. And really, it doesn't matter because nothing about any of this is all the way honest, not her hair or clothes or the way she paints her lips.

But the way his prick throbs against her tongue—that is honest. The weight of his balls in her palm, that's honest too. And so is Stella's desire to make this man explode for her.

"Lie down," she says.

He hesitates. She lets go of his cock, and it rises proudly to tap his belly. Stella unequivocally loves cocks, but there's no denying Captain Truax's is particularly lovely, and frankly, she adores that thick hardness she gave him with her touch. She loves how he shakes as he lies back, how his poor, fellatio-deprived prick pulses under the sweep of her tongue from the head to the base just before she settles herself between his legs.

"Shhh," she tells him when he starts to speak. "Just enjoy it."

"Do you want me to—"

"Shh," Stella repeats. "Not now."

She takes her time. She worships and adores his cock. Hands and mouth working together, she sucks and strokes.

She wiggles out of her dress and presses him between her breasts until he bucks and cries out hoarsely; then she eases off and watches his cock fuck the air.

Again and again she brings him to the edge, certain each time she's going to misjudge and finish him, but either her skills are just that fucking good—which is possible—or he's just willing to be teased, which might also be true. And the longer she goes, the wetter she gets. The harder her clit. The tighter her nipples.

Stella fucks him with her mouth and hands, every so often stroking herself, but it's the pressure of her thighs as she squeezes them together in rhythm that sends her hurtling toward her own finish. It would be easy to forget herself just now, lost in the pleasure, but Stella focuses. Sitting up, rocking her hips and clenching her muscles to keep herself edging toward her orgasm, she strokes his cock a few more firm pumps.

"I'm…" is all he says this time.

"Me too," she tells him, and bends back to take him in her mouth for that last, desperate thrust.

She comes in slow, rolling ripples that are so different from how it feels when she comes while actively rubbing her clit. The pleasure goes on and on while his cock pumps into her mouth and she swallows again and again. Breathing hard, Stella sits up again, her body still quivering with the force of what turned out to be a surprisingly strong orgasm.

Truax had been moaning, but is now silent. His softening cock is a reminder of how little Stella likes this part—what she thinks of as "the clash" because of that rock group's famous song. "Should I Stay or Should I Go?" Stella almost always votes for go, especially on nights like this when she still has a cab ride back to her own hotel and a plane to catch.

She takes a moment to fall onto the bed next to him. Staring at the ceiling, Stella says quietly, "I hope it was worth it."

Truax rolls onto his side and puts a hand on her belly. "Yes. It was. But…"

She looks at him with a smile. "Don't worry, Captain Truax. Your secret's safe with me, and it was a onetime offer, already redeemed."

He laughs gently but has the grace to look ashamed. "I've seen you before, you know."

"I know."

"You do this often."

"Yes," Stella says. "I do."

He brushes the hair from her eyes. "Because you want to."

"Yes."

He doesn't ask her why, and she's grateful, because in that moment, Stella thinks she might tell him all her reasons. Impulsively, she leans to kiss him. He hesitates for a moment, and she thinks she misjudged. That he might pull away, making this sad and awkward. But after that second or so, he kisses her too. His arms go around her. She breathes in time with the rise and fall of his chest and wishes that just for a few hours, she could relax here with him. Sleep. It's been so long since she shared her bed, and though most of the time she relishes having the bed to herself, there are times she misses someone to snuggle with.

But she doesn't really want to snuggle with Captain Truax.

"She's going to leave me," he says. "I'm pretty sure of it.

And my daughter… She knows too. She thinks her mother's right to want to go."

"I'm sorry." Stella doesn't really want to know.

"Sometimes…things just happen and you think you know what you're doing, and you wake up and realize that everything you thought was right, all the choices you made, they're all wrong. And everything's gone." His voice cracks a little but doesn't break.

Stella sits up to look at him. "I understand."

"I tried listening to her, but she says I never pay attention. I do," he says, too defensively. "But I'm gone a lot. It's part of the job. She doesn't seem to care when it comes time to spend the money, though. That, she has no problem with. She spends my money and turns my kids against me, but she can't be bothered to ever appreciate any efforts I make."

Stella doesn't want him to say more. She doesn't want to talk about the things in their lives that have gone wrong, all the broken things that have kept them in misery. That's not what this is about, this coming together. But when Truax swipes a hand over his face, Stella knows there will be no getting out of the conversation.

She should never have gone with him, no matter how charming the smile. No matter how appealing the damage. With a sigh she keeps locked behind her teeth, Stella puts a hand on his chest, over his heart. The steady thumping has eased to a normal pace. How quickly things go back to normal, she thinks, when the fucking's done.

"Men and women speak the same language, but different dialects," she says. Nothing more.

Truax blinks. Frowns. "Yeah. I guess you're right."

"I need to use your bathroom, okay?" Without waiting for an answer, she gets out of bed and goes to the bathroom. She takes her time, using the toilet. Rinsing her mouth. Drinking a glass of cold, clear water. She brushes her fingers through the blond wig, setting it more firmly in place though it hasn't even gone askew—she's gotten so good at securing it.

In the mirror, her reflection smiles. Grimaces. Bares its teeth. Frowns. Gives a sultry wink.

When she's able to put on her concerned and sympathetic face, Stella leaves the bathroom. Whatever gloom he was harboring has passed, at least a little bit, because he's turned on the TV. Good. It will make it all the easier for her to slip out if he doesn't expect to cuddle.

The late-night news is on, which surprises her into looking for a clock. What seems like a reasonable bedtime at home is ridiculously early when she's flying, but surely more time has passed than this? Truax has dressed in a pair of pj bottoms and a faded blue T-shirt, but he hasn't pulled down the comforter to make the bed more inviting. He's propped against the headboard, remote in hand.

"Well," Stella says. "This was great...."

He gets up. "You're going to go?"

"Yes."

"Do you...always go?" He looks uncomfortable.

"Yes," Stella says. "Almost always."

"So it's not me."

Her eyebrows rise before she can force her expression into compassionate neutrality, and before she can stop herself, she's stepped forward. "Oh. No. Wow. No, it's not you."

"Because I didn't fuck you? I mean, you said you wanted me to just enjoy it, but I could've... I meant to. I wanted to," he says. "I wanted it to be good for you too. I'm not a total caveman."

Men are so wrapped up in their cocks. How they work or how they don't. There are plenty of men who don't give a damn if they make their partner come, and a lot who take so much pride in their ability to get a woman off they lose sight of the important thing. Her pleasure is hers. Not his.

"My wife says I'm selfish in bed."

There it is, of course. Stella says nothing when he sinks onto the bed and puts his face in his hands. His shoulders shake.

Oh, she thinks. *Fuck.*

There is one Mother Teresa moment when she thinks about sitting next to him, maybe taking his hand. Letting him cry on her shoulder. She could reassure him that she came hard, and it won't be a lie. She can tell him he wasn't selfish, at least as far as she could see, because she chose to do what she did. That wouldn't be a lie either, but it also wouldn't matter.

"She always accuses me of fucking around. But I never have. Not until tonight." He shoots her an accusatory look from red-rimmed eyes.

Frankly, Stella's not in the mood to play nursemaid. She doesn't owe the captain anything. She seduced him; she didn't force him. She ought to feel worse about it, she supposes. Fucking a married man and all. There seems to be a line she shouldn't cross, some sort of responsibility she should take for this. But, while she owns her part in it, never ashamed and rarely regretful, Stella is unwilling to take on anyone else's burden.

"Look," she says, because she's not entirely a vicious

bag of dicks about this sort of thing, "your wife will never know."

"I'll know."

"Then maybe it will teach you something," Stella says, too harsh. "Happy people don't cheat. Trust me, I know."

He nods after a moment. "No. I guess they don't."

"She's fucking around on you. Isn't she?"

He nods again, and she thinks now's the time for him to cut his gaze from hers, but he doesn't. "Yeah. I think so."

"This won't change any of that." Damn, her feet hurt. She wants to get out of her heels and this dress and this wig. Wash away the makeup under a hot shower and crawl into the big, soft bed with its crisp white sheets and sleep until her alarm wakes her in time for a leisurely breakfast… alone…and then her plane ride home.

"But the next time she accuses me, I won't be able to say it's not true. Not without lying."

Stella's eyebrows go up again. "And?"

"And nothing, I guess." Truax frowns.

Stella sighs. "I'm going to head out. It's late and I'm tired. You get some sleep, okay?"

He doesn't answer her.

Stella gathers her things. At the door, she looks back at him, knowing she should feel pity even if he doesn't want it, and unable to find any. Something's cold in her. And broken. But it's her own fault, she supposes, for picking men she knows are already damaged because it feels easier to justify breaking them.

"Good night," she says, waiting for him to answer.

He doesn't.

She's not surprised the next day when Truax is the pilot on her flight back to Harrisburg. She's not even surprised when he doesn't say a word to her as she boards, and it's not because she's not traveling as a blonde. She is surprised, though, when he won't even look at her. It shouldn't sting her, but somehow it does.

She should've known better, Stella thinks, as she settles into her seat for the swift trip home, than to fly with someone she knew she'd have to see again.

CHAPTER TEN

"Didn't your dad say he'd be here by eight? Or do I have to drop you off?" Stella's phone buzzed in her pocket as she turned from the suitcase she was unsuccessfully trying to pack with everything she'd need for a week away from home. She'd been offered the chance to take a weeklong seminar on advanced Photoshop techniques in Chicago on the company dime, and she was taking it. She ignored the buzz. No time for a call right now.

"He'll pick me up."

Something in Tristan's tone made Stella look at him. He lounged in the doorway, headphones around his neck, a bottle of soda in one hand and a bag of chips in the other. She straightened.

"What time?" she asked.

Tristan shrugged. Stella looked at the clock. Her flight wasn't until tomorrow morning, but it left at the ungodly hour of 4:30 a.m., and it was inching on toward 9:00 p.m. at this point. It wasn't unheard of for Jeff to be late, of course, but something in Tristan's shifty gaze tipped her off to something going on.

"Tristan."

He scowled. "I'm going there after school tomorrow. Okay? Not tonight."

Stella scrubbed at her eyes, behind which a steady pressure had been building for an hour. "Why?"

"Because I wanted to stay here an extra night, okay? I like my own bed."

She couldn't blame him for that. Tristan had had his own room at his dad's house since the divorce. She could argue with her son that his bed in his father's house *was* his own bed, but she understood. And, truthfully, there was also a quiet sort of vindication that Tristan thought of her house as home, no matter how many presents Cynthia bought him.

"I have to leave super early," she told him now. "Can I trust you to get yourself off to school?"

"Don't I get up on my own every day?"

This was true, but it was different when she wouldn't be here at all, just in case he overslept or missed the bus. "Just making sure."

"I'll be fine." Tristan took a long swig from the bottle, then let out a long, reverberating belch.

Stella burst into disgusted laughter. "Oh. Nice."

Tristan, grinning, lifted a leg and prepared to let out a fart, but Stella made such a threatening gesture that he stopped and backed up into the hall, laughing.

"Yeah, that's it," she said, acting tough. "Don't you bring that in here."

So instead, he did it out in the hall. "Ten points! Gold medal stuff here, Mom!"

"You are repulsive, you know that?" she called after him.

Tristan stuck his butt through the doorway, wiggling it. "Shouldn't have made chili for dinner."

"No! Tristan, don't!" But it was too late. He let out another long, ripping fart that sounded like hands clapping. Stella shrieked, running after him, but he was already ducking away from her. She shook her fist at him instead, shaking her head. "You're a pig, you know that?"

Tristan pushed up his nose to look like a snout. "Remember that time he ate the chili dogs at the baseball game and farted so bad we had to roll down all the windows?"

All the laughter left her.

Carefully, Stella turned back to her suitcase, where she made an effort of sorting through her socks, tucking a couple pairs into an empty space in one of the packing cubes. "I think you should call your dad and have him come get you tonight. You won't have to get up as early tomorrow morning if you're at his house, and I'll feel better knowing you're not here alone."

Silence from behind her. Then a long, snuffling sigh. "I'll be fine. It's a few hours in the morning, God."

Stella kept herself focused on what she was doing. "Don't argue with me, Tristan."

"I want to sleep in my own bed tonight. It's already going to suck that I have to be there for a whole week!"

"It's only half a week," she pointed out. "You have your ski trip for the second half."

"Whatever."

She turned. "What's wrong at your dad's house? Is there something going on I need to know about?"

"No." But his gaze shifted from hers in a way that told her otherwise.

"Is it Cynthia?"

Tristan shrugged. "She's fine."

"Is it your dad?" His look gave that away, even though he shrugged again. Stella sighed and sat on the edge of the bed. "Is he giving you a hard time about something?"

"No."

"Then what is it?"

"I just like being here better." The stubborn set of his jaw was more Stella than Jeff. The resemblance wasn't often there except when he made that face.

"I understand that, but, sorry, kid, you can't be here by yourself for a week. Or even half of one. But, fine, you don't have to go tonight. Just…go to bed," she told him wearily. "I'm tired, and I have to be up early, and I have a lot to do before I leave tomorrow."

Tristan didn't move at first. The look he gave her was calculated, sort of aggressive, and somehow wary at the same time. "Cynthia told Dad I should see a counselor. I heard her talking to him about it."

Stella blinked rapidly against this unexpected news. "What the hell?"

"Yeah." Tristan's shrug looked casual, but she knew it wasn't. He wouldn't meet her gaze.

Stella shoved aside the suitcase and patted the bed. "Come here."

He wouldn't at first, but then did, dragging his feet. His recent growth spurt meant he was a head taller than her even while sitting, and for a moment the fist of emotion squeezed tight around her throat, making it impossible to talk. Instead of words, Stella put her arm around her son's shoulders and squeezed gently.

"You want to talk about it?" she asked.

"No."

"No meaning not at all, or no meaning not with me?"

Tristan shrugged. Incredibly, for a moment, he leaned against her, and all Stella could do was hold on to him as tight as she could. She stopped herself from petting his hair—Tristan had never been her snuggler.

"I just don't like going there as much as being here," Tristan said in a low voice.

"Why, honey? If it's a problem with your dad or Cynthia, you can tell me." It would've honestly surprised her to find out that Cynthia had ever been anything but sweet as sugar to her stepson. That was just how she was. Jeff, on the other hand, could be a pain in the ass.

"He never lived there with us," Tristan muttered, so low Stella had to strain to hear him.

She went cold inside. Involuntarily, her fingers tightened on him hard enough to make him shift. She let him go. They sat in stolid, awkward silence, side by side, for half a minute.

"I know, sweetie," Stella said finally. "But that doesn't mean it's not okay for *you* to live there."

Tristan looked at her, blue eyes narrowed against the tears he was bravely trying to hold back. Her heart ached for him, but when she tried to hug him, he pulled away just enough to make it clear he didn't want her embrace.

"If you need to talk to someone," she said, "we can find you someone to talk to, but only if you want to."

During the divorce, Stella had taken Tristan to a round of counseling, first with the school guidance counselor, then with a child psychologist who specialized in grief issues. Tristan had hated going then; she couldn't believe he wouldn't hate going now. Again, in this he'd been unfortunate enough to inherit the worst of both his parents. Jeff's quickness to dissatisfaction and Stella's reluctance to open up emotionally. But she had to offer it.

Something shifted in his gaze, something flaring brightly before it faded like a firework arcing through the sky and fizzling to darkness. He shook his head. "Cynthia just thinks I should, like, be going out with girls and stuff. And doing more than playing video games with my friends. She's too into social stuff."

"Hmmm. I can see that. I think she was one of those popular kids in high school." *Which was, like, last year,* Stella thought meanly, and was proud of herself for not saying aloud.

"Dad says my grades are shit too," Tristan added.

Stella frowned. "He thinks B's aren't good enough?"

"Yeah."

Stella sighed and patted his shoulder, then stood. "I'll talk to him. Are you doing your best?"

"Yeah," Tristan said.

"Then that's your best. And that's what matters."

He gave her a small grin, and it was better than nothing. "Thanks, Mom."

When he hugged her, Stella was too surprised to do more than stiffly accept the embrace for a few seconds, and by the time she moved to return the hug, Tristan had already broken away from her. He paused in the doorway to look back at her, his mouth open as though he meant to say more, but instead he shook his head and disappeared. She heard his door close, then the faint blare of music she was too tired to tell him to turn down.

Exhausted, Stella sank back onto the bed and rubbed at the pain between her eyes. She remembered her phone after another minute and pulled it from her pocket to find a message from Craig.

The voice mail was brief. "Hey, Stella, it's Craig. Just trying to catch you before you leave for Chicago. Give me a ring when you get this, or else I'll talk to you when you get back. Have a great night."

Totally bland and casual, but she knew him better than that. At least, she had known him, once upon a time. And, once upon that same old time, she'd have been answering him so fast it would've made a rift in the time-space continuum, allowing her to call him before he'd finished leaving his message.

But that had been then. This was now, and now she was tired. It was late. She had a week's worth of travel ahead of her, and she had to get up at two in the morning.

She called him back anyway, half hoping she'd get his voice mail. "Hey, you. Got your call."

"Stella." He sounded so pleased she was glad she'd answered. "I wasn't sure I'd hear from you before you left."

"Wasn't sure you'd still be up." She cradled the phone against her shoulder as she worked, shoving her suitcase full of everything she thought she might need and knowing she wouldn't use half of what she was packing.

"Just wandering around the internet, wasting time. What time do you leave?"

She told him, and the conversation predictably meandered to the disgustingness of having such an early plane, and traveling in general, and how horrible it was to work but how nice it was to have a job. She and Craig had used to talk about their dreams and ponder things like the existence of the soul. Not this mundane cocktail-party chitchat.

Then again, the sound of his voice had once been able to send her heart into pitter-pattering spasms.

"So...when you get back," Craig said just as Stella was trying to wrap everything up, "can we have dinner?"

"Like a date?" As soon as the words came out, she felt stupid.

Craig laughed softly. "Well. Yeah. A date. Dinner, maybe a movie?"

There'd been a time when even the option of this had seemed impossible, but she'd spent hours dreaming about it anyway. And now here it was, the opportunity dropped in her lap like it had fallen from the sky, and all she could do was stare at it. Stella cleared her throat.

"I...guess... I'll have to check my schedule, but..."

"If you don't want to..."

"No, no," she said hastily. "Of course I want to. Yes. Absolutely."

Craig hesitated before answering, "You sure?"

"Yes." She laughed, embarrassed.

"I don't want you to feel obligated or anything, I mean, if you say no, I'll just go back into my dark corner and listen to sad opera music."

"Oh, God. Don't do that." She remembered now how easily he'd always been able to make her laugh, and why she'd fallen so hard for him in the first place. "I will go to dinner with you."

"And a movie?"

"And a movie," she said.

"Good."

There was another pause, not so awkward this time. Stella yawned, hating to look at the clock but knowing she had to. "Listen, I have to get to bed. I'll call you when I get back from Chicago, okay?"

"Get to bed, crazy girl." The smile in his voice made her smile too. "Safe travels. I'll talk to you when you get back."

They said their good-nights and she disconnected, then put her phone on the charger as she went to take a shower. Under the hot water, though, it hit her. Nostalgia. Memory. The day on the riverbank, she'd been certain she'd never see Craig again.

But she had.

"I feel like I can tell you everything," Stella says as the rain pours outside, battering the roof of the car and turning the windows blank. Their breath has fogged up the inside just as much, making them invisible.

"You can. You know that." Craig's hand pushes her wet hair off her shoulder. His fingers linger, brushing down her arm to take her hand. Linking their fingers. He squeezes gently.

But she can't tell him everything. There's too much of it to say to anyone, and how can she expect him to understand? He can try, and she knows he would. But he will never feel what she feels. He will never know what it's like to have lived with what she has. And in that moment, staring at him across the expanse of his front seat, Stella wants to bare all of her scars to him.

But she can't.

Shuddering, Stella bit back a cry, then covered her mouth with both her hands to keep herself from letting out the sob that threatened to surge out of her mouth. She would not let herself break open. Once she started, she was afraid

she wouldn't be able to stop. Making herself stone, Stella
turned her face to the water as she twisted the dial to cold
and forced herself to stand under the frigid spray until everything went numb.

It took a long time.

Finally, teeth chattering, she got out and dried herself off,
ran a comb through her hair. Brushed her teeth. Dressed
in flannel jammies, she peeked in on Tristan, who was
sleeping, then got into her own bed, all without giving in
to the waves of emotion that threatened to pull her under
and drown her. She breathed, pressing her face into the pillow, thinking of how early the alarm would be going off.

Shit. The alarm. Stella reached to make sure she'd set
the alarm on her phone, and discovered a text from Craig.
Short and sweet.

Can't wait to see you.

This time, Stella didn't answer.

CHAPTER ELEVEN

It'd been a completely different experience, traveling to a destination for an actual reason. First of all, the price of the ticket had astounded her, even though it was being reimbursed by the company. Second, Stella was far too used to breezing through security with only her carry-on bag. Dragging her huge suitcase behind her and waiting to check and pick up baggage had been an unpleasant surprise. And third, on her weekend turnarounds she never had a schedule that could be derailed by something as stupid as weather or mechanical failure. If her plane was delayed or late or even canceled, she simply took another one or didn't go. Sitting in the terminal with a couple hundred grouchy strangers, watching the news and seeing the announcement board blipping planes one after another, Stella understood now why so many people hated to travel by air.

She'd already voluntarily given up her seat because of being overbooked when she had a few extra hours of leeway, but now she was barely going to get home in time for

Tristan to get back from his trip, and that was if she was lucky and he left later than he'd told her he was going to. Knowing her son and his friends, she'd counted on that, but even with that extra hour or so, she was still going to be late. She watched an irate man, his face getting redder and redder as he waved his arms and shouted, demand to be put on a plane leaving *now*. No point in that; the icy rain was making everything slow or late.

"Hey," she said suddenly when there was a break between the guy's sputtering threats and the gate clerk's apologies. "Give the girl a break. She can't control the weather."

It wasn't as though Stella made a point of being a champion of the weak or anything, nor was it that she'd never experienced her share of frustration with incompetent people who were supposed to be helping her. But losing your shit never helped. It only made people less interested in helping you. More than that, this guy was giving her a headache.

He turned on her. "This is a private conversation."

She made a point of looking around at all the staring faces. "Your voice level is making it very public."

"I'm not talking to you!"

"I know that," she replied patiently. "But we're all in the same place you are. We all want to get home on time. And I'm sure if you'll just let her help you without shouting—"

"And I'm sure," he snapped, "you should just shut up and mind your own business."

"Sir, if you'll just let me see what other flights I can find for you—" the clerk tried.

"I don't want another flight!" Spittle flew. The cords on his neck stood out. He leaned over the counter, getting in the clerk's face. "You obviously didn't hear me the first time!"

"I heard you, sir. But I can't make the rain stop." She shot a brief glance at Stella. "I'm sorry. I can only do my best to—"

"Your best is shit." The man slammed both hands on the counter, making the clerk and several other waiting passengers jump. "Your airline is shit."

With that he turned on his heel, presumably to stalk off in a snit. The toe of his shoe caught the edge of Stella's carry-on, but the impetus of his movement wasn't enough to send it flying as far as it went. He'd kicked it. On purpose.

"Hey!" She stood.

The man whirled on her, speaking through gritted jaws. Sweat stood out on his forehead. "I have to get home. On that plane."

Stella didn't bend to move her bag out of the aisle, not wanting to put her face near his possibly kicking foot. She nodded at the young guy who put it on her molded plastic seat, but didn't take her eyes off the asshole in front of her. "Yeah, I get it. We all do. But you're being a real jerk about it."

Some people were probably engrossed in their magazines or sequestered with their earphones blocking the shouting, but most everyone else at the gate was watching the drama. Sick sweat tickled her spine, and her fingers curled defensively. This guy looked crazy, and crazy people did crazy things. Like punching women who called them jerks in the face. She lifted her chin, sort of daring him, sort of caught up in the moment and crazy herself.

"I don't care about anyone else. It's very important I get home. That's all I care about." He looked her up and down with a sneer.

"I get it. You think you're more important than the rest of us."

"I *am* more important!" he shouted.

Stella sighed, no longer interested in this drama, not wanting to engage, wishing everyone would stop staring so she could sit down and stop being some kind of rom-com heroine. "Whatever. Do you see the enormousness of the fuck I do not give?"

He blinked rapidly, his chest rising and falling. Shit, was he pushing himself into a heart attack? She'd be forced to be some kind of freaking first responder, saving his life after she goaded him into a near-death experience. Stella cut her gaze from his and took up her carry-on so she could sit, praying he'd give up. Go away.

"My son is dying," the man said.

Stella froze. Around them, there was a collective intake of breath. A sense of waiting.

"He has terminal cancer. We thought he'd have another few months. My wife called to tell me they moved him to hospice care last night. He's going. I have to get home." His voice broke, but not in grief. Rage drove this man, evident in every droplet of sweat, every clench of his jaw, in his fists.

She waited for sympathy. For empathy. It should have come, swift and sure, to her of all people after hearing his words. Instead, all she found was anger of her own.

"Using your dying son as an excuse to treat anyone else like crap only makes you an asshole." She spoke quietly because she really wanted to open up her mouth in a siren-strength scream. Because she wanted to shatter him with the force of it like an opera singer breaking a glass.

"I just want to get home," he said.

"Sir?" The clerk's hesitant voice turned him away from Stella. "If you step over here, I'll be able to help you."

He leveled a stare at Stella. She waited for more anger. He shot her a look of triumph that turned her stomach so fiercely she thought, instead of screaming, she might spew hatred and bile all over his expensive, kicking shoes.

Everyone was staring at her and pretending not to, and she did them all the courtesy of letting them think she didn't notice. Instead, she stared at her feet so intensely she thought she might rupture something vital. She stared so hard she didn't hear the clerk calling to her until the little old lady sitting behind her tapped her shoulder and pointed it out.

Warily, Stella hefted her bag onto her shoulder and went to the desk. The plane had already been canceled, and she knew they were going to try to put her on another just as she knew she was going to be polite about whatever they offered no matter how irritated she was. The clerk smiled at her, and Stella managed to smile back.

"Thanks," the clerk said in a low voice. "For... You know."

"It's okay."

"I'm sorry, but your flight's been canceled, as you know. We were able to book you on a 5:00 p.m. flight and upgrade you to business class for your trouble." The clerk smiled and again lowered her voice. "And for what you said."

It did pay to be nice to people. "Five will be okay. Business class is great, thanks."

"No problem." The clerk busied herself with making the arrangements, then handed Stella the updated paperwork with a small frown. "Though, with the weather..."

Stella put a finger to her own lips. "Shh. Don't jinx us!"

They shared a laugh. Five o'clock was a few hours away,

and Stella didn't feel like sitting at the gate for that long. She pulled out her phone and sent Tristan a text message telling him she'd be home later than she'd thought and for him to send her a message when he got in. Typically, he didn't answer. She tried telling herself he was busy with his friends, that it didn't mean anything, that the bad weather keeping planes on the ground in Chicago didn't mean bad roads in Pennsylvania. It didn't mean their car had spun off the road into a ditch or any of the other hundred bad things her mind wanted her to imagine.

She found a bar the way she usually did, this one more crowded than usual. Probably because of the weather. People tended to seek out liquid refreshment when they were forced to wait longer than expected. That's why she ended up sitting at the bar instead of at one of the heavy round wooden tables set with chairs that looked like wagon wheels. What the hell? Since when was Chicago the Wild, Wild West?

The bartender looked vaguely familiar, but then they all sort of did. White shirt, black pants, black bow tie. He gave her a smile that made it seem as though he might know her too, but only if she was willing to acknowledge him. Shit. Had she slept with him? Stella eyed the dark, slightly too long hair, the crooked smile. It was entirely possible. Sometimes she couldn't find a businessman.

Of course she'd showered this morning at the hotel, but she hadn't straightened or even blow-dried her hair, and she'd barely bothered with makeup. Just a swipe of mascara and some powder. Her lipstick had long ago worn off on the rim of her coffee cup. Her slim-cut jeans and oversized cardigan were clean and comfy, but in no way anything close to the outfits she would wear on her turnarounds. Even if she had fucked this guy now sliding a paper napkin and a bowl of pretzels toward her, even if she looked as vaguely familiar to him as he did to her, there was no way he was going to remember her exactly.

Still, he kept staring at her even after she'd ordered her unsweetened iced tea and a plate of cheese fries. He wasn't subtle about it either. No cutting eye contact or anything when she caught him.

Finally, when he came over to freshen her tea, she said, "Do I know you?"

The bartender grinned. "No. But I think I know you. Diane Lane, right? You were in that movie with Richard Gere."

"And *The Outsiders,*" Stella said after a pause. "Don't forget that one."

"Wow! Wow, that's right!" He did a small, shuffling dance of excitement.

"I'm not Diane Lane," Stella told him, half wishing she was.

"No? You sure?"

She laughed, giving him credit for trying…whatever it was he was trying to do with the comparison. "I'm sure."

"You look just like her."

It wasn't the first time she'd heard it, though sometimes she got Julianne Moore and sometimes she got Kate Winslet, "that girl in *Titanic.*" She supposed it was better than only being compared to Lucille Ball. "It's the hair. We both have red hair."

"Huh." He wiped at the counter, not looking convinced, as if maybe she really was Diane Lane and was just trying to trick him. "Well. You really look like her."

"Thanks." Stella lifted her glass.

The bartender moved to take care of another customer. Stella sighed and dipped a fry in the cheese sauce. It was disgusting, and she grimaced. Served her right for ordering junk like that in an airport bar. She should've stuck to the onion rings.

"You don't look like Diane Lane."

Stella turned to the man on her left, who had a whiskey glass in front of him that hadn't been empty since she'd sat down. "Sorry?"

"You don't look like her," he said. "Not really."

Half a laugh snuck out of her. "I wouldn't mind if I did. She's gorgeous."

He hadn't looked at her when he spoke, both his hands wrapped around the glass and his gaze focused on it. Now he twisted, just a little, to settle his gaze on her face. It moved over her hair, tied in a messy bun. Briefly over her body. Then back to her face.

"So are you," he said.

Heat, all through her, just like that. Stella opened her mouth to speak but found no words. Her breath hissed out like a slow leak.

"I'm Matthew." He held out his hand.

She took it. "Stella."

Her real name slipped out without thinking, surprising herself.

He didn't seem to notice. He smiled. "Stella, can I buy you a drink?"

This was far from the first time a man in a bar had offered to buy her a drink. She almost always said yes. But that was when she was someone else, some other woman with a different name and hairstyle, a woman in stockings and garters instead of a stretched-out sweater and cotton granny panties, one who had a man at home waiting to take her to dinner and a movie sometime.

"I have a drink, thanks."

Matthew lifted his glass and tipped it toward the bartender for another. He looked at her again. He might've been drunk, but it was hard to tell. His eyes had a hint of red around the rims, some lines in the corners, but it could be exhaustion. She was sure she looked more than a little travel-weary herself.

"Your flight's canceled. If you're going to stay in the airport all night, you should have something more to fortify you than iced tea."

Stella turned her glass around in her palms and looked at the glisten of moisture it left on the bar. "It won't be all night. They booked me on a five o'clock."

Matthew shook his head as the bartender refilled his glass. He pointed at the television set, tuned to some news station. A blonde woman was talking, but silently, while her words scrolled across the bottom of the screen. "All flights will be canceled today and into tonight. I guarantee it."

She'd suspected as much herself, but hearing it said so firmly, no hint of doubt, set her back a little bit. "How can you know that?"

"I've flown a lot." He shrugged and sipped at his drink. Cut his gaze toward her again. "Hope you don't have someplace important you have to be."

"I have to get home to my son. He was away with some friends on a ski club trip. He'll be coming back tonight...." She pulled out her phone, but Tristan hadn't replied. She thumbed Jeff's number and typed a quick message telling him her flight had been canceled and to check in with

Tristan. He didn't answer her either. When she looked up, Matthew was watching. "How about you?"

"I have a flight to New York. But it will probably be canceled, and I'll just go home." He swirled the whiskey for a second before downing it and gesturing at the bartender. "One more."

That made at least his third, by her count. Not that it was any of her business how serious he got with his liquor. Stella studied him, though, with her practiced eye. He had a businessman's haircut, dark hair cropped short with glints of silver at the temples, but he wasn't dressed like one. No suit, no tie. He wore a pair of jeans and a plain blue T-shirt that clung to a nicely muscled back and showed off arms just as nice. She couldn't see his shoes, but his leather jacket hanging on the back of his chair looked beaten and worn by real use, not prefab distressing.

"You live in Chicago?" she asked.

He nodded and waved a hand at her glass. "Another tea for the lady. Can I at least make it a Long Island? In honor of my trip to New York. Maybe I'll get lucky, and it won't be canceled. Or, I know. How about a Manhattan? Even better. Corey, get the lady a Manhattan."

Matthew's smile transformed him, and she didn't have the heart to tell him she didn't want the drink. He was tired, she thought. Not drunk, at least not too much. When the drinks came, he clinked his glass to hers.

"What are we toasting to?" Stella asked.

"Bad weather."

She laughed and breathed in the aroma of liquor without sipping it. She'd never had a Manhattan. "Don't you want to toast to better weather?"

"Nope. Because if the weather was better, your flight

wouldn't be canceled, and we'd never be sitting here having this drink."

"Ah." Stella stared at her glass but didn't lift it to her mouth.

"Don't you like it? I can get you something else." Matthew was already gesturing at the bartender, but Stella shook her head.

"No. It's not that. I'm just not a big drinker."

"Oh." He studied her, then leaned a little closer. "Friend of Bill's?"

At first, she didn't know what he meant. Then she laughed. "Me? Oh. No, no, nothing like that. I just..."

But there was no explanation for it that could come out here, in a bar, with a stranger. There didn't really seem to be a valid explanation at all. Certainly not that she couldn't drink, if she wanted to. That she had some kind of drinking problem. She had no idea why she cared if this stranger thought she was an alcoholic, but all at once, it mattered that she prove the idea wrong. With sudden determination, Stella sipped and let the liquor warm her mouth for a second or so before it slid down her throat to settle in her belly. It rose in her cheeks too, and she didn't need to see her reflection in the mirror behind the bar to know she was flushed.

She wasn't prepared for this, but it was happening anyway.

They drank together. He charmed her, bit by bit, and if he was hitting on her he was so impressively subtle about it that Stella second- and third-guessed herself when she flirted in response. When she leaned a little closer, his eyes widened, just a little. His smile got a little bigger. He didn't lean in to her, but he bought her another drink, and his eyes never left hers when they were talking. He asked her questions, simple ones about her opinions on pop culture, music, television, the bar's decor. Nothing too personal. He gave her his entire attention but didn't stare so intensely she worried he was going to put her in a well so he could make a suit out of her skin—and she'd met a disturbing number of men in her turnarounds who'd made her feel that way.

Her second plane *was* canceled, just as he'd warned. Stella was sure Matthew would be gone by the time she got back from making the arrangements to leave tomorrow morning, along with the phone calls to her boss, to Tristan and to Jeff when her son didn't answer. She tried to pretend she wasn't disappointed when she went back to the bar and saw his seat empty. She also tried, without success, to pretend that when she saw him standing by the door with his coat on that she wasn't relieved and excited too.

"I don't like to brag," Matthew said, "but I was right, huh?"

"You were. How about yours?" She scanned the flight-board quickly, but couldn't find his flight.

Matthew didn't even look around. "I won't be flying tonight."

"I won't be leaving until tomorrow, ten-thirty in the morning. It was the first flight they could get me on." She shifted her bag on her shoulder. "I guess I might as well see if I can get a room."

"You don't want to do that," he said with a shake of his head and a solemn look. "I have a better idea."

Stella forced her breath not to catch. She'd done this so many times before, played this game, danced this dance, but now she felt as if she'd forgotten the rules. She might stumble on the steps. "Oh?"

She thought if he kissed her she'd turn her head so his mouth hit her cheek and not her mouth. If he touched her, she would pull away. One late night she'd fucked a man in a bathroom stall. Once she'd let a different man get her off under a table in a sushi place. She wasn't shy, she wasn't a prude…but those times she also hadn't been Stella.

Matthew didn't kiss her. Didn't touch her. He didn't even take a single step closer to her. "Sure. You can stay at my place. It's not far from here at all. And I don't have bedbugs. Do you want to come home with me, Stella?"

She ought to ask him what made him think she was the sort of woman to go home with a man she'd just met, except somehow he'd know she was. Or maybe just hoped she was. Maybe he could smell it on her, like a perfume.

Stella looked into his eyes, and though earlier she'd been not quite certain if he was flirting with her, there was no mistaking the gleam of desire in his gaze now. He had brown eyes, more like hazel. She imagined herself reflected there.

She opened her mouth to say no, but instead said yes.

Matthew, as it turned out, had taken a cab to the airport, so she didn't have to worry about driving with him in the icy rain after he'd had more drinks than she could keep track of. His apartment wasn't far, just as he'd promised, and though the frigid wind took her breath away and nearly knocked her over between the cab and the foyer, inside the building was delicious and warm. Beautiful too, with a lovely art deco feeling to the decor.

Matthew nodded at the doorman. "Evening, Herndon."

"Evening, sir." Herndon obviously knew how to be discreet, because he gave Stella a polite nod, then let his gaze slip away from her as though she were invisible.

In the elevator, both of them faced the door and stood with at least a foot of space between them. If he kissed her, she thought, she wouldn't open her mouth. If he touched her, she would put her hands on his to keep them still before she put some space between them.

The door opened. Matthew let her go first, then pointed to the left and down the hall. His key slid into the lock with a metallic click that sent a rush of sudden, trembling emotion all through her.

This was real.

This was *her*.

Before it could overwhelm her, this understanding that she really was going to go inside a stranger's apartment, Matthew got the door open and ushered her through. He closed the door behind them, locked it and tossed his keys into a small bowl set on an ornate table just inside the door.

If he kissed her, she thought... But he didn't.

"Let me hang up your coat. I'll put your bag here too." He opened a narrow door, a closet, and tugged on a string to light a bare bulb. There was just enough room for her things.

For one panicky moment, Stella almost didn't let him take her coat or give him her carry-on. In the bars when she was looking for a hookup, her suitcase was her anchor. Her excuse to leave if she wanted to. Here and now, there'd be no "oh, sorry, have to catch a plane." No quick escape, and it would be even longer to leave if she had to fish around for her belongings before she did.

"Stella?"

"Oh, sorry. Right." She shrugged out of her wet, cold

coat and let him put her bag on the floor beneath it, but out of the way to avoid any dripping. Her purse too. She rubbed at her arms with a nervous laugh. "Chilly."

"Come into the kitchen. It's usually warmer there. Hungry?" he asked over his shoulder as she followed him down the narrow, high-ceilinged hall and into the kitchen.

"Starving, actually." She put a hand on her stomach, which was jumping with nerves as well as hunger.

He smiled. "I can make something. Nothing fancy. Spaghetti? Garlic bread?"

Oh, exactly the right thing for an intimate interlude. She laughed, wondering again if she'd misjudged him. "Sure. Sounds great. What can I do to help?"

"Salad in the fridge, if you want to put that together."

They moved together expertly, stepping out of each other's way as he puttered with the pot of water and she rinsed the lettuce and cut the tomatoes to add to a large stoneware crock he handed her from the cupboard. He poured her a glass of wine she wasn't sure she wanted after two iced teas and an equal number of Manhattans, but she took it anyway and sipped. It was good, even to someone who didn't usually like wine.

They ate together from mismatched plates and flatware at an antique-looking table in the small dining room. Matthew kept her glass filled. His too. He twirled a fork of spaghetti and held it out for her. Later, when Stella did the same for him with a bite of the cheesecake he'd pulled from the freezer to thaw during dinner, he circled her wrists with his fingers and held her hand steady while he bit the dessert.

He didn't let go.

If he kissed her, she thought, she would slide herself onto his lap and straddle him. She'd taste wine and garlic and cheesecake on his tongue and it would be delicious. She would rock her cunt against his cock and urge his hands to grip her ass and hold her closer.

If he kissed her.

He let go of her wrist, but not her gaze. His tongue touched the center of his bottom lip for a second. He blinked, blinked again, something faltering in his gaze. He'd snagged her with it before, but now he was letting her go.

"Stella…"

She never gave them her real name, and this was one of the reasons why. When she was someone else, it didn't matter what they said or did, all those men who didn't know her. It didn't matter who they thought she was. Maria, Lavinia, Suzanne, Amy, Lisa, Karen, Debbie.

"Shhh." She shook her head, willing him not to say anything else. She didn't want to hear him tell her this had been a mistake, that she should go, or worse, that she could stay anyway. "Matthew. Shh."

He closed his eyes for a moment, brow furrowed against some small pain. When he opened them she saw desire, but also something else. Guilt, she thought. Anxiety of some kind. It alarmed her enough to push back a little, the legs of her chair squeaking on the tile floor.

"I want to kiss you so much right now," Matthew said in a low, rough voice on the edge of breaking. He blinked rapidly and licked his bottom lip again. "I just…want…so much…"

This she understood. This she knew. Stella drew in a breath, mind racing even as her heart thumped faster. "So kiss me, Matthew."

He gave his head the smallest shake, not quite a denial.

More as though he'd found himself not unwilling, but incapable. His fingers gripped the edge of the table. Stella got up carefully, making sure not to scrape the chair on the floor any more than she had done. Now he had to tip his head to look up at her, though he didn't otherwise move. She took a step back, then another. Matthew stayed motionless except for the rise and fall of his Adam's apple as he swallowed.

"I'll get a cab," Stella said quietly. "Thank you for dinner. It was delicious. It was nice…meeting you, Matthew."

The words felt stale and sour, certainly not sincere, but this was awkward enough without her trying to escape without at least an attempt at civility.

In the hallway, she let her hands shake as she tugged her still-damp coat from the hanger and lifted her bag. She screamed when she straightened and closed the closet door to find Matthew directly on the other side. He looked as startled as she was, and he caught one of her flailing arms to keep her from knocking into the mirror hung on the wall next to the closet.

Babbling words rose to her lips, a string of some senseless apologies on a stutter of breath. The adrenaline rush of fear pushed her heartbeat into an even faster, unsteady rhythm. Made her light-headed and spinny, her feet slipping a little on the wet floor.

"You scared me." She put a hand on her heart, fingers slightly curled, and gave a self-conscious laugh.

"I'm sorry." He ran a hand over his head, his hair too short to rumple, though she got the idea that maybe he was used to wearing it longer, that he was accustomed to pushing it out of his eyes. "I'm an idiot."

"You're not." She pressed her palm against her chest for another moment before touching his arm. "Really."

They both looked down at the touch of her fingertips on his bare skin. He was warmer than she'd expected, or maybe it was because she was so suddenly chilled. Her nipples tightened, and she was sure he could see them. The crisp, curling dark hairs on his skin tickled her knuckles. She wanted to let go, she knew she should let go, but as Matthew stepped closer and pulled her into his arms, all Stella could do was hold him tighter.

"I want to kiss you," he murmured with his mouth all at once so close to hers that every word he spoke sent a shivery breath across her lips. "I just…"

Stella didn't waste more time with words. She moved against him so there'd be nothing for him to do but let his mouth press hers. It was as sweet as it was strange, that first kiss. It lasted a few seconds before he broke it, eyes closed, not moving more than a breath away. She didn't have time to count even a heartbeat before he was kissing her again, harder this time, but not rough. Her mouth opened as her hands slid up and over his firm chest to link behind his neck.

He tasted as good as she'd imagined, maybe better because she'd been so sure she wouldn't find out. He backed her up a step, then another, his mouth never leaving hers. The wall pressed against her back, Matthew's body a delicious counterpressure at her front.

Whatever had stopped him before had gone away. His hands moved over her breasts, belly, hips. One centered on her lower back as the other cupped the back of her neck. His tongue stroked hers.

This kiss ended with them both panting, breathless. He

stared into her eyes, and she was close enough now to see the green ripples in his irises and the thick black fringe of his lashes. He licked his mouth again as he tilted his head to angle his mouth toward hers, but he stopped just before kissing her again.

"It's okay," she whispered. "I want to."

She never wondered what the men thought when she went with them to their hotel rooms or to shadowy corners. She never cared. She wasn't interested in knowing them any more than she assumed they wanted to know about her. Already she'd spent more time learning Matthew than she had any man since... Well, since Craig. And all of that in the past few hours.

Matthew's thumb stroked her jawline. The hand at the small of her back pressed her against the thickness in his groin. He brushed his mouth along her cheek to nuzzle at her ear, his breath hot. His shoulders lifted and fell with a sigh before he mouthed her neck. Her head tipped back at the wet slide of his tongue on her skin, then the nip of his teeth along her collarbone.

"Yes," she breathed, and gave herself up to each small pleasure. "Like that."

Desire had become the one true constant in her life, the only feeling she could count on never to disappoint her. Desire required nothing from her. No investment. No responsibility. All desire wanted was to be sated. It was physical, and therefore, could be killed.

She pushed his hand between her legs, the denim an inconvenient and unaccustomed barrier. Still, when his knuckles rubbed at the seam of her jeans, it pressed her clit so sweetly she bit her lip with the pleasure. His mouth returned to hers, the kiss teasing and taunting her until all she could do was open her mouth and let him take it however he wanted.

Matthew worked her button free, then the zipper. He slid his fingers into her panties and unerringly found her clit. He dipped a little lower to slide along her folds, then up again. She wasn't quite wet, and Matthew withdrew his hand long enough to slick his fingers with his mouth before sliding them again into her panties. It was such a simple thing, not showy, just practical, but lust pulsed through her, making her throb around his fingers as he pushed them inside her.

Matthew shuddered a little against her, his tongue dipping inside her mouth before he broke the kiss again. He pulled back enough to look into her eyes. Pinned by his hands behind her neck and between her legs, Stella could only return the look.

His mouth teased at hers. "Bedroom, down the hall."

She followed him, their fingers linked. His room was sparely furnished with a bed on a Hollywood frame, no head- or footboard, made up with a plain blue comforter and several pillows in white cases. A small bedside table, a match of the one in the hall, held a lamp with a plain white shade, a utilitarian-looking black clock with red numbers, and a tissue box. The dresser in one corner and the surprisingly beautiful armoire in the other were antiques too, of softly curving wood inlaid with a pretty pattern and equally lovely ornate handles. No curtains, just a plain white roller shade. Through another narrow doorway, past the black wooden door with the crystal knob, she could see what looked like a white-and-black-tiled bathroom. The hint of a claw-foot tub.

Inside the room, Matthew let go of her hand. He gestured at the bathroom. "If you want to…"

"Oh. Sure, yeah." She definitely could use the bathroom. She closed the door behind her and ran the water in the sink, which had the cutest old-fashioned taps. She didn't peek inside his medicine cabinet, though she wanted to. She blotted her face, studying her reflection.

She could still keep track of the number of men she'd fucked. She didn't need to know or remember their names to recall the taste of each of them. The length and thickness of their pricks. The smell of their cologne. She didn't have to be able to pick them out of a crowd for each one of them to have been imprinted on her in some way. They'd all left their mark.

But not on Stella. On someone else, whoever she was when she put on the lipstick and the lace. Stella didn't walk in those high-heeled pumps, but Stella's was the face that looked at her from this mirror now.

What the fuck was she doing?

Stella gripped the sink with both hands and listened to the rush of water with her eyes closed for a moment or two. She should walk out. Get her coat and purse and carry-on the way she'd meant to, call a cab. Leave this apartment and this man behind her, no matter how sweet his kiss. His touch.

She used the toilet and then automatically used the sink again to clean herself. She laughed, the sound low and shaky, as her fingertips moved in the heat of her flesh. She could tell herself whatever she wanted, but she was going to go out there and fuck him, because something inside her made her helpless to stop herself.

Because she *wanted* to fuck him.

She wanted to.

That was the simple truth of it, and she could be ashamed, or she could be honest. She could be brave and bold, she could be a little crazy, or she could embrace this desire, because she certainly could not deny it.

Stella looked at herself in the mirror again. This was who she was, even without the hair, the makeup, the clothes. Here she was.

She slipped out of her cardigan to be in just the tank top beneath, her nipples already jutting against the thin fabric. The blessing of small breasts meant she could go without a bra when she wanted, and though she normally didn't, she was glad she had done so today. The granny panties were going to be bad enough. If she'd worn the bra she'd packed, wash-worn and faded, she'd have been too embarrassed to take off her clothes.

Matthew hadn't taken anything off, but he had turned down the bed and sat on the edge of it with his head bowed. He looked up when she came out of the bathroom, and his smile looked sincere even if it was only half the brilliance it had been earlier. She moved to stand between his knees, her fingers brushing over the short scrub of his hair before she cupped his face in her hands and tipped his head back.

She didn't kiss him, not at first. She just looked at him. The bedside lamp had pretty decent light, golden, casting half his face in shadow. She traced the lines at the corners of his eyes, then the shallower ones bracketing his mouth. She touched the silver in his hair and the scruff of beard growing in on his chin and cheeks. This was a man who'd lived.

One fingertip moved over his eyebrows, one at a time. Matthew closed his eyes under her touch, still smiling. When she drew a finger over his lips, they parted just enough for her to slip the point of her index finger inside. He bit it gently, then sucked, and the sensation sent a delicious shudder all through her.

He opened his eyes. His hands slid up the backs of her thighs to cup her ass, though he didn't pull her closer. She thought he would lie back on the bed, maybe pull her on top of him. Instead, he pressed his cheek against her belly, just below her breasts. She'd noticed before the heat of his skin and felt it now through her tank top. He was a furnace. Her hand stroked the back of his head and found the back of his neck.

They stayed that way for what felt like a very long time, breathing in. Breathing out. She wondered if he heard her heart beating or if it was only the pulse in her throat and wrists, the rush of it in her ears that made it seem so loud.

Matthew murmured something she didn't catch and tipped his head back to look up at her. The phone on the bedside table rang just as she kissed him, but Matthew shook his head when she started to pull away. He shifted on the bed, tugging her down next to him.

"Let it ring." In the next minute, though, his pocket rang. He sighed, defeated, and moved to pull out his cell phone. He looked at the screen and frowned. "Sorry. I should've known she'd just keep calling until I answer."

Stella sat back on the bed, giving him space to answer the call. Awwwwwkward. As Matthew answered, she gestured, pantomiming that she was going to go out to get her own cell phone. She couldn't be sure he understood her charade, but he nodded.

"Yeah. Hi." He sounded brusque.

Stella ducked out of the room to get her purse. No messages from Tristan or his father. She shrugged off her worry, but it didn't go far. She sent another quick text as she walked back toward the bedroom.

"What do you want me to do about it? Well, buy them what they need. You take care of it. You don't need my… No. Of course not. Well, if they were with me, I'd do it, but they're not. Yes, I'll have them next weekend. You're the one who said they needed the stuff right now. If it can wait, sure, I'll take them. If not… Look," Matthew said sharply, "I don't see what the problem is."

Stella paused, not wanting to intrude. She typed another message to Jeff, and with reservations, added one to Cynthia too. She didn't like going to Jeff's wife for things, but the fact was Cynthia, God love her, did keep track of everything much better than Jeff did. Stella remembered how that had been.

"Just take care of it, then! Christ, Caroline. What do you want me to say?"

Silence. The creak of the bed. Matthew sighed. Stella gently pushed the door open, and he looked up.

"Hey," she said.

His smile looked tired. "Hi. Sorry about that."

She came in and sat next to him. "It's fine."

"It's my ex," he explained, though she'd figured that part out. "Something with the kids. I don't really know why she can't just deal with it, but she likes to mess with me, make me feel guilty under the guise of keeping me 'in the loop.'"

He made air quotes with his fingers, a gesture Stella would've found irritating but for the fact that he'd used the word *guise* correctly. She was such a sucker for a good vocabulary, it wasn't even funny. She shrugged and nudged him with her shoulder, teasing.

"No problem."

Matthew brushed some hair off her face, then over her shoulder. When his gaze went to her mouth, she anticipated the kiss and leaned in...just as his phone rang again. He muttered an expletive.

"I'm not answering it."

She laughed and kissed him, spoke against his mouth. "You probably should. Or turn it off."

"Yeah..." They melted into the kiss. His hands slid up her body to cup her breasts, and he thumbed her nipples.

His phone beeped with a voice mail. A moment later, a text. Matthew groaned and buried his face against the side of her neck while Stella laughed and petted his hair.

"Maybe you should call her back," she offered, taking a peek at the phone. The text was simple to read: ANSWER YOUR PHONE.

He sighed, looked at the text and frowned. He didn't listen to the voice mail, just tapped in a number. "What?"

Ouch. Stella settled back on the bed, watching Matthew as he got up from the bed to pace. He spoke with his hands when he got upset, his face expressive. Studying him was a guilty pleasure, since he looked very, very fine when he was angry. She was glad she wasn't on the other end of the phone.

"Why do we have to have this discussion now? Let me talk to them." He frowned and tossed up his hand. "Of course they're in bed, why would you call me when they're awake so I could actually talk to them? I did call them. I left a message. Christ, Caroline, if you don't answer the house phone, I figure it's because you're busy or, you know, out and about doing something that you should be paying attention to, not answering your damn cell phone. Like driving, maybe you should pay attention instead of answering the phone, right?"

He paused, cutting a sort of guilty-looking glance toward Stella. "No, I'm at home. Yes, I'm alone."

Stella considered feeling offended, but knew she'd have said the same thing if the situation were reversed. She carefully kept her eyes on her own phone. Matthew tossed his phone in the dresser drawer and climbed up on the bed.

"Sorry," he said.

She shook her head. "Really. It's okay."

He leaned in to kiss her.

Her phone chimed.

"Cock-blocked by technology," Stella said.

Both of them burst into laughter. It was cathartic, a release of sorts, kind of like orgasm in the way it built and built, then crashed. The bed shook with it, they gasped with it, it stole their breath the way good sex would have. It felt as intimate as sex. It felt real.

"You'd better check it."

She did. It was from Cynthia, of course, telling Stella not to worry. Jeff would pick Tristan up at the house whenever he got home and bring him to their place. She'd added a *hugs* at the end of the message, totally irrelevant and useless and also annoying. Cynthia added it to almost every message. It was probably her sig line.

"Important?" Matthew asked.

Stella tossed her phone into her bag and put it on the floor. "No."

Then they were kissing again, and his hands were moving over her. He pulled her tank top over her head and pushed her onto the bed at the same time. He covered her with his body, his mouth moving on hers, down her jaw and throat and finally to her breasts. Stella moaned when he took one nipple into his mouth and sucked gently. Then the other.

He moved off her just long enough to pull his shirt off too, revealing a chest and belly as nicely muscled as his arms. And hair, oh, she did like a man's chest to have hair. Not too much, not like a pelt or anything, but a nice pattern of it on his pecs and then a bit more down lower on his belly.

"What?" He'd stopped kissing her, noticing her looking.

"Just enjoying the view." She arched upward to take his mouth again, her hands moving over his skin. She tugged at the button on his jeans and slid her hand inside, remembering how it had felt when he'd done the same to her in the hall. Her fingers encountered cotton and hot, hard flesh.

His groan, muffled inside her mouth, sent a shiver through her. It seemed as if they'd been at this for hours and now neither one of them wanted to risk another interruption. Clothes came off. The golden lamplight hid a lot of flaws, but it wouldn't totally hide the scars.

And it didn't. Matthew traced the longest one, the ugliest one, from side to side across her belly but said nothing about it.

He bent back to kissing her as his hand moved between her legs. His cock was hard against her thigh, and when she stroked it, his hips pushed forward in that involuntary way most men seemed to have. She loved that helpless thrust, as though they couldn't stop themselves from fucking into her fist.

"Shit," he said under his breath, and sat up to look down at her. "I don't have anything."

Stella had been riding a lovely wave of arousal, but now

she blinked. At least he was assuming she'd want him to use something. "Um…let me check my bag."

She rolled to hook it with her finger and pull it toward her. She found the small plastic zipper case she used to store feminine supplies, not sure if she'd actually stuck a condom or two in there or if she was remembering wrong. This wasn't the purse she usually took on her turnarounds.

Matthew looked sheepish when he took it from her. "Sorry. I wasn't expecting this."

She thought of the way he'd tossed back his drinks and the way he'd looked her over, up and down. He'd hit on her pretty hard in the bar. He'd invited her back to his apartment. She had a hard time believing he had no idea this was where things were going to go. Then again, he'd been so hesitant to make a move when they finally got here. And she hadn't intended to go home with anyone on this trip either. Strange shit happened all the time when sex got involved, and she of all people should know that.

"Don't worry about it." On her back but propped on her elbows, she let her toes slide up his thigh to his belly. "We're good."

He fumbled with the condom wrapper, ducking his head in a way she found incredibly endearing. When it looked as though he might also falter putting it on, though, she pushed up onto her knees to take it from him. "Let me."

She sheathed him and looked up to find him watching her with an expression she couldn't read. His cock, nicely thick and full in her hand, bobbed. She kissed his mouth and nipped at his chin. Nuzzled his ear. Stella pushed him gently until he lay back, and she straddled him with his cock in her hand. Only his fingers moved, squeezing her hips gently.

She loved the look in their eyes when she put them inside her for the first time. Matthew's eyes fluttered closed as his back arched a bit. He bit his bottom lip too, but while all of those things were enough to melt her butter, none were what made her gasp aloud. She did that when he put his arms over his head, one hand gripping the other wrist.

Every. Button. Pushed.

She settled onto his cock until he filled her, all the way. When she leaned forward, she could kiss him and rub her clit against his muscled belly with every rocking thrust. She gripped his shoulders, letting her nails dig in the tiniest amount. He thrust a little harder at that, his teeth denting his lip, eyes closed, brow furrowed. But not in pain. No, not that.

She moved on him, slow and then a little faster. She'd been with men who tried to control everything about this. The pace, the rhythm, the depth of the thrusts. That could be fun, though usually it was so much harder for her to come that way she ended up giving up and just enjoying the fucking for what it was, finding her own pleasure later with her hand and her memories. But this…oh, this was so much sweeter. So much sexier. She rolled her hips, moving on his cock, her cunt slick and hot and her clit tight and aching with lust. Every time she rubbed herself against his belly, the pleasure spiked until she shuddered with it.

Mouth open, eyes closed, fingers digging deep into his skin, so hard it had to hurt him but he didn't tell her to stop. Her hair fell in her face, sticking to her skin with the sweat that came from really great fucking. Everything became pleasure; nothing else mattered. All she wanted to do was move with it. All she could do was let it overtake her.

She was kissing him when she came. Matthew breathed

in her cry. His hands went around her, unexpected but welcome. His fingers pressed a line of demand down her spine
until he settled again on her hips to move her a little faster.
A little harder. He fucked into her so hard it hurt, but it was
a small pain and overshadowed by the pleasure. She moved
a hand from his shoulder and pressed it flat over his racing,
pounding heart. He came with a shudder and a low shout.

With a low sigh of satisfaction, Stella leaned to press her
face against the side of his neck for a moment while she
timed the slowing pulse of both their hearts. He softened
slowly inside her, which was nice because he didn't slip
out right away. She got to spend a few precious seconds
snuggled up against him before she reached between them
to keep the condom in place as she rolled onto her back.

Stella yawned with the back of her hand against her
mouth. She was sleepy now, though it couldn't be much
past ten or eleven. She wasn't looking forward to heading
back out into the icy weather and finding a hotel room.

Matthew went into the bathroom. The toilet flushed.
He got back into bed and switched off the light, which was
enough to make her at least shift in the covers even though
she hadn't quite managed to rouse herself enough to move.

She hadn't adjusted to the darkness yet, so blinked rapidly to focus on him. "I should get going."

He was silent for a heartbeat. "Oh. If you want to?"

There'd been many awkward moments in her life, but
the men she picked up in her turnarounds generally knew
what was what. But this was not a usual turnaround.

"Sorry," Matthew said before she could say anything.
"It's just…I haven't, um… Well, I don't usually do this.
Haven't done this, I mean."

He paused, as if he was waiting for her to say the same

thing, but she couldn't very well tell him that, could she? Even if he didn't know it as a lie, she would, and just because her turnarounds weren't something she liked to brag about, it didn't mean she was ashamed.

"It's okay. You don't have to explain."

The bed dipped as he shifted his weight. "No, I do. I just wanted you to know that this isn't something I do all the time or anything."

"I'm not judging you, if that's what you're worried about." Stella pressed her head into the pillow and let her hands slide down her body to rest on her stomach. She could feel her hipbones, her belly concave between them, but the skin not smooth. The scale and the size of her jeans might show her to be "skinny," but she'd never have a flat, unblemished stomach again.

His low chuckle sounded a little embarrassed, and it was still charming. "I've been divorced for just over a year. I haven't been with anyone since then."

"I could take that one of two ways." Stella kept her voice light. "Either you just couldn't stand it anymore and you took the first thing that came along—"

He snorted laughter. "God. No."

"Or," she added, "I should feel special."

"I'd say definitely special."

She went a little tingly at the answer, even as she told herself it was all just talk. He could even be lying, though... she didn't think so. Or she didn't want to think so, at any rate.

"So, why me?" The only light in the room came from his alarm clock, so she couldn't see his face very well. That was fine. It was easier to ask things like this in the dark.

She wasn't even sure where the question had come from, or why she cared.

"It was the way you talked to that asshole giving the gate agent a hard time."

Stella was more awake now, but that statement seemed garbled and nonsensical, the kind you'd hear in a dream. It meant he'd been aware of her before she went into the bar. It meant that maybe he'd been watching her, which made even less sense if, as he was saying, he wasn't the sort to pick up women and take them home.

"People treat airline staff like crap all the time," Matthew said. "Guys like him get away with it because they can. I liked what you said to him. She couldn't say it, but you did. And you were right."

Stella cleared her throat a little, thinking of what she'd told that irate man and why his situation had resonated with her so strongly. "I should've had more sympathy for him."

"No, you were right."

She thought of the man's fury, and his explanation, and how hearing it had only made her all the more angry herself. "He shouldn't have used his grief as a reason to be a prick."

Matthew didn't answer, not at first, though in the silence she could hear him thinking how to respond.

She kept on, the words slipping out of her, one after another, aided by the dark. "Even in the middle of dealing with the worst thing that has ever happened to you, even when you think there is no possible way you can get through another minute, not another second, even if you're dealing with the most incompetent of idiots... Well." She cleared her throat, memories rushing to the surface on a wave of emotions. "Even when you're terrified that you can't take one more step or deal with one more thing, there's never an excuse for behaving like that. Because when you do, you make all of those fears come true."

His hands pulled her closer, till he was spooning her. His mouth found her shoulder, his breath her ear. He put his hand flat on her belly and held her, just held her without speaking for a few minutes. He'd ask her now. About the scars. She knew he would.

What surprised her was that she answered.

"We were coming home from a Christmas party. The weather had turned bad. It was an accident," Stella told him. "Just a stupid accident. Icy roads, someone going too fast. I woke up in the hospital with a broken collarbone and internal injuries. My husband and younger son were fine. They both walked away. My older son..."

"You lost him?" Matthew asked quietly when she didn't continue.

"Yes," Stella said. "But not for another half a year."

CHAPTER TWELVE

After that, there wasn't much to say. She really should rouse herself, but moving would destroy this quiet that had fallen between them. Force her to acknowledge that she'd told him the most awful truth about herself, and worse, she would have to force herself to wonder, why him? Dozens of strangers. Why now?

Maybe she'd just close her eyes for a minute or two. Just a few seconds. No more than that.

She woke with a start from a dream of falling, and sat up in a strange bed. A darkness she didn't recognize. Lumps and shapes of shadow loomed, but there was no familiar crack of light around the bathroom door to tell her anything else. No familiar anything, and she panicked for a couple moments until the bed creaked next to her, and warmth nudged at her bare skin. Breathing. The brush of a hand on her hip.

"You okay?"

Matthew. She'd fallen asleep; he'd turned off the lights;

there was nothing to worry about. Stella pressed a hand to her chest, her pounding heart an echo of earlier in the night. "What time is it?"

"Almost four."

She sat up to push her back against the wall since there was no headboard. She drew her knees up, blinking as her vision adjusted a bit to the dark. She felt sticky with sweat and sex. Her mouth cotton-dry. Her head whirled a little bit. Exhaustion and the drinks she wasn't used to, which might've been the reason she'd allowed herself to stay so long in the first place. At least it was an excuse she could use.

"I have to go."

"Right." Matthew sat up. "Let me call you a cab?"

"I have the number in my phone. Thanks, though." She rubbed her eyes, trying to get the energy and motivation to move off the bed.

"Let me at least make you breakfast.... Cup of coffee?" He shifted.

Charming, totally. She laughed a bit. "I'll grab something in the airport. I'll have plenty of time. Thanks."

"I'll walk you out. At least let me do that."

She laughed again. "Okay. You can walk me out."

Neither of them moved at first, and then he kissed her. Soft, sweet. Brief. "Thank you for this, Stella. I told you, it's been a while. I really...needed. Someone. I'm glad it was you."

It was horrifying to weep in the bed of a man she'd just met. Fucking aside, they were strangers. Yet the tears welled up, emotions overwhelming her though she fought to hold them back.

"Hey. Shhh." Matthew put an arm around her, pulling her against him. He stroked her hair.

Warm skin. Hot breath. She buried her face into the curve of his neck and shoulder, her own shoulders shaking as she tried to keep herself from completely dissolving. He would think she was crazy. He would think she was a mess.

Well.

Wasn't she?

"I haven't told anyone about Gage in a long, long time." Her voice was thick with tears, and she swallowed hard to keep them from flowing. "I'm sorry, it's not something I share with people I know really well, much less strangers."

"It's okay." His hand smoothed over her bare back. He kissed the top of her head. "Everyone has scars."

Stella said nothing to that, working hard to get herself under control. She breathed. In, out. She put her hand flat on his chest to feel the beat of his heart. It soothed her. They sat that way for some long minutes until her twisted position started to hurt and she had to sit back.

"I really should go."

"Stay," Matthew said. "What time's your flight?"

"Ten-thirty."

"And you're going to sit in the airport that whole time?"

"It wouldn't be the first time," she told him. "I usually find a nice spot in the preferred customer lounge. I'll be fine."

It was the perfect time for him to ask her why she flew so often, but he didn't. He nuzzled against her for a moment, then said into her ear, "You can sleep here, Stella. In the morning I'll make you coffee and maybe pancakes, if you're lucky. And you can take a cab to the airport with a few hours' sleep and something in your stomach. It'll be a lot nicer than sitting in the lounge."

She shook her head, but didn't say no. Matthew huffed quiet laughter against her. She wiped at her eyes, burning with exhaustion and emotion. The scene with the man in the airport had left her hurting and vulnerable; sharing the story about Gage had been a surprise and hadn't helped.

"Are you sure you don't mind?"

He laughed too, softly. "I don't mind. In fact, I insist. Does that make me kind of a jerk?"

"No. Not at all." Stella tilted her head, looking him over. "You're being unexpectedly kind."

Matthew moved closer then. His mouth found hers. His voice whispered over her lips, "I'm sorry that kindness is unexpected."

They clung together for a moment, less a hug than two people on a raft in a storm-tossed ocean holding on for fear of being swept away. She wanted to let go of him. Needed to, as a matter of fact, because clinging like this went against everything Stella had ever sought while flying. But she held on to him for just a few minutes longer anyway.

CHAPTER THIRTEEN

Stella had no idea what to wear.

Not for a real date. With Craig, no less. She pushed through her racks of clothes, setting aside dresses and skirts in favor of a pair of well-worn jeans that hugged her in all the right places and a tunic-style shirt.

She called Jen for moral support. "I hate what I'm wearing."

"So change. What do you have on?"

Stella described her outfit, adding, "And a pair of Converse."

"Girrrrl." Jen laughed softly. "Well, you're comfy, right?"

"Yes. And it's not like I don't know this guy. I mean, he's seen me dressed in all kinds of things already." Stella had told Jen the Craig saga in brief, leaving out the intimate details, saying only that they'd become friends before her divorce and then lost touch.

"Friends to loooovers," Jen teased until Stella shushed her. "Are you nervous?"

Surprisingly and tellingly, she was not. "No. It's a date, but...not. If that makes sense."

"He thinks it's a date," Jen said.

"Shit. Should I put on a dress?"

"Do you want to wear a dress?"

She did not. A dress meant heels and hose; it meant a different hairstyle and makeup. "No. I guess not."

"You're going to have fun tonight. And, girl, I'm proud of you, can I tell you that?"

It was Stella's turn to laugh. "Why?"

"Because you're getting out there. Getting you some."

For the first time, Stella thought about telling Jen at least a little something about her weekend turnarounds, but thought better of it. "It's one date, Jen."

"With a guy you used to think hung the sun."

Stella had never put it quite that way, but it was true. "It was a long time ago. Things have changed."

"Maybe they haven't," Jen said sagely. "You don't know until you try."

So Stella was trying, and she tried through dinner and the movie after it, and then the coffee and dessert that followed. All the time they'd spent together should've made this date less awkward than any other first date, but as Craig solicitously pulled out her chair for her and offered to add cream and sugar to her coffee, Stella could no longer deny that she *was* nervous.

But this was Craig. Her Craig, who, yes, she'd thought hung the sun, once so long ago. And he hadn't changed, had he? The same smile, same quirky sense of humor. He wore the same cologne, which did send a tingle through her, more from nostalgia than anything else.

Once he'd been all she could think about, and now... Well, he hadn't changed, but she sure had.

He'd picked her up at her house. Stella had stared straight ahead during the ride home, their conversation easy but vague. He walked her to the door, and everything felt surreal. The night was still young enough that she should invite him inside. Should she? Was he going to kiss her?

"Do you want to come inside?" She blurted the words before she could second-guess it.

"Do you want me to?"

Before she could answer, the front door flung open, Tristan on the other side. It startled Stella so much that she let out a short scream. Tristan started to laugh. Craig did too, after a second.

"Sorry. Didn't know you were here. I'm just waiting for Dad. He was going to be back in a few minutes."

"What are you even doing home?"

"Forgot my laptop," Tristan said. "Dad dropped me off and ran to get gas, said he'd be back... There he is."

"Perfect," Stella said through gritted teeth as Jeff pulled into the driveway, even though every other time he parked across the street. It wasn't enough for him to simply wait for Tristan in the car, nope, he had to get out and stride up the front walk.

"Hi," Craig said before anyone else could. "I'm Craig."

"Jeff."

They did not shake hands.

"Dad, let's go." Tristan gave Craig no more than a glance before leaping off the front steps and heading for the car.

Jeff didn't go right away. He gave Craig a blatant up-and-down assessment that had Stella taking him by the elbow to lead him off the porch. "Goodbye, Jeff."

"Nice to meet you," Jeff said over his shoulder with a face that said he was lying. To Stella he said in a voice thick with disdain, "Nice."

"I'm allowed to date, hello," she whispered fiercely, hoping Craig couldn't overhear them.

"And bring him back to the house?"

"I live here," she told him. "You don't. Remember? And Tristan wasn't supposed to be home."

"Dad," Tristan said. "C'mon."

Jeff's lip curled and he looked over Stella's shoulder. She didn't dare turn to see what Craig was doing. Jeff shrugged and got in the car, rolling down the window to say, "I'll bring him home Sunday afternoon. Do you want me to call first, in case you need to—"

"Go," Stella said. "Now."

Putting a smile on her face, she turned and went back to the porch. "Sorry."

Craig shrugged. "It's okay."

"So…do you want to come inside?"

"If you want me to," he said with a small grin. "Looks like we have the place to ourselves."

Stella waited for the rise of heat within her, but all she felt was a little tumble-tickle of anxiety in the pit of her stomach. Inside, she directed Craig to the couch while she brought out a pitcher of iced tea and some brownies she'd made earlier—never mind the dinner and coffee and dessert they'd already had. She put the food and drink on the coffee table, and they both looked at it, then burst into shared laughter.

"God, you always made me laugh," she said without thinking.

"I've missed you," Craig told her. "So much."

Her laughter faded. "I missed you too. A lot. For a long time, Craig."

He had the grace to look embarrassed. "I thought a lot about what happened, you know. I felt…so bad. So bad. I'm sorry, Stella."

Sitting next to him on the couch, she found it the most natural thing to let him take her hands, but she tensed when it seemed as if he was going to pull her closer. Instead, their knees touched and fingers linked. Craig looked at their hands, then at her face.

"Can you forgive me?"

"Yes. Of course. It's been a long time," she pointed out. "I'd have to be some kind of crazy, bitter bitch to hold on to that this long."

The truth was, it had taken her a long time to forgive him. Forgetting had been another matter. She hadn't been able to do that for a lot longer.

"Bumping into you that day at the coffee shop, it just felt right. You know?" He sounded so earnest, she didn't have the heart to disagree. "Like…fate."

He'd always been one to believe in that sort of thing. There'd been a time in their daily conversations when Craig had always shared her horoscope with her. And this, comparing what was meant to be for both of them. It was one of the things she'd found so wonderful about him, this disparity between his steady, solid corporate banking demeanor and what she thought of as the wibbly-wobbly timey-wimey stuff.

"It was bound to happen, sooner or later," she said, though the truth was she'd avoided that coffee shop for years for just that reason. The day she'd gone there had been on a whim, unexpected. Totally by chance.

Maybe it had been fate, after all.

Craig's thumb swept her palm. "I wanted to call you so many times, but I never knew if you wanted me to. I thought maybe you'd curse me out. I wouldn't have blamed you, I guess. But I couldn't face it. I was stupid. And the longer I waited, the less likely it seemed that you'd want to talk to me again, much less see me.... I was a coward. I'm sorry. I was afraid of what you were going to say, so I let it go until there was no way I could face you."

"There's a saying. 'The anticipation of the suffering is worse than the pain itself,'" Stella told him. Not meanly. She'd imagined herself being cruel to him, should she ever have the chance, but had no desire for that now.

"Yeah. I know. I was an idiot."

She shook her head. "It was an impossible situation. You weren't wrong."

"I *was* wrong," Craig said in a low voice, meeting her gaze without looking away. "I didn't have to be such a jerk. I was an idiot."

"Fine. You were an idiot."

"An enormous one," Craig said with a small smile.

Stella laughed, finally. "Yes. Gigantic. Huge. Do you feel better now?"

"I'd feel better if you let me kiss you."

And just like that, the air left the room. She tried to breathe, but got only a gasp for her efforts. Stella blinked rapidly against the sudden rush of heat in her face.

She didn't say no.

Craig kissed her, and she opened for it, helpless not to. Not after all this time. When his hand threaded through her hair, tipping her a little deeper into his kiss, Stella breathed out a sigh. Not a moan. A simple exhalation.

The kiss ended, but they didn't pull apart. Slowly, Craig let his fingers slide from her hair, but his breath still caressed her face. She opened her eyes to see him looking at her.

"I'm sorry," Stella said. "I can't do this."

She got up from the couch as soon as the words left her mouth. She didn't want to look at him. Wasn't sure what she'd see on his face, not certain she could handle whatever it was. The moment his mouth had touched hers, everything she'd told herself she'd gotten over had come rushing back to her.

"I'm sorry," she said again.

Craig stood. "Do you want me to leave?"

"Yes." She shook her head. "No. I mean…not like that. I mean…"

"It's okay," he told her. "I understand."

She looked at him then. "No. You can't. I mean, I don't even understand. It's just that it's been so long, you know, and really, you're kind of a stranger to me. I just don't feel comfortable taking this…there. Now."

He frowned and ran a hand through his dark hair for a moment before straightening his shoulders. "I get it. I just saw you and we had such a good time tonight. Or, I mean, I did. And I know it's been a long time, and I was an asshole when it ended—"

"Yes," Stella said suddenly, voice cold. Anger she'd been trying to deny rushed over her, twisting her guts. "You were."

Craig said nothing at first. Then he nodded. "I'll just go."

"I think you should. I'm sorry."

"Don't be sorry," he said, too sharply. Softer, he added, "Could I still call you, though? I'd like to see if we can be friends, at least."

Stella was wary of that. They'd tried it once before, after all, and it hadn't gone well. "I don't know. Sometimes when you give something up, you can't get it back."

"I understand," Craig said again.

This time, she didn't contradict him. "There were lots of times when all I wanted was for you to say you were sorry. So, thanks for that."

He smiled a little. "There were lots of times when all I wanted was for you to let me apologize. So…thanks for letting me."

They looked at each other with a distance between them that could not be crossed. She wanted to, if only because once being in his arms had made her feel as if she could face anything, though the comfort had been fleeting and not without a heavy price. But she could not make herself move now.

"I had a good time tonight. But I'm not ready for this with you. Don't," Stella added with a hand up, "say you understand again. Please."

He laughed with genuine humor. She joined him a few seconds later, a little more cautious but no less sincere. He shook his head and gave her a sideways glance, eyes crinkled in the corners in the way that had once set her heart pitter-patting. She walked him to the front door in silence and held it open while he went through. On the porch, Craig turned to face her.

"I won't call you if you don't want me to. And I'll completely understand if you don't want me to. But I hope that we can at least part on a good note." He held out his hand.

Stella took it. "Yes. We can do that."

For a moment, he looked as if he meant to say more than that, but common sense closed his mouth. He gave her a wave just as he got to his car, and there was a second or so when Stella thought about running after him, if for no other reason than for that long ago once-upon-a-time.

But in the end, all she did was watch him drive away the way she had done so long ago.

CHAPTER FOURTEEN

"I don't care," Stella said to her stubborn-faced son who was pouting by the kitchen counter, spreading crumbs as if he were trying to plant a toast garden from seed. "You're not staying here by yourself. Not overnight, and certainly for the whole weekend. No way. We've already had this discussion."

"They're having some sort of *party*." Tristan's expression made it clear what he thought of Cynthia's parties.

Stella looked at the clock. They had to leave or she was going to be late. She hadn't even showered yet.

"Did your dad say he didn't want you to come?"

"No. But I don't want to."

"Oh, Tristan, for God's sake. Stay in your room the whole time. It's what you'd do here anyway."

His gaze gleamed, and he waved his toast around. "Exactly! So why can't I stay here?"

"Because you're sixteen years old," Stella told him flatly. "And I'm going to be out of town."

"Where are you going, anyway?"

"Photoshop training workshop." She lied smoothly, without so much as a blink to betray her.

Tristan shoved toast in his mouth, chewing furiously. His anger hadn't ruined his appetite, at least. "You don't trust me."

"No," Stella said honestly. "I absolutely do not."

She'd forgotten how bad the traffic was in the mornings, what idiots the other parents were. Tristan gave her the silent treatment during the entire drive. Stella didn't try to get him to talk. She counted the minutes and estimated how long it would take her to get to the airport, what flights she'd be missing. If she should bother going at all. It was on the tip of her tongue to turn to her son and tell him it was fine, she'd change her plans, that he could stay home this weekend instead of having to spend it at his father's. But it had been two months since she'd flown, and she really wanted to go.

Stella was desperate to fly.

"I'll be home Sunday night," she called after him as Tristan got out of the car, ignoring her. "I can pick you up—"

"I'll have Dad drop me off," he said over his shoulder. "Wouldn't want you to bother."

He slammed the door behind him and stalked off, and Stella became one of those annoying mothers who waited to watch until their kid got inside the building before pulling away.

Of course, she missed the flight to Atlanta she'd planned to take. The others were too far—one to Houston, one to Denver. Her weekend policy had always been to not do anything with a layover because it made it that much harder for her to be sure she could get home on time. There was a flight she could just barely make, if she was lucky—and leaving from Harrisburg almost always meant she was lucky, since it was such a small airport.

Chicago.

It wasn't that she hadn't been to Chicago before. Of course she had, several times. But all Stella could really remember was the last time, when she'd met Matthew and told him not only her real name, but the secret she never told anyone. All she could really remember was Matthew.

There was almost no chance she'd see him there again, obviously. And though she could remember every detail of his apartment, she did not remember the address. She didn't know his last name. And even if she did, she wouldn't have looked him up in the phone book, much less showed up at his apartment. It had been, what, two months since she'd fucked him? He might not even remember who she was... though something told her that he would.

Chicago it was, though, unless she didn't want to go anywhere at all. She made her way through security and checked her watch. Half an hour before boarding. Plenty of time for her to hit the restroom and make a few cosmetic changes.

The woman in the mirror had wide brown eyes outlined in black liner. Full red lips. Glossy black hair in a short bob. The wig came off first, tucked into the special satin bag in her carry-on. She wiped her face with makeup towelettes, then pulled her cosmetics case from the bag and redid everything. When she'd finished, she checked over her outfit. Black wrap dress. Full cleavage. Stockings and garters beneath. Ankle-breaker pumps. The clothes would be fine, but her face and hair...those she wanted to be her own. She brushed out her hair to get rid of any tangles, then pulled it into a messy twist. Turning her face from side to side, Stella leaned on the sink.

"He won't be there," she mouthed at herself. "And even if he does happen to be in the same airport, the chances of you meeting him are so fucking small."

The ride to Chicago was uneventful. The businessman who sat next to her would've been a decent prospect, on a different flight. She did flirt with him, though, letting him lean close enough to smell the whiskey on his breath. The few times his knee bumped hers, she didn't pull away. She even let him get a number of long, leering looks down the front of her dress, and that was totally for her benefit. She liked watching a man's eyes widen, then narrow. The leap of his pulse in his throat. She liked turning men on.

But when they disembarked, he gave her no more than a second glance, pulling his briefcase from the overhead compartment and booking it out of the plane and down the corridor so far ahead of her it was almost comical. She'd have been insulted if she'd intended to seduce him. As it was, Stella took her time, allowing all the other passengers to get off the plane before she reached overhead for her bag. She thanked the crew, something most people didn't bother to do and she remembered as one of the greatest annoyances of working as flight crew.

In the airport, she went first to the Pegasus Airlines courtesy counter and had them check the available flights leaving on Sunday, making sure they put her down for the first available. Then she hit the restroom to freshen up. And after that, she went to the bar. She turned heads as she took a seat, and though she noticed, pretended she didn't. It was the same bar as before, the one with the wagon wheels.

"Iced tea," she said politely to the bartender. "Thanks."

"You should have something a little stronger than an iced tea," said a male voice from behind her, and everything inside her clenched and twisted and dropped.

Stella turned on her stool to favor him with a smile. "Hi. Matthew, right?"

"You remembered." His grin seemed easier this time than it had the first time they'd met. She guessed it was the liquor she could smell on him and the empty glass in his hand. "Stella."

"You remembered," she murmured.

At home, if she'd dressed herself up and gone to a bar, Stella would've been plagued with insecurities that never bothered her when she flew. But here was the conundrum. She was dressed up; she was flying. But against all odds, she was still Stella. If she'd met another man tonight, there'd have been a different name. Mannerisms, habits, whatever it was that made her into someone new. In front of him, though, this man who'd already seen her naked, who'd already felt her come, who'd already tasted her, Stella had to swallow hard against the sudden tightness in her throat.

Matthew leaned a little closer. His face was stubbled a little heavier this time, the lines at the corners of his eyes a little more pronounced. She caught the flecks of silver in his dark hair, cropped shorter than she remembered. Two months hadn't been entirely kind to him, she thought. Two months had worn him. Though he was still handsome.

"How could I forget you? Stella, Stella star."

She laughed at that. Not the first time she'd heard it. "Have you been here awhile?"

"Corey, have I been here awhile?" Matthew raised his

glass. "Long enough, I guess. For tonight. Hey, Corey, gimme another, would ya?"

Corey was happy to do it, and one for Stella too, though she hadn't asked for it.

"Corey," said Matthew, "makes a great Manhattan, as you might remember."

Stella smiled. "Yes. He does. Do you want to sit down?"

"Yes." Matthew slid onto the stool next to hers, not as unsteadily as she might've guessed from the way he was slightly slurring his words. "Stella, Stella, Stella. How did I know I'd see you again?"

She twisted on her stool to let her knees bump his and lifted her drink as well as an eyebrow. This was getting easier, making Stella a character the way all the others had been. "I don't know. How did you?"

"I just thought if I sat here often enough, waiting, you'd make your way back here. And I was right, wasn't I?"

She hesitated at that, not sure how seriously she should take him. "You were waiting for me?"

At that, his gaze shuttered briefly before he smiled at her. "Sure."

"Uh-huh." Stella could tell when she was being played, but it didn't matter because he was so very, very charming about it. She lifted her glass and sipped, eyeing him. She leaned a little closer, lowering her voice. "Well. Here I am."

"Here you are."

He might be well on his way to drunk, but he held her gaze for so long heat flamed inside her. His smile teased her own, until they both sat looking at each other like a pair of fools. It was enough to look at each other, it seemed, because Matthew didn't seem inclined to say anything for some long minutes, and neither did Stella.

Finally he spoke. "You want to go home with me?"

Stella smiled. "Why do you think I flew to Chicago?"

CHAPTER FIFTEEN

They took a cab the way they had done the first time, though this time she'd had only iced tea, not having touched her Manhattan before they left the bar, and could better remember the street names and path the cab took. Matthew sat close to her, holding her hand. His thumb stroked the back of it, over and over, until she had to clench her thighs together against the pulse in her clit.

He kissed her in the elevator. Backed her up against the wall. Slid a hand between her legs and found her slick and hot. He moaned a little when his fingertips encountered the garters, and he pulled open the slit of her dress to look. Then at her face.

"You are so sexy."

Stella's breath caught. Men had said that, or permutations of it, to her so many times she'd lost track, but something in the way Matthew said it left her speechless. When he pushed against her to nibble her neck, his hand still between her legs, she could only give herself up to his caress and pray nobody else was going to get on the elevator.

Nobody did, although when it stopped on his floor and the door opened, Matthew did withdraw fast enough to make her head spin in a different way. Holding her hand, he drew her out of the elevator and down the hall to his apartment.

Inside, he kissed her, long and slow and deep. His tongue stroked hers. His hand went between her legs again, this time to tug open her dress and explore the straps of her garters. He let out another of those shuddering sighs and pulled away to look into her eyes.

"Did you dress this way hoping to meet me?"

"Yes." It wasn't a lie. She'd dressed this way to meet someone—and though it hadn't been until the missed flight to Atlanta that she'd considered Chicago an option, there was no denying she'd hoped against hope she'd find him again.

And she had.

Matthew went slowly to his knees in front of her. The wrap dress came open with a swift tug. She stood in front of him in her fancy bra and pretty panties, the lacy garter belt and sheer stockings.

Men had varied reactions to this sight for the first time. Most loved the sexy lingerie, though there'd been a few who couldn't have cared less about what she wore so long as she had their dicks down the back of her throat. Most were properly appreciative, some went gape-jawed, a few blushed.

Matthew adored.

He ran his fingers along the backs of her legs, tickling behind her knees. Then the tops of her stockings. He nudged her thighs to widen her stance a little, and Stella obliged, going dry-mouthed at his attentions. Matthew nuzzled the inside of her thigh, just above the stocking. His fingers crept up to cup her ass as he nosed a little higher, higher. He breathed against her pussy, the heat of his breath making her squirm until he held her still. The pressure of his lips on her clit, even through the satin, was enough to urge a sigh from her.

"Fuck, I want to taste you," he said.

Stella had no answer for that but to shift her feet a little wider and tilt her hips toward him. Matthew hooked his fingers in her panties and eased them over the garters and stockings, then gently gripped first one ankle and then the other to help her step out of them. She had to put a hand on his shoulder to steady herself, and when he looked up at her from that place on his knees, his hazel eyes hazy with lust, his mouth already wet from where he'd licked his lips, she knew she'd better find something to hold on to, because when he put his mouth on her she was going to want to fall down.

Matthew pressed his mouth to her clit, sucking gently. Stella groaned. Her fingers tightened on his shoulder. With a low laugh that sent shivers of pleasure all through her, Matthew looked up at her. He kissed between her legs again, then pushed her gently back toward the couch.

"Sit. Open your legs for me."

He said it in such a way it was clear he expected no resistance. Not that she had any. Stella was more than happy to shrug out of her dress and toss it to the side and take a seat on the couch. Matthew gripped her hips and pulled her forward to the edge, then sat back to look at her.

Slowly, slowly, she did as he'd commanded, inching open

her thighs to reveal herself to him totally. There was always hesitation in this exposure. In making herself vulnerable and available. And this time, she wore her real name. Her real face and hair. The Stella who normally looked this way, aside from the lingerie and shoes, was not the woman who fucked in bathroom stalls or the backseats of cars. Or fucked at all, for that matter.

"So fucking gorgeous." He pushed himself between her legs before she could say a word, and his compliment sent another surge of heat through her.

When his mouth found her flesh again, Stella didn't even try to hold back her low cry of pleasure. She let her head fall back against the cushions. His hair was much too short for her to tug or pull. She had to settle for cupping the top of his head.

Matthew's tongue smoothed over her clit. Stella moaned at the tug of his lips against her. When he pushed a finger inside her, she moaned again, this time his name.

"Wanna fuck you so bad," he murmured against her cunt.

She couldn't hold back a breathless giggle at that. "No, no…you wanna fuck me so good."

The hum of his laughter felt so good that Stella squirmed. Matthew moved up her body to find her mouth. His tongue stroked hers while his fingers still moved inside her.

"Do you want me inside you, Stella?"

"Yes."

"Say it," he said into her mouth.

"I want you inside me, Matthew…." She trailed into a gasp when his thumb pressed her clit just right.

"I want to get you off first. Just like this."

That sounded delightful to her, especially since she was halfway there. "And then?"

"Then I'm going to fuck you until you come again."

"Such a gentleman," Stella breathed, and let him get to it.

Stella lost herself in the pleasure of his mouth on hers, his fingers deep inside her. Thumb pressing her clit. He added a little come-hither gesture with his fingers inside her that had her losing her mind. Everything went tight and tense, and finally her orgasm rippled through her and left her panting and spent.

Blinking, she kissed him. "Mmm."

Matthew eased his fingers from inside her and put his hand flat on her belly. He nuzzled her neck, nipping a little. "I felt you come around my fingers. That was so hot."

Stella laughed a little and pushed away to look at him. "You've never felt that before?"

Matthew hesitated, licking his lips. "No."

"Hmmm." She tilted her head to study him.

He looked down her body, and though his scrutiny made her feel a little self-conscious, Stella didn't move. "It's hard for women, sometimes. Isn't it?"

"Yes." She sat up on the couch, aware now of the nubbly fabric under her bare skin. Without the haze of impending orgasm to distract her, being half-naked while he was still fully clothed was becoming disconcerting. Not to mention that her bare ass and wet pussy were in direct contact with his couch cushions.

"But you...you," Matthew said as he kissed her again, "you don't have trouble."

That wasn't always true, but she was happy her ability to get off had pleased him. When he stood, pulling her to her feet, Stella put her arms around his neck for another kiss. With her heels on, there was no strain to reach his mouth.

"I think you promised you'd fuck me," she said against his lips. "Where do you want me?"

To her surprise, Matthew bent to hook an arm beneath her knees and lifted her. With a small shriek, Stella clung to him. She couldn't remember the last time a man had ever picked her up this way—if one ever had. Jeff hadn't carried her across the threshold. Matthew didn't even struggle as he carried her down the hall and into his bedroom, where he kicked the door shut behind them in a totally caveman way that had her squirming all over again.

They were both on the bed before she knew it, rolling. She ended up straddling him. Stella sat upright, to work at his belt. She could feel him, hard as brick through his jeans. She had him free in a minute or so. His cock pushed from the top of his briefs, and she was overwhelmed by the desire to take him in her mouth. She didn't get a chance, though.

With his hands on her hips, Matthew rolled them both again so she was beneath him. He reached to pull open the drawer of his nightstand and grab a box of condoms, which he tossed onto the bed next to her. Last time he'd been unprepared. Either she'd taught him a valuable lesson in preparation, or he'd been fucking other women during the past two months…which wasn't any of her business and not something she wanted to think about right now.

Not with his mouth moving down her throat to the swell of her breasts and him shimmying out of his jeans. Not when he pushed up on his knees to pull his shirt off over his head and toss it aside, leaving him naked and erect and between her legs. And certainly not when he shook a condom from the box and opened it carefully, then slid it over his lovely, thick cock and poised himself at her entrance.

He pushed inside her slowly until he was seated so deep it

hurt, just a little. Stella drew in a breath and shifted to ease
the angle. She drew her knees up to press to his sides. Her
hands slid up his chest, pressed flat over the thump of his
heart. Matthew, supported on his arms, didn't move at first.

"You feel so good," he said in a low voice.

There wasn't an answer to that. Not a verbal one. She
murmured encouragement and pressed her knees against
him, urging him to move. She tilted her hips. His cock
throbbed inside her, and she let out a small groan.

Matthew began to move. Slow, so slow at first she wanted
to wriggle in frustration, but after a few minutes, she wanted
to writhe with building desire. Every time he pressed into
her, his body gave just enough pressure on her clit to tease
her. When he slid out, adding a twist of his hips, his cock
hit her in all the right places. In. Out.

"Harder," she whispered.

Something shifted in his gaze. His mouth twisted. Matthew's brow furrowed, and he did move faster. Harder.

"Harder," Stella said.

His hand slipped behind her neck to dig his fingers into
her hair, bringing her to his mouth. His kiss bruised as his
thrusts got faster. Stella wrapped herself around him and
held on tight, eating at his mouth and hooking her heels
around the backs of his calves to urge him even deeper.
Matthew buried himself against her neck.

Stella turned her head, offering him the soft skin of her
throat. "Use your mouth...."

He didn't, at first. When the tentative press of his teeth
had her gasping though, he seemed to gather courage and
bit her. Not hard enough to leave a mark, but hard enough
to make her hips buck and her clit pulse. Her cunt throbbed

and she concentrated on her internal muscles, clenching on his cock.

"Oh, fuck," Matthew breathed.

"Fuck me harder."

He did.

Whatever hesitation he'd had was gone now. Matthew fucked her so hard the bed slammed the wall. Stella cried out at the slam of him inside her, but she welcomed the pain. It sent her up and up, over into a short and sharp climax that surprised her into a hoarse shout.

Matthew came a moment later and collapsed onto her, squeezing out her breath for a moment before he rolled off her and onto his back. Breathing hard, he flung an arm over his head and stared up at the ceiling in silence. Stella turned on her side, tucking an arm under her cheek to prop herself. She put a hand on his flat belly, admiring the muscles there. She still wore her bra and garter belt, though she suspected her stockings were a ruin. She sat up.

"Where you going?"

She looked at him over her shoulder with a small smile. "Girl's gotta take care of things after. Is it okay if I use your bathroom?"

"Of course. Absolutely."

Her panties and dress were in the living room, a tiny fact she'd forgotten. Without getting off the bed, Stella quickly unhooked her stockings and rolled them down her legs—one was shredded, as she'd suspected. She undid her garter belt too, sliding the thin scrap of lace through her fingers. Then she sat, sort of stuck. Being totally naked would feel less awkward in this moment than wearing only a bra, but why would she take it off, only to put it back on in a few minutes? But to walk to the bathroom in only her bra would make her entirely self-conscious.

Spotting Matthew's T-shirt a couple inches from her foot, Stella grabbed it. If he was offended by her borrowing his shirt, she reasoned, he shouldn't have put his cock inside her. Tugging it over her head, she stood to let the fabric fall around her thighs, then went into the bathroom, where she found a clean washcloth from a stack on a shelf next to the shower. She washed herself carefully and rinsed the cloth several times before wringing it out. She searched for a laundry basket and didn't find one, so settled for hanging it over the edge of the sink.

She was rinsing her mouth when Matthew, still naked, came into the bathroom. He weaved a little, then went to the toilet and pissed in a long, hard stream, one hand gripping the wall for balance. She eyed him in the mirror as she ran the water and cupped a hand under the stream to scoop another mouthful. She was still watching him when he finished, flushed and made his languid way toward her.

She stiffened a little when he came up behind her and put his arms around her to nuzzle against her neck. The embrace, intimate and unexpected, warmed her and prickled the back of her throat. It had been a long, long time since a man had hugged her at the bathroom sink.

She turned in his arms, the sink's marble edge pressing her lower back. "Hey."

"Hey." Matthew kissed her. "Are you trying to run out on me again?"

"Again…" She laughed. "I don't have to leave until Sunday. But I wasn't assuming—"

"If you don't want to stay, you don't have to," he said

after a second, pulling away but not letting go. "I just thought—"

"If you want me to—" she began, and stopped.

They looked at each other. Then they both smiled slowly. Matthew pulled her close again and looked into her eyes. She knew he was still a little drunk. That he might regret waking up next to her in the morning. But at that moment, Stella liked the way he was looking at her.

"You should stay."

"If you want me to."

"You have a better offer?"

She laughed. "No. No way."

"Good." He kissed her, yawning in the middle of it. "Shit, I'm wiped out. I'm going to jump in the shower. You want to shower?"

"Um…sure."

"You want to go first?"

Considerate, she thought with something that tried to be nonchalant but was as squeeful as a giddy fangirl seeing her favorite crush up close. He was considerate. "No, you can go ahead. I'll get my bag. I have some things I need."

He nodded and turned on the water while Stella went to the front entry to get the bag she'd flung there while Matthew had been kissing her. She had pajamas—a pretty cotton babydoll set that wasn't exactly a merry widow corset, but was comfortable and cute, if a little lightweight for January in Chicago. In the bathroom, she brushed her teeth while he showered.

He sang in the shower, she discovered. Or rather hummed. A mishmash of classic rock and show tunes that somehow worked together. She washed her face while staring at her own reflection and sometimes at Matthew's shadow in the shower, and couldn't stop herself from being charmed.

Her stomach turned.

She should leave right now.

Find her dress, find her panties, get her coat. She should take her bag and get out right now, because this was not a one-night stand. This, she thought, was dangerous.

"All yours." Matthew pulled a towel from the rack and wrapped it around his waist before heading for the sink. He caught her looking at him. "What?"

"Nothing. Just… You sure you're okay with this?"

Matthew wiped at the water droplets trickling down his face. "Stella, I just went down on you on my couch and then fucked you hard enough to almost break my bed. What kind of asshole would I be if I didn't let you stay overnight? And besides…don't I owe you pancakes from the last time?"

She nodded, another burst of prickly emotion trying to choke her. She focused on brushing her teeth, watching him from the corner of her eye as he went about his bed-time routine as though they were longtime lovers instead of nearly strangers. Then she helped herself to his shower while he left her alone.

She knew the taste of him. How he kissed. How his face twisted when he came. She knew the length and girth of his cock. She knew the scent of his skin and now of his soap, that he used an electric razor and not a blade. She knew his brand of toothpaste.

But sleeping next to him on purpose, that was going to be something else altogether.

The lights were out when she came out of the bathroom, but there was enough of a glow coming in through the cracks in the curtains that she didn't worry about tripping on her way to the bed. Matthew had left her the side closest to the bathroom, whether out of courtesy or because his usual side was the other one, it didn't really matter. She slipped under the heavy comforter, grateful for its weight.

The pillow was soft. The sheets were luxurious. She waited to fall asleep, but though she turned on her side and curled into her normal sleeping position, though she counted backward three times from one hundred, Stella could not sleep.

"Are you sleeping?" Matthew's drowsy, almost silent whisper drifted to her in the dark.

"No."

He moved to her, spooning. His body fit hers as naturally as though it had been made to fit her. His mint-scented breath warmed the back of her neck, and his fingers curved to her belly.

It was what her body had been waiting for. That embrace, as unexpected as the one at the sink, but as needed. Stella relaxed into him. Her breathing slowed. Her eyes closed. She began to drift.

"I kept waiting for you to come back," she heard him say, and his words ought to have startled her into wakefulness, but instead they eased Stella into dreams.

CHAPTER SIXTEEN

The scent of coffee and bacon woke her in the morning, and for some long moments Stella luxuriated in the big, warm bed without opening her eyes. Then, remembering where she was, her eyes shot open and she sat up. Scrubbing at her face, she looked around the room, still disoriented, looking for a clock. How long had she slept?

Swinging her legs out of bed, she fumbled in her bag for her phone, which she usually didn't let out of her sight. Funny what an exemplary round of fucking could make you forget. No messages, thank God.

She took a few minutes in the bathroom to run her fingers through her hair, brush her teeth. She didn't go so far as to put on makeup, but she did at least try to make it look as though she hadn't...well...rolled right out of bed. She found an elastic in her bag and pulled her hair on top of her head, as well as a cardigan to keep herself warm, along with a pair of socks. His apartment was still so freaking chilly.

With her hand on the doorknob to the hall, Stella

stopped. She heard voices. The distinct rise and fall of a woman's voice, and then a few seconds later, of two childish voices. Also female. She did not go out into the hall, but she did keep the door cracked.

There was the clatter of silverware on porcelain. The scrape of the chairs on the tile floor. Domestic sounds, so normal and unremarkable, except that Stella was lurking in the bedroom like a dirty secret.

Maybe that's what she was.

She listened hard at the door, too aware of what her mother had always said—if you don't want to hear things you don't like, don't listen at doors. But she had no choice, really. She couldn't exactly saunter out into the kitchen wearing her pj's and help herself to a mug of coffee if Matthew had houseguests. And, she had to be honest, at ten o'clock on a Saturday morning, who were those guests likely to be?

Oh. Fuck. Ex-wife. Kids.

What sort of man invited a woman back to his apartment and then insisted she stay the night when he expected his ex-wife to drop off his kids in the morning?

The kind who wasn't expecting a visit from his ex-wife and kids, Matthew told her forty minutes later when the front door finally closed and he opened the bedroom door. "Louisa—she's my oldest. She wanted to stop by and get something she left here. So Caroline brought them by."

And had stayed for breakfast.

"They saw me making pancakes," Matthew said after an awkward silence had grown between them. Stella didn't say anything. What could she have said? "Beatrice, my little one, she wanted to stay. I didn't know what to tell them."

"Not that you had company, apparently." She understood, of course, on the surface. She was still essentially a stranger, and she wouldn't have liked to be paraded out in front of his ex-wife and kids anyway. She respected the fact that he didn't just shove strangers in front of his children. But that was the surface. Underneath, it still felt kind of shitty to be stuck in the bedroom for forty minutes while he entertained.

"I'm sorry," he said after another awkward pause. "I should've at least come back to let you know, but she kept talking to me and she has a habit of following me if I walk away before she's finished."

Stella softened. It had taken her a while after her divorce to consider dating again, and in the brief time when she'd actually gone on actual dates before deciding it wasn't worth the effort, she'd been careful about exposing Tristan to her new "friends." Of course, she flew hundreds of miles from home to fuck men. That might've had something to do with how much easier it had been for her to keep them from meeting her son.

She smiled at him. "It's okay. It's hard to juggle an ex and kids and dating.... Not that we... Well."

Matthew smiled slowly. "Yeah. Still, I should've checked on you."

"So long as there are some pancakes left," she began, half teasing, but stopped at his expression. "Are you kidding me?"

"I'm sorry, they ate..."

"You—" Stella stood and poked him in the chest "—better get me some pancakes. And bacon. And coffee."

Matthew pulled her into his arms and kissed her. Long, leisurely and sweet. It sent chills all through her. He looked into her eyes. "I will take you out. How about that?"

She pretended to give him the stink eye. "Where?"

"Diner. Best in Chicago. And the bonus of that is, they'll serve us hash browns. I wasn't going to make hash browns."

"Are they greasy?"

"Greasiest I ever ate."

She held out her hand for him to shake. "Deal."

He shook it firmly, then pulled her close again. This time, his big hands cupped her rear. He ground his thickening cock against her. "How hungry are you?"

"Oh, no." Laughing, Stella backed away from him. She'd taken the time while waiting for him to clean herself up and dress in case she needed to make an abrupt getaway. She shook her finger at him. "No way. Food first. You can't expect me to fuck on an empty stomach."

Matthew snorted softly, looking at her from the corner of his eye as though he couldn't quite figure her out. She liked that look, Stella thought. That she kept him on his toes. She darted in for a quick kiss of his mouth and added a nice, firm squeeze of his ass.

"Move it," she told him. "I'm starving."

The diner turned out to be perfect. Stella ordered a thick stack of buttermilk pancakes oozing with butter and syrup, a side of bacon and sausage links too. A platter of hash browns arrived along with a pot of coffee. Matthew watched as she arranged the food and sighed happily at the sight of it.

"Breakfast is my favorite meal," she told him. "I could eat breakfast all day long."

Matthew had ordered only coffee—he'd already had his breakfast. That didn't stop him from giving her sausage links a longing look, though, and she could've taken pity on him. Offered him one. Stella stabbed the sausage with her fork and lifted it to her lips, watching Matthew watch her eat it.

"What else do you like?" he asked.

She thought about that for a moment. "Birthdays."

"Yours, or other people's?"

"Both," she said. "I love giving presents, and I love getting presents, and I like a party where everyone is trying to be nice to someone on their special day."

"I hate my birthday. I never celebrate it. As far as I'm concerned, it's just one more day closer to death."

Stella sat back to ponder this, uncertain if he was joking. "Wow."

Matthew shrugged. "Also, I never buy anyone the right present, so I suck at that part of it too."

"So...what do you like?"

"Breakfast," he said. "Especially with a beautiful woman who gave me one of the best nights of my life. And I like that you like breakfast. I like to watch you eat."

Stella pointed at him with her fork and gave him a raised brow. "That's creepy."

Matthew put a hand over his eyes for a moment. "You are...something else."

"Something else that's good, I hope." She took her time chewing, washing down the delicious pancakes with swallows of perfectly brewed coffee. He had no way of knowing how much of this was bravado. An act she'd perfected during so many flights—she was Stella to him, but he didn't necessarily know who Stella was.

"Definitely good." He watched her dig into the pancakes again. "I meant that I like that you like to eat."

"Instead of nibbling at a piece of dry toast, huh?"

He paused, an expression she couldn't quite interpret flickering across his face. "Yes. Something like that."

"I haven't eaten in over twenty-four hours," she reminded him.

"Something about you tells me you're not a dry toast sort of gal."

Stella sipped at her coffee and sat back in her seat, mirroring him. They stared at each other in comfortable silence. He smiled. So did she.

"No," she said after a minute. "I guess I'm not."

"Good," Matthew said, and signaled for the check. "How do you feel about museums?"

It was the nicest day Stella could remember having in a long time. As far as dates went, one of the best she'd had, ever. If you could consider it a date, and she wasn't sure that's what it had been.

Matthew had taken her to the Field Museum. Then for a walk along the riverfront. Then dinner at a restaurant nice enough to show he was making an effort, but not so fancy she felt out of place in her jeans and the T-shirt she'd borrowed from him that morning. In the cab he took her hand so nonchalantly that she let him hold it all the way back to his place. And once there, she let him take her inside his apartment without making so much as a peep about how she really needed to find herself a hotel.

The fact was, Stella didn't want to find a hotel or an earlier flight home. She didn't want to find another man either. She liked him.

Oh, shit.

She did have to ask, though. "Do you want me to go?"

Matthew looked up from the drinks he was mixing and frowned. "No. Do you want to?"

"No." She moved closer, leaning on the counter to watch him shake and strain and pour. "But I had to ask. Didn't want to just assume. Or wear out my welcome. I mean, especially since…"

He slid a fat tumbler full of greenish-tinged liquor toward her. The ice cubes clinked. "Since what?"

"Well, you weren't expecting a weekend houseguest. And we just met." Stella curled her fingers around the glass but didn't drink from it.

"We met months ago," Matthew pointed out. He lifted his glass. "Cheers."

Stella lifted hers, though she wasn't sure about drinking it. "What is it?"

"Gin rickey."

She sipped it. It was good. But that was the problem, wasn't it? It was all good. And if one was good, another would be better. And after that a third, until before she knew it, she'd be blotto if she wasn't careful.

"Not a big drinker," Matthew said in a low voice, watching her. "I keep forgetting."

Stella turned the glass around and around on the countertop. She watched the liquor slosh over the ice cubes. She breathed in the scent of lime and the stinging, junipery smell of gin. "It's not that I don't like it. I guess if anything I like it too much."

Matthew paused with his glass to his mouth. She watched his throat work as he swallowed. Studied the wetness left behind on his lips when he pulled the glass away. He licked them. "Oh?"

"I'm not an alcoholic," Stella said.

"You just like to drink."

"I like to be drunk," she said. "I don't *have* to be drunk, or feel any burning desire to be drunk. I never think about drinking when I'm upset. I've never used it to escape my feelings or anything like that."

"Sounds like you've done a lot of research into what makes a person a drunk or not." Matthew drained the glass and set the tumbler on the counter. He moved the bottle of gin closer to his glass as though considering pouring some more.

Stella wondered if he would.

When he didn't, at least not immediately, she said, "I guess I did. And I know that someone who does have a drinking problem would be the first to say she doesn't, it's the truth. I just like to be drunk."

"Most people do, which is why they drink." Matthew smiled. Then he poured another shot into the shaker and uncapped the bottle of sweetened lime, adding a few shots of that too.

Stella laughed, rueful. "Yes. I guess so. It's fun, you know? I mean, hangovers aren't fun. And neither is being out of control."

"Ah." Matthew poured the contents of the shaker into his glass and topped it off with club soda. "And that's the part you don't like."

She looked up at him, into his eyes, trying to see if he could guess anything else about her.

"Is it because of the accident?" Matthew said.

She didn't have to tell him. She could've made up any sort of excuse. He didn't know her, even if he'd guessed she wasn't the sort to suffer dry toast and he'd spent the day learning her mind and habits as well as he'd started learn-

ing her body the night before. She'd already told him the
worst of her secrets. What was one more piece of the story?

"I wasn't driving."

"But you were drunk?"

She nodded. "I figured it was safe enough, you know?
Christmas party, hanging out with friends. Jeff, my ex, was
there to drive us all home. So I had a few drinks, just enjoying myself. Being a mom to small kids takes a lot out of
you. I let loose a little. And Jeff drove us home."

"Was the accident his fault?"

The question, so blunt and to the point, set her aback
but didn't offend her. "I blamed him for it."

"But it wasn't really his fault." Matthew drank deeply.

Stella took another sip, relishing the crisp flavor of citrus
and the sparkling carbonation. "The roads were icy. We
rear-ended someone and were sideswiped by an eighteen-
wheeler. There was nothing Jeff could've done. Or any of
the other drivers, for that matter. Bad weather, bad roads.
Bad luck."

"But if you'd been sober and driving, you might've been
able to stop it, right?"

Stella straightened and took a step back, still holding her
drink. She moved so fast it sloshed over her hand. "There's
no way to know that. Maybe it would've been worse."

"But that's what you think, isn't it?" Matthew said quietly. "If you'd been driving, it never would've happened. If
you'd been in control, you could've changed things. That's
what you think. Right?"

Stella's throat closed with emotion, so tight she couldn't
answer. Her hands shook so that the ice cubes clattered,
and she set the glass on the counter, then tucked her hands

in her pockets. She looked at him, trying to think of what to say, how to answer. How to leave.

Matthew put his own glass down and came around the island. He took her in his arms before Stella could even think about pulling away. He stroked a hand down her back, then up again to cup the back of her neck. He breathed warmth against the top of her head.

He held her. That was all.

"There's no way to know what might've been different." Stella's voice caught like silk on barbed wire, shredding. "There's no way to ever know. And it's useless to blame myself...."

"But you do," Matthew said. "All the time."

"Yes," she said.

"I understand," Matthew said.

It would've been easy to brush off his answer as trite, but the sound of his voice stopped her. She listened to the sound of his breathing for a moment. She believed him.

Stella drank the rest of her gin rickey, but not another. That one was enough to give her a pleasant buzz, and that made the movie Matthew put on that much funnier. Sitting next to him on the couch with her legs curled under her, occasionally holding his hand or resting her head on his shoulder, sometimes with him leaning against her, it was companionable. And sweet. And...normal.

Normal like brushing her teeth at the sink next to him, like showering and putting on her pajamas and climbing into bed next to him. When he spooned her, that also felt normal. Stella waited for him to slide his hand from her belly to between her legs, to nip or nuzzle at her neck, but

Matthew's breathing slowed and he did neither of those things. He fell asleep, and that felt normal too.

She woke in the morning better rested than she could remember being in months. Longer than that. Years. Funny how toward the end of her marriage she'd yearned with a burning fire to no longer have to share her bed, and yet it had been the warmth of a body beside her and the soft shush-shush of Matthew's slight snores that had soothed her to sleep so sweetly.

Maybe it was just him, Stella thought as she rolled to face him. Maybe he was special. Different. She thought of Craig, how often she'd dreamed of how perfect it would be if they'd found their way back to each other, and yet when they had, how very obvious it had been to her that he wasn't what she wanted anymore.

Matthew still slept, both hands curled beneath his chin under the pillow. Practically angelic. Definitely hot. She wanted to slide down his body, take his cock in her mouth and wake him that way. Or at the very least, kiss him. But, ugh, morning breath, and a quick look at the clock told her she didn't have time for any of that. She settled for tracing the line of his bare shoulder and pressing a kiss there. He didn't wake, and she didn't do it again.

Stella slipped from Matthew's bed and dressed quickly. She didn't need a shower, and she brushed her teeth in double time. If she didn't move her ass, she was going to miss the only direct flight back to Harrisburg. She'd be lucky as it was to get a seat on it.

In the bedroom, Matthew had rolled to face the other direction but didn't appear to have woken at all. Stella packed her bag and slung it over her shoulder and debated about kissing him again, at least to wake him enough to tell him goodbye. But what would she do if he pulled her into bed and wanted to fuck her one more time?

More important, what would she do if he didn't?

She settled for scrawling a note for him, thanking him for the wonderful weekend. She signed her name, her real name, though writing it down made her feel stranger than telling him had. What she did next, though, made her palms sweat and her stomach leap and twist and threaten to climb out up her throat.

She left her phone number.

CHAPTER SEVENTEEN

Getting up in the dark sucked. So did getting home in the dark. It was one of the few things Stella despised about her otherwise pretty fantastic job.

What made it worse, of course, was pulling into her driveway with no outside lights on to greet her. Or any inside the house either. Tristan obviously wasn't home and probably hadn't been home either, Stella thought, since the kid couldn't enter a room without turning on all the lights or exit without leaving them all burning.

She pulled into the garage and gathered her things, juggling her travel mug and the giant water bottle she always had the best intentions of finishing but never did. The mail slipped from her fingers as she slung her bag over one shoulder, keys dangling from her other hand. Her jacket snagged on the car door and she almost had to do an entire dance routine just to get herself inside the house—everything made more complicated by the lack of welcoming light. Maybe she ought to get some timers.

In the kitchen, Stella dumped everything on the kitchen table and considered the task of making dinner. She'd left some leftover meat loaf defrosting in the fridge that morning—a quick glance showed her it was still there. With some instant mashed potatoes and a salad, it wouldn't be a bad dinner, but suddenly a peanut-butter-and-jelly sandwich and a handful of chips sounded ever so much better. If her son were here Stella would've made the effort at a real dinner, but alone…what was the point?

Stella sorted through the mail while she ate her sandwich and mentally ran through all the tasks she still needed to get through tonight. Laundry. Balance her checkbook. Pay bills. Find out from Tristan what his upcoming schedule was like and what weekends he'd be with Jeff. She had a phone call from her mother to return, along with one to her best friend from high school, Lisa. They'd been playing phone tag for weeks.

Which was why, when her phone pinged with a text message, she swiped at the screen without bothering to see who it was. At the single word—hi—from an unrecognizable number, Stella paused. The area code said it was from Las Vegas. Well, whatever had happened there was going to stay there, because Stella had never been to Sin City and didn't know anybody there either.

The second message came a few minutes later as she put her plate in the dishwasher and was pouring herself a glass of iced tea.

Stella?

She paused, then typed Who's this?

It's Matthew. From Chicago.

As if she knew dozens of Matthews. For all he knew, she might. Or it had been so long—another couple of weeks—that she'd forgotten him. Stunned, Stella stared at her phone while heat rose inside her, burning up her throat and into her cheeks. Her heart pounded. She blinked rapidly, for the moment finding it difficult to breathe.

Carefully, she put down her tea and the pile of mail she was intending to go through while she ran a hot bath upstairs. She cradled her phone in both hands, willing herself to be calm. Not an idiot. At least he couldn't hear her. Or see her, thank God, there was that.

Hi! What a nice surprise, she typed.

I got your note.

Obviously, she thought, but didn't type. Great. I'm glad. It's nice to hear from you.

The front door creaked open, and she went through the living room to greet her son. Her phone pinged again as she found Tristan in the entryway, kicking off his sneakers but, typically, leaving them where they fell as he headed toward the kitchen through the shortcut of the dining room. He'd almost bypassed her entirely, making this like some kind of Benny Hill farce, but she just caught him.

"Hey," Stella said. "First, put your shoes where they belong, please."

"I will. Starving." Even in his sock feet, Tristan's steps sounded like the boom of a marching band.

Her phone pinged again, and she pulled it from her pocket to peek at the messages. Matthew had sent her a picture of a platter of spaghetti and a glass of wine. It made her laugh, along with the caption—

Bachelor's feast.

"Hey," she said again, heading after her son after the brief distraction of her phone. "Shoes. Now. Not later. There's..."

He'd already discovered and pushed aside the meat loaf in favor of a foil-wrapped helping of pizza from the weekend. Stella cringed, imagining it as a playground for food poisoning. She shook her head.

"Tristan, throw that away. Or at least heat it up!" Her phone pinged, but Stella didn't grab it up right away. As much as she wanted to get back to her conversation, she needed to get things straight with her kid first. "Didn't your dad feed you?"

"Wasn't at Dad's." Tristan spoke with his mouth full, pizza sauce smearing around his lips. He chomped noisily, a habit he'd picked up from his dad and one Stella loathed.

She paused, looking up from her phone where she'd been about to reply with something lame like *LOL.* "What? Where were you?"

Tristan pushed past her, pizza in hand. She reached to snag his shirt, but he was too fast, and she clutched at empty air. He started for the stairs.

"Tristan!"

He stopped. Turned. Gave her the longest, most annoyed sigh a teenage boy could give his mother. "What?"

"First, don't talk to me in that tone of voice. Second. Shoes. Third, you know the rules about food—" Before she could even finish, Tristan gave another huge sigh, this time with a grunt attached to it. He stomped through the living room to the front door, where she heard the thump and thud of his shoes being flung against the wall. Then his pounding feet heading back toward the stairs. "Hey!"

She hadn't even needed to go to the front hall to see that

he hadn't put his shoes where they belonged, since they belonged in his room or in the closet. "Tristan!"

"What, Mom? Jesus!"

"What is your problem?" Stella put a hand on her hip, aware of her phone pinging in her palm and wanting more than anything to get back to that and not have to deal with this. "And where were you?"

"Went with Steven and Joey to the mall."

They stared each other down. Tristan gave her a wide-eyed and somehow also sullen look of faux innocence.

Stella frowned. "You didn't tell me you were going there, nor did you ask permission."

"Dad said it was okay."

Stella rubbed her tongue against the back of her teeth to keep herself from blurting out an answer. Tristan wasn't with his dad until the weekend; therefore Jeff was not the person to ask for permission. Tristan knew that. More important, Jeff knew it.

"Did your dad pick you up from school and take you? Because I know you didn't come home first." She also knew that Jeff couldn't have picked Tristan up from school, since he'd have been at work. Cynthia could have, but it was unlikely that Tristan would've asked her.

Even if she hadn't known that, the guilt on his face would've given him away. "Steven drove."

Stella said nothing. A mother's silent stare could be more effective than any amount of screaming. Tristan stared back with uncharacteristic defiance.

"Dad said—"

"It's not up to your dad," Stella said through a tight jaw. "When you're staying with your dad, he gets to decide. But not when you're with me. And you know how I feel about

Steven driving you, and you knew what I'd say if you asked me, so asking your dad is the same as disobeying me, as far as I'm concerned. You're grounded from the computer and PlayStation for the rest of the week."

Since she was ninety percent positive his haste to get upstairs was so that he could get online and play games with his friends and not so he could do some homework, Tristan's response was not a surprise. The vehemence of it, however, was. Tristan pounded his fist on the railing and barked out his dismay so loudly that Stella stepped back.

"What? Not fair!"

"It's more than fair." She forced herself to remain calm, not to raise her voice. *Don't show fear,* she thought suddenly, thinking of a documentary she'd seen on feral dogs. *Keep eye contact.*

Muttering a series of words she definitely ought to rebuke him for, Tristan turned and stomped up the stairs. He went into his room and slammed the door behind him so hard she heard the crash of something from inside. She thought for a moment about following him, yanking open the door, demanding his respect. She knew better. Still, her heart was pounding and her stomach churned.

Her phone pinged. Is this a bad time?

Sorry, Stella responded. Was dealing with my son.

A few minutes passed after that without a reply, which she thought was fair since it had taken her the same amount of time to get back to him. The next message that came through made her smile and clutch her phone to her chest. He was asking if he could call her.

Of course. Anytime. That's why I gave you my number.

Her phone rang a scant minute after that. The caller ID didn't list a name and read Las Vegas again, not Chicago, but it had to be him. Taking a deep breath, Stella answered, "Hi."

"Hi," Matthew said. "How are you?"

"I'm fine. Tired. Long day." She didn't even want to look at the clock now, the promise she'd made to herself of a long, hot soak in a scented tub with a few chapters of her book not looking so promising. "You?"

"Something like that. So," Matthew said after a few seconds of silence. "Trouble with your son?"

Stella climbed the stairs, pausing at the top to listen for any noise of computer games coming from inside Tristan's room. She thought wearily of opening the door and taking the computer away altogether, just to be sure, but honestly if she couldn't trust him to obey her when she disciplined him, taking the laptop from him would be the least of her worries.

"His dad and I don't agree on some things," she said lightly. "So he likes to ask his dad for permission to do the things he knows I would say no to. And he thinks I won't figure it out."

"But you do. Moms always do."

"Of course." She laughed a little and went into her own room, where she closed the door firmly and sank onto the bed with a sigh. "And I don't really want to have another argument with his father about it, but I guess I'm going to have to."

"Uh-oh. Sounds bad."

She hesitated, lying back and toeing off her shoes as she settled into the pillows. She knew her reluctance to let Tristan drive with his friends was directly tied to her own issues. She knew there were plenty of parents who either didn't worry as much or who managed to put aside their

concerns to allow their kids some freedoms. She knew how
it would sound when she told Matthew the issue…as if she
was some kind of crazy helicopter mom who couldn't let go.

"I don't like him to drive with his friend Steven," she
said flatly. "The kid's only just reached the point where le-
gally he can take passengers, and he wrecked his mom's car
once already. Didn't total it or anything, but he did rear-end
another car. I don't like them joyriding around aimlessly.
Tristan's dad doesn't seem to have the same concerns, and
he's a lot…" Stella cleared her throat, trying to think of
what to say that wouldn't come out sounding like total bit-
tersauce. "Well. Jeff is always more concerned about what
will make his life a little easier than maybe what's the best
choice. That's all."

"Ah." Matthew cleared his throat. "Makes me dread the
teen years."

"How old are your girls?"

He didn't say anything at first, for so long Stella watched
the numbers on her clock change. It hadn't seemed like too
personal a question. Not to someone who'd had his mouth
on her pussy and his dick inside her, anyway.

"Six and eight."

Her breath came a little short. "Louisa is eight? Beatrice is six."

"Yeah… How'd…? Oh. Yeah, I guess I told you?"

Stella smiled. "Sort of."

As silence fell between them, Stella remembered one
more reason why she preferred flying to going on dates.
Getting to know someone was like navigating a room full
of broken glass in bare feet and a blindfold. It was way too
easy to step on something that would make you bleed.

"So...long day?" he asked, breaking the silence. "What do you do?"

That was the sort of neutral question that it was fine to ask even of strangers. And she'd already told him the worst thing of all—the memory of that admission, that unburdening, painted her throat and cheeks again with heat. "I work for a company that retouches photos."

"Really?"

He sounded so surprised that Stella laughed. "Yes. Really."

"People still need that?"

"We deal with companies that take school and church pictures. Things like that. Sometimes I'll get someone's wedding pictures, senior pictures, things like that, but most professional portrait photographers use Photoshop and stuff to do their own retouching. I get stuff that comes in bulk."

"Huh." Matthew made a soft noise.

"What do you do?"

"I look for work."

She blinked at that, not sure what to say until he laughed; then she laughed too, although she wasn't sure what, exactly, was so funny.

"I teach some adult education classes," Matthew said. "Night school."

"What do you teach?"

"English."

Stella made the same noise he had. "Huh."

"So...retouching. Sounds sexy." Matthew laughed.

He was flirting. She settled deeper into the mountain of her pillows. "Does it?"

"Yep. All that touching. And retouching."

She laughed out loud at that. "Oh. Sure. Smoothing wrinkles and erasing moles. Totally sexy."

"Do you like it?"

"The hours were good for part-time, which is all I could manage at first. And now I have the option of working four tens and having a Friday or a Monday off, so I basically get three-day weekends all the time. It's great. Not what I imagined myself doing, I guess." She paused. "But it pays the bills. There are a lot of advantages."

"What did you imagine yourself doing?"

She had no good answer for that either. "I went to college for... You'll never believe it. Chemistry."

"You were a chemistry major?" Matthew hooted soft laughter. "I didn't think anyone was a chemistry major."

"Well, I was. Don't ask me what I wanted to do with that. Work in a lab, I guess. I never worked in my field."

Matthew cleared his throat. "Why not?"

"I got married." Stella thought about that for a few seconds. "My husband was a few years older. Met him at my first job out of college, which was first flight crew, then office work for Pegasus Airlines."

There was silence. Then, "Is he a pilot?"

She laughed. "Oh. God, no. Thank God. He's the CEO. I'd never date a pilot."

"No?" Matthew paused. "Would you be too worried?"

"Pilots are so arrogant. Kind of like surgeons," Stella told him. "All that responsibility. You'd think it would make them humble, but it doesn't."

"So you married a CEO. Because they're never arrogant, huh?"

Stella laughed again. "You got me on that one. What about you? Have you always been a teacher?"

"No. But like you said, it pays the bills. I like making a difference. I was an English lit major," Matthew said abruptly, as if his own words had surprised him. "What the hell I thought I could ever do with that, I don't know."

"So you like to read?"

"Yeah. Do you?"

"Love it. What's your favorite book?" Stella looked at the overflowing bookcase next to her bed. With Jeff gone, she'd taken over what had been his nightstand, as well. A stack of favorites towered there, scraps of paper and bookmarks keeping her place in novels she'd read several times each. Sometimes she just liked to pull out an old favorite and skim the best bits.

"How can you ask me such a thing? That's like asking me which is my favorite hand!"

They laughed together.

"What were you going to do before I called you?" Matthew asked. "What would you be doing right now if I hadn't?"

"Hmm. I'd probably be in the tub with a book." Stella looked at the clock. It was getting close to bedtime. She got up and went to the door, but Tristan's door was still firmly shut, and she hadn't heard so much as the creak of hinges since he'd disappeared inside. "Maybe some soft music. Couple candles. You know. Romantic."

"So, what's stopping you?" His voice dipped low.

"You." Hers did too.

"You can talk and take a bath at the same time."

Stella closed her bedroom door and locked it. Cradling the phone to her ear, she went into the bathroom. "Yeah?"

"I'll take a bath too, how's that? We can take a bath together."

Her heart skipped. Her mouth remembered the taste of him, her body his shape and length. An answering pull centered between her legs. "That sounds like trouble."

Matthew's low chuckle tiptoed over her every nerve ending. "It will be fun. Good, clean fun."

Stella turned on the taps and toyed with the button of her blouse. "What if we drop our phones in the water?"

"Put it in a sealed plastic baggie," Matthew said.

"Have you done this before?" She tucked the phone against her shoulder and slipped the rest of her buttons free, then shrugged out of the blouse and tossed it in the hamper.

"No. But it makes sense, huh?"

She had a plastic bag in her drawer. She always kept a few there for packing her carry-on supplies. She wouldn't trust it to fully submerge her phone, but for protecting it from stray splashes... "Sure. Okay. Let's do it. Gotta put you down for a couple seconds while I get ready."

"Me too. Meet you back here in ten."

Laughing, giddy, feeling ridiculous, Stella quickly stripped and added a couple caps of bath oil to the water. She lit her scented candles—lavender, which she always found so soothing. She pulled her hair up in a messy bun and dimmed the lights before slipping into the heated water with a sigh.

Pressing the plastic-protected phone to her ear, she listened for Matthew. "You there?"

"I'm here. It's been so long since I took a bath, I had to clean out the tub first."

She heard splashing. "Not a bath fan?"

"I usually take showers. Faster that way. But this..." He hissed and sighed. "This could be good."

Stella leaned back against her bath pillow. "I take a bath

most every night, if I can. It's relaxing. If I try to read in bed, I usually fall asleep. So if I get a few chapters in while I'm in the tub, that's good."

"I do a lot of reading in the bathroom too. But not in the tub." Matthew splashed.

Stella giggled. "Nice."

"So I'm keeping you from your reading. I'd say I'm sorry, but…"

"It's okay. I'm glad you called. I didn't think you would."

"No? How come?" Matthew splashed a little more, then seemed to settle.

Stella rubbed the top of her foot along the back of her opposite calf, enjoying the way the oil had made her skin so slippery. "Just a feeling."

"But you left your number. You wanted me to call you."

She'd regretted it almost as soon as she was out his front door, so much that if it hadn't locked behind her she might've gone back in and stolen the note so he never found it. "Took you long enough."

Matthew didn't take offense. "You ducked out of my apartment without saying goodbye. I was surprised you left a note at all, to be honest. I was afraid maybe you'd be having second thoughts. I didn't want to call and make an ass of myself. But then I realized you didn't have my number and couldn't call me, so if I ever wanted to talk to you again, I'd better call."

That was so close to the truth, the part about second thoughts, that it gave her pause. "You must've really wanted to talk to me."

"So much," Matthew said at once, voice rasping. Lower. Sexy. God, he was sexy. Stella closed her eyes again, letting her free hand travel along her oil-slick skin. Collarbones. Breasts. Her nipples tightened under her fingertips. Down lower, over her belly, to dip between her legs and stroke her clit gently, just a few times.

Her voice, when she answered him, rasped too. "I'm glad you did."

"Stella...would it make me a creep if I were imagining you naked right now?"

"I am naked, Matthew."

"And wet," he whispered.

"Oh, yes," she said. "All over."

He made a sex noise, half a growl from the back of his throat. It sent a shiver through her; her nipples had already been teased erect, but at that noise, they tightened even more. The sensation echoed in her cunt, almost as if a chain connected the two places on her body. Stella's rolling hips made waves, and she held her phone up to keep it away from the sudden splash.

"Stella..."

"Yes, Matthew."

"Do you think I could see you again?"

It wasn't exactly what she thought he'd ask her, but it did put a smile on her face. She slipped a little lower in the water. "Do you want to?"

"I wouldn't ask if I didn't."

"I think...that could be arranged." She mentally ran through her schedule of upcoming weekends. "What were you thinking about?"

"How hard is it for you to get to Chicago?"

"I live in Pennsylvania," she told him, then laughed. "So it's not easy."

"Oh...I didn't realize..." Matthew laughed and splashed. "I'm getting out of the tub. My head's spinning, I ran the water too hot."

She could've stayed in longer, and would have had she been reading a good book. But a peek at the time told her she should get out too. Get into bed. The thought of that… getting into bed with him still on the phone…had potential.

"I live a couple hours outside Philly. Amish country." Stella carefully climbed from the tub and stood dripping, listening to him breathe. "You okay?"

"Yeah. Fine. Just had to sit down for a minute. Now I remember why I don't take baths."

"It helps if you don't pretend you're a lobster in a pot," she said.

Matthew snorted softly. "Philly, huh? Cheesesteaks are good there."

"You've been there, huh? How about shoofly pie? You ever try that? It's a local delicacy." She dried off and padded naked to her bedroom, where she pulled a clean nightgown from the drawer and slipped it over her head, missing half of what he'd said.

"…travel to Philadelphia."

"Sorry, I missed that. I was getting dressed."

"Nooooo," Matthew said in protest. "Why you wanna do that?"

Stella laughed. So much could've been awkward about this conversation, or it could have so easily devolved into nothing but a mutual wank session—not that she'd have minded, not exactly. "Because I don't like to sleep naked."

"That's not totally true," he tried to say, but her laughter cut him off.

"I barely slept with you. It doesn't count."

"True. We didn't do much sleeping. So what are you putting on now?"

Stella looked down at the lightweight plaid flannel

granny gown. "A sheer black nighty with matching lace panties."

Matthew gave a soft growl. "Wish I could see that."

"Maybe you'll get lucky." Stella opened her bedroom door to check on Tristan, whose door was still closed. No light from underneath. She thought about knocking, but frankly couldn't face him. She closed her door again.

"So. It would be hard for you to get to Chicago."

"No harder than it was before. I could come see you. If you really wanted—" She stopped herself. He wanted. He'd asked. "I mean, yes. I'd like to come see you again."

"We had fun, huh?"

"Yes. We had fun."

There was silence, though not awkward or uncomfortable. She heard the rustle and shuffle of him doing something. Perhaps pulling a T-shirt over his head. Maybe getting into bed the way she was, snuggling into the covers.

"Stella."

"Yes?"

"Are you happy I called you?"

"Yes," she said, and held back a yawn. "Are you happy I left my number?"

His voice was a little hoarse with sleep, the way hers was. "Yeah. Can I call you again?"

"Whenever you want." Stella turned off the light and tucked her blankets around her.

"It's late. I should let you go."

No, she thought. *No, I don't want you to let me go.*

But that was too much for a first phone call, even if they had already fucked their brains out, and more than once. Stella smiled into the dark, remembering. "Yeah. Well. Goodbye. Thanks for calling."

"We'll talk again soon."

"Whenever you want," she told him, though she was far from old-fashioned and would have no problem calling him.

"Well. Goodbye," he said again.

Neither of them disconnected. Both started laughing. Stella tried to keep her voice low, not wanting Tristan to hear her in here guffawing like a lunatic.

"You hang up," she said, then in a slightly different voice, mocking, "'No! You hang up!'"

"We can count to three," Matthew said. "One. Two. Three..."

She waited, but he didn't disappear.

"Good night, Matthew," she said, amused by his reluctance to end the call.

"Good night, Stella. Dream in color."

She'd been a second away from disconnecting, but this stopped her. "What?"

But it was too late. He'd already gone.

CHAPTER EIGHTEEN

Stella had woken this morning with a pounding head and twisting stomach, certain that the flight she'd booked would've filled up, leaving her stuck in Harrisburg. But nope, the Gods of Getting Laid had seen fit to smile upon her, because not only was the plane not full, but she got to sit in business class.

"Why not?" Carla, a petite blonde who worked almost all of the zone-three flights, said as Stella gladly took a seat in the empty row. "Nobody else is in them, right?"

It was a great way to start the morning. Stella had opted to aim for the most ungodly early flight she could get so as to maximize her time in Chicago.

She was already exhausted.

She and Matthew had spent the past two weeks either chatting online or on the phone, or sometimes, if he didn't have his girls, on video chat. The conversations had ranged from serious—the importance of financial planning, for example—to silly—why did pepper make people sneeze?

They'd flirted. Matthew was a tremendous flirt and Stella an aficionado of the double entendre. Some of their conversations had left her head spinning and her panties soaked. But they hadn't sexted. Not even on video chat, when sometimes all he did was stare at her with that look, and her cunt clenched. The suspense, as Gene Wilder's Willy Wonka had said, was terrible. Unlike the chocolate maker, Stella didn't hope it would last.

There was no question she was going there fully with the intent of fucking him again. It was all she'd been able to think about, as a matter of fact. Days and days of fantasies had consumed her. She'd been distracted at work, losing herself in memories of the slide of Matthew's cock inside her. At home, her patience with Tristan had been greatly extended, which in turn had made his attitude a little better, so a win-win all around. She'd hesitantly told him about her new relationship, emphasizing that it wasn't a big deal, and bracing herself for blowback, but Tristan hadn't seemed to care very much. She hadn't said anything about it to Jeff.

Every night for the first week after she and Matthew had gotten off the phone, Stella had touched herself. She had a drawer full of sex toys, many of them accumulated from the spate of home parties that had been popular a few years ago, when all her friends had been suckered into hostessing and they'd all spiraled into this incestuous orgy of "if you come to mine, I'll come to yours." She had waterproof vibrating bullets, realistic dildos in several different flesh tones. She had one or two vibes with animals on them, a beaver and a rabbit. She had all these "toys," but when she thought about Matthew, all she needed was her hand.

Hell, barely that sometimes. Lying in bed with the phone

pressed to her ear, all she really had to do was squeeze her thighs together and roll her hips, and she could bring herself to the edge of orgasm just listening to his voice. She always waited until she was off the phone to finish, though, in case her moans gave her away.

She didn't want him to think she was creepy, after all.

Still, she hoped that their talks had led him to do the same things she had done. To take his cock in his fist and stroke it while he thought about her. The heat of her mouth or of her cunt. The thought of her on her knees in front of him. The taste of her...

"Get you something to drink?" Carla smiled curiously. "Are you too warm? I can bring you something with ice...."

"Oh, I'm fine." Stella reached up and turned on the air vent, tipping her face toward the burst of cool but still stagnant air. She gave Carla a wide, bright grin. "I could use some orange juice, though, if you have any. And coffee."

"We have some muffins and fruit, if you're hungry. The flight's not that long," Carla said apologetically, and swept a hand around the empty business-class cabin. "But as you can see, we don't exactly have a full house."

"Don't worry about it. A drink's fine." There was no way she could eat, anyway.

The trip took about two hours, but because of the time change, she got there only an hour later than when she'd left. She'd offered to take a cab to his apartment, but Matthew had promised to pick her up.

"Have a great trip. What time are you coming home on Sunday?" Carla asked as Stella hung back, waiting for the rest of the plane to empty before she got up to pull her bag from overhead.

"I have the last afternoon departure."

Carla grinned. "I'm working that one. I'll see you then."

Stella went first to the restroom, where she smoothed her hair, powdered her nose and refreshed the lipstick she'd nibbled off during the trip. She had faint circles under her eyes from lack of sleep and anxiety; she pressed her hands flat to her stomach and turned from side to side to look at herself from all angles.

She had not dressed the way she usually did for flying. She wore a cute royal-blue dress of soft fabric and a pair of complementary leggings, along with her favorite pair of black-and-white floral Converse, the ones she'd custom-designed and treated herself to for her fortieth birthday. It was a comfortable outfit, and cute. Flattering. It was sexy if you already liked her, she thought as she smoothed the fabric over her hips. It wasn't an outfit meant for seduction, even though beneath it she was wearing new lace panties and a matching bra.

Stella drew in a deep breath. She couldn't stay in the bathroom forever. She washed her hands carefully and dried them, but they were still shaking when she took the handle of her rolling bag and pulled it behind her through the terminal.

Everything seemed brighter, clearer, louder. All the kiosks, the people passing her, intent on their own destinations. How many of them were going to meet their lovers? Longtime or brand-new, how many were on their way to a reunion?

She saw him before he saw her, and was glad of it because it gave her a minute or so to calm herself. This was Matthew, she reminded herself. She already knew him. This was going to be a great visit, she told herself. *Stop worrying, Stella.*

He caught sight of her and waved. He pushed through the crowd. And then he was there in front of her.

He was real.

They hadn't talked about how they'd greet each other— who would? But now Stella wished she had asked him if he intended to kiss her. If she should brace herself for a hug, or if they would simply stare at each other with foolish grins painted all over their faces while everyone around them thought they looked like morons.

Matthew kissed her. A quick peck on the cheek, just at the corner of her mouth. Almost nothing, but then she was in his arms and he was holding her so tight she could barely breathe.

"Hi," he said into her ear.

Stella found her voice. "Hi."

They smiled and smiled, and then she pushed up on her tiptoes to angle her mouth across his for a proper kiss. Long, lingering, the quick slip of tongues before she pulled away with flushed cheeks. She hadn't let go of her carry-on's handle, and it made standing so close to him a little awkward, but she didn't want him to let go.

"Hungry?" Matthew asked.

"Starving." Suddenly, she was. She'd woken just before dawn, too anxious to sleep longer than that. Tristan had been at his dad's already. She hadn't eaten breakfast, declined food on the plane. Her stomach was in knots, but at the sight of Matthew's smile, all the tension had begun to drain away.

He took the handle of her bag from her with one hand, and her hand with his other. Fingers linked, he led her toward the exit. "Breakfast?"

"I can always eat breakfast," she told him.

"I remember."

He'd parked in the garage, which was far from empty at this time of morning. Somehow that didn't matter when he pushed her up against his car and kissed her, hard. Stella's arms went around his neck, holding him close. The kiss almost bruised her; she didn't care. They gorged themselves on each other in those few minutes, until her knees got weak and her breath caught so tight in her chest she had to break the kiss or faint.

Matthew pressed his forehead to hers. "You taste so good. It's all I've been able to think about. Kissing you again."

"Wow." Stella laughed a little self-consciously. "You sure know how to make a girl feel welcome."

"Breakfast. I promised you breakfast. I'm a terrible host," he murmured against her mouth.

"Kiss me just a little longer," she told him. "And I'll forgive you."

He did kiss her, and more than that. Matthew slipped a hand between them to press between her legs. Swiftly, only for a few seconds, but the pressure sparked pleasure through her, and she shivered. The staccato blare of a passing car horn pushed them apart. Matthew looked a little guilty, maybe embarrassed, and Stella gave a mental chuckle. She'd done more than make out in a parking garage before...but she didn't want to think about what she'd done with other men now. Not when she was standing with this one.

He opened the car door for her, and shut it when she got inside. In the few seconds it took him to round the car and get in the driver's side, Stella stole a glance in the rearview mirror. Her mouth was wet, lipstick a little smeared, but the weariness that had plagued her expression for the past few weeks had vanished. Bright eyes, pink cheeks. She pushed some stray hair out of her eyes and turned toward him as he got in the car.

"Let's go, Jeeves!"

"Call me Alfred," Matthew said. "It sounds better."

"If you're Alfred, then that makes me Batman." Stella made a face. "I don't want to be Batman."

"Who doesn't want to be Batman?" Matthew asked as he backed out of the parking spot and eased his car into the line of others waiting to get out of the garage.

He drove a BMW, Stella realized as she looked at the dashboard and the logo on the glovebox. She hadn't noticed before, so busy with his mouth on hers. It didn't impress her, exactly. But it did sort of surprise her. "You should be Batman. Not me."

"Then does that make you Catwoman?" He shot her a grin.

Stella lifted an eyebrow. "Meow, Bruce Wayne."

Matthew was not a patient driver. She saw that within the first few minutes as he muttered about the other cars in line and even flipped off, albeit discreetly below the level of the dashboard, one car that cut him off. What she hadn't been expecting was that he drove like a Nascar racer with something to prove. Once he hit the highway, it was pedal to the metal and no brakes.

Stella tucked her fingers into the door handle, squeezing it. Her other hand gripped the side of her seat. With both feet on the floor, staring straight ahead as Matthew wove in and out of traffic, it took everything she had not to "brake" every time he came up too close behind another car.

There aren't many cars on the road this time of night, and in this weather, but the red flash of taillights up ahead reminds her of the lights on Brad and Janet's Christmas tree. So do the traffic lights up ahead, glowing green, glowing yellow. The orangish-white of the streetlamps overhead. Everything is bright, everything glows, and she tips her head back against the seat and laughs and laughs at how good the world feels. From the backseat comes the shuffle and grumble of two little boys up way too late past their bedtime.

"He's touching me!"

"He's looking at me!"

"He took my guy! Mama, make Tristan give me back my guy!"

"Gage," Stella says, twisting in her seat to shake a finger at him. "Can't you share?"

Then there is the squeal of brakes, the crunch of metal and glass and everything is cold.

Everything is dark.

"Hey. You okay?"

She'd closed her eyes against the sudden wave of nausea brought on by memory, too much coffee, not enough sleep, not enough food. Stella looked at Matthew, intending to smile and lie, but the ache in her fingers from where she gripped the door handle distracted her. The road ahead of her swarmed with cars and the flash of taillights, but it wasn't night. The roads weren't slick with ice.

Matthew wasn't going to rear end a pickup truck and, in turn, be sideswiped by a tractor trailer.

And there were no children in the backseat.

He eased to a stop at a red light at the end of an off-ramp and turned in his seat to put a hand on her leg. "Stella?"

She jumped at the touch, her breathing slowing through

force of will, and gave him a weak smile. "You drive really fast."

"I do?" The light turned green, and Matthew took his foot off the brake, his attention still on her.

"Eyes on the road," Stella snapped. It was too harsh, she heard that at once. It embarrassed her, and she shut her mouth with a painful click of her teeth.

Matthew had been reaching for her, but now he put both hands on the wheel with a nod, and focused his gaze on the road in front of them. They drove in silence for the next five minutes or so, getting away from the highway and onto local city streets. Each minute that ticked by left her feeling more and more embarrassed about her outburst, until by the time he'd pulled into the parking lot of the diner he'd taken her to last time, Stella was full of anxiety again.

"I'm sorry—" she said as he turned off the ignition, but his mouth on hers stopped more words from coming out.

"No. I'm sorry." Matthew cupped the back of her neck, his fingers beneath her hair. "You told me about the car accident. I should've thought about that. My wife tells me all the time I drive like a maniac."

Stella didn't miss the word *wife,* but she didn't point it out. She let him kiss her. "I've gotten a lot better. When I'm driving, I never have a problem. It's only when I'm in the passenger seat."

"I understand." He pushed her hair off her face and over her shoulder.

He didn't, not really. He couldn't. Nobody could, not even Jeff, and he'd been in the car too.

"It's about being in control," she told him. "When I'm driving, I feel like I'm in control, so it's okay. But when I'm not, sometimes it all comes back."

Matthew didn't say anything, which was the perfect response. He kissed her again, lightly. Then he took both her hands and simply held them for a few minutes until they stopped shaking. "Ready to go in? Or we could go someplace else."

"No," Stella said, linking her fingers in his. "This place is perfect."

CHAPTER NINETEEN

"I need to grab a drink." Matthew shaded his eyes against the sun, looking out over the tents and stages set up all along the Riverwalk. "Will you be okay here?"

Stella nodded, relaxing in the sunshine. The breeze off the water was brisk and would've been too chilly without the fierce overhead burn. She was glad for the sweater she'd tied around her waist but didn't need right now. "Nope. I'm good. I'll wait here for you. Enjoy the music."

It wasn't her sort of music, actually. The Riverwalk was featuring some kind of indie rock festival along with charity and business booths, as well as carnival-type foods like corn dogs and fried dough. But it had been hard finding this spot on one of the benches, and she didn't want to give it up.

Matthew gave her a quick kiss and headed off into the crowd, where she lost sight of him after a minute or so. Stella stretched her legs, nodding along with the music and watching the people come and go. Five minutes passed.

Then another five, and though she searched for him, she couldn't find Matthew. She tapped out a quick text to him, then checked her emails, her Connex page, read a few of the blogs she liked to follow. Still no Matthew, and no reply to her text either.

When almost half an hour had passed, she got up from the bench, squinting into the brightness to see if she could catch a glimpse of his red-and-black plaid shirt. Still nothing. She checked her phone to see if she'd missed his reply, but nothing had come through.

For a moment, the pancakes she'd stuffed herself with an hour or so before threatened to make a reappearance. What if something had happened to him? It was unlikely in the middle of a music festival, in broad daylight, but...

Stella's high school friend Denise's mother, Rosemarie, had epilepsy. Growing up, Stella had spent many nights sleeping over at Denise's house, many hours hanging out in her rec room watching MTV and playing board games. She'd seen Rosemarie have several seizures, all of them scary, even though her family treated them pretty matter-of-factly. But one thing had always stood out in her mind, not something she'd seen but a story Denise had told her about how once Rosemarie had experienced a seizure while shopping at the local mall alone. She'd been seizure-free for several years by that point, able to drive on her own. She'd gone out looking for some new curtains and hadn't come home for close to six hours, because after having the seizure she'd been unable to tell the EMTs who she was, and someone had been shitty enough to steal her purse while she lay fallen.

What if something like that had happened to Matthew?

How would she know? Pacing, Stella kept her phone in her hand, sending another text that was quite a bit less casual than the first had been.

WHERE ARE YOU?

She saw him then, cutting through the crowd with a look of determination on his face that scared her only a little less than how long it had taken him to return. He saw her looking for him and headed for her. He had an empty water bottle in his hand, which he tossed into a garbage can as he passed it.

"Are you okay?" she cried. "I was getting really worried."

Matthew looked over his shoulder. "Yeah. Sorry. I—"

She was so relieved, she hugged him. Hard. He hugged her back, after a few seconds. Stella pulled away to look into his face.

"I texted you, and when you didn't answer—"

"Oh. Shit. I didn't hear it. I'm sorry, Stella. I ran into someone and couldn't get away."

She stepped back at that. "You were gone almost forty-five minutes. You didn't think I might be worried? You could've texted me. I'd have come to meet you."

His expression told her that would not have been an option.

Stella's shoulders straightened. Her jaw tightened. "You could've texted me to tell me you were caught up. At least answered my texts to let me know you were all right."

"I'm sorry," he repeated. At least he looked sorry. "I told you, I didn't hear my phone."

As if on cue, his phone chirruped with a truly obnoxious ring tone. Stella looked at his pocket. Matthew pulled out his phone and swiped the screen to check the message. She waited, eyebrows raised, for him to say something, but all he did was put his phone back in his pocket.

"You didn't hear my text," she said.

Matthew looked guilty. "I... Your number... It connects to an app on my phone. I don't always have it set to notifications, so I missed your messages. You're right, I should've texted, but I was... It would've been noticeable if I whipped out my phone and started texting. It would've been hard to explain."

"An app?" That would explain why he had a Nevada phone number but lived in Chicago. The rest of it didn't take much more figuring out either. "It was your ex, wasn't it?"

"We're all still on the same phone plan. It was complicated for her to set up her own, and we have shared minutes and I keep meaning to get her on her own plan, but I just haven't yet."

"And you don't want her seeing that you're calling or texting me. Because she checks that sort of thing?"

His face said it all. Stella blew out a long, irritated breath. She forced herself to take a few more steps away from him, untying her sweater and shrugging into it, because now the wind was starting to give her the chills. Or maybe it was her anger. She hadn't been here more than four hours, and she was already calculating if she could make it back to the airport and catch a flight home.

"Hey. Hey, Stella. Don't." Matthew took her by the upper arm, turning her to face him. "I'm sorry. Really."

"I understand if you didn't want to parade me around in front of her, but it's incredibly rude of you to leave me here for all that time without even a message. I'm your guest, Matthew. If nothing else, I'm that."

Anger flashed in his eyes, but she didn't care. Let him get defensive. She was pissed off, and not afraid to tell him.

"No. I didn't want to parade you around, as you put it. Caroline had the girls, and it would've been ugly. That's all. Not just for them, but for you too. I didn't want to subject you to that. When you meet them," Matthew said, "I don't want it to be at random, okay? Is that hard to understand?"

Stella's lip curled a little. "Oh, no, it's crystal clear. I understand it just fine. But the point you seem to be missing is that I don't care if you ran into your ex-wife. You could've run into your fifth-grade schoolteacher, your priest, your chiropractor or the guy who cleans your lobby. I don't care who it was. You left me. Sitting. For forty-five minutes. Without telling me where you were. I thought something had happened to you."

She shook her head, crossing her arms to keep herself from pacing or making more of a scene than she already was.

"You're right." He softened, reaching for her. "Shit, Stella. I'm really sorry."

She softened too. She let him pull her close, though she didn't offer her mouth for a kiss. He looked sorry. He sounded sorry. The wary part of her still wanted to go home, but the other part, that darker, greedy part, had not yet had her fill of him.

"You want to get out of here?" Matthew didn't look over his shoulder as though he were being pursued, but that was the vibe she got from him.

Stella, who'd lost her taste for sitting in the sun, nodded. "Sure."

In the car, he didn't turn on the ignition. He sat staring straight ahead for a minute or so while Stella waited for him to speak. She wasn't going to pry it out of him, whatever it was.

Finally Matthew turned to her. "The divorce has been really hard on her."

Stella said nothing.

"It's hard on everyone," he added. "I'm sure you know what it's like."

"Yes," she said warily. "But I don't still share a cell phone plan with my ex-husband. Nor would I ever have to hide from him who I'm texting or calling or visiting, quite frankly."

"What about your son?" Matthew said sharply. "Would you just randomly introduce him to strangers, just because you're…"

She waited for him to finish, thinking that if he said "fucking them," she'd get out of the car and go home, even if she had to leave her bag behind.

"My girls are young," Matthew said instead. "And I haven't dated anyone since the divorce. Caroline hasn't either. I guess neither of us wants to be the first one to bring anyone around."

"But you are divorced, right? I mean, it's official. Papers signed and everything?"

"Yes." He shrugged.

"And she didn't want it?"

"No," Matthew said, looking surprised. "She's the one who asked for it."

Stella sat back in her seat, arms crossed. This relationship was too new for this sort of drama. This relationship, she reminded herself, wasn't even a relationship, really.

"I'm sorry, Stella. Really sorry. I've been a dick."

"Yes. You have," she said, then turned toward him. "Look. I'm not interested in swooping in on your life and wreaking havoc, okay? We all have our own shit to shovel. I understand how you'd want to be careful with your girls. I'm not so clear on why you're still tied to the ex-wife so that you have to act like you're cheating on her."

He looked startled at that. Then a flush of guilt. Maybe he'd cheated on his wife, maybe that was why she'd asked him for a divorce. Stella wasn't about to get into it.

"I don't need to rub her nose in anything. And she would check the bill to see if I was texting strange numbers. She's done it before. And then she freaks out. I just don't need the hassle. That's all."

Stella sighed and rubbed at the swelling headache pressing behind her eyes. "I think you should take me back to the airport. I'll grab a hotel room—"

"No!" Matthew reached for her. "Shit, Stella. Don't do that. Can't I make it up to you? I feel like shit. Really."

She eyed him, trying to gauge his sincerity. Matthew hadn't yet impressed her as the sort of guy who'd run roughshod over her in pursuit of what he wanted, but he did have that charm she'd found so many men knew they could use to get their own way.

It was against her better judgment, but she smiled a little. "You're going to have to work for it."

"Okay. I can do that." Matthew grinned.

"Work hard. Realllllly hard."

Matthew sat up straight, giving her a firm nod. "As hard as I have to. In fact, I'm kind of semihard right now."

"Bad. You're very bad, you know that?" Stella shook her head.

Matthew leaned in to offer his mouth for a kiss she didn't give him right away. "Yeah. I know."

Stella let him kiss her.

"I'm stuffed." With a groan, Stella dropped onto Matthew's couch. "I don't know where you put all that food. Do you have a hollow leg, or what?"

He'd taken her to the movies, then shopping and to the Skydeck in Willis Tower. Then finally out to dinner. It had been a whirlwind of a day, cram-packed with all the sorts of touristy things she imagined he thought she wanted to do, and they'd been fun. But what she really wanted was to spend time with him. Maybe he was trying to impress her. Maybe he was trying to fend off any more possible awkwardness by keeping them both busy until they collapsed.

At least Caroline had left him alone. Mostly. A couple of bland texts Stella hadn't asked to see, but Matthew had felt compelled to share with her.

She eyed him now as he poured himself a nice measure of whiskey.

"You want?" Matthew held up his glass.

"No, thanks."

"I have wine."

"I couldn't," Stella said. "I'll explode. Seriously."

Matthew, glass in hand, joined her on the couch in a swift, graceful motion, so smooth the liquor didn't even slosh. "I don't want you to explode."

Watching his gaze light up and travel over her, Stella felt an answering pull of heat. After the debacle at the River-walk and the discussion in the car, he'd been lovely to her all day. Holding her hand. Nuzzling her occasionally. Pulling her close for random hugs. But he hadn't looked at her like this until just now, and it was what she'd been waiting for since he'd pushed her up against the car in the parking garage and plundered her mouth.

When she kissed him, she tasted whiskey. Smoky. It reminded her of fall. When she sucked his tongue gently, Matthew gave a soft moan. Stella moved onto his lap, taking his face in her hands to kiss him harder.

"Gonna spill your whiskey," she mouthed against his lips. "You better drink it."

Matthew moved the glass between them, eyeing her over the rim. Watching his tongue swipe his mouth, Stella shifted to press herself against him. Her clit pulsed when he drank and swallowed; he offered her the glass and she sipped. Shuddered at the burn.

Matthew laughed and drained the glass, then reached behind him to put it on the sofa table. His hands found her hips. His lips, her lips. The kiss deepened, tongues searching. He put a hand on the small of her back to press her to him, and in minutes they were both grinding against each other.

Stella broke the kiss with a gasp. "Matthew…"

"Yes." He didn't let her say another word, capturing all her sighs with his mouth and breathing them back into her. He rocked his hardness against her, and it felt so good Stella forgot what she meant to say, if anything.

Maybe she just liked the taste of his name.

Somehow she got a hand between them and undid his belt, his zipper and button, to free him. The head of his cock pushed free of the denim and his briefs, and she pressed her palm to its heat. His hands had moved beneath her dress, his thumb finding her clit through the soft fabric of her leggings. He stroked her once, twice, until she shuddered.

"Feels good," she whispered.

He looked into her eyes. "I want to make you feel good. I want to watch you come."

"I," Stella said, sitting upright, "would love for you to watch me come."

"I can feel your heat. And right here…" He stroked her clit again. "You're hard. I can feel it. Fuck, that turns me on."

Her muscles leaped as he touched her. Stella let her head fall back for a second with a moan. "That feels so good. Just like that."

Stroke. Stroke. Back and forth, the pressure almost so light it shouldn't even have registered, yet drove her crazy for just that reason. Stella wanted to writhe from it, to whimper. She kept herself still only so she didn't wiggle herself right off his lap, but she curled her fingers in the front of his shirt.

"You like that."

She laughed breathlessly and leaned in to kiss him. "Yes. I like that."

She wanted to ask him to put his hands inside her panties, sink his fingers deep inside her, but she didn't move. Matthew opened his mouth, his tongue delicately stroking hers. His thumb kept up the slow, steady and frustratingly light pressure while the pleasure built up and up inside her until Stella let her head drop to his shoulder. Trembling, she strained toward climax, every muscle tight.

He stopped.

Stella let out a groan but didn't move. It would take so little to send her over the edge right now, but she felt helpless to even shift her hips and press herself against him. All she could do was concentrate on that flickering flame of desire between her legs.

Slowly, he swiped his thumb across her clit again. His other hand gripped her ass, kneading. Pressing her against him. Then he slid his hand up her back to anchor it in the hair at the base of her skull, fingers tangling, pulling her head back. Matthew kissed her throat, baring his teeth against her skin. Biting gently.

"Oh," she breathed. And again, "Oh, oh…"

"Come for me," Matthew said. "I want you to come for me."

She did. Up, up and over. Sometimes she came hard like falling into an abyss, but this time her orgasm lifted her. Flying. She rode the waves of pleasure in silence but for the tortured gasp of her breathing, and when it was over she collapsed against him.

Matthew stroked his hands down her back, then held her close. They stayed that way for a minute or so. Stella forced her eyes to open, made herself sit up, though she could've stayed like that forever.

"Wow," she said.

Matthew grinned. "Good?"

"Um, yeah." She wriggled a little, putting a hand between them to cup his hard cock. Every part of her felt loose and sated, but there was more to come. Literally, she hoped.

Matthew's eyes went heavy-lidded at her caress, but he shifted her off his lap, then urged her onto her knees facing the back of the sofa. He bent over her back, arms along hers, to press her hands to the sofa cushions, curling her fingers to grip. Stella looked over her shoulder at the sound of his zipper going down. In the next minute, Matthew flipped the hem of her dress to her hips and eased down her leggings and her damp panties, then put his hands on her hips and pulled her to the edge of the couch.

"Bend over."

She did, closing her eyes again, waiting for his touch. At the stroke of his fingers along the seam of her cunt, then inside her, Stella moaned. Matthew found her clit and stroked that too before withdrawing.

"Hold on a second." He pulled open a drawer in the end table.

She heard the rustle of him opening a condom. Tense, she waited for the press of his cock and wasn't disappointed. Matthew rubbed himself between her legs, getting himself slick, then pushed slowly inside her. This angle made the friction a little odd until she bent forward more, widening her knees on the couch and tipping her hips to allow him to get inside her even deeper.

"Fuck," Matthew breathed as he seated himself inside her. "Oh, Stella. Shit. You're so fucking wet."

She knew it by the effortless slide of him inside her, but hearing him say it as though she'd presented him with some sort of gift sent shivers of pleasure all through her.

He fucked her like he owned the patent on getting her off. Slow, then harder and faster, short and sharp, followed by leisurely and long. He was teasing the fuck out of her, and she loved it. Every so often he reached around to tweak her clit, sending fresh waves of desire coursing through her, but again, Stella didn't worry about whether or not she was going to come again. The journey was as delicious as the destination.

He fucked her that way for what seemed like forever.

Stella let her face press into the cushions as she pushed back against him. The slap of their bodies turned her on. So did the sound of Matthew's low moans when she ground herself on his cock, and the smack of his hand on her ass. Not hard enough to hurt, just enough to warm her skin. The unexpected pressure of his thumb on her asshole startled her into rocking forward, and that was enough to surprise her into another orgasm.

"Oh, shit, I can feel you coming," Matthew said. "I'm gonna…"

Stella let out a long, stuttering sigh and rocked her hips to get him deeper into her. Matthew's hoarse shout put a smile on her face. So did the way he collapsed onto her back for a few moments before getting off her and falling, splayed, on the couch, with one arm flung over his face.

Stella moved, her dress falling over her hips. She wriggled her panties and leggings back up and peeked at him. "Mmmm."

Matthew cracked open an eye. Without moving, he waved his hand in the general direction of the end table. "Could you…get me…"

Stella laughed and reached for the box of tissues, which she handed him so he could take care of the condom, then took the box and the mass of tissues from him to throw away in the kitchen. There she drew herself a glass of cold water from the tap and drank deep, cataloging all the lovely aches he'd given her. Her knees hurt most of all, but something had pulled a little in her neck and shoulder too. Wincing, she rubbed it.

"You okay?" Matthew said from behind her. He opened the fridge and pulled out a beer, offering it to her. Stella shook her head.

"Just a little neck spasm." Stella rubbed at it, watching him crack the top on the beer and swallow a long, thirsty pull. "It's an old injury but still acts up sometimes."

"Sit." Matthew indicated the kitchen chair, and she obeyed. He set his beer on the table and put his big hands on her neck. "Here?"

"Lower... Yeah. There. Ouch."

"You're really tight there." He worked the muscles gently but firmly, hitting the trigger points in a way that made her want to cry even though it felt good at the same time.

Before she knew it, Stella *was* crying. Small gasping sobs at first that she tried to hold back, but then the tears came along with deeper, breathy groans as she tried to hold them back. It wasn't only from the pain in her neck and shoulder, though it could be bad enough sometimes to make her cry.

It was... Well, she didn't quite know what it was, only that as he worked on her tense muscles, the stress and fear of earlier came slamming back into her and the euphoria of the hour they'd spent on his couch had worn away her walls enough that she had no chance of holding back any emotions at all.

"Hey," Matthew said when he noticed. "I'm sorry. Did I hurt you?"

"I'm sorry. I'm sorry. I just... I feel stupid now. I'm sorry." Stella swiped at her eyes and pressed her fingers there to hold back the tears still threatening. She'd managed not to burst into braying sobs, but only barely. She breathed, concentrating on pushing away the sudden onslaught of emotions threatening to overwhelm her. All of this was so much more than she'd been looking for, and what was she supposed to do with it now that it had found her?

Matthew didn't say anything else; he just pulled her close,

her face to his shirt. He stroked her hair. And that was really all she needed, not words or platitudes, but the unspoken comfort of his touch.

"I wish you didn't have to go." Matthew said this against her neck.

They'd made a tent of his blankets, the light filtering through the windows casting shadows through the sheets. Stella moved her knees slowly against the soft fabric, watching the way the light changed. The tickle of his lips on her skin sent a shiver through her, peaking her nipples, but she didn't want him to move away.

"I have to, though."

"I know." He sighed and nuzzled closer, one hand on her belly. Teasing lower, through her curls. His fingers found her clit for a second, but only that.

Stella rolled to face him, kicking the covers off so they could lie naked and untangled. She touched his face, then kissed him. "This was a great weekend, Matthew. Thank you."

It had been, even with the awkwardness at the Riverwalk. She kissed him again, lingering a little before pulling away when he started to make it deeper. She laughed, shaking her finger at him as she got up.

"I have to go. I need to shower and get to the airport…."

Matthew groaned and flung himself against the pillows. "Ugh."

Stella laughed again, her heart beating a little faster at the thought he might really want her to stay. She went to his side of the bed and put a knee on it, looking down at him. "You can call me, you know. Anytime. It's not like we won't talk again."

"What if we don't? What if you walk out my door and I never see you again?" Matthew sat up, his back against the wall.

He was so fucking beautiful when he was naked. He looked damn good with clothes on too, but clearly so comfortable in his bare skin, he was glorious. He took her breath away, and she had to force herself not to pounce on him again. She couldn't miss her flight—there wasn't another until tomorrow.

"You'll see me again," Stella said, aiming her tone for breezy and not quite making it.

Matthew gave her a slow smile that kindled fire inside her. "Promise?"

She hesitated. Making promises was the fastest way to end up telling a lie. "Well, I'd certainly like to. And I'm sure we can make it happen, if you want that too. You could come to see me in Pennsylvania. Fly into Philly. I'll take you out on the town."

He stared at her a long moment, not answering. Just when it started to feel awkward, he reached for her hand. Pulled her closer. He kissed her, long and sweet and slow, until her head spun and she lost her sense of direction.

"You could come back here," he murmured against her mouth, "and we could just stay in."

She laughed as she kissed him. "Well...if you insist."

"I do," he said. "I absolutely do."

CHAPTER TWENTY

That was how it began, this thing between them. With a promise she'd been unable to make a couple months ago. Technically, Stella thought as she once more boarded a plane home from Chicago after another whirlwind weekend with Matthew, it had started in a hotel bar, where she'd once more picked up a stranger…only it had been different with him from that first meeting. Different ever since.

A little over two months wasn't such a long time, especially when she'd only managed three visits in that span of time. But they talked on the phone or video-chatted every day, which was nowhere as fulfilling as seeing him in person, but better than nothing.

Her phone booped in her pocket as she settled into her seat, and she pulled it out, grinning to find a message from him. Miss you.

They'd both downloaded an app called Kik to use for their messages. It irked her, a little, to have to dance around his ex-wife's neurosis, but she had to admit there were a few functions of the app that she liked better than texting.

One of them was the ability to see at once if he'd read her message, and also if he was replying, both functions regular texting couldn't provide since Matthew was a heathen who didn't use an iPhone.

Quickly, Stella entered a series of emoticons. A smile blowing a kiss, a heart, a woman's face. Then a man's. It was their code. She glanced at the man taking the aisle seat next to her, who was blatantly looking at what she was doing. Stella sent the message, then turned off her phone in preparation for departure.

"Hi," the man said.

Businessman. Just her type too. Stella reached in her bag and pulled out her book without giving him more than a polite, distant smile.

Things really had changed.

At home, things hadn't changed. Stella walked in the front door to the blare of music coming from the speakers connected to Tristan's iPod, and a kitchen full of teenage boys in various stages of stink. The fridge hung open with one foraging inside. The sink had been piled high with dirty dishes. The table groaned under the weight of pizza boxes and other trash.

Well, at least none of the cans scattered around and over-flowing the recycling bin were of beer, and she couldn't find any evidence they were shooting heroine into their eyeballs or any place else. And, she noted, there was a distinct and obvious lack of girls.

"Hi, guys," she said, and was greeted with a chorus of "hey" and "hi, Mrs. Cooper." She gave Tristan a raised-brow look. "I sure hope you're going to clean this all up."

"I didn't think you'd be home until later," Tristan said.

"Clearly." Stella looked around the room again, calculating how long the group must've been ruining her kitchen. It didn't take long, she knew that, but it still looked longer than a few hours, which it should've been if Tristan had been with his dad until this morning. "I'm going upstairs to unpack. Tristan, if you have laundry, please bring it down so I can get a load started before tomorrow."

Behind her, the room erupted again into laughter as she left the kitchen. She wasn't happy about the idea that maybe Jeff had fallen down on the parenting job again, or that Tristan had been home by himself this weekend. For the most part, his friends were good kids, and she'd rather have them hanging out here than someplace else. Still, it wasn't a good idea for her empty house to be where they did it.

She thumbed in Jeff's house number, knowing Cynthia would be the one to answer it. The situation with Matthew and Caroline had made Stella even more careful about how she dealt with her ex-husband and his new wife. "Cynthia. It's Stella."

"Oh, hi, Stella!" Cynthia always sounded so chipper. So perky. It was disgusting.

"Hey. Is Jeff around? I need to talk to him about Tristan."

"Jeff went to Atlantic City for the weekend for a poker tournament. He won't be home until late tonight." Cynthia sounded slightly less perky about that.

Stella paused in sifting through her dirty laundry. "Was Tristan with you this weekend?"

"No." Cynthia sounded hesitant now. "Was he supposed to be?"

"Yes, actually. I was out of town."

"Oh. Stella, I'm sorry. I didn't know. I guess Jeff didn't know either. Do you want me to leave him a message?"

"No," Stella said. "I'll call his cell phone."

That set Cynthia off. "Oh, oh…"

"I'll handle this, Cynthia. Thanks." Stella disconnected before the other woman could say anything else, and dialed Jeff's number. Typically, he didn't answer, but that's what voice mail was for. "Jeff. Please tell me you did not go to Atlantic City knowing your teenage son was left home alone for the weekend. I'm sure you won't call me back when you get this, but don't think we're not going to talk about it."

Downstairs, the look on her face scattered those boys like leaves in a brisk autumn wind. She barely had to say a word before they were all making stammering excuses and fleeing, leaving a guilty-faced Tristan to stand in front of her among the detritus of what had clearly been a weekend-long orgy of takeout food and video games and whatever else it was teenage boys did when they were alone. She didn't want to think too hard about it.

"You have something to tell me?"

"I was going to clean it all up before you got home," Tristan said.

Stella lifted an eyebrow. "You realize that's not the point I'm trying to make. Right?"

Tristan stayed silent, which was probably smart. She gestured at the kitchen. "Clean this up. Now."

Upstairs again, her phone alerted her to a message from Matthew. She thumbed in his number instead of replying via the app. "Hey."

"Hey." He sounded wary.

Stella paused. "Bad time?"

"The girls are here. Caroline's just dropping them off now."

Well, at least he'd answered her call rather than letting it go to voice mail. "Ah. Sorry I didn't warn you I was going to call. I just got home and found the house a mess. Tristan was here all weekend with his friends. Apparently his dad blew off his parental responsibilities in favor of a boys' weekend away."

"Uh-huh. Uh-huh."

She paused again, closing her eyes and pinching the bridge of her nose. "Caroline's still there, huh?"

"Yes. Yeah. Uh-huh."

It would've been funny, maybe, if Stella weren't already annoyed. Or if it was, in fact, humorous instead of slightly insulting. She breathed out a low, irritated sigh and caught sight of Tristan trying to sneak past her door unnoticed.

"I'll talk to you later. Maybe," she amended. "I'm sure you'll be so busy with the girls you won't have time."

"Hey, that's... Yeah, okay. Sure. Sounds good." His voice, so carefully neutral, curled her lip.

"Whatever," Stella said, and disconnected. Tucking her phone in her pocket, she rapped on Tristan's door, waiting for him to answer before she opened it. "Hey. We need to talk."

Tristan sighed, head hanging. "I knew you'd be mad."

"So why did you do it?" She'd have sat to talk to him, but as usual, every open inch of space in his room was covered with crap she didn't have the strength to yell at him about. "You know how I feel about you being here alone."

"I'm gonna be seventeen, Mom! I'm fine! I can take care of myself."

"It's not that I worry you can't take care of yourself, Tristan. I don't want a house full of boys here while I'm gone and can't be here in case something happens. And I'm sure that your friends' parents don't want them hanging around unsupervised either. I'm a mom. I know this stuff."

Tristan didn't say anything, though at least he looked ashamed and not belligerent. It could go either way with him, these days.

With a sigh, Stella leaned against the bedpost. "I want to trust you, but stuff like this is exactly why I can't."

"We weren't doing anything bad," he said defensively. "All we did was play *Honor Bound 3* and watch movies."

"When did you find out your dad wasn't going to be home?"

"Friday afternoon. After you were gone."

Stella frowned. "He didn't tell me he'd changed plans."

"I didn't want to hang out there with Cynthia. She doesn't care if my friends come over, but it's weird, Mom. She makes us sandwiches and is sort of…annoying."

Stella could completely see that. But that didn't change anything. "You should've texted me right away."

"Would you have come home?" Tristan tossed the question at her, and Stella fumbled it. "No. I didn't think so. You're too busy with your *boyfriend* to bother."

Stella had not yet started calling Matthew her boyfriend; they hadn't talked about what they were. But she'd made no secret of him and hearing her teenage son say it in that snide tone didn't make it sound very good. "That's not fair."

"Well. It's not fair that you're always running off to spend time with him so that I have to deal with it either!" Tristan shoved at a pile of papers on his desk and sent them fluttering to the floor.

This raised an eyebrow. "I'm hardly always running off to spend time with him, Tristan. I've been to Chicago three times in two months."

"You're on the phone with him all the time."

"You talk with your friends all the time," she pointed out, calmly, she thought, though the idea that her son might've heard the content of her conversations didn't settle too well in her gut.

"That's different."

"Because you're the kid and I'm the mom? I'm not allowed to have friends?" Stella shook her head. "Tristan, that's not fair. And, look, I'm sorry if you think my attention's been taken up too much with Matthew. I'm sure it might seem that we spend a lot of time together, but we really get very little—"

"All the time," he said sullenly. "You're always on your phone, messaging him."

Coming from the boy who practically needed to be surgically separated from his phone, this was pretty rich. Stella didn't laugh, though, too aware of how this argument could spiral out of control. She was tired and angry and annoyed, and coming down off the high of the weekend was hard enough without all this stuff too.

"And that's my business. Not yours." Stella looked around the room. "Clean the house up, or I swear to you, Tristan, you won't like what happens."

He didn't answer her, didn't say a word until she was at the doorway, when he muttered, "Whatever."

It was exactly what she'd have said, and she had to bite back a snarky reply. Instead, she turned to face him. "When you're done, we can watch a movie or something, okay? If it's not too late. I was thinking of ordering Chinese. You can drive with me to pick it up."

This turned his head. He needed a certain number of hours' driving experience before he could test for his license, and he wasn't quite there yet. "Really?"

"Yes." It felt a little like rewarding him for bad behavior, but she didn't want to fight with him.

"Great!" He bounced up, and Stella lifted a warning hand.

"Clean up first," she said.

Tristan nodded. "Got it."

Back in her room, still trying to get her suitcase unpacked, Stella pulled out a T-shirt that wasn't hers. Oh, she'd worn it to sleep in, but it was Matthew's. Sinking onto the bed, she pressed her face into it, breathing in the scent of his cologne that still clung to the fabric. *Breathe. Breathe. Breathe.*

She shouldn't miss him this much so soon. He shouldn't mean so much to her...but he did. And as she breathed in the smell of him, she thought of him touching her. Kissing her.

"Mom?"

Embarrassed, Stella tucked the shirt into her lap as casually as she could. "I'll be ready in a few minutes. Okay? Is the downstairs clean?"

"Yeah."

"Will I think it's clean if I check it?" Tristan grinned sheepishly. Stella laughed. "Go back and finish up."

When he'd gone, she pulled her phone from her pocket, not expecting a notification of a message from Jeff and not surprised there was none. She opened the app and typed in a message to Matthew—the woman's face, a cloud thought bubble, the man's face.

Thinking of you.

But although the D alongside the message turned to an R, indicating that he'd read the message, Matthew didn't answer.

"Ready now?" Tristan asked from the doorway, and Stella put away her phone, determined to give her son the attention he'd claimed he was lacking.

CHAPTER TWENTY-ONE

"Girrrrrl! You look so good!" Jen waggled her eyebrows up and down and made Stella turn in a circle. "Feels like it's been forever since I saw you. How's tricks?"

"Good, good. You look good too. I like your skirt, totally cute." Stella impulsively hugged the other woman, whom she hadn't seen in weeks. Jen had quit to take a job at an art gallery in downtown Harrisburg, and now that they no longer worked together, it had been harder for them to get together.

"So, how is it back in the old place?" Jen helped herself to a bread stick. She gave Stella a small grin. "Miss me?"

"Oh, hell yes. You thought it was quiet before? Now it's like working in a graveyard." Stella shrugged and took a bread stick for herself. "I shouldn't eat this."

"Yes, you should."

Stella laughed. "I've been eating way too much lately, that's all. And not working out."

"Working out, gross." Jen laughed, and gave Stella a knowing look. "He's a good cook?"

"Oh, no. But he likes to eat out—in restaurants!" Stella shook her head before Jen could say anything. "Perv."

"I bet he likes to do the other thing too."

He did indeed. Thinking of it now, Stella flushed. It had been a long week and a half since they'd seen each other, and she was looking forward to heading to Chicago tomorrow.

"So it's going well?"

"Yes. I almost hate to say anything, so I don't jinx it."

"Long-distance stuff can be hard," Jen said.

Stella nodded. "Yeah. But it's easier than it used to be, I think. I mean, we talk every day. Video-chat, stuff like that. Can you imagine what it was like before the internet and cell phones? I had a boyfriend in college. Over the summer I was lucky if I got to talk to him once a week or got a letter in the mail."

"I had a boyfriend like that." Jen waved the bread stick. "Found out he was banging some skank when he sent me the wrong letter."

Stella made a face. "Ouch."

"Not that I think you should worry about that," Jen said hastily.

Stella laughed. "I'm not. I mean, we haven't talked about being exclusive or anything. We didn't get that serious about it."

They hadn't had to. Between Caroline and the girls and the time he spent with Stella, it would've been unlikely for Matthew to be tomcatting around, and Stella hadn't ever told him about her previous flying turnarounds. They'd fallen into their relationship like old friends falling into step along a path leading to… Well, she had no idea what lay around the bend, but she was willing to find out.

"You get all dreamy-eyed when you think about him. Looks kind of serious to me," Jen said.

"I like him."

"And he's your boyyyfriend," Jen teased. "Thought you didn't want one of those pesky things."

Stella chewed the inside of her cheek for a second. "I didn't. But it happened. And it's perfect, really. We see each other when we can, but we can't possibly see each other all the time, so we each get our own space without having to fight for it, you know what I mean? We talk all the time, but we can be doing other things too. He's got his life, I have mine, and so far we don't have to really make a lot of changes to either of them."

"But...don't you miss him when you're not with him? Don't you hate not being able to just see him whenever you want?"

"Sure. I miss him." More than she wanted to admit, actually. "But it is what it is, and what can I do about it right now? He's got young kids, so he's not going to move here, and I won't move anywhere until Tristan's in college, at least, so that's another couple years."

"But you've thought about it!" Jen seemed tickled by this, leaning over the table. "You have, I see it on your face."

"Well, sure, I've thought about it," Stella said. "We haven't talked about it or anything, but, yeah. I think about it."

Jen leaned back in her chair with a smug grin. "I knew you'd want a boyfriend sooner or later."

"Pffft." Stella rolled her eyes, but laughed along with her.

The conversation turned to other things. Jen's relationship, for one, which was also getting serious. The art show opening on Sunday at the gallery. Jen had some pieces in the show, and she wanted Stella to come and bring Matthew.

"I'm going out to Chicago this weekend, damn. How long will they be in the show?"

"Couple weeks. Maybe next weekend," Jen said.

"We only see each other every other weekend," Stella explained.

"Ah. Well…bring him the weekend after next. It'll be the last weekend of the show."

"Oh…well, he'd have to come out here, then."

"That's kind of the point," Jen said. "You mean he's never flown out here any of these times?"

"I get free travel, remember?" Stella said. "Courtesy of Pegasus Airlines. It's the one thing I fought Jeff to keep. So, no, Matthew's never come here. How could I ask him to spend that kind of money for a weekend, when I can just as easily go out there? And Chicago has a lot more going for it than good old Lebanon, PA."

"Amish country," Jen said with a snap. "Or you could bring him up here to Harrisburg. Show him the sights."

They both burst into laughter at that—Harrisburg was the state capital and a city, but a small one with not much to see. Still, it would've been nice to go to the gallery show with Matthew. Show him off to her friends.

"I'll ask him," she said.

Back at work, Stella settled into her chair and pulled up her queue. Today she had only a handful of photos to work on, each requiring some detailed work but not much. By two o'clock she was finished. She thought about clocking out early, but honestly didn't want to lose the hours, and besides, more work could come in if she left, and it would pile up. Since tomorrow was Friday and she wouldn't be in, there was the potential to come in Monday to a shit-ton of zits and wrinkles and saggy chins, something she'd rather not have to face while still coming off the Matthew high.

Instead, she did something she hadn't done in ages. She opened up her instant message window. Back when she'd first started, she'd had her IM open all the time to keep in touch with Jen and the couple other coworkers she'd liked, as well as a few online friends.

She hadn't been thinking of Craig when she clicked open the program, though his user name was still in her contacts list. It was kind of like a time machine when she saw the names, some of them she'd forgotten ever knowing. It took her back to those days in the coffee shop, the hours she'd spent looking for work and chatting online with strangers. The hours she'd spent chatting with him.

And there he was.

Hi!

The message icon bounced with his name until she clicked on the message window.

Hi, she typed. How are you?

She hadn't heard from him since their disastrous date. She'd half expected him to call her, but he hadn't, and she was relieved. And then things had started heating up with Matthew and she'd shut Craig out of her mind almost totally. Until now.

Good. Busy at work. Saw your name pop up and took a chance on saying hello.

Stella typed, Glad you did.

She meant it, she realized. Sure, things with them had

been weird and awkward, and she supposed there would always be some residual emotional tie between them—how could there not be? But though she'd been angry at him for a long time, she wasn't anymore.

He sent her a smiley face without words. Then, a few minutes later as she toyed with fixing a shadow on a picture that the client hadn't ordered just so she could practice and also look as if she was keeping busy, the IM window bounced again. Craig again.

So, two chips were on the playground, and one chip punched the other one in the face.

Stella paused in what she was doing, watching the little pencil icon blink in the box, telling her Craig was still typing. It was a joke. He'd always been able to make her laugh.

I'm NACHO friend! the chip said.

Stella burst into stifled laughter, but he wasn't finished.

That's not fair, the other chip cried. Can't we TACO 'bout it?

Funny, she typed.

Glad we had the chance to chat. Got to go, talk to you another time?

Yes, she answered, but he'd already signed off.

The joke kept making her laugh, so much that she sent it to Matthew. It was his night to have the girls, so she didn't expect an answer until after they went to bed, but when hours passed and she was getting ready for bed herself, he still hadn't replied.

"I hate it when you don't answer me," Stella said aloud to her phone.

Her house was silent. Tristan had gone to his dad's house tonight because he didn't have school the next day and Jeff had promised to take him for his driver's license, finally. She'd thought about asking them to wait for her. It seemed like something they should do together, something she wanted to be a part of, anyway. But they weren't a family anymore, and Tristan had been so excited at the prospect of getting his license that she hadn't been able to bring herself to be so selfish as to deny him that just because she wanted to go see Matthew.

And she would see him, tomorrow afternoon. Heat washed over her, as it always did. In her bed, Stella stretched out, almost too wired for sleep. She didn't have to get up superearly, and it wasn't even late.

The house was too quiet.

She sat up, considering pulling out her book to read a chapter. Or going downstairs to her computer and surfing the internet for a while. Maybe even watching a movie. But all of that stuff smacked of effort, and though she wasn't quite tired enough for sleep, she wasn't awake enough for any of that other stuff.

She was lonely, Stella thought. And bored. With a frown, she burrowed into her pillows and forced her eyes to close. Other nights she'd have been yawning her way through a conversation with Matthew that stretched on too late, wrecking her for the morning. But on the night she could've easily spent an hour chatting with him, he was nowhere to be found.

His girls were in bed by now, tucked into the cute twin beds in the room he hadn't had to tell her Caroline had helped decorate. His apartment was only two bedrooms, so they shared a room while in their mother's house they each had their own bedrooms. The house he'd shared with her. Stella hadn't met Matthew's daughters or his ex-wife yet, but she'd seen plenty of pictures on his phone. She pictured the house they'd shared in the suburbs pretty much the way Caroline looked—sort of bland, everything matching. Decorative balls on the coffee tables. That sort of thing. Matthew's apartment, in comparison, was still so bare of anything but the most basic of furniture and decor that if Stella hadn't known he'd lived there for almost two years, she'd have thought he'd just moved in.

She checked her phone, but there was no message. She'd see him tomorrow, she reminded herself. There'd be time enough for conversation then. If they bothered to talk, she thought with a small smile, already imagining all the ways they'd use their mouths for other things.

And then, just before she drifted into sleep, came the ping.

GNS.

GNM, she replied and got no reply, but this time it didn't bother her as much because a good-night from him was what she'd been waiting for. Now she could sleep. Now she could dream.

But she didn't dream of him.

"Maybe you'd just be happier if I moved out." This is Jeff, mouth twisted. Arms crossed. He looks mad enough to punch a hole in the wall, and she wouldn't be surprised if he did. He has before.

They've been arguing about laundry. Something stupid. He tossed his filthy clothes into the basket without paying attention, ruining the clean clothes Stella hasn't mustered the energy to put away.

"Yes. That's what I want." She imagined herself shouting the words, but they whisper out. Defeated. She looks him in the eye when she answers, though. "Yes. Go. Please."

"Why? You have someone lined up to take my place already?"

Guilt should stab her, but she refuses to let it. Stella lifts her chin. "No. That's not what this is about."

She could ask the same of him, after all. She knows that when he stays out late and comes home smelling of smoke and perfume, it's very likely her husband has been fooling around, if not outright fucking other women. It's been months since they had sex, and the last time was horrific. Jeff turned from her scars and lost his erection, and Stella stumbled to the bathroom to dry-heave with grief.

"Then what?" he demands.

"I don't love you anymore." There. She's said it out loud, what she's been thinking for close to a year. "I don't want to be married to you. I want you to move out. I want a divorce."

The truth of what her husband feels for her is evident in the way he doesn't sag or protest or try to change her mind. Jeff only nods. Once, sharply. They stare at each other across the laundry, and Stella knows she will never be able to forget this moment.

And later, weeks later, when she is tired and sad and the house is quiet because Jeff has taken Tristan for the night, she stumbles down the hall and sits outside the closed bedroom door she's been unable to open. She puts her hand on the knob but does not turn it. And then she dials Craig, whispering fiercely for him to meet her somewhere. Anywhere. Just meet her so they can talk.

The rain started before she got in the car, and it makes her late. It's normal rain, not icy, nothing that needs anything more than normal precaution, but in this state of mind, she can't deal with it. She pulls into the parking lot of the diner where they agreed to meet twenty minutes later than she said she'd be, expecting him not to be there.

But he's there.

And instead of eggs and hash browns, which is what she thought she wanted, even instead of pie and coffee, Stella sits in the front seat of Craig's car and shakes. And shakes. And shakes.

"I lost him," she says over and over again, unable to explain that she doesn't mean Jeff.

She means her boy.

Her Gage. Her firstborn, her mini-me. She lost him, and nothing that has come after could possibly compare to this pain she can't bring herself to share.

There aren't even any tears. Just dry, staring eyes and chattering teeth. Her hair is wet and sticks to her face. The rain falls outside, heavier. Shielding them. Craig could reach for her over the center console, but he doesn't, and Stella's not sure if she's grateful or angry that he doesn't offer her that comfort.

"I don't know what you want me to say," he tells her finally, when she falls silent.

Blinking, Stella can finally focus on him. "You don't have to say anything, Craig. Just kiss me. Please."

But when she leans to kiss him, he recoils. Just enough to wound her. Just enough to sting.

"Look. Stella. You know I like you a lot. And I was really surprised you called me, after... Well."

She knows what he's referring to, what he means. The day they'd walked along the river. "Things have changed. Jeff moved out. I asked him to."

"I don't know what to say," Craig says.

"You don't have to say anything. Just kiss me."

But he doesn't. He can't; she sees it on his face, and the rejection is too much for her. Stella withdraws, hand on the door, ready to flee into the rain. She can't look at him. What had she been thinking? That he would still want her when he could finally have her? That wasn't how things like this worked.

"I feel like I can tell you everything," Stella says as the rain pours outside, battering the roof of the car and turning the windows blank. She can't see through the window; the fog of their breath has made it impossible.

"You can. You know that." Craig's hand pushes her wet hair off her shoulder. His fingers linger, brushing down her arm to take her hand. Linking their fingers. He squeezes gently.

But she can't tell him everything. She wants to, but she can't. Not like this, after months and years of their friendship have become something else even when they didn't want them to. How can she tell him what happened now, after all this time of keeping it a secret?

She finally pushes her way out of the car, slamming the door behind her. She's halfway to her car when he catches her. Turns her. Takes her in his arms. The rain batters them both now, hard and stinging, and she opens her mouth to it because he still will not kiss her.

"But I want to be a choice, not something you fall into," Craig says. "Maybe you can patch up your marriage—"

"No." She shakes her head violently. "No. That's not going to happen."

Now, she thinks. *Tell him now how you lost your son. How you blame your husband, and he won't take any responsibility for any of it. Tell Craig how you wake in the night listening for the sound of Gage's breathing and in those few moments before your brain is fully conscious, sometimes you still hear it.*

"What do you want from me?" he asks her.

"I want you to kiss me," she says one more time. Aching for it. "And take me somewhere. Take off my clothes. Fuck me, Craig. I want you to fuck me until I forget."

How can he say no to her yet one more time? But he steps back, letting her go. Shaking his head. "I don't think that would be right."

"Goddammit, Craig," Stella cries into the night, the rain, in a diner parking lot like something out of an episode of bad reality TV, "any other man wouldn't have to think twice about it!"

"Then find yourself another man!" Craig shouts. "I don't want to just fuck you, Stella! Because what happens after that?"

She has no answer. Can't know the future, wouldn't try to guess it, anyway. This is Craig. Her friend. The man for whom she's yearned for so long she can't remember a time before she wanted him, and now she's offering herself to him.

And he won't take her.

"I know you think all guys are just a hard-on waiting for

pussy," Craig says. "But if I just wanted to get laid, I'd find someone else. I don't want that with you, Stella."

"You don't want me?" She's shaking again. Teeth chattering. She thinks she will fly apart with the force of her shudders.

"I want you. But not like this. Stella...I love you."

No. No, no, she can't have this. Not now. Not like this. Because the moment he says it, Stella thinks of waking up next to him. Going to bed beside him. She thinks of standing with him, holding his hand, of making a brand-new life. It all spreads out in front of her, all the opportunities. New chances. New life.

And how can she do this? How can she put the past away, when the past is the only place where she can be with her son? How can she move forward without leaving him behind?

"I...I have a great emotional attachment to you," Stella says. The words are bitter and clog her throat.

Craig nods, face shuttering. "I get it. Right. Well, listen, Stella, I'm glad I was the one you called when you were desperate for an empty fuck, but maybe next time, just lose my number. Okay?"

She should tell him to wait. Call after him. She ought to explain, but all she does is watch him walk away.

The letter comes a few days later. She's never had a letter from him before, and she doesn't know his handwriting, but the moment she sees the way her name is written on the envelope, she knows it's from Craig. It isn't very long, but it is very brutal. Honest. Unflinching. Stella knows she deserves all of it, every word.

There's not much she can do to make it right except call him to explain, but Craig never answers the phone. She leaves messages he never returns. When she tries to email him, she gets no reply, and the fact that she no longer sees him on her instant message list tells her he's blocked her.

Craig shuts her out of his life, and Stella can't forgive him.

CHAPTER TWENTY-TWO

"You look tired." Matthew kissed her mouth, then each cheek. He took her bag from her so she didn't have to carry it.

"I didn't sleep very well," Stella admitted. "Bad dreams."

She'd tossed and turned, dreaming of the past and mistakes she'd made. Some would never be fixed. Some no longer mattered. Still, reliving those memories had left her with a headache this morning. Puffy eyes. Sore throat. Or maybe she was coming down with something, which would be just her luck, to be sick during her weekend with Matthew.

She was quiet on the drive to his apartment. About halfway there, Matthew reached for her hand and held it the rest of the way. That felt right, Stella thought, looking at him when he focused on the road. Watching him when he wasn't watching her. Her hand in his, no need to force conversation.

"It's nice to just be with you," she said when he had to let go of her hand to pull into his spot.

Matthew shut off the ignition and turned toward her. "Yeah?"

"Yeah." She smiled. He smiled back.

He leaned to kiss her. "Welcome to Chicago, by the way. What do you want to do today?"

They'd spent so much time talking since that it felt impossible they hadn't spent more time in person. "I'd like for you to light a fire and make me breakfast foods. Then I'd like to lie around all day and watch movies and read. Oh. And you can make out with me, in between."

Matthew's eyebrows rose. "Oh, I can, huh?"

"Yep." Stella brushed her mouth against his and shivered at the contact. "Maybe, if you're good, I'll let you touch my tits."

"Awwww, yeah!" Matthew punched the air a little before kissing her again. Harder, with a slip of tongue. "Missed you."

It always warmed her when he said stuff like that. Suddenly, strangely melancholy, she clung to him for a long moment, her cheek pressed to his. Breathing him in. His hand cupped the back of her head, but he didn't say anything, and it was perfect.

"You don't want to go anywhere?" he murmured when they pulled apart. "You sure?"

"I just want to be with you. Hanging out. I'm tired. It was a kind of rough flight, and I'd like to just...be. With you. Is that okay?"

"Sure. Of course." He gave her a curious look. "Are you okay?"

She was, and she wasn't. By the time they got upstairs and she'd dropped her bag in his bedroom, used the bathroom and freshened up, Matthew had turned on the gas fireplace and set up a small tray with a bowl of strawberries and two glasses of what she assumed was champagne. He handed her one as she sat next to him on the rug.

"It's early," she said, but sipped it.

"Never too early for champagne. Besides, we're not going anywhere. Right? We have all day to indulge ourselves." He stretched out his long legs and plucked a strawberry from the bowl, offering it to her mouth.

Stella leaned to take it, mouthing his fingertips. She watched his face, his pupils dilating, the press of his tongue on his lower lip for a second or so. The champagne was smooth and bubbly at the same time, tickling as she swallowed it. The strawberry's sweetness lingered.

Somehow they were kissing, and he'd pulled her next to him. Aligning her body with his, Matthew cradled the back of her head and slipped a knee between her thighs. He was slow and thorough in his attentions to her mouth. Relentless, even. Every time she tried to move or shift, he kept her still with a gentle but steady pressure, until at last she gave up and let him have his way with her.

His tongue slid along hers, and he gently sucked it. Nibbled along her lips. Then her chin, and down her throat to nibble and suck there as his hand slid between her legs to press upward. She'd worn jeans, and the denim was too thick to feel much except the steady press and release of his knuckles, but that teasing sensation built and built until she had to break the kiss with a gasp and the murmur of his name.

"Let go," Matthew whispered into her mouth. "Come for me, Stella."

It was more of a request than a command, and it sent her, trembling, over the edge. Her orgasm rippled through her as relentlessly as his kisses had and left her just as breathless. Stella's eyelids fluttered as her body arched, shuddering, into the pleasure. The aftershocks continued for a minute or so as she pressed her face against his neck and breathed in his scent.

When she'd quieted, Matthew said into her hair, "I love it when you come. It's so easy for you, isn't it?"

"Not always." Stella nestled closer, using the tip of her tongue to taste him briefly. She didn't want to move.

"Just with me?"

He sounded as if he was teasing, but there was an undercurrent of something else there. Jealousy? Insecurity? Stella pressed her teeth against his flesh, not quite biting, then kissed him before looking into his eyes. "Just with you."

It wasn't a lie. She hadn't been with another man since meeting him. Couldn't imagine it, actually. And this thought, that it wasn't that she hadn't met anyone but that she'd stopped looking, made Stella sit up.

"I need a drink of water," she told him, then kissed him to take away anything sudden or strange about how fast she needed to get away from him in that moment. "And some lunch. Can we order something in?"

"Of course." Matthew watched her get up. His hair was endearingly rumpled. He adjusted himself in his jeans, and Stella thought about getting on her knees for him.

Taking him in her mouth. Giving him what he'd so generously given her. She wanted to make him feel good too. But something stopped her, and it wasn't selfishness but self-preservation at the moment. She needed to get herself under control.

Matthew didn't seem put out. He got to his feet and pulled her close for a brushing kiss, then looked into her eyes. Stella cut her gaze from his, unable to face him with what she knew must be her every emotion all over her face.

"Hey," he said quietly, and waited until she looked at him. "You okay?"

She forced a smile. Fake it till you make it. "Yes. Yep, absolutely. Starving, though. Too much champagne, too early. I'm ready to fall asleep too."

He grinned at that, hands sliding down to grip her ass. "I can wake you up."

"Feed me first," she told him, relaxing into his embrace, "and we'll see what happens next."

They decided on sandwiches from the insanely delicious deli around the corner. One problem—their delivery guy was out sick. But Matthew, hunching into a sweatshirt and leather jacket overtop, promised to be back in twenty minutes, and Stella, happy he was willing to go out into the rainy spring chill and even more grateful to have some time alone to compose herself, kissed him at the door.

"Hurry back," she said.

Ten minutes later as she hummed to herself in the kitchen, heating up some water for tea that might chase the chill from her bones, the front door opened.

Two minutes after that, shit hit the fan.

"Who're you?" said the little girl with Matthew's eyes and a mop of tangled dark hair. "Mom! There's a lady in Dad's kitchen."

Oh.

Fuck.

Caroline looked almost exactly the way she did in the wedding picture Matthew had never deleted off his Connex photo album. Ash-blond with dark roots and dark eyes.

Subtle makeup. She wore a sleek pair of capri-length yoga pants and a matching slim-fit hoodie sweatshirt. Perfect soccer mom...except for her expression, which was that of a woman who'd just stepped in an enormous, steaming pile of dog crap.

"Hi," Stella said when Caroline simply stared. "I'm Stella. A friend of Matthew's. You must be Caroline. And you," she said to the little girl, "must be Beatrice. And Louisa."

The older girl standing beside her mother gave Stella a long, careful look. "Where's my dad?"

Stella waited for Caroline to say something. Anything. But the other woman only stared with her lip curling.

"He ran out to get some lunch." *Don't fidget,* Stella told herself, trying desperately to think if she'd buttoned her blouse all the way, if her hair was sex-mussed, if her mouth looked as though she'd been kissing for an hour. If the stink of sex clouded her like perfume.

"He didn't tell me he had...company." Caroline spoke at last. Her gaze swept Stella up and down in that way women have with each other that's supposed to leave scars.

Stella gave Caroline the blandest smile she could. *Not in front of the kids,* she thought. *Don't you dare.* "He didn't mention that you'd be stopping by."

Because, of course, Caroline hadn't called ahead. Because she hadn't been invited. Because Matthew's ex-wife felt so comfortable in his new apartment that she could walk right in, Stella thought with another neutral smile designed not to taunt.

"We were heading to the movies and the girls wanted to see if their father wanted to come along." Caroline's chin lifted, just a little bit.

"Ah." Stella smiled warmly at the girls, who were still

staring at her, though without the suppressed bitterness their mother had. Nope, Louisa and Beatrice were full-on glaring their hostility at her. "I'm sure that would've been fun."

"We only want him," Beatrice said. "Not you."

Stella's smile didn't waver. Behind her, the teakettle hissed, and she turned to take it off the heat and turn off the burner. She pulled open the cupboard and found a mug, then a second she held up toward Caroline, who blanched, then shook her head. With another small smile, Stella put the rejected offer on the counter and found the teabags. She poured hot water into her mug, too aware of the weight of three sets of angry female eyes on her back as she did. Finally she turned around, mug in her hands. She leaned against the counter.

"He should be back soon," she said. "You're welcome to wait."

Caroline's eyes said it all. Of course she was welcome to wait in her ex-husband's kitchen, and she didn't need permission either. Stella sipped the hot tea, risking a burned tongue rather than an embittered one.

"Hey, I bring you food—" Matthew stopped in the doorway, brown paper bags held high. "Caroline?"

The girls ran squealing to him, and he put the food down to hug them. Over the tops of their heads, he caught Stella's gaze. She couldn't read his expression, but she took another sip of tea before putting the mug in the sink.

"Excuse me, I need to check my email." She pulled her phone out of her pocket and held it aloft. Without another word of apology or explanation, because fuck that, she pushed past Matthew and went down the hall into his bedroom.

Ten minutes later, he came in to find her propped on

the bed playing an intense round of *Diamond Dash*. "Just a minute," she said mildly. "Let me beat this level."

"Stella…"

She let the time run out and tucked her phone back into her pocket to give him a look. Matthew ran a hand over his head, then rubbed at his mouth. He came closer and sat on the bed, but didn't touch her.

"The girls…" he began, and trailed off.

Stella raised both eyebrows. When he didn't say anything else, she drew her knees to her chest and linked her fingers together. "You're not going to the movies with them."

He didn't answer.

"Are you?" Stella shook her head, stunned. She was halfway off the bed before Matthew grabbed her wrist.

"No! Stella, sit down. Please."

She did, but gave him a narrow-eyed stare. "She walks into your house like she owns it. Or at the very least, like she lives here. And she had no idea I was here. Or that there was even a…me. Which, okay, fine, you don't want to rub it in her face or something, but, Jesus, Matthew. You might want to fucking give her a clue that you're dating. Or that you're not available on the weekends when I'm here. Something. She walked into that kitchen and looked like I'd stabbed her in the throat."

Stella paused, frowning, then said softer, "And your kids, Matthew. That's not the way I would've liked to be introduced to them either."

"I'm sorry." He didn't sound sorry. Or chastened. He sounded defensive, which made Stella sigh.

"You haven't told her you're dating?"

He made a low noise. "I'm not dating."

"No. I guess you're not. You're just fucking me every

few weeks." She yanked her wrist from his grasp, but his arms were longer, and he snagged her shirtsleeve again as she moved away. He didn't try to hold her, not when she pulled again, but it did stop her.

"That's not what I meant, and you know it."

"Actually," Stella said, "I don't know it."

They stared at each other, awkward silence rising between them.

"I'm not sure what you want from me," he said finally.

There it was, the inevitable. Stella sighed and shook her head. "You know what I want from you, Matthew? Just don't be a dick to me. Really, that's all I ask. Don't be a dick."

He blinked and recoiled slightly but didn't say anything.

Stella's chin lifted. Jaw tight. Keeping her voice as neutral as she could, she said, "Look. I don't have any grand notions about what this is, okay? We're both grown-ups. We get along. We like fucking. There doesn't have to be... This doesn't have to mean..."

Her voice cracked and she cut herself off before she could embarrass herself with breaking down. This had been a cluster fuck of a day already. She didn't need it to spiral into anything else.

Matthew's phone chimed. He put his hand automatically to his pocket, but then stopped himself. It chimed again.

"Aren't you going to answer it?"

"It's Caroline."

Stella crossed her arms and cocked a hip, giving him a look. Matthew looked back. The phone chimed again with another text.

"I'm sorry," Matthew said. "Stella, I feel like I say I'm sorry to you an awful lot."

Her stance softened. "Do you think I'm demanding?"

"No," he said, but with enough of a hesitation that she thought he might not be telling the whole truth.

The first step toward him was the hardest, but she made herself take it. Then another, and a third until she sat on the bed next to him. They were close enough that she could shift a bit and touch him, but she didn't.

"I like you, Matthew."

"I like you too."

There was something important she needed to say, if she could find the words to express it. If she wanted to try. It would be easier to walk out the door now instead. Leave him behind.

"I don't think there's a point in playing games," Stella said. "You know, those dating games, where I play coy and you have to chase me. Or where I expect you to guess what I'm thinking or feeling, or what I want from you. Whatever this is, I like it, and I'd like to keep doing it."

"Me too," Matthew said.

She looked at him. "What is this, Matthew?"

"I don't know. What do you think it is?"

"Good sex." She nudged him with her shoulder. "Good food. Fun. We have great conversations. You make me laugh. I like the way we fit together."

Matthew chuckled softly. "I like that too."

"Look. We don't have to put a name on this. I'm okay with that. But I'm not okay with being a dirty secret. It's early to be part of your life with your kids, and I surely don't expect you to have me over for the holidays—"

"What if I wanted to?"

She let her knee press his for a second or two. "We could talk about it. If you really wanted that."

"You're not a dirty secret, Stella. I just didn't know how to tell her."

"And she clearly has no boundaries," Stella said. "You might want to think about that."

Matthew frowned.

"I should never have to guess how you feel about me, or how important I am to you, Matthew. Not as a lover or fuck buddy or a friend or anything else. And I don't need to settle for not being important."

His scowl eased into something softer. "I'm not that great with expressing myself. It's one of the reasons why she left me."

Caroline might've divorced him, but she'd far from left him, Stella thought but didn't point out. She put her other hand on his other arm, gripping both his biceps lightly. She went on her tiptoes to kiss him, offering her mouth but letting him close the gap. He did, thank God, the kiss brief and sweet.

"You never have to tell me how you feel about me, so long as you never make me guess." She kissed him again, murmuring against his lips.

His arms went around her, pulling her close. The kiss got deeper. His hand curved around the back of her neck, fingers tangling in her hair. They kissed harder while he walked her back toward the bed and laid her down, then covered her with his body.

But this time, Stella rolled over to straddle him. Breathing hard, she ran her hands up his body over his shirt. Then under it, feeling his warm skin. She let her nails scrape him lightly and smiled when he twitched.

Bending, she kissed him while she worked open his buttons. She nibbled his jaw, then his throat. His collarbones.

Opening his shirt, she moved her mouth down his chest, taking her time to run her tongue around his nipple, which tightened nicely under her attentions.

He didn't say anything, but she loved the rise and fall of his chest with his breathing. The low rasp in the back of his throat when she nipped at his hipbone. When she moved lower to rub his thickening cock through the denim, she loved watching the way his mouth twisted and his eyes closed.

Stella unzipped his jeans and tugged them open, then found his erection through the soft fabric of his briefs. She stroked him, watching his face. His mouth parted, his tongue swiping lightly along his lower lip before he bit it. His cock edged its way from his waistband, and she let her fingertips stroke him, just a little, loving how his hips bucked.

She moved lower, letting her tongue flicker along the exposed flesh. "Shhh," she said against him when he started to talk.

Slowly, she worked his jeans and briefs down his thighs, then off. She took a few seconds to admire him—that lovely cock, so hard. She stroked him, but when he arched into her touch, she stopped and bit her lip on a smile at his muttered groan of frustration. This was going to be…fun.

So the morning had started off all wrong, but this felt right. Taking her time, Stella moved her mouth over Matthew's thighs, nuzzling inside each one and letting her breath caress his balls without actually touching him there. Her hand moved slowly, stroking, every so often palming the head of his cock while she licked and nibbled at the soft skin of his inner thigh. When she let her fingernails brush upward along the skin between his balls and inner thigh,

Matthew twitched and sighed, and Stella paused. His cock throbbed in her fist. He pushed upward, but she didn't move.

When he'd stilled, she stroked again. Licked and kissed, teasing, until finally she let her tongue trace a delicate pattern on his balls and around the base of his cock. His groan was so satisfying that she eased off again, tickling him with her breath as her fingers gripped him but didn't move along his shaft. Over and over, she used her mouth and hands to edge him close to coming. She lost herself in the pleasure of giving him pleasure, until finally Matthew breathed a single word.

"Please…"

Stella ceased her teasing. Taking him in her mouth, she kept up the pace and pressure until he came with a shout. Then she eased him down and moved up his body to tuck herself against him. She wasn't usually much of a snuggler, but she pressed her face into the curve of his neck and shoulder, her hand flat on his belly, feeling the residual twitch of his muscles.

His phone, which had slid from his jeans pocket when she pulled them down, buzzed from its place on the bed between them. Matthew let out a soft groan but didn't reach for it. Stella did, holding it out to him.

"You should answer it."

He cracked open an eye to look at her and, without saying a word, checked the text. Whatever it was made him laugh, though without much humor. He sighed and sat, rubbing between his eyes. Then he turned the phone to show her the message.

ANSWER YOUR PHONE. I DON'T CARE IF YOU HAVE A GIRLFRIEND, JUST ANSWER ME.

Stella sat up to prop herself against the headboard, pulling her knees to her chest, then resting her chin on them. She shrugged, not offering an opinion. Matthew frowned and turned away to make his call.

"Hey. Yes. Sorry, I was busy. Yes, I know. I'll pick them up. Yes. I got it. I sent it. I'm sorry, you're right, I should've told you. That's not... You know what? Yes. That would be great if you could start doing that. Fine," he said at last in a tight voice. "No, but if that's how you want to take it, that's your business. Yes...I'll take care of it."

He held the phone out from his ear to look at it with an expression of mingled disgust and amusement, then looked at Stella.

"She hung up on me."

Stella chewed the inside of her cheek, still not speaking or moving. Matthew slid closer to her to put his chin on her shoulder, nudging her with it until she looked down at him. He grinned up at her, sprawling naked without seeming to care or be embarrassed. She touched his eyebrows, smoothing them with a fingertip.

"She said she's going to call before she comes over from now on."

Stella smiled, silent.

"She's pissed," Matthew added.

"I can't blame her," Stella said. "It would've been nice for both of us not to meet unexpectedly. I mean, let's face it, any woman you brought around would probably have to go Godzilla versus Mothra with her."

He laughed. "No..."

Stella's eyebrows rose. "Um, yeah."

He looked at the phone in his hand, swiping to bring up

the text messages. He held it up to show her again. "She said she doesn't care if I have a girlfriend."

"Oh, she cares. She cares a lot." Stella smiled again. "It's a good thing you don't have one, huh?"

Matthew kissed her. "Yes, I do."

"Do you?" she asked against his mouth.

Matthew took her face in his hands to look into her eyes. "Yeah. I think so. Do I?"

"Do you want one?"

"Will you go with me? Circle one," he said. "Yes, no, maybe."

"Yes," Stella said. "Yes, yes, yes."

CHAPTER TWENTY-THREE

Wrapped in a blanket, her feet on Matthew's lap, Stella dozed to the sound of the movie on the television. Matthew had plied her with a few glasses of wine while he drank his whiskey, and the heat from the fireplace, the earlier great sex and the general stress of the morning had wiped her out. When her phone pinged from her purse on the chair all the way across the room, she blinked but snuggled deeper into the warmth and ignored it. Except, of course, that her phone wouldn't stop chiming until she answered it.

"I'll get it for you," Matthew said when she sighed and grumbled. And he did too, gently setting her feet aside and bringing her the entire bag.

Stella thumbed her phone to bring up the text from Tristan. It was a picture of him, grinning ear-to-ear, standing next to a car she didn't recognize. Jeff stood next to him, hand on Tristan's shoulder. He had the same grin. No text, just a picture.

Furrowing her brow, she studied the picture, then replied, What?

Dad bought me a car.

Fuck.

"Oh, he did not," Stella said aloud. "What the hell?"

Matthew gave her a curious look. She showed him the photo. He looked confused.

"My ex-husband bought our sixteen-year-old son a Mustang. He just barely got his license, but Jeff bought him a thirty-thousand-dollar car. What the hell?" Stella repeated.

"I wish my dad would've bought me a car when I turned sixteen."

Stella got off the couch. She needed to move. Shift, pace. Run. Her heartbeat had slowly started thumping faster and faster since the text came through, and she pressed a hand to her chest in a useless attempt at slowing it.

Brake lights. Red, flashing. The wipers cut the color, back and forth, and Stella wants to tell Jeff to slow down, but instead she laughs because it's all so funny. The boys from the backseat start to argue and bicker, and she twists in her seat to tell them to stop, but somehow that's funny too. She's drunk. How long has it been since she's been drunk, or even more than tipsy? Long years, many years, since before Gage was born, for sure. Long time.

"Stop it," she says, or tries to say, but giggles break the words and she can't explain why everything is so light and bright and merry. "It's Christmas."

Tristan lets out a wail and bats at his brother, demanding to hold the toy Gage picked from the pile Brad and Janet had placed under the tree. Each kid picked one. Tristan got a truck, but Gage got a cool action figure, and Tristan wants it. He kicks at the back of Stella's seat and grabs with pudgy fists for the plastic guy, but Gage holds it out of his reach.

"Stop," Stella repeats, but Tristan doesn't.

She unbuckles her belt to turn around and reach into the backseat, both to pick up the truck Tristan threw to the floor and also to get her hands between them to separate them. She's halfway into the backseat when Jeff lets out a hoarse shout.

When the horn blares.

When the red brake lights stop flashing and turn a solid, steady red in front of them.

"Hey, babe, you okay?" Matthew's hand on her shoulder steadied her, but not enough.

Stella shook her head. "Jeff and I never talked about getting him a car. And a Mustang. He's sixteen. He's reckless. He's not in control, he barely has his license…."

Matthew pulled her close, saying nothing. Just holding her. It wasn't enough of a comfort, but she let him do it even though she wanted to keep pacing.

His hand stroked her hair. "He'll be fine."

Stella tried to relax against him, but it didn't work. "I need to call Jeff."

"No," Matthew said. "Not if you're going to lay into him."

Angrily, she pulled away from him. "What?"

"You want to call him up and bitch him out? Look, I don't know your ex, but how well do you think that's going to go over? What do you think he's going to do, sell the car? And your kid… He's over-the-moon about it. Are you going to take it away from him? What do you think he'll think about that?"

Blinking rapidly to force away the tears, Stella took a step back, jerking her arm free of his grip when he tried to hold her. "I hardly think I need to take relationship advice from you."

"You sure don't mind handing it out, though, do you?"

Stung, she crossed her arms over her chest but said nothing. Whatever words she had wouldn't be kind. That he had a point only made her angrier.

Matthew, also silent, sat back on the couch and picked up the remote to switch through the channels, and after a few seconds, Stella joined him. But not with her feet on his lap, not snuggling. She made a place for herself as far from him as she could get while still being on the couch. She sent a text to Jeff.

We never talked about this.

A moment later, I got a bonus.

He's too young for a car. And a Mustang?

No answer, which only infuriated her more. She did not, however, text her son. It wasn't his fault his father overcompensated by spending too much money, and though the thought of him racing his way through dark streets sent her heart pounding into her throat again, she couldn't bring herself to take away what she knew had to be his exhilaration.

Matthew got up from the couch and went to the bar to pour himself a fresh drink. "You want something?"

"No, thanks." Stella didn't look up.

Minutes passed, neither of them speaking. Matthew ran through all the channels. Then again. Stella ignored him and the TV, instead scrolling through her phone and catching up on all her social media. When she opened her Connex app and saw the video from Tristan halfway down the page, she let out a muttered curse.

It was tame, as far as videos went. Clearly shot from his cell, it was of him behind the wheel of the Mustang, then a cut to the road stretching out in front of him and the music playing loud. Laughter. A blurred shot of Steven in the seat next to him.

Oh, hell no.

Stella typed in the website for Pegasus Airlines, searching for flights. There was a flight to Harrisburg leaving in a few hours. She could be home by 11:00 p.m. She typed in her customer number and booked the flight. Then she stood.

"I have to get home."

Matthew looked up, ice clinking in his glass. He swallowed the rest of the liquid and set the glass on the coffee table, then sat back against the couch. "Now?"

"Flight leaves in a couple hours, so pretty shortly. Yeah." Stella lifted her chin to stare at him.

He stared back. Then, very carefully, he looked back at the TV. "Okay."

"I'll go get ready. Don't worry," Stella added in an overly sweet voice. "I'll take a cab."

Fighting tears, she took her stuff from the bathroom and packed her suitcase. With shaking hands, she splashed her face with water, refusing to think about Tristan driving that Mustang too fast. Or worse yet, inattentively, shooting a video as he drove.

Refusing to imagine the crunch of metal and glass, the blare of a horn. The smell of exhaust and gas and blood. The taste of tears.

She had time to hang out here, but with things the way they were with Matthew, she didn't want to. Pulling her bag behind her, thumbing the number of the cab company into her phone, she placed the call as she went into the living room. The cab would be there in fifteen minutes.

"Shit," Matthew said, sitting up straight. "You're really going?"

Stella frowned. "Um, yeah? I told you I was. Look, my son is out joyriding in his new car, no evidence of any parental supervision, and posting videos of it on Connex. I'm freaked out. And really, I just need to get home. Judge me if you want, Matthew, but this is my son."

He stood. He'd made himself another drink, she saw, this one half-finished. He swayed a little when he got up, which made her take a step back.

"Not judging you. Wish you didn't have to go. I didn't really think…"

"I said I was," she repeated stiffly. "Maybe it's been your common experience that women like to play games and whatever, but I told you. That's not me."

"No. I can see that. At least let me take you to the airport."

She laughed without humor. "Wow. No. How many drinks have you had?"

"I'll come in the cab with you." He moved toward her, meaning to, what, kiss her? Embrace her?

Stella shook her head, stepping back. "You don't have to do that. I think it's best if I go by myself."

"Stella."

She could not bring herself to look at him. If she did, she was going to burst into ugly sobs, and she would not give him that. As many orgasms as he wanted, but no more of her tears.

"I want to go with you to the airport. I don't want you to leave like this." Matthew sighed and reached to tug at her sleeve, though he didn't try to pull her closer. "Can't I convince you to stay until tomorrow?"

He thought she was being irrational, and the worst part of it was, Stella *knew* she was being irrational. There was nothing she could do to stop it. "Come with me."

"What?"

"Come with me," she said. "I'll pay for your ticket, if that's the issue, but you could come with me and…I could…" She shook her head. She could what? Use his support? Need him to be there for her?

"I can't come with you, Stella, not last-minute like this."

Of course he couldn't, yet the way he cut his gaze from hers made it seem like an excuse. Stella blinked back the sting of tears and took a few deep breaths to try to get herself under control.

"I'll feel better if I can get home. See him. I just…"

"You're not going to stop him from driving," Matthew told her. "Not for the rest of his life."

"He's sixteen!" she cried. "Do you know the statistics about teenage drivers? Boys in particular? Boys in sports cars?"

"Not specifically. No. But I know that no matter what you do, you're never going to stop worrying about him. And…honestly, no matter how much you worry, it's not going to change anything. You can't stop an accident from happening by worrying about it ahead of time. All you'll do is make yourself sick with it."

She swallowed bitterness. "Then I'll be sick with it. I'm going home to my son. I have to. I'm not asking you for your advice. I'm sorry to cut the visit short, but I need to get home. I need to make sure he's okay. I know it's crazy. I know it—"

"I never said it was crazy," Matthew said quietly. "Will you please let me come with you to the airport?"

Stiffly, she nodded. She let him carry her bag for her too. In the cab, they sat without speaking. He surprised her by getting out of the cab, paying the driver and sending him on his way.

"You don't have to—"

"I can get another one," he told her.

At the Pegasus desk, Stella confirmed her reservation and got her ticket. Matthew followed her to security, where she turned toward him. Without a ticket, he wouldn't be able to get through.

"Well," she said, "goodbye."

He hesitated. It would've been the perfect moment for her to tip her face toward his for a kiss. At least a hug. But Stella didn't move toward him, nor he toward her.

"Call me when you get home," Matthew said. "So I know you made it okay."

"Okay."

She waited, hating this hesitation. When he made no move toward her, Stella shifted her shoulder bag and gave him a stiff nod. Then she turned around and went through the security checkpoint. By the time she had the chance to see if he was still watching her, Matthew had gone.

The flight was uneventful, made longer because she

couldn't sleep and had forgotten her book on Matthew's nightstand. In Harrisburg, her eyes grainy, she had a panicked moment when she thought she'd forgotten her car keys. That's when she broke into tears. Brief but harsh, they stung her throat and clogged her nose before she got herself under control.

She drove to Jeff's house, her anxiety mounting. There was no Mustang in the driveway, and her guts twisted. Her hands shook when she got out of her car and rang the front doorbell. If something had happened, she told herself, Jeff would've called her. He would have.

Cynthia answered the door in her pajamas, cracking it open only far enough to peek out before seeing it was Stella and opening it the whole way. "Oh. Hi? What...?"

"I came home early."

"Jeff took Tristan to the movies. Um, in the new car. Do you want to come in?" Cynthia stepped aside.

Stella had been inside her ex-husband's new house a handful of times. She preferred to avoid it. There was no non-awkward way to be a guest there. In the foyer, she took note of the enormous portrait of Jeff, Cynthia and Tristan that hung against the far wall.

"That's new," she said.

Cynthia looked surprised. "Oh. Yeah. I thought Jeff might've told you about it."

"He doesn't seem to tell me very much about anything," Stella said.

Cynthia had the good grace to look embarrassed. "Can I get you a drink or something?"

"When will they be home, do you know? I just..." Stella let out a long, shuddering breath. "I needed to make sure he was okay. I just needed to be sure he was all right."

Cynthia nodded. "Come into the kitchen. They'll be home soon. Let me get you some water. Or something."

She was acting crazy, Stella realized. She shook her head, the heat of embarrassment making her cringe. "No, I should head home."

"Stella…" Cynthia said hesitantly. "You can wait for him, if you want."

It was already close to midnight. Stella shook her head again, wanting to hate Cynthia for seeming so understanding. Wanting to hate her for a lot of things, and as always, finding herself unable to.

"Just have him call me when he gets in, okay? I want to congratulate him."

Cynthia nodded. "Of course. You sure you don't want to stay?"

"No. I can't, really. I'm tired."

With that excuse, Stella escaped. At home, she forced herself not to give in to the swell of emotions threatening to bring her to her knees. She couldn't afford it. Wouldn't allow it.

In the hallway, she peeked into Tristan's room. No reason for it, just habit. The other room, the one with the never-opened door, beckoned, but she ignored that impulse. In her bed, Stella pressed her face against the pillows and checked the clock every few minutes as the time ticked by and no call came in from Tristan.

Finally it buzzed in her hand. "Tristan. Hi."

"Mom! Did you see the picture of the sweet car Dad got me?" Tristan paused, then sounded puzzled. "How come you came home early?"

"Oh…I wanted to. That's all." She closed her eyes against

a fresh spate of tears, ones of relief this time, and of a love so fierce it threatened to consume her.

They chatted for only a few more minutes, with Stella mostly listening while Tristan rhapsodized about the car. By the time he finished, the sick feeling in her gut hadn't abated by much, but she'd managed to get it under control. After confirming what time he'd be home tomorrow, Tristan said goodbye.

Then, "I'll give you a ride, Mom. We can go out to dinner. My treat."

A sudden image of him in a pair of short overalls and saddle shoes, a binky in his mouth and a stuffed bear in his hands, assaulted her. Those days were over. He was growing up.

And she had to let him.

Sleep, surprisingly, came easy after they disconnected, and with nothing to do the next day, Stella didn't bother to set her alarm. The buzzing of the phone, which wouldn't ring while settled in the dock, jerked her from sleep, and she grabbed at it with blind hands. Frantic. She couldn't remember what she'd been dreaming, but her mind at once had turned to bad news.

"What is it? What happened?"

"You said you'd call me when you got home." The slurred voice was barely recognizable as Matthew's.

Stella rubbed at her eyes, checking the clock. *Shit.* It felt as if she'd been sleeping forever.

"Sorry," she said.

"I was worried, Stella."

"I'm sorry," she said, more sincerely this time. She knew what it was like to worry.

When he didn't answer, she listened hard. There was

noise in the background, not the TV or music playing, but the clink of glasses and murmur of voices. It was just past two in the morning. She lay back on her pillows.

"Where are you?" she asked.

"I'm at the bar where we met."

Stella frowned. "At the airport?"

"Yes."

"What are you doing there?" The slur in his voice curled her lip a little.

"Drinking."

And what else was he doing? What had he been doing the night they'd met? Drinking and picking up women, maybe. Or one woman. All it would take was one.

"At the airport," Stella said.

"Yeah. Yes. This place, here. It's like Cheers. Everybody knows my name."

She frowned. "Nice."

"It is nice," he said. "I was waiting for you to call me."

"Why are you at the airport?" she asked again, confused. He could drink at home, or the neighborhood bar. But... "How'd you get through security without a ticket?"

"I got a ticket."

Stella sat up in bed. "Why? Where are you going?"

"I was gonna come to Harrisburg." It came out slushy. *Harrishburg.*

A different sort of heat spiraled through her. Not embarrassment. Not arousal. Sort of fear, as if something terrible was about to happen. Or something miraculous.

"You were going to randomly fly to Harrisburg?"

"To see you," Matthew said. "I wanted to make sure you were okay."

"So why aren't you here?"

"I couldn't make the flight."

She thought about this, him wanting her so much he'd fly to her without even letting her know. Him wanting her that much. She didn't want her pulse to quicken and heat to gather in her lower belly, but when she thought of the taste of him, the throb of his cock on her tongue, she slid a hand between her legs for a moment.

"And," Matthew added, "I don't know where you live."

A burst of strangled laughter escaped her; she clamped her jaw tight to keep the hilarity inside. "That would make it hard, for sure."

"You know what else is hard?"

Stella wasn't falling for that one. "You're drunk. Go home."

"Wish you were here with me."

She couldn't stop herself from thrilling to that simple statement, no matter how irritated she'd been with him earlier. No matter how much the drink was influencing him...or not. She sighed.

"No, no, I'm good," Matthew said, but not to her. "I'm going home now. Home alone, to my lonely bed. All alone."

"Come to me next weekend," Stella said impulsively. "I'll tell you where I live and everything."

Matthew muttered something into the phone, but she couldn't tell what he'd said or if he meant it for someone else. Then, louder, he added, "I'll talk to you tomorrow. 'Kay?"

"Yes. Okay. You call me when you get home," she told him. "I want to make sure you got in all right."

"I'll tell you I will. But maybe I won't."

She sighed. "Then call me tomorrow."

"I'll call you tomorrow. Tomorrow. Okay?"

"Matthew," Stella said, not sure what she meant to say, but he'd already disconnected.

CHAPTER TWENTY-FOUR

"So, you made it through your first fight." Jen dug a chip into the queso sauce.

Stella sipped her iced tea. The waitress had tried valiantly to tempt her with an enormous margarita, but Stella's appetite for liquor had waned considerably without Matthew there to encourage it. She shrugged.

"I'm not sure I'd call it a fight, exactly. I was upset, hormonal. Things hadn't gone well. Trouble with his ex."

Jen made a face. "Ugh."

Ugh was exactly the right word to use, as far as Stella was concerned. "Everything got awkward, that's all. And now I haven't heard from him for the whole week. Not a fucking word. Not a text, a call, a Kik, nothing. I sent him a message the next morning, checking to see if he was okay. He didn't answer."

"I hate that!"

"Me too. And I know he read the message, but he didn't reply. I thought about sending another one, but..." Stella shrugged again.

"Hmm." Jen bit into a cheesy-soaked chip. "That sucks."

It did suck. The entire week, Stella had been left with a sick feeling in her stomach. "He's ignoring me."

"Fuck that noise," Jen agreed.

Stella took her own chip, though in truth she wasn't hungry and hadn't been all week. "How do you go from 'miss you, wish you were with me' to just flat-out blowing someone off?"

"'Cause men are dicks," Jen said cheerfully.

"He's the one who brought up me being his girlfriend. He's the one who invited me to come to visit him. He's the one who said he'd been waiting for me to come back to that bar. I mean, he was probably full of shit. Maybe he says that to all the women he picks up there...."

But that didn't feel right, and Stella knew it. Matthew had told her there hadn't been anyone since his marriage, and she believed him. She didn't think he was out there looking to get laid now. Maybe she was naive, but she'd done more than her share of flying. She knew what it felt like, how it made a person act. Matthew had never been like that with her.

"I'm sorry." Jen frowned in sympathy.

"Me too. I thought... I don't know what I thought."

"You could try him again?"

Stella's mouth thinned. "I don't need to chase him."

"No. Of course not. But you could just try him again. Maybe he thinks you're mad at him."

"And what if he blows me off again? What if he says he's been busy?"

"Maybe he has been busy," Jen said. "Not that it's an excuse, but you know, dudes are stupid."

"I hate games," Stella said flatly. "I sent him a message. He didn't answer it. I'm not some desperate, cling-ing, crazy bitch."

"But you really like him. Don't you?"

Stella sighed, deflating. "Yeah. I'm crazy about him, actually."

"So, message him. See if he'll come visit you. Just talk to him," Jen urged. "The very worst that can happen is he'll blow you off again, and honestly, if he already is, at least you know you tried. That doesn't make *you* the asshole."

It made sense, though Stella didn't want to admit it. Right there at the table, she pulled out her phone and opened Kik. She sent off a brief, Hey, how are you? Haven't heard from you, hope all is well. Then she held up the phone to show Jen the screen and tucked it back into her bag.

Matthew didn't answer her.

Not through dinner. Not through the movie. And not through the ride home.

Her phone did ping with a text though, just as she was walking in the door. Craig, as it turned out. His timing was impeccable.

Stella waited to answer him. Giving Matthew the chance to answer her. Giving herself time to shower and get ready for bed. To think about what she should say, or if she wanted to say anything at all.

At last, when it had grown almost too late to reply for the sake of politeness, she typed in a quick response to Craig. Hey! Everything's great here, hope all is good in your world.

Just checking in. Haven't seen you online lately.

It's nice to hear from you, Stella wrote, and meant it. There was nothing then, for just long enough that she

was sure he wasn't going to answer. Then a smiley face
came through. Three words that made her smile.

Good night, Stella.

But though she checked for a message from Matthew,
there was none.

CHAPTER TWENTY-FIVE

Ten days. That was how long it took him to answer her, and by that time Stella had been on the verge of erasing all his contact information about a dozen times. Each time her finger had hovered over the delete button, indecisive, and she'd changed her mind.

When he messaged her, she thought, she would tell him to fuck off.

When he finally replied, she would be distant.

When he at last decided to answer her, she thought, she would act as if nothing at all had ever gone wrong.

Please, she bargained with the universe. *Please, just let him call.*

Her phone beeped from her bag while she was paying bills, so faint that at first she was convinced she'd imagined it. It beeped again a minute or so later, and she pulled out her phone to see the small red 1 of a notification. She closed her eyes, letting out a long, long sigh of relief.

Can I call you?

Stella?

Of course, she typed.

The phone rang a minute later, and she answered without letting it ring more than a couple times. No games. "Hi."

"Hi, Stella. It's Matthew." He said nothing for such a long time she was certain he meant to say nothing at all. Then, "How've you been?"

"Fine. You?" She hated this stilted, awkward, bland and neutral conversation. They'd never spoken to each other this way even in the beginning. The words tasted bad.

"Okay. Busy."

"Uh-huh."

Silence.

"Well," Stella said after another half minute of listening to him breathe, "I guess I'll let you go."

Damn the tears making her voice shake. She swallowed against the tightness in her throat, but couldn't stop herself from drawing in a shaky breath. She waited for him to say something. Anything.

Please, she thought. *Say something.*

And then in the last three seconds before her finger stabbed the screen to disconnect, Matthew said, "Wait."

"Yes, Matthew."

"Can't we taco 'bout it?" Matthew asked.

Stella leaned her elbow on the kitchen table where she'd been sitting with her laptop, her hand pressed over her eyes. "I'm not sure we have anything to talk about, really."

"I don't know why you had to run out without talking to me about what was going on. That's all."

She sighed. "It was for a lot of reasons. I don't know what to tell you. There was all that stuff with Caroline. And then my kid... I know it might be hard for you to understand, Matthew, how an accident can change the rest of your life. What happened colored everything that came after it, and probably always will. I don't like it, but I'm not going to apologize for it."

He was silent for another long moment. "Don't assume I don't understand you. I'm not asking you to apologize. But I didn't know what was going on. One minute you were all into me. Then you were pissed off and not talking to me."

"I wasn't... Being upset isn't exactly the same as being pissed off," she said. "And you're the one who wasn't talking to me. Ten days, as a matter of fact. That's how long it's been."

He was quiet for a moment. "I wasn't sure you wanted to hear from me."

"I messaged you, didn't I? I thought maybe we'd talk about you flying out here to visit me." She heard only silence for a long moment. "Look," she said. "Can we video-chat? I need to see your face."

A minute later, they'd connected. Maybe it had been a mistake, she thought at once, seeing his smile. That face. She was helpless against the sight of him. Without thinking, she touched her laptop screen, caressing the line of his jaw.

"I missed you," Stella blurted.

"I missed you too."

It was the right thing for him to say.

There's a difference between treading water and swimming. In one you're keeping yourself from drowning. In the other, you're making it to shore.

Two steps backward, one step forward. That's what their relationship had become, and Stella couldn't say she minded it. Having a certain wariness suited her, she supposed, and though they'd started talking almost every day again, if one passed without hearing from him, it was easier not to fret. Easier not to miss him.

"The shine is off the penny," she told him, phone cradled against her shoulder as she washed dishes one night after dinner.

Tristan had gone on a date. Dinner and a movie. Stella knew the girl, a pretty blonde who liked video games and had been in Tristan's class since kindergarten. The thought of the two of them in the Mustang hadn't given her an easy time, but she'd tried to, as Tristan put it, "breathe through it, Mom."

"C'mon. Don't say that."

She laughed as she dried her hands. "I'm going to watch a movie. Want to watch one with me?"

"Sure. Got my whiskey. You gonna have some?"

She looked automatically at the clock, but it was just past seven. Not too early for a drink, especially if he was at home. But she didn't have any whiskey, anyway.

"Nah. What are you in the mood to watch?"

They settled on a horror flick that had good reviews, both of them logging in to their Interflix accounts and starting at the same time, also while logged in to video chat. With her laptop propped on the coffee table next to her as she stretched on the couch, it wasn't anything like having him there with her, but it was better than nothing.

"Date night," Matthew said midway through the movie as he lifted his glass toward her. "Thank God for technology."

Stella laughed. "Right?"

"Wish you were here."

She hesitated. It wasn't that she was glad they weren't together, or that she didn't want to be with him. But it had been a long week, and if she'd known Tristan was out on a date while she was seven hundred miles away and unable to get to him in less than a few hours, she'd have been anxious. Breathing through it or not.

It had only been a week since she and Matthew had started talking again. They'd gone longer than that between visits without any tension.

The movie was ending, so she turned the computer to face her.

"You could come here," she told him.

Matthew pointed the remote and pushed a button, then leaned forward to look into the camera on his computer. "I thought you liked coming here."

"And it's free for me. I know. Or at least cheaper." Stella frowned. She'd never asked Matthew about his finances, though judging by the car he drove and the apartment he lived in, she'd assumed he was doing fine. Divorce could be expensive, though.

"It's not that." On-screen, he was fidgeting, running a hand over his head. He looked uncomfortable, but then he said, "I could come to you. Sure. Yeah. Next weekend?"

She sat up. "Yes. Matthew, I'd love that."

"Let me see what's going on and let you know, okay?"

Already excited, thinking of having him here in her house, Stella grinned. "It's not as exciting as Chicago, but I'd love to see you again."

Matthew smiled at her. "In the meantime..."

"Hmmm?" It took her a few seconds, but then when he

tipped the computer screen downward to show his hand on his crotch, she laughed. "Ohhhh. Uh-huh."

Matthew leaned close, filling the screen with his mouth. Oh, those lips. "I've reallllly missed you."

She had missed him too. Stella checked the clock. Tristan wasn't due home for another few hours. He hadn't even texted her to let her know they'd gotten out of the movie yet. She leaned close to the camera too.

"How much?" she whispered.

He showed her how much, and her breath caught. So fucking beautiful, that was Matthew's cock in his fist. When he pumped it slowly for her, Stella had to squeeze her thighs together. She took the laptop upstairs and locked her door, watching him stroke himself.

"You too," he said. "I want to watch you."

"I'm getting there." She stripped slowly, putting on a show for him. It should've felt ridiculous, but the gleam in his eyes and the way he licked his lips while watching her, the sound of his stuttered moan when she slipped her fingers inside her and showed him how wet he was making her... All of that made this anything but silly.

"You are so sexy," Matthew said.

If she hadn't before, his clear appreciation of her would've made her feel it. Stella lay back, fingers moving on her clit, letting the pleasure overtake her. It was hard not to be distracted by the sight of him doing the same. It had been long enough that she reached the edge within minutes, but she eased off to wait for him.

"Feels...so...good," he said on a groan. "Are you gonna come with me?"

"Oh, yes," she murmured, tweaking her clit lightly to keep herself close. "Wanna watch you."

There was something so powerful but almost feral in watching him get off. When they were together, Matthew was a skilled and considerate lover who made sure she felt as good as he did—but alone, all he had to worry about was his own pleasure. She loved the way his gaze went unfocused. How his hand twisted around the head of his cock before sliding all the way down to his shaft. How prettily his prick changed color the closer he got.

She didn't forget about her own orgasm, but it definitely moved to the back of her mind as she watched Matthew making himself come. When he did, crying out hoarsely, all she had to do was press herself a little harder and she was tipping over with him. She shook with it, watching his cock throb, his fist covering the head as his stroking slowed, then stopped.

Breathing hard, Matthew let out a small laugh. "Fuck. Wow."

"Mmmm," Stella said. "That was great."

"Be right back. Don't go anywhere."

She didn't, though she did pull her clothes back on. When he padded back into view, still naked, she propped her chin on her hand to watch him as he went to the dresser and pulled out a pair of pajama pants. He looked over his shoulder at her, shaking his ass a little until she laughed and shook her head.

"Come see me," she told him. "I can't stand this much longer."

"I'll see what I can do," Matthew said. "I want to see you too."

From downstairs came the sound of the front door opening, followed by "Mom! Me and Mandy want to play some *Hazard Station,* okay?"

"Shit," Stella said. "Tristan's here. He didn't text me. Gotta go. Let me know about this weekend."

"I will," Matthew promised.

As it turned out, he didn't.

A couple days passed. Stella waited, patiently at first. Then not so much. Finally she sent Matthew a message. Call me?

He did. "Sorry. Got caught up with stuff. I can't make it this weekend. It's my turn to have the girls."

"Ah."

"I should've told you sooner," Matthew said.

Stella frowned. "That would've been nice. Do you not want to come visit me? Is that it? Are you worried about meeting Tristan? Because we could arrange it for when he's with his dad."

"Of course I want to visit you. Don't say that. You're overreacting. What can I do? It's my turn to have the girls."

Oh, how she hated being told she was overreacting. "Didn't you know that when I asked you? You could've told me then."

"I thought I could rearrange."

This rang so false she had to take a moment before she could reply. "Matthew, I'd rather you be honest with me than ever try to save my feelings with a lie. Okay?"

"I'm not lying about anything." He sounded mad, and she didn't really care. She was mad too.

"I'd rather have a no than a maybe that you already know is a no. For anything."

Matthew sighed. "It wasn't a no when I said I would check. Okay?"

"Okay." This had the feeling of becoming a second nonargument, so Stella changed the subject toward something lighter.

After a bit more awkwardness, the tension eased. They joked. They laughed. They shared stories about their days— Stella had some funny things to share about her job and the sorts of crazy photos she'd been asked to retouch. Matthew spoke with fondness of some of his students in the adult education class.

"We're doing poetry," he said. "Limericks. Hey, it's an art form, really."

"What's your favorite? The only one I know is about Nantucket."

"All the good ones are about Nantucket," Matthew said.

He talked more about the class, how his students had gone from barely being able to put together coherent sentences to publishing pieces in a chapbook. The obvious pride in his voice moved her.

"You've made a difference in their lives," she told him. "That must feel so amazing."

Matthew was quiet for a few seconds. "I don't think of it that way. I'm just trying to show them there's more than one way to look at the world."

"That's a beautiful and important thing to do for anyone, Matthew."

"It's not… Thank you. I guess I never thought of it as being beautiful. Or important."

"Well," Stella said, "it is."

CHAPTER TWENTY-SIX

Stella's heart jumped at the familiar boop-boop tone of an incoming Kik. Up to her elbows in dishsoap suds, she needed a minute or so to dry her hands and fish her phone from her pocket, then to open the app, but when she did, she burst into low laughter. Matthew had sent her a picture of his dinner—macaroni and cheese. With ketchup. A hot dog, sans bun, peeked at her from the corner of the shot.

Father of the year, she typed and watched the tiny D turn to an R.

Matthew is typing, the app said at the top of the screen. What? It's delicious. And has all the food groups.

Stella, in reply, took a picture of the inside of her oven, the chicken and potatoes baking inside. Also her table's two settings. The bowl of salad and basket of rolls. She sent them all, one, two, three, without commentary.

Nice, Matthew said. Next time you come to Chicago, will you make me chicken?

If you're good. How are the girls?

Louisa has a cold. Beatrice is having a fight with her best friend. God help me when they get to be teenagers.

Stella laughed, but ruefully. Tristan had come home from school an hour or so ago and pounded right up the stairs to disappear into his room without little more than a word for her. He'd been up there ever since, not a peep, which she had to admit was better than the bass-beat thump of his music being played too loud or the steady back-and-forth thud of the weights or treadmill.

What's on the agenda for tonight? she typed.

The *D* became an *R*, but Matthew didn't type. Stella watched the screen for a minute longer than necessary, then put the phone back in her pocket so she could finish scrubbing the rice cooker and Crock-Pot crocks—the ones she'd asked Tristan to take care of last night. He'd been out with Mandy when she got home, so she couldn't yell at him about forgetting, or deliberately refusing to do it. And she'd been too tired to do it herself until now, which was why now it was like completing an archaeological dig.

"Tristan!" she called as she rinsed the final bits of crusty rice and soggy carrots into the drain strainer so she could empty it into the trash. "Dinner in half an hour! Gather up your laundry and bring it down!"

No reply seemed to be the theme of the night. Frowning, Stella went to the bottom of the stairs to shout again. This time, the muffled shout from her son's room seemed to be an answer of some sort, and, too weary to make herself climb the stairs, she went back to the kitchen.

Boop-boop.

Movies and popcorn at home. Early morning tomorrow. Museum for a birthday party, then bowling party in the afternoon.

Busy girls, Stella typed. Have fun.
She paused, then added, Call me later, when they're in bed?
D.
R.
No answer.
Stella waited.

Matthew is typing...

He typed for a long time, with no message coming through. Until at last: I'll try.

She knew better than to let it sting her, but it still did. Stella put her phone away, vowing not even to look at it again even if it did boop-boop at her. She poured herself a glass of wine, then busied herself sorting the piles of mail and cleaning up the disaster of her kitchen, until the timer on the oven went off, signaling that the chicken was done. She shouted for Tristan, then again when he didn't answer or come down. A third time, her voice cracking, blood pressure rising, and finally he thumped down the stairs with a tread like an elephant and flung himself into his chair with a sigh so heavy it was as if she were asking him to stab himself in the eyes with the fork.

Boop-boop.

Stella ignored it, but another ping a moment later made it impossible for her to pretend she hadn't heard it. Tristan scowled as she set the chicken and potatoes on the table, then pulled out her phone. He didn't say anything, though.

Louisa forgot her inhaler. And I think she might have a fever.

Do you have a thermometer?

Yeah.

Take her temp, Stella said. Then you'll know.

"Tristan," she said aloud. "Get the iced tea. C'mon, I shouldn't even have to ask you."

"I don't even want to eat this," he muttered.

Stella looked up from her phone, where Matthew had not yet replied. "Excuse me?"

"I told you, I'm going out with Mandy tonight. Remember? I have to leave in, like, ten minutes."

She had forgotten, but shouldn't have been surprised. Friday night, no reason for him to hang around at home with his mother. Still… "Where are you going? You don't even want to eat dinner first?"

"We're going to see a movie. We'll get some pizza or something after."

"And after that?" Stella asked slowly, looking at the meal she'd prepared. Admittedly, it was no gourmet fare. It hadn't taken hours or anything, but if she'd known he wasn't going to be home she'd have made herself a sandwich and been done with it.

"Probably hang out somewhere."

She pursed her mouth at this. Her phone booped, but she ignored it to focus on her son. "Where?"

Tristan shrugged. "Don't know."

"Well, you need to know, Tristan. I don't want you just wandering the streets looking for a place to go." She paused. "Why not come here?"

He gave her a shifty glance. "But you'll be here."

"Um, yeah," she said tightly, trying not to be offended and failing for the second time in less than half an hour. "That's kind of the point. But you call me and tell me where you're going after the movie. I mean it. And wherever it is, I'll need to know there's going to be an adult."

"Fine!"

He was gone, out the front door, slamming it behind him before she had time to say another word. Not that she had any to say, Stella thought with a sigh. She looked around the kitchen. She drank the rest of her wine. Friday night, alone at home.

Hooray.

Her phone booped again. She'd forgotten about Matthew's message. Pulling her phone out again, Stella swiped the screen to pull up the app.

Fever. What do I do for that?

The next message had come only a minute or so after, according to the time stamp. Caroline's bringing her inhaler and some children's Tylenol.

Caroline.

Stella's lip curled. She looked at her phone for a long, long minute before she thought of how to respond.

Louisa will be fine. She has a cold, right? Kids get colds, Matthew. How high is her fever?

The *D* became an *R*, but Matthew didn't answer.

Stella poured herself another glass of wine. She cleared off all her counters and scrubbed out her sink. She turned her music up loud, dancing alone in her kitchen, though she wasn't actually in the mood for dancing. She set her phone on the counter, but it stayed frustratingly silent.

The wine had made her the tiniest bit hazy. Her need for a cigarette suddenly became a gnawing ache.

How's Louisa? she messaged Matthew and watched the *D* stay solid for a few minutes while she sat and drank her wine and did nothing else. At last, the *D* became an *R*. He'd read the message. He saw her talking to him; he saw her concern for the daughter she hadn't yet been allowed to know.

But he didn't answer her.

"Fucker." The wine spoke for her. The rational part of her mind told her to chill out. That he was with a sick kid, probably worried. Maybe she'd thrown up or something, and he was dealing with that. But it was bullshit, and Stella knew it. She could make excuses for him all night, but the simple fact was, Matthew was deliberately not replying to her, and not for the first time, and yes, oh, yes, it fucking pissed her off.

Not for the first time, she thought how much easier flying was than this…this supposed relationship with Matthew. No phone number exchanges, no repeat visits, no expectations.

No disappointments.

The third glass of wine didn't seem like a luxury, but a necessity at that point. And finally, so did the cigarettes she pulled from way back in her dresser, inside the vintage tin where she'd kept her "emergency" pack for years before quitting. Somehow even after she'd long given them up, knowing that pack was in there was like a lifeline. Except when she pulled out the tin and opened it, all she could do

was stare at the crumpled and clearly empty pack of cigarettes she most definitely had not smoked.

Stella let herself sink onto the bed, empty pack in one
hand, wineglass in the other. There was no sipping or sa-
voring now. She gulped the wine and put the empty glass
on the nightstand that had once been Jeff's. A little too
close to the edge, but she caught the glass as it fell, spat-
tering her white bedspread with dots of purpley crimson.

"Shit," Stella muttered, but had nobody to blame but
herself. She sat there for a few minutes, staring at the empty
pack. It was possible Jeff had, at some point, taken the cigarettes, though he'd never smoked and wouldn't have snuck
them anyway, if he had. Which meant her son had been
sneaking around in her drawers and stealing. And smoking. Dammit.

Standing in front of Tristan's door, Stella took a few deep
breaths. Stella's mother had thought nothing of coming into
her room, snooping around in Stella's private things. Reading love notes, journals, school papers, whatever. Stella had
vowed she would never do that to her kids, that she would
treat her children with respect for their privacy.

But what if it wasn't just cigarettes, but something worse?
She'd smoked a few joints in her teen and college years.
Experimenting with pot and booze was a part of growing up. She knew that. And she had no reason to believe
that Tristan might be into anything more hard-core than
that, other than his recent surliness, which she'd chalked
up to teenage angst and the strain of his parents' less-than-
amicable divorce. Privacy was important, respect was important, but she had a duty as his mother to make sure he
wasn't in trouble.

Still, she hesitated. She could go into Tristan's room and

riffle around, but if she found something she was going to have to confront him on it, and then he'd know she snooped. She'd have to call Jeff too. Deal with shit from him, even if she'd prefer to deal with it on her own. If she found nothing, she'd know she snooped for no reason, and that would be bad too.

The wine was making this decision less of a no-brainer than it normally would've been. Here she stood in front of the closed door, wondering if the missing cigarettes—which could've been snuck years ago, for all she knew, when Tristan was a rebellious middle schooler trying to look cool to his friends—were worth fucking with the already fragile relationship she had with her son.

She pulled her phone from her pocket, thumbed the screen to bring up the app. No reply from Matthew. She tried again.

How's the kiddo? I'm standing here in front of Tristan's door, trying to figure out if I should snoop around in his room. I think he stole some cigs from my drawer from ages ago. She added the emoticons for an embarrassed face, then a frowning one with a tear. Having a teen IS hard.

D became *R,* but he didn't answer.

She imagined his phone boop-booping, Matthew pulling it from his pocket, seeing her message and putting it back in his pocket. She closed her eyes at that vision, and leaned against the wall with a heavy sigh and hanging head.

"Matthew," she said aloud. "You know I hate it when you ignore me."

Stella squared her shoulders, took a deep breath and opened Tristan's door. The stink wrinkled her nose. Sneakers, stale laundry, the pungent and unmistakable odor of teenage boy. She had to shove the door open against the pile of laundry she couldn't tell was dirty or clean, and remembered that she'd asked him to bring it down to the laundry room before dinner. Obviously, just like with last night's dishes, he'd forgotten or ignored her. Stella kicked aside four damp towels and stood in the center of his room, then turned in a slow circle.

Standing in the middle of what looked like an explosion of dirty clothes, books, papers, video game and DVD cases, a myriad of broken bits of wood and tools... What the hell had he been doing in here? Building an arc? With a snort of disgust, she toed up the edge of a body pillow on the floor and found a tangle of socks and underwear beneath.

Where are you? she texted quickly. I told you to call me when the movie was over.

On top of his dresser, Tristan had lined up a diorama in a shoe box, circa the fifth grade. Inside, a clay horse she remembered him crafting at the kitchen table. Seashells from their last vacation to the shore. He'd done a report on the wild ponies of Chincoteague. Got an A, she saw from the score sheet still stapled to the back. Next to the diorama were several small trophies from when Tristan had played baseball. Cheap plastic things, one of them broken. Littered over the dresser top were nubs of crayons, pencils without erasers, pens with the ends chewed and split. Garbage, all of it, and she was tempted to sweep it all into the overflowing trashcan next to his desk.

She held herself back. First of all, none of this was what she'd come in here to look for, and second, if anyone was going to clean up this junkyard, it would be Tristan. The kid who was steadfastly not replying to her texts.

She wasn't even sure what she was looking for, other than proof he was actively smoking. Or doing drugs. Or oh, God, shooting heroine into his eyeballs or something like that.... It was the wine talking again, but suddenly she was yanking open his dresser drawers to search through the mess of unfolded clothes to find....something. Anything to help her understand where her sweet boy had gone.

She found it.

Tucked into an empty shoe box beneath a pile of video game magazines, Tristan had left a couple of empty lighters and a half-empty pack of Marlboro Reds. It wasn't pot or drugs, but it didn't make her feel much better to think of him as one of those boys who hung around the outside of the mall, shoulders hunched against the wind, smoking. And it was enough to keep her looking through the rest of his stuff. In the bottom drawer of his nightstand, the quickest glimpse of bare flesh and blond hair on a glossy magazine had her closing it right away.

But, bolstered by her discovery and probably that third glass of wine, she kept looking until she found other things. Things that weren't worse but that made her stomach churn uncontrollably.

First, a handful of photographs collected in a battered manila envelope. She shook them into her palm and gasped at the sight of two small boys, arms around each other. Identical striped shirts. Identical gap-toothed grins. Tristan's teeth had straightened after years of orthodontia, but Gage's never would.

Gage would never wear braces.

Gage would never grow out of that shirt.

Gage would never steal her cigarettes from her dresser.

Gage would never do anything. Ever. With trembling fingers, Stella pushed the photos back into the envelope and replaced it. The room spun a little, her head woozy.

She almost didn't open another drawer, but when she did she found a layer of smoothly folded sweatpants and T-shirts, so incongruous with the rest of his room that she knew there had to be something beneath them. Lifting them, she found another layer of clothes. These much smaller. Folded just as neatly. She picked up one shirt and held it to her. Gage's. Beside it, his favorite sweatshirt, the one with Cookie Monster on it. And next to that, the soft, folded square of pale blue waffled fabric edged with satin.

Gage's blanky.

Stella let out a low, strangled sob and pressed the soft blanket to her face. Shoulders shaking, she wept broken glass and razor blades. She sank to the floor and rocked with it against her for a long time.

She hadn't seen this blanket in...years. Long, long years. The last time she could remember seeing it, it had been in Gage's bed beneath his pillow where he kept it even though he'd outgrown the need to take it with him everywhere long before.

Months ago, she'd found a soft stuffed baby that used to be a favorite toy of Gage's in Tristan's bed. She'd pushed aside her discomfort at the time, but this...this... It meant that Tristan was repeatedly going into Gage's room. The room that had been closed since she'd lost him, her brilliant boy, her firstborn. Tristan was going into Gage's room and touching things. Taking them. How many things had he stolen?

Stella tossed the mattress, dumped the drawers, dug into the back of Tristan's closet to pull out crates and boxes of old school papers and keepsakes. She texted him every five minutes, getting no reply, until finally she stopped in the middle of the chaos. Panting, weeping, she gathered up all of Gage's things—his blanky, his baby, the small clothes. The photos. She took them all from Tristan's room and stood in front of Gage's closed door, but could not make herself open it.

Grief swelled and tore at her, making her shake.

Stella pressed her forehead to the painted wood. She put her hand on the knob but didn't turn it.

Earlier she'd given herself a pep talk to convince herself that not only did she have the right to search her son's room, but she had the responsibility to do it. Now there was nothing she could do to make herself open the door. It had been closed for too long. She couldn't bring herself to go inside and see how everything had been left unchanged, minus the things Tristan had taken. Everything but their entire lives.

She took Gage's things and put them in an empty cardboard boot box she pulled from the top rack of her closet. A noise in the hall outside drew her attention; on unsteady feet and with swollen eyes, she opened her bedroom door to find Tristan standing in the hall, staring into his room.

His face, pale but for two bright red spots on his cheeks, swung toward her.

"What the hell did you do?" he cried.

Mandy paused on the stairs, not daring to come up any higher. Tristan backed away from his mother, shaking his head. Stella came out of her bedroom, aware too late that she needed the support of the doorframe to keep her from stumbling.

"Your room was a mess," she told him. "And you didn't call me like I told you to! I texted and texted you! You're in big trouble, young man!"

Too late, she noticed the other couple of kids behind

Mandy, all of them giving each other guilty-eyed glances. Tristan gave her a look of such horror, such disgust, that Stella had to back up a step.

"You're...drunk," Tristan said. "I didn't text you because you said we could come back here, so that's what we were doing.... But I'm out of here! You trashed my room! You trashed my stuff! What were you doing in my room, Mom?"

"Looking for cigarettes!" she cried, triumphant at the instant look of guilt and chagrin on his face. "Did you think I wouldn't notice that you stole mine from the dresser?"

Tristan looked so blank-faced for a moment that she was sure she'd been wrong. Then his expression twisted. Full of disdain.

"I stole those, like, forever ago." He looked so much like Jeff right now that it kind of made her want to puke.

Stella looked past him, to his shuffling, embarrassed friends. She *was* drunk, she realized. The floor beneath her was tipping, tilting, and she reached for the doorframe to steady herself.

"Your friends should go home now, Tristan. We have some things we need to talk about."

Shaking his head, he backed away from her. Down the stairs. "I'm outta here."

"What? Wait a minute—"

But he was already at the bottom of the stairs, and though Stella would've said that there was no way a single one of those teenagers could've moved without footsteps of thunder, the four of them were almost completely silent as they left.

"Where are you going?"

"Dad's," Tristan shot back, voice already faint and distant and disappearing.

The front door slammed shut. Stella sank onto the top step and put her face in her hands. She ought to have stopped him. Right? Gone after him? But she'd been unable to make herself. *Let Jeff deal with him,* she thought, swallowing convulsively. *Let his father handle it for a while.*

She needed to lie down. Or take a shower. Her stomach was churning. She could see Gage's closed door from where she sat. She could see it when she closed her eyes.

How long had Tristan been going inside, helping himself to his brother's things? And what should she do about it? Stella shuddered, suddenly chilled.

She forced herself to her feet, swaying, nearly taking a tumble down the stairs before she caught herself on the railing. In her bedroom, she looked at the spatter of wine on the bedspread and thought about pulling it off to put in the wash before the stain could set, but the best she could manage was to pull it to the foot of the bed, where it stuck from being tucked beneath the mattress.

Stella sank, sank, sitting with her back to the edge of the bed and her knees pulled up. She pulled out her phone, opened the Kik app. Typed. Matthew. I need you.

D, D, D... Minutes passed while Stella let her head fall onto her knees. Tears burned and choked her. When she looked again after ten or so minutes had passed, the *D* had become an *R,* but Matthew had not replied.

She dialed his number this time. She listened to it ring, twice, then got his voice mail, which meant that he hadn't missed the call. That would've taken at least six rings. No, he'd sent it directly to voice mail. On purpose.

"Matthew, please call me. I'm having a really rough

night. I had a fight with Tristan, and…" She drew in a breath. "I found out he's been smoking, and he stole some things…from Gage's room."

The weight of Gage's name pushed her to silence after that. She breathed into the phone, eyes closed, knowing this wasn't like the days when someone could hear a voice on an answering machine and choose to pick up a call they'd previously been ignoring. She could wait forever, and Matthew wasn't going to pick up this call.

"Please call me back," she whispered. "I hope Louisa's feeling better. I need to talk to you. Please."

Stella disconnected the call and put her phone in the alarm clock dock. She dragged herself to the shower, which she ran hot enough to scald. She lay on the shower floor with the water pounding all over her.

Her grief rose and slaughtered her.

And when the shower ran cold, she let the needle-prick of the frigid water abuse her while she shivered and twitched, until finally her head cleared and she forced herself to get out. Wrapped in her thick robe, towel on her hair, Stella went to her bed. She pulled back the covers and got underneath them, still shuddering with cold. She looked at her phone, but there were no messages.

Eventually, she slept.

CHAPTER TWENTY-SEVEN

Matthew didn't call her back or even Kik her until four o'clock on Saturday. The Kik came through while Stella was busy folding all the sheets and towels she'd collected and washed from Tristan's room, and at first, she didn't even reach to pull her phone from the dock where it had been since the night before. She could see the alert message from where she stood on the other side of the bed, but even if she'd been unable, she knew it was from him—Matthew was the only one who ever Kik'd her.

She'd woken earlier than normal for a Saturday in which she had no plans. Clearheaded, not hungover, but wide awake just the same. She'd spent the morning stripping her bed and Tristan's, gathering all the laundry and working on getting the stain out of her comforter. It had faded to a pale pink, but she was never going to be rid of it. That's what happened with stains; they were reminders of the mistakes you'd rather forget.

She hadn't heard from Tristan at all, though she'd put a

call in to Jeff to make sure their son had indeed gone to his father's house. Cynthia had left a message while Stella was in the shower that Tristan was there, that he was fine and he could stay as long as he wanted. Stella had not returned Cynthia's well-meaning but slightly bewildered call. Stella needed to talk to Jeff about everything, and much like with the night before in which she'd known what she ought to do about her son but had been incapable of making herself do it, all Stella could do was listen to the answering machine and delete the message.

Her phone booped a few minutes later as she was fitting her pillow into a new case, and because she was standing next to her nightstand, she took the phone from the dock. She swiped the screen, bringing up the app and the messages Matthew had sent. As she read them, Stella's lip curled.

Hi.

Then, later, Louisa's fine. Fever gone. We passed up the birthday parties for movies at home all day.

He would be able to see that she'd read the messages, just as she could see when he did, and Stella strongly considered not replying—except that she refused to play those stupid games, wouldn't be the woman who held herself hostage for spite. She sat on the edge of the bed. Her fingers moved over the phone's keyboard.

Good, she typed. I'm glad she's feeling better. Sorry you're missing the birthday party madness.

D became *R*, but Matthew didn't answer.

"Fuck you," Stella said aloud. "Fuck you so much."

Sunday, she kept herself busy catching up on the miscellany of household chores she always put off. Dusting the baseboards, washing curtains. Spring cleaning. It was the sort of work that should've left her feeling content at finishing it, but by six o'clock, all she felt was grimy, exhausted and pissed off. She reheated leftover chicken and ate it at the kitchen table while she read, which was at last enough to soothe her jangled nerves.

By seven, she'd cleared away her dishes and wiped down the kitchen table and counters, and taken her book upstairs to read in bed. Fresh sheets, the scent of the lavender she'd sprinkled on her pillow, clean pajamas. Soft music playing from her phone in its place on the speaker dock. It was a perfect Sunday evening alone, Stella told herself, though she couldn't stop herself from looking at the clock every few minutes, noting the passage of time.

The girls would be home with Caroline by now. And yet her phone didn't ring. Didn't ping or boop or buzz. Eventually, she was able to lose herself in the powerful words of Margaret Atwood's *A Handmaid's Tale,* a classic and one of Stella's favorites.

The message was waiting for her when she came back from the bathroom, where she'd gone to empty her bladder one last time before going to sleep. She hadn't heard the Kik come in, but she caught the flash of her phone's lit screen, showcasing the alert. A minute later and she'd have missed it.... But she knew better than that. She'd have checked her phone one last time before turning out her light anyway.

You awake?

It would've been easy enough for her to ignore it. Easier than answering, anyway, because by now she'd become convinced that no matter how their conversation began, it was going to end in an argument. But again, Stella didn't want to play those sorts of games, making him guess at her mood, biting her tongue to keep the peace. She'd spent too long with Jeff in that sort of back-and-forth, passive-aggressive battle. She refused to do it again.

For another few minutes, she replied. I'm in bed.

Video?

Automatically, she considered her appearance. No makeup, hair a mess, dressed in pajamas. Not exactly her best look. Still, it had been days since she'd seen his face. How could she say no? Sure.

A moment later, Matthew's face appeared on her phone. She wished she'd taken the time to have him call her on her laptop, where at least his face would be bigger.

"Hi," he said at once.

"Hi."

Matthew was also in bed. He sat propped against his headboard on a mound of pillows. Everything about him looked good.

"Busy weekend," he said after a moment when Stella didn't speak. "I'm wiped out."

"I bet. How's Louisa?"

"She's fine. Had a fever of a hundred, that's all. The Tylenol brought it down."

A hundred was barely a fever, as far as Stella was concerned—her boys had always suffered with outrageously high fevers when they came down with colds. One hundred and three wasn't uncommon. But, she reminded herself, Matthew hadn't been raised by a nurse the way she had. Lots of parents overreacted to their kids being sick.

"But Beatrice, she was kind of out of control. Super-hyper," Matthew said. "She was upset that we decided not to go to the birthday parties, so she was really acting up. Caroline had to send her to time-out three times."

Silence.

His expression, small as it was held captive in the tiny rectangle of her phone screen, nevertheless showed her that he knew he'd fucked up.

"Caroline," Stella said into the awkwardness.

"Yeah…she came over to bring the inhaler and the Tylenol…" Matthew paused. "I told you."

Stella kept her face as neutral as possible. "Uh-huh."

"And then when we decided it would be too much for Louisa to go to the parties, and we were going to stay home, she just hung out to watch movies. That's all," he added, too quickly. Sounding too defensive.

"Why didn't Caroline take Beatrice to the party while you stayed with Louisa, since it was your weekend to be the primary caregiver?" Stella asked in what she hoped was an entirely reasonable tone of voice. It didn't feel reasonable. It kind of felt like barbed wire slashing at her throat and gums and tongue. "Or why didn't she take Louisa home, if that would've made her feel better? Then you could've taken Beatrice to the parties."

Matthew didn't say anything. His mouth twisted. She watched his face work, as though he were trying hard to think of something rational to say, but failed. "It was my weekend to have them," he said finally. "My responsibility. I couldn't just pawn them off on her."

"But you did, didn't you?" Stella swallowed the bitterness she wished she could get past. "And I bet Caroline was right there, wasn't she? Ready to help out."

"She's their mother," Matthew said, stone-faced. "Of course she was."

"And she's not married to you anymore," Stella told him. "Yet she's still your wife."

She disconnected the call.

Her phone rang a minute after that. She thought about sending it to voice mail, but answered it instead. Braced herself for Matthew's anger—ready to own her words. They'd been bitchy, yes. But true.

"I'm sorry," he said, surprising her. "I was worried about Louisa. That's all. I didn't know what to do."

"I told you what to do. Take her temp. Give her Tylenol. Let her rest."

Matthew huffed into the phone. "I was anxious about it, okay? Caroline's the one who always takes care of them when they're sick. She handles it much better than I do."

"You know you're not incompetent, right? Even if she makes you feel that way?"

"She doesn't—"

"Caroline could've dropped off the inhaler and the Tylenol and gone home." Stella paused to keep herself from launching into a full-on bitch attack. "But I bet she didn't. Did she?"

Matthew coughed. "Stella…"

"How was the couch?"

"Hard on my back."

She snorted laughter. "Uh-huh."

"It got late," he said defensively. "What was I supposed to do? Tell her she had to go home?"

"Yes!" Stella cried so loud her voice echoed in the phone's

speaker. "Goddammit, Matthew. Yes. You were supposed to tell her she should go home, and you were supposed to take care of your girls like the competent and capable dad I know you are. And you were supposed to call me. You were supposed to *be here*," she added, voice breaking. "I needed you."

More silence. This time it stretched on and on, beyond awkwardness. Stella drew in a sobbing breath, hating that she was giving him this.

"Nothing happened with me and Caroline," he said quietly.

Stella's laugh hurt her throat. "You think that's what this is about?"

"Isn't it?"

"No," she told him. "But should I be upset that you completely ignored me when I needed you?"

"You knew I was with my kids. You know they keep me busy, that they're my priority...."

"I needed you," Stella repeated. "I was having a really hard time."

"How was I supposed to know that?"

She didn't know how to answer that, at first. "You didn't listen to my message?"

"No... I just thought you were calling me to say goodnight or something. But I told you I'd try to call you," he added hastily. "I just didn't have a chance, so I figured you were—"

"What? Checking up on you? Desperate?" He didn't answer, and Stella went on. "I am not Caroline."

She waited for him to hang up on her for that one, but Matthew only made a low, disgusted noise. "Nice."

Stella gritted her teeth. "I needed you. I wouldn't have called otherwise."

"I was busy, I'm sorry. I had the girls—"

"And Caroline," she said with a snarky laugh. "Don't forget her. And I certainly wouldn't know about busy, would I?"

"You don't get it," Matthew said sharply. "You have one kid, and he's a lot older. It's a lot more complicated with two."

For a moment, the sheer arrogance and insult of what he'd said to her didn't fully sink in. Stella pulled the phone from her ear to look at it before pressing it back to her head. She blinked rapidly, trying to form the right words, trying not to let her emotions run away with her. Trying not to simply lose her shit all over him.

She failed.

"I know what it's like to have two children, Matthew. I know how hard it can be with two little ones, close in age. I know how complicated it is."

"Stella, oh, God. I'm sorry, I'm so sorry. I didn't mean—"

"I found his blanky in Tristan's room," Stella said in a low, numbed voice. "I was worried he'd taken up smoking, but instead I found out he's been taking things from Gage's room. I can't go in that room, Matthew. Do you understand that? Do you understand what it's like to walk past that closed door and be unable to open it because I cannot face the thought of packing away all his things? It's been over ten years, and I can't open that door because I'm somehow terrified that it will let out the smell of him. That everything will be gone. I can't open the door, I can't pack away his clothes and toys and furniture and make that room empty. And, yes, I know what fuckery that is. I know it's not healthy. And I still can't make myself do it, Matthew, because once I open that room I will have to let him go, and I can't bear the thought of losing him all over again. So don't you dare tell me smugly how I don't understand what it's like to deal with two. Don't you dare whine to me about how anxious and stressful it is to deal with a hundred-degree fever. When you've held your child in your arms and prayed not for him to heal, but for him to finally just die so that he won't hurt anymore...then maybe you'll have one small, infinitesimal inkling of what it was like for me, and why I needed you last night. But you weren't here. You are never here. I come to you, and you don't ever come to me. I am there for every bitch and moan and hand-wringing emotional breakdown you ever have. And you were not there for me for one. Fucking. Night."

This time, when she disconnected, Matthew didn't call back.

CHAPTER TWENTY-EIGHT

Stella and Tristan weren't completely estranged. She spoke with him on the phone or texted him. Once or twice a week she picked him up after school and took him to dinner before dropping him off at Jeff's, but Tristan would not come home, and Stella didn't ask him to.

"He's welcome here, you know that," Cynthia told her on the phone. "I don't know what happened, but…"

This was the woman who opened her house to Stella's son. The one who'd end up doing his laundry and making sure he got up for school, who would feed him and be there when he got home, because surely Jeff would not. "He likes his dad better."

Cynthia laughed softly. "I don't know about that. Things will work out, Stella. I'm sure."

Stella wasn't so convinced.

The balance had shifted—where once Tristan's home had been with Stella and he "visited" Jeff, now it was the opposite. It ate away at her, day after day. The gallons of milk in the fridge she kept buying automatically and had to toss because nobody drank them, the regular supply of hot water, the small extras in her bank account at the end of the month that normally would've gone to dinners out or Tristan's spending cash. The silence. Everything she'd once imagined she'd adore once her son went off to college had now become her reality, and Stella far from loved it.

It might've been easier if she had something to distract her, but that would've meant contacting Matthew and she was done with that. Maybe, she thought as she let herself into the dark kitchen and tossed her keys and coat onto the table, he was just as relieved to be done with her as she kept trying to convince herself she was.

The trouble was, everything reminded her of him. She couldn't share the funny joke she'd heard, or the new song she loved and played on repeat, or send him pictures of her food. Without Matthew, there was a giant gaping hole she kept falling into whenever she tried moving forward.

Missing Tristan was different. She'd always known someday her son would move out and away; she hadn't thought it would be so soon, or on such magnificently bad terms. But no matter how angry they'd been at each other, there was nothing that couldn't be undone. Tristan would always be her boy.

She waited for the urge to fly to hit her, but it didn't.

Another week passed, and one night in the shower, washing herself, Stella cupped her breasts in her hands and thumbed the nipples tight, waiting for arousal to find her. She slipped her fingers between her legs and sought the same thing, but all she found was numbness and disinterest.

Another week.

Another.

The days got longer. The sun hotter. Her flowers bloomed, but Stella wilted.

She unfriended Matthew on Connex. Deleted his number from her phone. There was nothing she could do about the message application but block him, and that felt unnecessarily antagonistic and stupid, especially since he wasn't bothering to message her in the first place.

He'd made her nothing, so she made him a stranger.

She moved through her days without much drama. Work. Chores. She took Tristan to dinner or to the movies or shopping the few times she could convince him to let her. She still did not ask him to move home.

She was alone, and it was more terrible than she'd ever imagined it to be, and yet there was a kind of pleasure in that pain of her solitude. Clarity in her thinking. Or maybe, Stella thought as she slipped into bed without a word from her son or her lover or anyone else, she was just numb.

She is still drunk and reeling when they wheel her into the E.R., but even without the liquor in her blood, Stella knows she would've been blurry and blinded by what happened. Blood has run into her eyes, and though she knows she's crying harder than she ever has cried in her life, her vision will not clear. There's pain, but it's faint and far away, sectioned in parts of her body that no longer seem to even belong to her. She can't feel her legs, and something in her brain tells her that's probably a good thing.

Stella's throat is raw from screaming, but she reaches for Jeff. For Tristan. For Gage. Her boys were in the backseat. Jeff, driving. She remembers this but can't make sense of it.

"Ma'am. Do you know where you are?" Someone shines a light into her eyes; if she weren't blinded already, she would have recoiled from the glare. "Do you know your name?"

"Stella Andrews." No. That is her maiden name, but she can't remember what she should've said. "I think I was in an accident."

"Yes, ma'am. You were in a car accident. We're taking you back now. Try not to struggle—"

"My boys," she cries. "Where are my boys?"

"Your husband is already in an examination room." It's a man's voice, rough but kind, and his hands are also rough but kind as they push her back onto the gurney or whatever it is.

Stella can't see, and the sounds are echoing and wavering. Her hands paddle at the air, struggling. Someone holds her down. The taste of eggnog coats her tongue, along with the taste of blood. She's going to be sick. She's going to pass out. The world spins, and Stella screams when someone straightens her legs and the pain is thick and wild and terrifying.

"Where are my sons? Where are my boys?"

"Shh." This voice, female, tries to be soothing. "They're being taken care of."

That's all Stella knows for a time, and when she comes back to herself, all the pain has fallen on her and the hangover has too. Her first thought is to struggle up from the blankets and sheets binding her so tightly to the bed, but she can't manage to do more than work one hand free. The other is pinned by a needle and tubing attached to a plastic bag of some kind of clear fluid hanging from a hook. Her second thought is guilt and fear—she's been unconscious, clearly, incapable of getting to her boys. She has failed them. Mama has always been there for every bump and bruise and bad dream.

She needs to get to them.

The nurse who comes at the call of her bell looks tired. She is not particularly kind, and her hands are calloused and rough on Stella's when she pushes her back against the pillows. But her eyes are understanding. "Shh. Lie back. You've had a bad accident. You have stitches, and you need to be careful."

"My boys—"

"Your younger son is at home with your husband." The nurse tucks in the blankets again, checks the bag of fluids, smooths and straightens it.

Relief floods Stella, but only for a moment. "And Gage?"

The nurse looks Stella in the eye, and she will always be grateful for that honesty. "Your older son is in ICU with multiple injuries. He was operated on to relieve swelling in the brain, but he hasn't regained consciousness yet."

Stella lets out a long, low cry and falls back against the pillows. "But he's alive. Oh, thank God. He's alive."

The nurse pats her, adjusts some things and leaves. Stella, against her will, sleeps. She wakes to pain. Throbbing, grinding, burning agony all through her in every part. Behind her eyes. Her throat and tongue so dry when she swallows it's like rubbing a hand the wrong way on a fish's scales.

Time passes without her knowing how much or how long, only that it's measured in the ebb and flow of pain. Later, she will discover it's been three days since the accident before she's allowed to get out of bed. Jeff and Tristan visit her in the hospital, Tristan bearing a tiny bandage on his precious forehead and Jeff without any signs of damage at all but the rings of sleeplessness beneath his eyes and the way he grips her hand.

"I'm sorry," Jeff says, over and over, and Stella can't begin to think what he's apologizing for.

She cannot begin to forgive him.

When she's allowed to see her son at last, she's in a wheelchair with her bandages and stitches and the hanging bags of liquids and medicines. She's not allowed to go into the room, and can't see him through the observation window without struggling to her feet. The world tips and spins as she grips the windowsill hard enough to bend a nail; that small pain is nothing compared to the rest, and it won't be until later when a blood blister forms that she even notices.

Gage is very small among all the tubes and wires, and Stella looks at him for a long time without saying anything. Jeff is not beside her, not this first time, though later there will be times when they stand side by side and look through the glass without saying anything to each other. Without offering each other the comfort of their touch. Without even looking at each other.

"I'm sorry," Jeff says every time he leaves her.

She thinks he means because he's going home to their soft bed, their warm sheets. She thinks it's because she and Gage were injured and he was not. She thinks it might even be because it's the only thing he can think of to say, maybe the only thing he thinks she wants to hear.

"Stop," she tells him finally, the day she is getting ready to go home and leave her son behind. "Stop saying you're sorry."

And at home, in their bed, where Stella gingerly stretches out with a sigh at the comfort of the mattress, the quiet of the room, the ease in the ache of all her muscles, Jeff moves next to her and tries to hold her. The weight of his hand is more than annoyance, it's pain on the remaining stitches that are soon to become scars. His breath is too hot. The way he shifts and shakes the bed when he moves makes her want to scream.

"No," she tells him when he tries to nuzzle against her.

"I don't want to *do* it," he says, meaning he doesn't want to make love. "I just want to—"

"No," Stella says again. If she could turn onto her side away from him, she would, but there's still too much pain in the wound on her hip and belly. She stares at the dark ceiling and listens to the sound of her husband's affront at this rejection, knowing she should have been kinder and incapable of finding anything to be kind with.

He moves away from her in a shuffle of sheets, flinging himself onto his side and pulling the covers almost completely off her so that she has to sit up and rearrange them. This hurts too, stretching her rips and tears, but she supposes it's less than whatever agony Jeff's feeling at being rejected. And again, Stella searches herself for any scrap of kindness and is unable to find any. She lies back to stare at the darkness and listens for the telltale whistle-snort of Jeff's snoring to tell her he's fallen asleep.

And then, only then, does she allow herself to weep.

She woke in the night to the sound of nothing.

No soft hush-hush whisper of the respirator, no rattle gasp of breath from down the hall. Stella blinked against the darkness and the scald of sudden tears. Even in sleep, she always knew he was gone, but waking this way slammed the memory into her with the weight of a fist.

She sat up in her bed, drawing her knees close. The covers tangled, making it hard at first, and she fought them. She didn't want to weep, but there was no stopping it. And, at least at this grief, there was no shame. The tears welled up and out of her, the claws of the grief beast shredding her into pieces.

Stella pressed her face to her knees, linking her fingers to the back of her head. Weeping, weeping, weeping. The empty house took her grief and swallowed it all.

For so many years when the boys were small, she and Jeff had made love in whispers and sighs instead of shouts; for so many years Stella had given up to her sorrow in the same way, too mindful of her husband beside her in bed and her son down the hall to ever fully give in to it.

But now she was alone, and there was nobody there to hear or judge her pain. Nobody to share it with either, and she'd grown accustomed to that. But somehow now it seemed worse than ever, not because she wasn't used to it but because at least for a little while she'd had Matthew to turn to and now he was gone too.

The pain of that loss was still fresh, still raw, but she'd get over it. She'd had her heart broken before, more than once. There would be another man. Probably a lot more, at least if she decided to start flying again. And if there weren't, she'd had her share, hadn't she? Men could be replaced.

Her son never could.

In the early days after the accident, confined to her bed with her own injuries, Stella had gone insane with trying to get to her boy. Tristan and Jeff had been treated and sent home. Jeff's mom had come to stay and help take care of them. At six, Tristan was old enough to miss his mother and brother, but being taken care of by Granny made it seem more like a vacation than a hardship. Stella might have her issues with her mother-in-law, who meant well but could be overcautious and hovery, but that only made her feel better about knowing Tristan was in her care.

It was knowing that she couldn't get out of her bed and go to her son, who needed her. Nightmares of him crying woke her repeatedly, along with the pain of her injuries as well as the constant bustle and regular interruptions of the hospital, until Stella had gone hours without restful sleep. Psychotic from sleep deprivation and in agony, she'd broken down more than once, sobbing into her hands without anyone to help her. She'd wept so fiercely she'd vomited.

She kind of felt as though she could throw up now. Deep breaths calmed her, though they didn't stop the burn of the tears. She swallowed hard, again and again, and pressed the heels of her hands to her eyes in a vain attempt at getting herself to stop. And then she simply gave up to it, all the grief and sorrow, all the loss.

Stella let it sweep her away.

Shaking with it as if she'd been struck by fever, she curled in the blankets and clutched a pillow to her face. She screamed into it. Then louder. Hoarse and brutal, the scream shredded her throat and left her with the taste of blood. Yet she felt better when she'd done it, once, twice, again. Then more. Until finally, wrung out and slaughtered from the force of this grief that would never, never ease, never cease, Stella rolled onto her back and looked up at the ceiling.

She went down the hall to Gage's room. She stood outside the door with her hand on the knob the way she had so many times before. But this time, with the darkness to shield her, to offer its comfort, she opened the door.

Inside, the faint glow of his night-light illuminated the

square shapes of dresser, desk and bed, and Stella stopped herself a few feet inside the door. It hadn't occurred to her that the light would still be on. At eight, Gage had no longer been afraid of the dark, but both he and Tristan used the lights, which turned on automatically in darkness so they could find their way to the bathroom in the night. The one she used in her bathroom had never gone out in all these years, so it should've been no surprise to find this one still worked too. Now Stella stood in the middle of the room with the faint green glow casting shadows on everything.

It might've been scary, that green light, but Stella remembered how it would've led her son safely around any obstacles that threatened him, and something lifted inside her. She thought about turning on the overhead light, but for now this was enough.

Stella went to Gage's bed. The mattress crinkled when she sat on it. The comforter and sheets, patterned with the faces and logos of his favorite cartoon show, had been expertly made up. Jeff's mother would've been the one to do that, sometime before Gage had come home from the hospital. Margery had slept here and left it looking as though she never had.

Stella pressed Gage's pillow to her face, but there was no smell of him. Nothing left. Something twisted and broke inside her at this, though it was no surprise. She clutched it and waited to be overtaken again by her tears, but there weren't any left. She'd worn herself out.

Stella curled up on Gage's bed, the pillow beneath her head. She slept almost at once.

She woke in the morning feeling a little as if she'd been hit in the face with a shovel. All over her body, as a matter of fact, all her normal aches and pains somehow exacerbated and emphasized as she swung her legs over the side of the bed and tried to force herself to her feet. Stella scrubbed at her face and pushed herself up with a wince.

In the pale light of morning, Gage's room looked so much smaller than she remembered. Stella went to the dresser, running her fingertips along the dust on the surface. His collection of toy cars was still lined up along the back of it, though there were empty places in the lineup. Tristan had taken those cars, and Stella closed her eyes against a fresh spate of tears that threatened to pull her under.

She'd lost Gage to an accident, but she'd lost Tristan to her own stupidity and selfishness.

Stella looked around the room, feeling sick to her stomach again. For more than ten years she'd left this room untouched, not as a monument or a memorial, but as a punishment to herself. And even that had grown into self-indulgence.

Sorrow is as insidious as water; if left to its own methods it will fill in every crack and crevice. Water can break apart rocks and sorrow can break a person. Stella's sorrow had worked its way into every part of her and had tried to drown her, but it had not yet completely broken her.

It was too early to be awake, but she didn't want to sleep anymore. Not in this bed, this room. Stella rubbed her face over and over until she scrubbed the dreams away, but still yawning, she went down the hall to her own room. She sat for a moment on the edge of her bed, contemplating snuggling under her own blankets or getting into a scalding shower. She'd set her alarm the night before, and if she were going back to sleep, it would wake her in an hour. She took her phone off the alarm clock dock to switch the settings, and noticed the text that had come in sometime during the night.

Of course it would be from Matthew.

Of course all it would say was HEY.

Because it would impossible for him to tell her he missed her, right? That he'd been thinking of her late at night, watching his phone for a message from her, disappointed when nothing came? He certainly couldn't tell her that, could he?

And it was ludicrous of her to expect it from him, Stella thought as her fingers hovered over the phone's keyboard, typing out a reply she then swiped to delete. She knew that man inside and out, upside and down, and it only made her the asshole to expect him to change.

She either loved him the way he was, which was no good for her, or she stopped loving him. But there's the problem with love—also like water, it works its way into every crack and crevice of a person, and it can break you worse than any sorrow. She couldn't stop herself from loving him, not just like that with a snap of fingers and an iron will, but she could refuse to let it break her.

She needed Matthew right now, but reaching for him would only start them both on that same old tumble down the rabbit hole. No Wonderland at the bottom. Only rough and jagged rocks, only dank, dark water. Only frustration. Only grief. Only that sharp and biting love that ate her from the inside out.

Stella deleted Matthew's message without answering.

CHAPTER TWENTY-NINE

Jeff had insisted Tristan attend counseling, which Stella didn't entirely oppose. Enforcing the visits to the counselor as a requirement for Tristan living in Jeff's house, however, she found utterly despicable and yet so typical of her ex-husband that all she could do when she found out was shake her head. Because Tristan had been grounded from his car for coming home too late—a punishment she did approve of, even if Jeff's other ideas were lame— Stella picked up her son after the session to take him to dinner. She found him sullen, nails bitten to the quick, unable to look at her. When she'd asked him how the session went, the truth came out of him in a choked, desperate voice that made her want to weep in sympathy.

"I'm sorry," she said. "I didn't know he was making you go. I thought you wanted to."

"I don't."

She'd pulled into the parking lot of his favorite burger joint, but now stared ahead, thinking hard. Her relationship with her son had faltered and misstepped, and navigating it was like tiptoeing through a mine field. But she was still his mother. He was still her son. That had to mean something, even among all the mess.

"I'm sorry, Tristan. For all of this. I know I've been a really shit mom." She took a deep breath. Cleared her throat. "I know you think I wasn't giving you enough attention because of my relationship with Matthew—"

His laugh stopped her. "No."

She looked at him. "No?"

"I was glad you had a boyfriend."

"You were?" Frowning, she twisted in the front seat toward him.

Tristan hesitated, then nodded. "Well…I mean, it was sort of gross, but yeah. And I know I gave you a hard time about it, but…I didn't want you to be alone, Mom. Dad has Cynthia. And then, you know, I met Mandy. I didn't want you to be alone, especially 'cause I'm going off to college in a couple years. I just didn't like him because he was an asshole."

"Oh." Stella blinked, then burst into startled laughter. "Oh, God. Tristan, he wasn't. I mean, he was, he could be, but…"

"He made you go there all the time. And he ignored you." At her next startled look, Tristan shrugged. "I could tell. He was a jerk to you."

"Sometimes. Yes. He could be."

"He made you happy sometimes, though. Didn't he? So I'm sorry you guys broke up. And you're not a shit mother." Tristan's voice cracked. "You're kind of the best mom. I mean, even though you get on my case about a lot of stuff, you also leave me alone to make my own decisions and things. You let me be my own person."

How had this happened? This boy in front of her, how had she and Jeff managed to make this? When the pair of them had done everything wrong, how had Tristan still turned out so right?

"You don't have to go back to counseling if you don't want to. I don't care what your dad says. I'll talk to him about it."

Tristan hesitated, then nodded, looking out the window. "It's not so bad. But maybe you and Dad should come in with me too, sometimes. You don't have to do it together."

"If you want me to... If you need me to do that, I will."

He gave her a smile, a small one, but it was enough.

"Hey, what do you say instead of junkie burgers, I take you home and we can have lasagna? I made a pan last week. I can defrost some. We can rent a movie too." Stella took a brave breath; this was more anxiety-making than asking a new guy out on a date. She braced herself for rejection, but instead Tristan smiled wider.

"Can we rent *The Resurrected?* It's supposed to be bad-ass."

"Zombies," Stella said. "Ugh. But okay."

Dinner was consumed—it was hard to believe that she'd forgotten how much he could eat, but she had. The movie turned out to be excellent. It was getting to be time to take him back to Jeff's, something she was not looking forward to at all and Tristan didn't seem to be either.

"Can I just stay here tonight?"

She kept herself from grinning, not wanting to make this a big deal. "Sure. Of course. Anytime."

Following him upstairs a few minutes later, Stella paused

in the hallway to stare past Tristan's open door to the one that was closed. She knocked on his doorframe. "Hey. So, listen… Tomorrow I have something I think we should do together."

It took them only a few hours to clear away what had been a small boy's lifetime. The clothes she donated to charity. Tristan took a few of the books, a couple toys, but as Stella sorted through boxes of building blocks and toy cars, she was surprised to learn she had no desire to hold on to any of it.

Gage had owned these bits and pieces; Gage had loved them. She had loved Gage. There could be no substitute for the loss of her son in the keeping of his things.

She had to let it all go.

Tristan put his hand on her shoulder when he saw her weeping. He knelt beside her. "I miss him too. Dad won't talk about him. You never wanted to talk about him either, but Dad… He makes it like Gage never existed. At all."

"People grieve in all different ways, Tristan. I'm sorry for letting my issues get in the way of you being able to talk about your brother." Stella drew in a hitching breath, wishing the tears in her throat would escape so she could be rid of them.

Tristan sat with a toy car missing a wheel in his hand. "He liked this one a lot. I always wanted to play with it, but he wouldn't let me. It's just junk now."

"You can keep it if you want to," she told him.

Tristan looked at it, then nodded and tucked it in his pocket. "Remember when we used to play superheroes? He always let me be Batman, even though he was older."

"He always held your hand when you crossed the street,"

Stella said on another surge of tears. "You hated it, but he always made sure you were safe."

Tristan nodded, staring at the carpet for a moment before looking at her with tears in his own eyes. "Once, on the playground, some bigger kids tried to push me down, and Gage punched one in the nose."

"I never knew that," Stella said.

"He made me promise not to tell, because you'd have yelled at him for fighting."

But inside, she'd have been proud of him, Stella thought. For protecting his baby brother. She'd have scolded him for fighting, but she'd have been proud of him too.

"I miss him, Mom. But sometimes I don't really remember him. It's like I've been an only child my whole life. I know I wasn't, but it feels like that." Tristan hitched out an embarrassed sob and covered his face. "I'm a shitty brother."

"No," she said, pulling him closer. "No, honey. You are not a shitty anything. You were a great brother to Gage, and you are the best son I could ever ask for. You don't have to remember him every single minute to keep him in your heart. And it's okay, sometimes, if you don't think about him at all. Loving someone doesn't mean you have to make your whole life about remembering him."

Then he hugged her, and Stella hugged him back.

CHAPTER THIRTY

The phone rang, of course, when Stella was wrung out, exhausted from the day of dealing with Gage's room. The trunk of her car overflowed with bags and boxes of things she was donating to charity, and she'd thrown a lot of it away. Tristan had put a few things in his room, an act that had given Stella hope he might decide to come home permanently, but which she didn't dare mention in case it urged him to be more adamant about staying with his dad. He'd gone back to Jeff's an hour before.

She wasn't ready for Matthew's call, but she answered it anyway.

"Hi," he said.

She wanted to tell him to fuck off, but all she said was hi.

He talked then. Several minutes of bland chatter that set her teeth on edge and made her head pound. It was nonsense. It was nothing.

"Enough," she told him. "You call me up after all this time, you want to talk about the weather? Sorry, I'm busy. What do you really want?"

He sighed. "I want to come to see you."

"No," she said immediately. "And also, fuck you, Matthew."

He was silent but did not disconnect. She could have, but waited for him to be the one to end it. Instead, Matthew sighed again.

Voice rasping, he said, "Stella, I have to tell you something that's really hard to say."

She waited. He said nothing. She waited some more.

"I can't fly," Matthew said.

Stella didn't sit so much as her knees gave out and she folded onto her couch. For an evil moment she thought he'd somehow found out about all the times she'd flown, what the term had always meant, privately, to her. "What?"

"I can't fly. I'm not capable of it. I…I was a pilot," Matthew said. "Something happened."

"I'm listening," Stella said when he fell silent again.

Matthew began to speak.

"There was nothing different about the day. I got up. Ate breakfast. I kissed my wife and girls goodbye, and caught a cab to the airport. I was going to be gone just for the day, a quick turnaround with an overnight stay. Nothing I hadn't done a hundred times, a thousand times.

"I had no reason to suspect anything bad might happen. The weather was good on both ends of the flight. My crew was one I'd worked with so many times we'd become a family. The only difference was that I'd been at my buddy's birthday party the night before. I'd been drinking, but I wasn't wasted or anything like that. A little hungover, but nothing serious. A headache. A little tired. And I had a little bit of a cold coming on.

"We were on the approach to Philly a few hours after sunset. My first officer and I were talking about where we wanted to grab dinner when the first bird strike happened. We both looked at each other like 'what the hell—'

"That's when the rest of the flock hit us.

"You never think a bird can do so much damage to a plane, even a Canada goose, which is big. A bird, right? Against a plane?

"Usually a bird strike is one, maybe two. Later, they counted more than ten strikes. The mechanics who worked on the plane said they'd never seen that many strikes at once, but all we knew at the time was that something was hitting us, and we couldn't see what it was.

"My first officer reacted first. He's the one who shouted, 'Geese.' He's the one who started the emergency protocols while I sat there like an idiot for a minute and a half. You don't think that's a long time, a minute and a half, but count it out while you're in a plane, in the dark, losing one of your engines, and you'll see it's both an eternity and a heartbeat.

"Jim was looking at me like I was a ghost, and I could see him talking, but it was like I couldn't hear him. I knew he was making sounds, but nothing made sense. He was looking to me to take over, to get it under control, and I sat there without doing a damn thing. He shut off the engine that had been compromised, but we had no idea if the other engine was okay. We could smell smoke, but there was no sign of fire. All we knew was that we'd been struck repeatedly, that we'd lost an engine, that we had to get safely to the ground.

"Because we were on approach and the birds hit all at once, the rocking of the plane got passed off as the landing gear coming down too hard and some turbulence. I could've done so much more in that minute and a half. I know it. I should've. But I froze. All those simulations, the training, everything I'd prepared to handle…and I couldn't make myself move. All I thought about was how this was it. Everyone on this plane, everyone who'd entrusted themselves to me, all of us were going to die, and it would be my fault because I hadn't been able to get my shit together in time. I'd left it up to someone else, when it was my responsibility, and now we were all going to die.

"When I finally managed to get my shit together, we went through the rest of the emergency protocols without any problems. My first officer radioed ahead to be met by the fire department. We alerted the passengers of a possible issue. And then we white-knuckled that plane to the ground.

"Only two people were hurt, and that was from improperly stowed carry-on baggage. That can happen even on a regular bumpy descent. But still, they got hurt because of me.

"It took a year for that plane to be put back on the line. That's how much damage it took. If it had taken us only a few minutes longer to react, if we hadn't been on the approach, if we'd been in a regional jet, if my first officer hadn't been so on the ball… If, if, if. If any one of those things had been different, we'd have crashed.

"Nobody thinks about how little keeps a plane in the air until you see how little it would take to knock it out. I'd always known, of course. You don't get your commercial pilot's license without knowing it. But knowing and experiencing it are two different things, and all I could think of after that night was everything that could've gone wrong and about how long it had taken me to take charge and do my job. All I could think of was how it felt to know there was something wrong, but I couldn't do anything about it. And what would happen the next time I had to react? What if the next time I didn't make it at all, or I was with someone who didn't pick up my slack?

"What if the next time, I killed myself and everyone on board that plane?

"I took a medical leave two years ago. I went on extended disability a year ago. That's when I started teaching adult ed.

"I haven't flown since.

"I can't."

"Is that why you asked me if my ex had been a pilot?" Stella asked.

"Yeah."

Stella's head pounded. She wanted to get off the couch and pace but couldn't make herself. Shudders twitched her until she pulled a blanket from the back of the couch and wrapped herself in it. Her teeth chattered.

"Everything turned out all right," she said after half a minute. "You saved them. You didn't choke. You landed the plane."

"Yes."

"Nobody died," she said quietly.

"That should make it better, shouldn't it?" His laugh sounded more like a bark, harsh and without humor. "Nobody died."

She understood, or at least thought she did, how coming so close to what might've been could have affected him so much. What she did not understand was something altogether different. "Why didn't you just tell me this, instead of letting me think you'd actually come to see me?"

"I wanted to come see you, Stella. I tried. I booked the flight. I went to the airport. And when the time came, I just…could not get on that plane. I know I wasn't going to be the one flying it, but even that, not being in control… I couldn't. I can't." He sounded broken.

She tried to find sympathy for him, and found only more of the same numbness that had covered her for weeks. "The first night we met, I told you my pain. I don't know why. Why you. Why any of it. But I did, so you've known since that first night what makes me who I am. Why I do what I do. And all this time, you couldn't tell me this?"

Matthew made a low noise. "It's shameful. I'm embarrassed. You're right. Nobody died. How could what happened to me possibly compare to what happened to you?"

"My pain," she said slowly, "doesn't mean that I can't understand someone else's."

"You weren't too nice to that guy in the airport," Matthew said. "And I didn't forget what you told me. 'Even when you're terrified that you can't take one more step or deal with one more thing, there's never an excuse for behaving like a prick.' That's what you told me. I didn't want you to think I was being a prick."

She laughed sadly. "But that's what you were."

"I was embarrassed," Matthew said sharply. "It was intimate, Stella."

"Too intimate? You could put your penis in me, but you couldn't be honest with me?" The words choked out of her, and finally she got up on shaking legs. She needed to move.

When he said nothing, Stella let out a small, wounded sigh. She swallowed her bitter words, though the taste of them made her gag. She straightened her shoulders and forced herself to be calm.

"Is that why your marriage ended?"

"She accused me of pulling away from her. Then of cheating. Which I didn't do, ever," Matthew said. "She didn't understand why I was spending so much time in the airport bar. The drinking...got out of hand. I wasn't there for her when she needed me. Or the girls. I missed school plays. I missed holiday dinners, trying to get on a goddamn plane, just once. And I couldn't do it. My marriage ended because I was an idiot."

"The question of whether or not your marriage actually ended is still up in the air," Stella said coldly. "Do you want to get back together with her?"

"No." He sounded stunned. "No, God. Never. We went to counseling. It didn't help. A lot of shit came up, stuff that might not have made a difference if not for what happened, but it did. Sometimes things don't work out. Doesn't mean I don't feel like shit for the way I behaved toward the end of our marriage. But I don't want to be with her. I want to be with you."

"I told you everything. Every fucking thing about me. And now I find out that I don't really know you at all. Do I?"

"You know me better than anyone ever has," he said in a low voice. "I'm sorry if you can't believe me."

She breathed in through her nose, out through her mouth. Breath after breath, until she could keep herself calm. When she could speak without sounding like a raging bitch, she said, "Why did you tell me this now?"

"Because I missed you so much I couldn't stand it anymore," Matthew said.

Stella's breath caught in her throat. Despite everything, despite all the pain he'd caused her, that water had seeped into every crack and crevice. There was no denying it.

"Please come to Chicago," he said quietly. "I can't come to you, but I miss you. I know it's a lot to ask of you to come here. But I want to make it up to you. Please, Stella. I want to try."

And what answer could she give him, Stella thought, other than yes?

CHAPTER THIRTY-ONE

Matthew greeted her at the door with a bunch of flowers that ought to have made all the pain of what had happened between them go away. Stella took them. Smelled them. They were mostly lilies, the smell of which always made her want to gag, but she found a smile for him anyway.

A kiss too.

"I should put these in water," she murmured against his mouth, not moving out of his arms as his fingers went to the special spots on her hips that still felt as though they'd been made to fit him. Always would, she imagined.

Matthew backed her up against the wall. Slowly, not rushing. The press of it against her back echoed the similar press of him against her front, and laughing, Stella turned her face to hold out the flowers to keep them from getting crushed.

"This," Matthew said against her neck. "This neck. This is what I want."

The press of his teeth. The hiss of breath. His fingers, tightening. Stella closed her eyes. The flowers fell. Matthew kissed her neck, her throat, then skimmed his mouth along her jaw to finally get at her mouth again, and his hand was between her legs. Under her skirt, inside her panties. His fingers were inside her a moment after that, and all she could do was arch into the touch.

She found the back of his head and held him against her. "Bite me."

He did.

"Harder," she said.

He did that too.

It felt so good. It always did. And so she let herself sink into that place where pleasure and pain were indistinguishable. Later, she thought when his teeth scraped her skin, later the memory of this pleasure might make the pain easier to bear.

Something would have to.

Matthew pulled away, dark eyes gleaming, breathing hard. He pressed his forehead to hers, his eyes closed. "Hey."

"Hey." Stella turned her face so she could nuzzle against him for a moment. "I think I ruined the flowers."

"I can buy you more."

She laughed, not because it was funny but because her throat had gone suddenly tight and the burning prick of emotion was stabbing her eyes. "You don't have to."

Matthew pushed the bulge of his cock against her. Made her breathless. She turned her head again, and he bent back to her neck. Nuzzling. Licking. Kissing gently while she tensed, waiting for him to use his teeth again.

Waiting, always waiting.

When he bit her, Stella cried out, low. His fingers moved again inside her, then on her clit. His touch shifted, too fast. Too slow. Teasing, though not on purpose, and she moved against him in frustration. Her fingers dug into his shoulders. The hand not moving between her thighs hooked beneath her knee, lifting her leg to hook around him. The pictures on the wall rattled in their frames as he pushed against her.

She could've reached for his belt. Unzipped him. Pulled out his beautiful cock and touched him the way he was touching her. She would have, in the past. She always did. But she didn't now. She put a hand between them to cup him, to rub him, but she didn't do more than that.

Matthew shuddered against her. Moaned her name. The sound of it, those two syllables broken in the middle by the hitch of his breath, the soft rasp of desire making it rough, echoed inside her. She pressed her knee to his hip and pushed herself against his fucking fingers.

"Make me come," Stella murmured. "I want to come for you."

He went to his knees in front of her and pushed her skirt up past her hips, then pressed his face against the lace of her panties, his hot breath caressing her hotter flesh beneath. Matthew hooked his fingers in the lacy fabric and pulled it over her thighs, exposing her to the rapid, flat stroke of his tongue against her clit. A second later he spread her with his fingers to get deeper inside her and she gasped at the invasion.

"Oh. Fuck. Yes," she said.

He muttered something against her, words she couldn't make out. They didn't matter. He could be reciting the alphabet or the motherfucking Declaration of Independence against her cunt; all that mattered was that his lips and tongue kept moving on her flesh. That he didn't stop.

Stella looked down at the man on his knees in front of her. He'd closed his eyes, his face buried against her. He gripped her ass, moving her against his mouth, then slipped a hand beneath her knee again to hook it over his shoulder. Open that way, exposed, she felt embarrassed, but only for a moment because the magic he was working with his tongue on her clit made it impossible for her to think of anything but how good it felt.

"Matthew," she breathed. Then again. His name. She loved the way it sounded. It had never been a name she liked until she'd met him, and then it had become the sexiest name she'd ever known. "Matthew, make me come."

He murmured again, soft sounds of assent. Maybe her name. Maybe terms of adoration, words of love, the ones he never said to her any other time than when he was between her legs. She wanted to grab something. Needed to. Her hand skimmed the top of his head, seeking purchase, but his hair was too short for her to grip. She settled for bunching his shirt in her fingers for a moment before she put her hands on the wall beside her.

Coiled springs of pleasure built inside her. The flicker of light in the corners of her vision reminded her to breathe, breathe. Stella rocked herself against his mouth. The flat of Matthew's tongue stroked her clit in a smooth, steady pattern until there was no more thought. Nothing but desire.

Her orgasm flooded her. Swept her away. And when she could open her eyes and focus again, there he was, looking up at her with that secret smile she'd come to know so well but never understand.

Matthew stood. Stella's dress fell down around her thighs again. When he kissed her, she tasted the memory of her own pleasure. When he tried to pull away, she held him close for a few more seconds until his muscles tensed beneath her, and she had to let him go.

★ ★ ★

In Matthew's kitchen, Stella pulled out eggs, butter, bacon. Bread for toast. She found some sweet orange and yellow peppers in the fridge. She sliced them and added them to the omelette while Matthew watched from his seat at the center island, glass of wine in his hand. She caught him staring and turned.

"What?"

"Nothing."

"What?" she said again, a little annoyed this time when he only gave her an enigmatic smile and shrug.

"I just like seeing you here, that's all. I like it when you're here."

It was a sweet thing to say, and she ought to enjoy it. Stella concentrated on flipping the omelette and sliding it onto a plate, not looking at him. She pulled the toast from the toaster, added it to the plate. She pushed all of it toward him across the island and took the glass of wine he handed her.

"You're so good to me," Matthew told her.

And she was. She knew it. Her choice, always, to be good to him. He'd never asked her for it, yet there it was. Given and taken, over and over.

She stiffened but didn't pull away when he moved behind her to nuzzle at the back of her neck. When he pushed her skirt up again, past her hips. Tugged her panties down. When he shifted her so that her hands skidded, flat, on top of the island and kicked a foot between hers to spread her wider for him, she bent her head. Closed her eyes. When he pushed inside her, she was still so wet from his earlier attentions that there was no friction. His cock filled her, pressing deep. At this angle, it hurt a little, but she'd never minded before and didn't now.

She wasn't surprised—he'd eaten her pussy so nicely twenty minutes ago, she'd have been shocked if he hadn't wanted to get a little something for himself too. She wasn't surprised when the phone rang either. But when he moved to answer it, Stella reached behind her to grip his hip.

"No," she said. "Don't stop."

One, two, three more rings before the answering machine picked up. The same number of slow thrusts inside her. She pushed back against him as his recording began to play, the only message the buzz of the dial tone. Predictably, a minute after that, his cell phone rang.

Again, Matthew tensed, but when he pulled out, Stella turned and grabbed him by the shoulders. Stroking him, she fit him back inside her, this time with the edge of the island digging into her back.

"Don't stop," Stella said.

Matthew groaned and kissed her. He lifted her onto the edge of the island, which meant he had to strain to keep fucking into her, but she guessed it didn't matter because he shuddered against her. He buried his face against her neck. She gripped his shoulders.

His cell phone pinged with a text.

Matthew kept fucking her. Harder now. Almost desperate, as if he was trying to finish fast.

Stella took him by the chin and forced him to look into her eyes. She clamped her knees to his sides. "Slower."

His kiss bruised her mouth; she didn't care. Matthew fucked her harder. Faster, despite her command. The fierceness of his thrusts slammed his pelvic bone against her clit, and there it was again. That helpless pleasure. That mindless need he always created in her.

They came together, him with a gasp, Stella in tongue-bitten silence. Matthew clung to her for a moment before pulling out and reaching for a clean dish cloth from the drawer, which he handed to her while he put himself back in his pants. He didn't look at her when he picked up his phone.

"Shit," Matthew said wearily. "Guess who."

Stella hopped down from the island and used the dish cloth carefully before pulling her panties back up and adjusting her dress. She tossed the dish cloth into the open washer, then went to the sink to wash her hands as Matthew answered the text from Caroline.

When she turned at last to look at him, his expression told her everything. Without a word, Stella took the plate with the omelette and toast on it. She pushed past him and dumped it in the trash. Then she put the plate in the dishwasher.

"It's the smoke detector. It's beeping, and—"

"And she's incapable of changing the battery," Stella finished for him, her voice steady. Without any evidence of the emotions tearing her up inside. "Yeah. I figured."

"I won't be long." Matthew's mouth thinned. "I'll be back in an hour."

Stella looked at him. "Take as long as you have to."

Matthew hesitated before giving her a tentative smile. "It won't take me long at all, I promise."

"It doesn't matter how long it takes," she said. "I won't be here when you get back. Stay all night, for all I care. You might find it hard to explain to her why you can't get it up so soon, but then again, maybe you won't have a problem."

He stared at her, mouth open and working, for a few seconds before his teeth clicked together. He scowled. "That's a shitty thing to say."

"You know what's shitty? I came here. I flew to Chicago to be with you, and we only get so much time, and you're wasting it!" Stella cried, loud enough to send him back a few steps.

"What am I supposed to do, just tell her to let it keep beeping? Keep the girls up all night?"

"Yes!" Stella shouted. "Yes. That's exactly what you're supposed to do. Tell her to figure it the fuck out. It's her house, not yours. Her smoke detectors. Her problem. You are not her husband anymore. Remember?"

Matthew said nothing.

"But I forgot. You feel guilty. You owe her." Stella pushed him away. "Go."

"Did you mean what you said? You won't be here?"

"Yes," she told him. "Does that change your mind?"

"Don't push me," Matthew said warningly.

"I'm not pushing you. I'm telling you. Go and do whatever it is you do over there. Play at whatever it is she wants you to play at. I'm done, Matthew."

With that, she pushed past him and headed for the front door. Her bag was still there. Before she could grab it he'd snagged her elbow. Turned her.

"Wait."

It was more than she'd expected from him, and it was enough to stop her from yanking open the door. Stella turned. She waited.

Matthew sighed. Stella didn't soften. Didn't budge, not even when he put his arms around her and pulled her close to nuzzle at her neck. She did not sink into his embrace.

"Don't leave—" His phone pinged with another text.

Stella waited, but he didn't pull it from his pocket. Finally she put her arms around him. They stayed like that for a minute or so, until she said quietly, "She manipulates you, Matthew."

"I know."

"She uses your children to do it, which I find despicable."

Matthew said nothing.

"She left you. Not the other way around. I know you feel like it was your fault, and maybe a lot of it was, but the fact is, whatever the reasons, you are not married anymore. She doesn't get to have the benefits of having a husband without the husband part of it."

He backed away at that. "Wow. Thanks for making me feel like shit about trying to be responsible."

"That's not what I'm talking about, and you know it. Or you should know it." She swallowed hard to keep her voice steady, already knowing there was no point to this conversation. He wasn't going to hear her, no matter what she said or how she said it. She reached for him, hating herself for it but trying to give this one more chance. One last time. "Look at me."

He did, though the belligerent set of his jaw and narrowed eyes didn't give her much hope of him being willing to listen.

"I love being with you." At her words, something gleamed in his eyes, giving her hope enough to link her fingers with his, to pull him a little closer. "I love the way we fit together. How I feel against you. I love the way you make me laugh."

"I love all those things too."

It was the perfect time for him to say something more,

even if it was a kiss. Matthew only stared. And Stella began
to break.

"Matthew, I love you," she told him.

Matthew looked startled. Then, for the briefest of moments, pleased. But he still said nothing, and from his
pocket, his phone gave another bleat.

Stella stepped back. Let him go. She waited for him to
choose her, to choose them, but Matthew pulled his phone
out to look at the message. He grimaced and tucked it
away again.

"Will you be here when I get back?" he asked.

"Do you want me to be?"

"Yes. So we can talk." He kissed her cheek. Gave her
shoulders a squeeze. He grabbed his coat and keys from the
rack by the door. He did turn back in the doorway to look
at her. There was that. "I'll bring home takeout from that
Indian place you love. Okay?"

"Sure." Stella nodded.

She waited until he'd closed the door behind him before
she let herself begin to shake. Then her knees gave out and
she went to them on the cold, hard tile of his entryway.
Her hands slapped flat on the floor as her shoulders bent
and she tried to hold back the sobs splintering her throat.
Scalding her eyes. She couldn't, of course. Her grief surged
up and out of her, Cthulu rising from the depths to destroy
the world and everything in it.

She got to her feet before she was done weeping, but
she couldn't stay there on the floor forever. In his powder room, she washed her face and drank cool water from
her cupped hands, gulping it until her stomach protested.
Then she leaned over the toilet, waiting for her guts to
erupt…but she breathed her way through the sudden nau-

sea. Got to her feet again. Smoothed her hair. Her clothes. The woman in the mirror was pale, with shadowed eyes. Her smile a grimace. Stella touched her fingertips to the glass for a second, but yes. That was her. No through-the-looking-glass moment here.

She didn't write a note to go along with the key she left in the bowl on the hall table. There were no words. He'd figure it out. Then she let herself out the front door, took the elevator to the lobby. Had Herndon call her a cab.

She left him.

Because loving Matthew was like trying to fill a cracked glass—she could pour and pour and pour, and the glass would always be empty. There would never be anything for her to drink.

She would always be thirsty.

CHAPTER THIRTY-TWO

There's no explaining fate or serendipity. It happens, most of the time unrecognized, but when Stella ran into Craig again at the same old coffee shop where she'd stopped after work to pick up a box of muffins, all she could think was how often and how hard the universe had tried to push them together.

She asked him to dinner. "Not a date," she told him. "But I'd like us to talk."

"I'd like that," Craig said.

She took him to a nice little place with dim lighting and soft music and an eclectic menu. Not a date, though it could've been, she thought as they both ordered glasses of wine and their knees bumped under the table. If she'd reached for his hand, he might've taken it. She didn't reach.

"Why do you think we didn't work?" she said bluntly. "Was it as simple as me being married? If we'd had a chance, if we'd met each other when I was alone…would it have been different?"

Craig sipped from his glass and studied her. "Yes. Maybe."

"I don't believe in soul mates or anything like that. I don't believe in one true love. I'm not sure, to be honest, that I even believe in monogamy." Stella broke a bread stick into small pieces she arranged on her plate without wanting to eat them.

"Yeah." Craig laughed. "Well, it's easier, though."

She smiled at him, and that was when she reached for his hand. A quick squeeze, no linking of fingers, nothing to indicate romance. He looked surprised and squeezed back.

"I do still miss you sometimes," she told him. "We always had fun together. I always felt like you'd listen to me, no matter what I ever had to say."

"I would."

Stella's smile tightened. "I should've told you lots of things, Craig. I was so dishonest with you. Not a liar. Just never fully truthful about me, my life, my feelings. I wonder if it would've made a difference."

"You can't ever know what might've been, Stella. Do I wonder? Yeah. Would I have liked something different? Yes." Craig shrugged. "But you can't spend your time second-guessing."

Stella took a deep breath. "I lost my oldest son in a car accident. He was almost nine. My younger son and ex-husband were fine, but I had a lot of injuries. My son Gage never regained full consciousness. He was on a respirator and feeding tube in the hospital. We decided to take him off both a month after the accident. He kept breathing on his own, so we took him home. He lived another five months."

Craig reached for her hand and, this time, held it tight. "That must've been really hard for you."

"It was hard for everyone. Not just me. I blamed my

husband for the accident. I blamed myself for not being the one who'd been driving, thinking maybe if I had been, I'd have been able to stop it somehow." Stella drew in a cleansing breath and found a shaky but sincere smile for him.

"I'm sorry you didn't feel you could tell me back then."

"I didn't want you to feel sorry for me. You were one of the few people in my life who didn't know. To you, I was not 'that woman who lost her son.' I liked that feeling, that anonymity. But, Craig," she said, "I am that woman who lost her son. I will always be that woman."

"You'll be a lot of things," he told her.

The call from Jeff surprised Stella, but warily, she accepted his invitation to breakfast. Just the two of them. He took her to their favorite place, the diner where they'd gone while they were dating, when they'd often stayed up so late night became morning.

It had been a long, long time since she and Jeff had spent any time alone together without Tristan between them. Stella watched him salt and pepper his eggs the way he always had done. She passed him the ketchup before he asked for it. You couldn't live with someone for fifteen years without memorizing at least a few of his habits.

"You should eat something more than that," Jeff said brusquely, pointing with his fork toward her pair of eggs-over-medium and toast. "You're getting too thin again."

He paused to look closely at her before she could even take a bite. "What's he done to you?"

At first, she thought he meant Tristan, but then she understood. "We broke things off. That's all."

"Does he need a kick in the balls?"

Stella burst into startled laughter. "You're going to kick my ex-lover in the balls for me?"

"If he needs it." Jeff laughed too.

They hadn't laughed together in far longer than they'd eaten breakfast together, and though the humor was bittersweet, it was better than being solely bitter. To appease him about her breakfast, Stella had ordered French toast in addition to the eggs. Jeff passed her the syrup before she asked for it.

It was nice.

"I have something to tell you," he said when they'd finished eating and were sitting, sipping coffee.

"I figured you did."

Jeff looked embarrassed but proud. And something else. True to form, he didn't try to soften his words. "Cynthia's pregnant."

In the space of one heartbeat to the next, Stella waited for pain or grief, but all she found was…well, not joy. Not exactly. But happiness, for sure. And it was also bittersweet.

"Congratulations," she said.

Jeff started to cry. His shoulders hunched, his eyes grew red. He covered his face with a hand, turning toward the window, while Stella sat, uncertain of what to do. She couldn't reach for him and wasn't sure she would have, even if she were sitting closer.

He got himself under control in under a minute, typically Jeff. He swiped angrily at his eyes and then blew his nose with a napkin. He cleared his throat.

"Sorry."

"Don't be sorry," she told him. "A baby is always good news, Jeff. Was it a surprise, or…?"

"No. She wanted a kid. I just… It feels… Shit, Stella. Shit."

Then she did reach across the table to take his hand. Once they'd stood in front of a priest and made their vows with their fingers linked. She didn't have to love him anymore to want to offer him compassion.

Jeff squeezed her hand as if she'd offered him a lifeline. "It feels wrong. What if I can't love it? What if it's a boy?"

In all the darkness, Stella had never allowed Jeff to be her light. Now all she could do was try to make up for it. "Then you'll have another son. And you'll love him. You won't be able to stop yourself, Jeff. And it will be all right."

"There are days I can't remember his face," Jeff said. "There are days I don't think about him at all."

Stella fought her own tears. "It's okay."

"Is it?" He gave her a stare so naked in its grief that Stella had no reply.

In the parking lot, she thought about hugging him, but instead they stood at an awkward distance. The sun had burned through early spring clouds that had hinted at snow. The light caught the threads of silver in Jeff's hair and showed the lines around his eyes. It probably did the same for her.

"I wanted to tell you first. I thought you should hear it from me. We'll tell Tristan later this afternoon. I think he's going to want to move back in with you," Jeff said. "If that's all right."

"Of course it is. And, Jeff…really sincerely, you and Cynthia have my congratulations." This time, she forced herself to move and hug him.

He hugged her back. For half a minute too long, his arms went around her. His face buried in her neck. If she closed her eyes, she could imagine they were young again, and in love, and their life together was just beginning instead of long over.

He let her go, his eyes suspiciously red again. "That guy? The one Tristan told me about? He's an asshole."

"Well. Yeah." She laughed. Shrugged. "But maybe so am I."

"So we all are," Jeff said.

CHAPTER THIRTY-THREE

To: Matthew Shepherd
From: Stella Andrews Cooper

You're Invited!

What: It's Stella's Birthday
When: Saturday, August 11
Where: Stella's house, 609 Aspen Drive

Your presence is your gift
Please RSVP by July 24

CHAPTER THIRTY-FOUR

Fifty people at a birthday party, all there to support and celebrate with her, and Stella was about to do a Leslie Gore and "It's My Party" all over them.

She didn't want to.

She didn't want to let Matthew make her cry any more than he already had, but there was this pesky thing eating away at her insides that wouldn't let her stop thinking about him. Stella locked herself in her bathroom and force-breathed until she felt dizzy, but at least she'd chased away the tears. She stared herself down in the mirror, looking fierce but, thank God, not too haggard though last night she'd been unable to sleep more than a couple hours at a time. She turned her face from side to side—misery had been good to her cheekbones, even if it had royally fucked up everything else.

Smoothing her dress over her hips and belly, Stella straightened her shoulders. "It's over," she told her reflection. "He doesn't love you. He doesn't want you. Not enough."

It was the shittiest of pep talks, as far as they went. But it worked, because it was the truth, and the sooner she got used to facing it, the sooner it would stop hurting. Or some such bullshit, anyway. She didn't actually believe that part about the pain fading faster, but the truth was better than trying to tell herself lies that would never come true.

He didn't love her.

Not enough.

Raking her fingers through her hair, she fluffed it over her shoulders. She swiped her face with powder and refreshed her lipstick. She looked a little less like Death, even if she still felt like it.

She needed to get out to the party, to mingle and smile and greet her guests and be gracious to all of those who'd come to see her. She had to oversee the food, though she was sure Cynthia with her bulging belly was bustling about Stella's kitchen in a tizzy, trying to be helpful while all the time silently clucking her tongue at the disorganization of someone who couldn't be bothered to separate her baking utensils from the serving spoons.

Slipping into a pair of sandals, Stella let herself out of the bedroom, closing the door behind her. From downstairs came the hum and buzz of conversation, the throb of music. Through the high windows in the family room she could see into the yard, where people were mingling and standing around the grill, where Jeff had taken up the apron and tongs. *Oh, God,* Stella thought with a shake of her head. *Worlds colliding.*

Still, it was nice of Jeff and Cynthia to have helped her with this party, no matter what their reasons. It was good for Tristan to have three parents who could work together to do something important for him. Something beyond the selfishness of themselves. Lifting her chin, taking a long, deep breath, Stella went downstairs.

Tristan and his friends had already set up the volleyball net, spending more time trying to spike the ball into each other's heads than any real scorekeeping. The girls clustered around the edges, watching, shaking their heads at the boys' antics, not even the sporty girls stupid enough to try to join what was becoming more of a war than a game. Stella set up the mental countdown to the first bloody nose at thirty minutes or so, and that was being generous. She watched them for a few minutes from the sliding glass doors to the deck, then turned to the kitchen.

Cynthia had indeed been bustling, as evidenced by the artfully arranged platters of veggies and dip, cut fruit, also with dip, and the cheese and crackers. With more dip. Cynthia loved dips. But Stella forced away the snarky thoughts about her ex-husband's current wife.

"This looks great," Stella said sincerely. "Thanks so much for this, Cynthia."

Cynthia, her face gone round and pink-cheeked from the heat and her pregnancy, looked uncertain. "I just set out the things I found in the fridge and whipped up a few dips."

Stella held back a snort of laughter.

"You didn't have any special platters or anything, did you? I didn't want to go digging around."

"No, no. It's fine." Stella pulled open one of the drawers to find a set of dip spreaders topped with old-fashioned shoes. They'd been a wedding gift from one of Jeff's relatives. She'd never even taken them out of the clear plastic box, but they'd be perfect now. She watched Cynthia's eyes light up at the sight. "You know...you should take these with you."

Cynthia looked confused. "Where?"

"When you go home. They came from Jeff's aunt and uncle. Really, I never use them, and you...you would."

"I would," Cynthia said with a wide, incredulous smile. "Look how perfect they are for the dips!"

Stella pressed the entire box into Cynthia's hand. "Take them."

Cynthia smiled hesitantly. "You sure you don't mind?"

"I have never in my life used a special utensil for a dip," Stella said, "but I'm sure you will use them all the time."

Both women started laughing at the same time, softly at first, then a little louder. Cynthia took the box of dip knives and tucked it into her oversized designer purse taking up a lot of room on Stella's counter. Her smile softened.

"Thanks, Stella."

"Thank you. For everything." For a moment, Stella was convinced she might burst into tears again, but she forced them back by biting hard on the raw spot on the inside of her cheek. It hurt like hell, which was the point.

Cynthia moved a little closer. "It's been a tough few months, huh?"

"Yeah." Stella turned to the food laid out on the center island, pretending to rearrange some of it, though Cynthia had done such a wonderful job there was really nothing to change.

"Hey." Cynthia put a hand on her shoulder, gentle fingers squeezing for a second or two before letting go. "I just want you to know that I'm sorry about your...friend. Jeff told me you broke up."

Stella stiffened, not turning. "He said that?"

"Yes. Jeff is too nosy. He should mind his own business." Cynthia sounded annoyed. Stella turned, completely understanding how it felt to be annoyed by an ex's too-close interest in a former spouse, but Cynthia went on. "Whatever goes on in your life isn't a reflection on him, and I keep telling him that you're a grown woman and you should be able to do whatever you like in your private life, that he needs to just accept that he's no rose garden and not everything was your fault."

Stella didn't know what to say.

Cynthia smiled a little, both hands resting on the swell of her belly, but didn't say any more than that. The women shared a look, bonding over the ass-hattery of the same man. It wasn't quite friendship, but it was the closest it had ever come to being something like that.

"I need to pee," Cynthia said abruptly, and waddled off toward the powder room.

The moment of camaraderie had occurred in a rare few minutes of quiet with no witnesses, but as was common with all kinds of parties, people tended to congregate in the kitchen. Stella was bombarded in the next few minutes with friends and relatives, some bearing gifts of food, some with more traditional birthday presents, which she directed them to put on the dining room table. Once the party was in full swing, there was no time for Stella to lose herself in her misery. It hadn't disappeared. But it was not the worst grief she'd ever suffered, and eventually it would go away.

Her parties had always been open-door—expansive guest lists, nothing formal. So when the doorbell rang while she was in the living room collecting empty Solo cups and discarded napkins, Stella at first didn't do more than look up. The party had spilled over to both the front and back lawns, so even if there was an oddball guest who felt shy about walking right in, he or she could surely walk around to the back. She dumped the trash into the pail she'd set up in the corner of the room for just that purpose, not that anyone seemed to have noticed it...and the bell rang again. Dusting off her hands, Stella went to answer it.

On the step stood Matthew, in all his glory. "Hi," he said. Stella closed the door in his face.

She opened it again a moment later, finding him still standing there, this time with his mouth open and brow furrowed. She'd imagined this moment in so many different ways. Playing it cool. Jumping into his arms. Telling him to get lost. But when it was real and true, when he was right in front of her, all Stella could do was stare.

Gently, Matthew reached for her wrist and pulled her forward a few steps onto the front porch. The door closed behind her. Stella stared. Matthew smiled hesitantly.

"It took me twelve hours to get here. Aren't you going to say anything?"

He'd driven here. Not flown, then. But still, he was here. Baby steps.

"It's just that I thought...I thought I would never..." The tears came then. Fat, burning, sliding down her cheeks and wetting her lips with the taste of salt. Stella drew in a sobbing breath, embarrassed but incapable of holding any of it back. "I thought I'd never see you again."

"Aww, now, now," Matthew said as if this were all some kind of joke. A fucking joke. "How could you think that?"

Stella drew herself up. "Because you made me think so!"

They stared at each other in silence pierced by the sounds of the party and Stella's hitching breaths. Then by Matthew's small, sad sigh. He reached for her but didn't grab.

Didn't pull or force. He reached and waited for Stella to let him take her.

Had there really been a question of her refusing him?

They clung to each other on her front porch, neither of them speaking, her face pressed into the hollow of his shoulder. She breathed in the scent of him. Fabric softener, soap, that distinctive smell of him that she'd been so sure she'd never breathe again. She shook a little, and his hands smoothed down her back, until at last she looked up at him.

"Shhh," Stella rasped, her own swollen eyes and streaked cheeks making this ironic, "don't cry."

Matthew held her close. "Stella," he whispered in her ear. "I just drove twelve hours on gas station coffee and determination. I need to use your bathroom and get something to eat, or I'm going to pass out on your front porch."

Stella laughed and wiped at her eyes. "Come inside. There's plenty of food."

"In a minute," Matthew said. "I can wait another minute."

Then he kissed her. And again. He kissed and kissed and kissed her, and suddenly everything felt as though it was all going to be all right.

★ ★ ★ ★ ★

32953012518413